PROJECT
DOMINIUM

PROJECT
DOMINIUM

RONALD MONTGOMERY

authorHOUSE®

AuthorHouse™
1663 Liberty Drive
Bloomington, IN 47403
www.authorhouse.com
Phone: 1-800-839-8640

Published by AuthorHouse   04/24/2012

ISBN: 978-1-4685-6104-3 (sc)
ISBN: 978-1-4685-6103-6 (hc)
ISBN: 978-1-4685-6102-9 (e)

Library of Congress Control Number: 2012904452

In this novel there are a few chapters that have multiple characters giving first person points of view.
The characters are distinguishable though different font styles or Italicized font.

Chapter I

TRAVIS: THE HOMESTEAD

April 29, 2007

I laid there in the park beside her, waiting for her to say something, anything. All I wanted was to know that she was okay with my decision. Both of us staring into the sky, I could only think about what I had just told her . . . I joined the army.

That was the best lie that I could think of to explain why I was going to be gone for the next few years. I wasn't sure if she would be able to handle the truth let alone comprehend it. I believed lying to her was the right choice. Telling her the truth would have only made the situation more complicated. I never wanted to leave her, but it was the only way that I could try and do anything with my gift.

"How long will you be gone?" She asked with fear and sorrow in her voice.

"About two years, minimum," I told her. "But I will write you every day and I'll try and call you whenever I can. Unless you just want to end it here. I would understand. I don't expect you to wait for me."

She sat up and rolled on top of me and began to kiss me.

"I never want to call it quits with us, Travis," she said. "If you think this is the right path for you, then I will follow your decision and I will wait for you."

"I didn't think you were going to be this supportive. I mean, I hoped you would have been," I said to her. "I love you, Amber, more than you know."

"I love you too, Travis," she kissed me again and rested her head on my chest. "When do you leave?"

"I'm leaving in three days. We are flying to Cincinnati and from there going to Fort Rucker," I said lying through my teeth.

"That's so soon," She said with her eyes tearing up. "We barley have any time left together."

"That's why we have to make it count."

TWO DAYS EARLIER

April 27, 2007

"Do you want to make this world a better place? Do you think you were born to help the world? Then click here NOW."

That's what the blinking advertisement read. The words seemed to jump off of the screen. The swirling colors in the background drew me in. I thought, why not see what it's all about? I might as well check it out, maybe a good job opportunity. I clicked on it and all this information popped up and then ones and zeros started running down my screen. Then my computer turned off.

"What?!" I yelled trying to turn it back on, but nothing worked. "Damn viruses, I should have figured as much."

I packed up my things and drove to school. There were only two more days of my high school education left. Soon I'd be off to Penn State with Amber. When I arrived at school I met up with my friends in the cafeteria until the bell rang. While in class, all I could think about was that damn popup. How could I have been so stupid to click it? That was like asking for a total computer meltdown. At the time, it seemed like I had to. Like my body had no other option, but to click it. The bell rang and the rest of the day passed by quickly.

The next morning I had to walk to school because my car wouldn't start. First my computer, now my car, what else could happen, I thought. All of the sudden, two white vans came out of each street surrounding me.

I stopped and watched as men in black suits came out of them, and towards me. My heart was racing. By the time I had decided to try and run away one of them had already grabbed me. I attempted to break loose, but he was stronger than me. Another man grabbed my feet. I tried to struggle, but there was no use. They were too strong. They threw me into one of the vans. I blacked out.

A light turned on, as if someone had shined a flashlight in my face. I was tied to a chair with, what felt like, rope. There was a man sitting on a chair in front of me. He seemed comfortable, as if he had been sitting there for a while. He was wearing a tan suit and a black tie. It didn't look cheap, so I knew it was no ordinary kidnapping. I could have as figured that out by the team of men that picked me up. He seemed about thirty or forty years old, he had very short hair, slightly longer than a standard military cut.

The ropes were tied tight around my wrists. I tried to get free, but it was pointless. Both my feet were bound as well. I didn't know what to do. I assumed there was no point screaming. The room was all white and the door was about ten feet away from me, the man was about five.

"Hello Mr. Travis Hartman. Five-eleven, one-hundred and eighty-two pounds, dark blonde hair, brown eyes . . . looks like we got the right guy. So, how are you this fine afternoon?" the strange man asked.

"Where am I? What is this place? Who are you people?" I asked angrily.

"Now now, calm down. Don't worry, you're fine. Actually, you are better than fine," he said with a chuckle. "So Mr. Hartman, how do you think you can make this world a better place? Why do you think you were born to help this world?"

Immediately, I remembered the advertisement that I clicked on my computer. The questions were strangely similar. "What is this place?"

"So, let's cut to the chase. What can you do? What's your power?" the man asked.

"Power? What are you talking about? I don't have a 'power'. I'm just an ordinary kid."

"Actually, you're not. The advertisement that you clicked on was designed to attract the energy in people that gives them strange and powerful abilities and ward away those who do not. Therefore, only people with abilities will click on it. You clicked. So I'll ask again, what's your power?"

"I don't know. I've never done anything special."

"No flying, no super speed, maybe moving things with your mind?"

"No! What is going on here?"

The man looked back behind me and nodded his head, I heard the snap of someone's fingers. Black. I opened my eyes again and the same man was still sitting there looking at me. I was groggy, as if I was waking up from a long nap.

"What's going on? What just happened?" I said in a dazed tone. I tried to look to the corner of the room, but due to my angle. I couldn't see it.

"Do you know your power?" The man asked with his violent temper flaring.

"No, I have no idea. I don't know what you're talking about. I'm sorry?"

"Well then, I guess that I'm going to have to kill you. You've seen too much."

He looked to the back of the room again and I heard another finger snap. Black. I opened my eyes, awaking with the same groggy feeling. No one was in the room, the door was open, and I was untied. I got up, wiped my eyes with my fingers, and took a second to look around the room. There was a symbol painted on the back of the wall. It was a black circle, which was no more than the size of a basket ball, surrounded by three rounded black trapezoids. The trapezoids weren't evenly sized. One surrounded about one half of the circle on the left side. Moving clockwise, the following trapezoid bordered about one-sixth of the circle, and the last one bordered roughly two-sixths. The remaining portion was the total space between the trapezoids. I had never seen it before. After staring at the symbol I turned around and ran out the door. At the end of the long hallway I could see a cracked door. I was sure it was a trap, but it was the only chance that I had to get the hell out there. I ran for it, hearing footsteps, lots of them. I looked behind me and I saw a bunch of soldiers . . . with guns. I ran faster, as fast as I could.

They started to shoot. I burst through the door while they opened fire. I started to run to the right after I got out of the building. I was outside surrounded by trees. It appeared as if I was in a forest somewhere, or a thick wooded area. There were trees and plants that I had never seen before. I thought, where in the hell did they bring me?

It only took a moment for them to be outside with me. I laid down into some brush. I had no plan, no idea where I was, and no idea how to escape.

There were a number of soldiers after me. I could hear them talking.

"We should split up, we will cover more ground that way," one said.

"Good idea," another said

I poked my head out of the brush, seeing one approach my hiding spot. I saw a branch in front of me, I planned to knock him out and steal his gun. I was scared; I knew if I made the slightest error he would kill me. I reached for the branch, and my hand began to feel weightless. I touched the branch and watched as my hand changed to the same color as the branch. I quickly pulled it back, touching it with my other hand. It felt coarse and jagged, but not sharp. My hand somehow became wood. I didn't freak out, but I was confused. My hand slowly turned back to normal, starting from my wrist then working up to my fingertips. I was in shock. I heard the soldier coming very close. I grabbed the branch, stood up, and smashed him in the face with it breaking the branch into two pieces.

He instantly fell to the ground. I grabbed his gun along with the knife from his vest. I took the knife out of its sheath and concentrated on my hand, attempting to repeat what I had previously done. It began to turn a clear white, nearly transparent, but foggy. I touched the knife and could feel my hand start to change, feeling cold and hard. I heard another guy running in my direction. I hid behind a tree. He ran by the tree and me, then over to the soldier I had knocked out.

"Are you okay? Hey man, are you okay? Wake up."

I walked up behind him quietly.

"Hey," I said, right behind him.

He turned around and I punched him in the head, cracking his helmet. He started to bleed from his forehead. I kicked him, he seemed unconscious.

"Stop it! That's enough," a voice said. "They're using empty clips. They're not a threat to you. It was only to scare you to make your ability awaken."

I turned around to see the man that had me in the room earlier.

"What are you talking about?" I said as I pointed the soldier's gun at him.

"I told you that they are empty clips. Please come with me and I will explain everything."

"They were shooting at me in the hallway, those didn't seem like empty clips" I stated.

"No, those were real bullets. You were in a confined space. It was easy to avoid you and only shoot at the walls to frighten you. So please, put the gun down and just walk with me. I'm not your enemy."

"I'm not going anywhere with you," I yelled as I pulled the trigger of the automatic gun. Nothing happened. There were no bullets in the gun. He was telling the truth.

"We never had any intention of killing you," the man said. "I just said that to scare you. My idea worked. There are cameras all over this place. I watched you discover your power, and it's a good one from what it seems. Come on, I'll explain everything."

I dropped the gun and walked over to him.

"So, where are we?" I asked. "What day is it? How long have I been here?"

"Well right now, we are on an island. This island is called The Homestead. This is where we test all of the new comers' powers and rate them on a scale of one to five," he explained as we entered back into the building. "A level one ability is a weak or uncontrolled power. A weak power for example, being able to melt. A level two ability being a somewhat honed power, being able to use your power at will or a useful power, such as being able to melt other things. A level three ability is a more advanced and even more honed power. A level four is an extremely advanced, possibly dangerous power, Such as telekinesis or being able to dehydrate the body."

We were walking down a hallway with a bunch of dark rooms.

"And what about what a level five power?"

"Well, a level five, there are only a few level fives that we know of and he is one of them." We stopped in front of one of the doors.

"I don't see anything."

"One minute, we just have to wait for my assistant to show up."

A door opened down the hall and a man came out and started walking towards us.

"This is Zander; he can generate a dark field up to ten feet in diameter and up to twenty feet away. While in the field you are unable to stay awake. That is why you kept falling asleep when we met earlier. Oh and by the way my name is Jacob Perin, but please just call me Perin. It's nice to formally meet you, Travis." I shook his hand and his assistant was now next to us. "When he first came here Zander's power was only to see perfectly in the dark and with time and training his power developed into what it is today. He is a great asset to us here. Hopefully, you will be just as valuable to us, Travis."

"Hey, nice to meet you, Travis," Zander said. "So what can you do?"

"I'm not to sure how to explain it. I can show you. Watch."

I stuck my hand out and tried to do what I did earlier. Nothing was happening. I tried to force it. I concentrated so hard.

"Hey, don't hurt yourself. You just figured out that you can do something extraordinary. You have a long ways to go before you can do it at will. I've been here for five years and I just recently perfected my power," Zander said.

"You're right," I stopped trying.

"Zander, could you please remove the field around this room?" Perin asked.

"Yes sir. No problem," he said and then snapped his fingers.

The room became visible. There was a person in the corner of the room, curled into a ball. He seemed about fourteen years old.

"Now, don't get upset, Travis. It's not what it appears to be. We aren't holding him captive; he wanted to be put to sleep for a long time. It is for the best. Merrick is very dangerous. Luckily, we knew about Merrick before his power developed," Perin asked.

"Why is that?"

"Well, this young man is the cause of some of the natural disasters from 2003 to 2005."

"How is that?"

"His body has effects on the planet. For instance, if he loses control of his power and his body starts to shake, then there is an earthquake." Perin explained.

"Can't you teach him to keep it under control?" I asked.

"Merrick lost control for just a minute on August 23, 2005. That's the date that Hurricane Katrina formed off the east coast," Zander said.

"Are you sure that it's not just a coincidence?" I asked them.

"There are countless other things that have happened due to Merrick, but we won't get into that. Merrick is one of few people with a level five power that we know of," Perin stated. "Now to answer your other questions from earlier, you've only been here for a few hours since this morning. It just seemed longer because you were asleep."

"Will I ever get to go home?" I asked. "Do I have to stay here?"

"Well, the decision is completely up to you. I mean, you won't be able to hone your skills without help. That's what we offer here," Perin said.

"Honestly, Travis, this is the best place for people like us. Without them I never would have been able to control my power. I used to be a thief, but they helped me. Your life will be better here," Zander told me. "After they think that your power can no longer be developed then they will let you go, or you can stay and work for them helping them find other people with abilities. Then, if you want, you can help train others. Assuming you're good enough."

"What do you say, Travis, will you join us?" Perin asked.

"Yes, but is it okay that you bring me home so that I can say goodbye to my friends and family?"

"Yes, of course. We will bring you home today and in four days we will come pick you up from Lehigh Valley International Airport. We'll call you the day before we pick you up," Perin said, "Under no circumstances can you tell anyone that you are going to an island to help hone your special powers. You need to think of an excuse."

"I told my parents that I was going to war. It's an easy lie to cover and I still write them every day," Zander recommended.

"That's not a bad idea. Thanks Zander."

"No problem."

"Will there be other people like me?"

"Yes. The ages of the other students vary. We like to get the students as young as possible, so we can train them for longer. We don't look for many older people to recruit into the project. If we do, we usually train them to be instructors. It's harder to convince older people into joining. It's also harder to train them with their power. Our targets are usually around your age," Perin explained.

"I guess that makes sense. What exactly am I going to be trained for? Like is it a special mission or something, fighting off evil aliens or something crazy like that?"

"No, Travis, nothing like that. When you get back more will be explained."

We continued walking and Perin told me that once I came back things will be different. It would be very strict, but he would explain that on enrollment day. Zander and Perin compared it to a boot camp or a military school. It is grueling, but the end result was worth the work. We went to the take off and landing zone for the island's helicopters; all of us got in and began to fly back to Leigh, Pennsylvania. Perin informed to me that the helicopters they used weren't ordinary ones, they had been greatly modified. They had a very powerful technopath at their disposal. She helped make more than half of the equipment they used on the islands. Without her he wasn't sure how successful the islands would be.

At about 4:30 p.m. we landed at Leigh Valley Airport. We got out of the helicopter and security guards approached us.

"I just need to see your identification sir."

Perin took out his I.D and showed it to the guard. "Last minute stop. Call your superior, the landing should have been processed through your system."

"Already taken care of, just had to check your ID," the guard said.

We walked away from the guards, through the airport, and out the exit. A black car was outside waiting for us.

"Here you are sir," the man standing in front of the car said as he handed Perin the keys.

"Thank you," Perin took the keys and unlocked the doors, walked over to the driver's side, and got in. Zander and I got into the car as well. Zander took shotgun while I got in the back. The whole ride there nothing was said. It was kind of creepy. We arrived at my house and my mom's car was in the driveway.

"Now remember what I said, don't tell anyone where you are really going. Under no circumstances can you let out the truth," Perin emphasized. "Also, don't forget to be ready in four days. We will pick you up at your house at 2:30pm. Have all the things you want packed."

"Okay."

"By the way, don't bring any electronic devices, such as cell phones, ipods, mp3 players, things of that sort. The less distractions the better."

"No problem."

"I'll see you in four days."

I got out of the car and they drove away. I walked into my house, took my shoes off, and put them next to the door.

"Mom, I'm home," I yelled as I walked straight into the kitchen.

"Hi honey, how was school?"

"It was good. A little boring, but good," I answered as I opened the fridge.

"Liar. The school called and said you didn't go in today," she said as she walked down the stairs and into the kitchen. "I know that you are eighteen now, but you need to think about your education. It's very important."

"I'm sorry, Mom. I wanted to wait to tell you, but I guess this is a good a time as any," I said closing the fridge.

"What is it? You better not have dropped out."

"No, Mom, it's not that," I took a deep breath. "I joined the army. Don't be mad. I think that it was the best choice for my future. I'm sorry."

Her eyes filled with tears. Slowly, they began to fall down her face. I felt so bad lying to her, but how would she look at me if I told her that I had a super power and was going to a strange island to learn how to use it. She'd probably call a psychiatrist and they'd put me in a straight jacket.

"Why would you do this?" she asked as she wiped her eyes.

"Because they will pay for my college and I can help the world."

"Travis, there are other ways of dealing with all of that. Your father left enough money for at least a year of school for you, and the rest you were already approved for loans. This is a terrible idea. Can't you see that?"

"Mom, this is something I want to do. I love you, but you can't change my mind."

"You're going to be a part of a war that shouldn't be happening."

"That's not the point. The point is that I'm doing what's best for you and me."

"Worrying about my only son everyday for the next four years is not what's best for me, Travis. It's going to kill me inside."

"Mom, I'm not even going to Iraq. I'm going to be at Fort Rucker. Just as a guard after I go through boot camp."

"I don't believe that for one minute, and you shouldn't either."

"It's all in my contract," I said continually making things up as I went along. I expected her to be more supportive of my choice.

"And what about all your friends, what about Amber?" She wiped her eyes again.

"I'm going to tell her tomorrow. Hopefully, she'll take it better than you did."

"I just think you're making a huge mistake."

"I've put some real thought into this; it's what I want to do. After my service I'll go to Penn State just like I always dreamed; following in dad's footsteps."

"If your father was still alive, he'd probably approve of your reckless decision. You know that whole 'being your own man' speech he always gave you."

"I know Mom, I miss him too, but you won't lose me as well. I promise."

She began to tear up again and hugged me.

"So if I can't stop you from going, then you have my blessing. When are you leaving?"

"In four days."

"WHAT! Why so soon?"

"I need to start the military training as soon as possible," I wanted to tell her the truth. I wanted her to know that I was going to be okay, but I couldn't.

"This isn't fair, that's just too soon."

"I'm sorry, but it's what I'm doing."

"I know, Travis. But you should tell Amber soon."

"I know. I wanted to tell you first. I figured if I could tell you, then I could tell anyone. I'm going to go call her now if that's okay."

"Yeah go ahead. I love you, Travis," she said as I left the room.

I turned around "I love you too, Mom," and proceeded down to my room. When I got there I grabbed my cell phone and tried to call her, but she didn't pick up. I started to pack all of the things that I needed. There really wasn't much, basically just clothes.

After a half an hour I tried to call her again, but still no answer. Then I realized it was Friday. Amber had dance class Fridays after school. I left a voicemail telling her to give me a call after dance. I laid down on my bed thinking about the island and how long I was going to be there for. Two to four years was a long time. It would help me a lot though. On the other hand, what if something bad happened while I'm gone, I thought. I have to stop talking myself out of this. I made my decision.

I wanted to try and use my power again. I held my left hand out and concentrated. My hand began to turn clear white again. I put it on my table and it turned brown. I lost concentration because I got too excited, it turned back to normal.

I tried to concentrate again, but with both hands, nothing happened. Then I tried my right hand, nothing. Finally, I made my last attempt with my left hand again, still nothing. The islands would be good for me, I knew it. I'd gain complete control over my power and hopefully be able to save hundreds of lives. I laid down on my couch day dreaming about all of the things that I might be able to do after I got back from the islands.

I woke up lying on my couch, getting up, and looking at the clock. It was 9:23 a.m. I had slept all night. I went over to my cell phone. Three missed calls, one from Derrick and two from Amber. I called Amber back. The phone was ringing, she picked up.

"Hey, Travis, how are you?"

"Good thanks. How about you? How was dance yesterday?"

"I'm good and dance was good too. You missed a party last night. Derrick and I tried to call you and went by your house, but your mom said you were sleeping. She seemed a little sad, did something happen?"

"No, well kind of."

"What is it?"

"I'd rather tell you in person. Can we meet at the park in a little while?"

"Yeah sure, I'll see you there in about a half hour. I love you."

"That's perfect, I love you too, bye."

I got off of the phone and hopped in the shower. While in the shower I couldn't help myself, I had to try and use my power again, first with my right hand, concentrating intensely, and it worked, my hand turned clear white and then into water. I kept my concentration longer the second time, then it turned back to my regular hand. I got out of the shower and dressed. I had fifteen minutes to get to the park. I locked up the house and went into the garage. I looked at my car, remembering it wasn't working. I hoped that it would start.

I got inside, put the key in the ignition, and turned the key. It started. I was super excited. I opened the garage door and drove off to the park to meet up with Amber. When I got there, I saw her sitting on a bench. I parked my car, walked over to her, and she ran to me, hugged me.

"Hey baby," she said before kissing me.

"I have something to tell you," I said cutting to the chase.

"Is it bad?"

"Kind of," I answered "Let's go lay down in the grass."

We walked over to the middle of the field and laid down.

"Amber . . . I joined the army."

Chapter II

Travis: Others

April 29, 2007

Sirens. Four fire trucks zoomed by the park. I rolled Amber off of me.

"I have to go try and help," I said standing up.

"What are you talking about? You can't do anything; you should just leave it up to the firefighters."

"I have to try," I said running out of the park. "I'll be back."

I ran after the fire trucks. It wasn't that hard to figure out where the fire was coming from, thanks to a giant cloud of black smoke in the middle of town. I ran as fast I could to get there. When I arrived the firefighters still hadn't started to put out the fire.

"Something is wrong with the fire hydrant," one yelled.

"Try the one across the street," another suggested.

Suddenly, it began to rain. I held both my hands out, absorbing the water.

"MY BABY! MY BABY BOY IS STILL INSIDE ON THE THIRD FLOOR!" a woman yelled.

I ran into the burning apartment building. It radiated with a heat unlike any I had experienced. I could feel my hands evaporating, returning them to normal, and not taking the chance of finding out what would happen if they actually did. I got to the third floor of the building and the stairs collapsed behind me. There was a hallway to my left and a door to my right, flames surrounding them both. I heard a little boy yelling for help from behind the door.

"Hold on, I'll save you!" I yelled to him. "Just move away from the door."

I turned my hands clear white and absorbed the fire. I tried to knock the door down, but my hands couldn't get close enough. I held my hands out and I could feel fire wanting to escape from them. I relaxed my hands and a ball of fire flew out of my hands, blasting a hole through the door.

"STOP IT! DON'T MOVE!" someone yelled behind me.

I turned around and saw a girl walking down the hallway. All the fire around her was dying down and there was no fire behind her.

"WHAT ARE YOU DOING?" she screamed.

As she got closer the fire around us was almost completely gone. I wasn't sure if she was a friend or foe. I tried to keep my guard up, but when I looked at my hands they were no longer fire.

"Your hands were on fire."

"How did you put all the flames out?"

"Did you cause this fire?" she asked. "Someone did, and you look like the best suspect."

"What? No, of course not. I'm trying to save this boy."

I turned around, kicked the door in, and ran in the room seeing the boy curled up in a ball on the floor. He was covered in smoke coughing. I ran over to him.

"Are you okay little man?" the boy lunged at me and wouldn't stop crying. "It's okay, you're safe."

I stood up, walked out of the room, and passed by the girl.

"Wait, I'm sorry. I didn't mean to accuse you of starting the fire. It's just, your hands were on fire and so was the building," she said. "My name is Callia."

"I'm guessing that you have an ability," I said as I walked down the hallway holding the young boy.

"Yes, I do. I can stop fire by cutting off the oxygen from it. What can you do? You obviously have a power. Your hands were on fire."

"I can absorb . . ." a fairly dark skinned man came out when I was walking down the hallway. I had no time to react. He had a sword drawn right to my face.

"Stop," the man said coldly.

"It's okay, Saeed, its okay. He's a good guy," the man, Saeed, put his sword back in its sheath.

"I didn't mean to startle you," Saeed said.

"It's fine. Just get out of my way. I need to get this boy back to his mother," he stepped aside.

I walked out of the building holding the boy and it was no longer raining. Everyone stared at me for a moment then ran over to me. I handed the boy over to his mother.

"Thank you so much for saving my boys life. How could I ever repay you?" the mother asked.

"It was nothing, really," I said to her as I started to walk away.

News crews began to run after me.

"Sir, please, just a few questions!" one group yelled.

I started to run away from them around the corner, and was grabbed. It was Saeed and Callia.

"You don't want to be spotted, stay calm. I won't hurt you," Callia stuck her head out of the alleyway and didn't see anyone.

"It's safe," she said.

Saeed let go of me, and I started to walk out of the alleyway.

"Wait, can we talk?" Callia said as she ran after me. "I want to help you. I know a man and a place that can help you with your powers."

I stopped walking.

"Perin and The Homestead, you know about them?"

"Yeah we know about The Homestead, but we don't know anyone named Perin," she said. "The man that we know is named Franz. We are going there in three days."

"So am I, but I'm leaving with Perin at Leigh Valley Airport."

"That's where we are leaving from as well. He's picking us up from our homes."

"Okay, we can talk."

We walked to the park where Amber and I were at about an hour earlier, but she had already left. We sat and talked about our powers and how we figured out that we could use them. Saeed could make it rain whenever he wanted, just by thinking about it. Callia could stop fire. I told them about my power and showed them by touching the grass and turning one of my fingers into it. I tried to change my whole hand, but couldn't. It started to get dark and we left. I went back home, called Amber, and told her what happened.

The next three days I spent with my mom and Amber. The day finally came when I had to go. Perin came and picked me up from my house and I said my good byes.

"Travis, please write me, or call whenever you get a chance," Amber asked before she kissed me goodbye.

"I will. When I come back, things will be just like before. I'll love you even more than I do now. Good bye, Amber."

I threw my bag in the trunk of the car, got into the backseat, and watched my loved ones tears as I drove away. We went to the airport and Callia and Saeed were there along with eleven other people. They all seemed about my age if not younger. Except for two who were at least in their twenties. They were all standing with an older person. There was another kid with Perin. He must had been picked up by Perin like I was.

"Who are all these people?" I asked Perin.

"They all have powers. You already know Callia and Saeed."

"Wait, how do you know that we met?"

"You don't think that I would just let you go and not keep tabs on you. I know it is an invasion of your privacy, but we didn't want you to reveal any information about the islands," he said. "I could tell you everything that you did over the past four days, what you ate, who you talked to, how long you talked to them. I could even tell you how many times you had sex with your girlfriend."

"Are you kidding me!?" I yelled trying not to make a scene. "I can't believe that you couldn't trust me for four days."

"I'm sorry; you weren't the only one that was watched. We watched everyone. We had to, to protect the safety of the islands and us."

"That doesn't give you any right to spy on me and my family. To be perfectly honest, I don't know anything about you or this island. You're even lucky that I decided to come with you guys in the first place."

"Don't make a big deal out of this. I have already apologized for spying on you. Can we please just forget about this and focus on what is important, which is your training," he said in a convincing tone.

"Yeah, I suppose."

"Okay, let's go."

Everyone got on the plane I sat next to Perin and the other guy. He didn't say anything, not even when I tried to introduce myself. There were so many people that had powers and I couldn't help but want to know all of them. A man in a black overcoat came out of the cockpit. On the left side of his over coat was a white patch. It was the symbol that I saw from before, in the holding cell, but his was just a little different. One of the trapezoids was white, the medium one. I wondered what it stood for.

"Now everybody, you already know that most of the people on this plane have a power. Yes, I am one of them. My power isn't important. You all know about the islands and what we do there. You have all made the commitment to the islands just by getting on this plane," he explained. "All of you have been assigned an instructor, which is who you are sitting next to. He or she knows everything about you and is assigned to help you hone your powers. Each of you has been put into a category. First Grade's barely know how to use their power. Second Grade's have control over their power and can use it well. Third Grade's, are one's with complete control over there powers. You will be put in different buildings according to skills. On the island fighting is not permitted under any circumstances and if you're caught fighting there will be severe consequences.

You will only associate with your instructor and roommate. If you are not in your room by 8:00 pm we will send someone to find you and apprehend you by any means necessary."

I sat there listening to all the rules that he was listing off. I was amazed on how strict the place actually was. I thought that it would be fun, but it didn't sound like it. I didn't come to have fun, but it would have been a nice addition.

"You will not be staying at The Homestead; you will be staying at another island called The Industrial. This is where your training will occur. Now that you know all the rules we will take off to The Homestead."

He walked back into the cockpit and the plane took off. I fell asleep. When I awoke we were there. Everyone got off the plane and stood next to their instructor. Perin had to go take care of something. He walked over to the man that gave the big speech on the rules and regulations of the islands and said something to him. They waved me over to them.

"Travis, I have to go take care of something very important and it can't wait. I'm going to leave you with him for now. He'll get you all set up, alright?"

"Yeah that's fine," I answered. "But what do I call this guy? Does he have a name?"

"Just call him, Sir. Oh, and, Sir, don't forget to watch Adair as well," Perin said to the man as he walked away.

"Okay everyone, follow me and we will register you in to the database and assign you a room," the man said.

On the outside of the building was the symbol again. Just like on Sir's jacket, the largest part wasn't black. It must have meant that this was the building he was from. We all followed him into the building. There were tons of people in black coats, just like Sir's everywhere. They were a little shorter and tighter though. Each of the people had the same exact patch as Sir's, but they all didn't have it in the same place. Some had it on their arms, backs or somewhere on the front. They all seemed very busy. A few feet in front of us were metal detectors, and a conveyer belt. It was exactly like airport security, except more high tech.

"Okay, now this is a simple procedure. Put your bag on the belt and step through the x-ray machine. This machine is designed to make sure that you aren't bringing anything unwanted onto the islands. Then just walk into the room on your immediate left and you will be entered into our database. Then you will be escorted to the boat that will bring you to The Industrial," the man explained followed by a brief pause. "Any Questions?"

No one said anything. The building shook violently and quickly subsided.

"Don't worry everyone. Just a storm brewing outside, it should soon diminish. Now get in a single file line and we can get moving."

Each person went through the x-ray machine with no trouble and the bag checks were good too. No one brought anything hazardous onto the islands. Then I went into the room to the left. They had me go into a separate room and show them my power. After I used my power, with some trouble, they told me to exit the room. When I got out a person gave me a number. It was a one. I wasn't sure what it meant, probably that my power was weak and undeveloped. I walked out of the room and met my escort. He was in his thirty's with long spiked back brown hair and wore a tan tight jacket with the islands symbol on the back.

"My name is Sven Hitry. I'll be your escort to the docks."

"I don't mean to sound rude, but why do I need an escort."

"It's just precaution. If you haven't noticed already that's one of the big things around here."

"Yeah," I laughed.

"Let's get on the move. It won't take long."

We began walking to the docks. We made it to the second hallway and an alarm sounded and red light flooded the long hallway. Hitry stopped and looked around. He seemed scared.

"Hold on," he said.

"What is it?" I asked.

"Something bad is happening."

"I could've figured that one out on my own. Do you know what?"

"Someone has escaped containment, but that's impossible. How could Bastian have escaped? He doesn't have any of his masks."

"What are you talking about?"

"Nothing, forget I said anything. Let's just get you to the dock quick."

The doors in front of us started to close and the alarm got louder. The lights started flashing at a faster rate.

"Damn, it's a full lock down. Not on the first day. This is just great," he said. "We have to get out of here and back to the lobby."

The doors were still closing in front and behind us. I turned around and saw someone walking in our direction. He was dressed in a black lab coat like the man on the plane was wearing. The coat went past his knees.

His face was obscured by something. The door closed, no longer being able to see him. I turned back around to Sven.

"There was someone coming," I said. "But the door stopped him."

Sven turned around and said, "It doesn't look like it."

My heart started pounding. I saw the same man walking. "That's impossible." Another door closed and I couldn't see him again.

"That was close. He was almost here."

The next door in front of that was nearly closed as well. The doorway kept getting smaller and smaller. The door closed, I let out a sigh of relief. Then I saw this gray face with blood red eyes come through the already closed door, followed by the rest of his body. My heart nearly stopped and I was unable to look away from him.

"What the hell? He can move through things?"

"It looks like it," Sven replied. "That is the guy I was talking about earlier, the one that was in containment, Bastian."

Another door closed, but it wasn't even going to slow him down.

"What do we do?" I asked. "Is he going to kill us?"

"I don't know."

He kept coming, walking through each sealed door.

"If I can't protect you, I'm sorry, but I'll try."

His arms started to stretch out to at least four feet. The man was about to walk through the last door between him and us. I backed up to the door behind me. This Bastian had full control over his power and I didn't. There was no way I could protect myself from this villain. He was now in our sealed off section.

"I'm going to stop you right here, Bastian," Sven said with his arms stretched out.

"I don't know who you are, but I'm not going to let you guys study us and use us for your sick and twisted experiments," Bastian said in a deep darkened voice.

"I have no idea what you're talking about."

"Deny till you die, right?" Bastian asked.

Sven threw his arms at Bastian, he then wrapped them around him, but Bastian made himself intangible and passed right through them. Sven tried to hit him, but his arms kept moving through Bastian. He walked right in front of Sven, putting his hand through the escort's chest, then pulling it out. Sven fell to the floor. Bastian's hands were bloody along with the tips of his sleeves. He walked toward me. My back was already against the wall. There was nowhere else to go. He grabbed my throat. I was terrified staring into his masked face. I didn't know what to do. I had to do something. I wasn't completely helpless, I could fight back. I had a power. I turned my hand clear white and put it on the wall, absorbing the metal. I was about to punch him in the chest.

"You have a power?" he asked as he let go of my neck and backed up.

"Yeah," I said as I stuck my hand up.

"You're as old as me."

"So?"

"Were ya kidnapped?"

"No, well, yes and no. I was at first, but it was just to awaken my power. Then I came here by choice to learn to control it."

"Ya have to get away from the islands. It's not safe here." Bastian said. "I was asked to come here and when I said no they tried to capture me. I eventually decided to go, because a man asked me to. Damn you, Faxon."

"Wait, what?"

The doors started to open quickly.

"I have to go. Ya have to get off these islands or else you will regret it. They will kill ya. They will use ya and when they are done, they'll kill ya. GET OFF THE ISLANDS!!!"

My hand went back to normal and he took off running through the doors before they fully opened. Soldiers came running down the hallway and Perin was with them. They stopped and looked at the escort's body. Perin stood next to it.

"First McGrand, now Hitry," he muttered.

Perin looked over at me.

"Travis, what are you doing here?"

"My escort was taking me to the dock when the lock down happened."

"How did Hitry die?"

"That guy put his hands through his chest."

Perin turned around and faced his men.

"Someone go check on Merrik. This storm didn't just come out of nowhere," two of the soldiers left back down the hallway. "Let's go, we have to get Bastian now. We are running out of time. Travis stay here. I'll come back for you."

Okay, I don't think I'd know where to go anyways."

Perin and the soldiers took off down the hallway going the same way Bastian did.

My thoughts raced, who is McGrand? Was everything that Perin told me a lie? What was the real purpose of the islands? Was this masked character, Bastian, telling the truth? What should I do? Should I somehow try and escape this place and go home. Why should I even trust Bastian's words?

I paced the hallway and gathered my thoughts. I had made up my mind. I knew exactly what I was going to do.

Chapter III

BASTIAN: CREATION

March 18, 2007

"I woke up, got dressed, and ate breakfast. It was a normal day, and then I went to school. I was in my wood design class workin' on a project. I went to go get a piece of wood from the back room. I saw a log in the back corner and went back to go take a look at it. I picked it up and started headin' back to the room. Then, all of the sudden, my hands started to shake. It got to the point where my whole body was shakin'. My head started feelin' heavy. My eyesight began to blur and I blacked out.

When I came to, I was in the nurse's office with the shop teacher standin' above me. They told me that I passed out and hit my head on the floor. The teacher handed me a mask and said that he found it next to me on the floor. The mask was oval shaped. Its eyes holes were really small and the face had a very stern expression. I immediately grabbed it and said that it was mine. I didn't even think about it, it was just an impulse. After they sent me home, I put the mask away. To be honest it gave me the creeps. I had no recollection of makin' it, but I knew it belonged to me. I went down stairs to get somethin' to eat because I still felt light headed, then went back up to my room, and took a look at the mask. It looked like it needed a little color. I went into my closet, grabbed some paint, sat down at my desk, and opened my paint kit lookin' at the mask. I looked right in its eyes. My head started to feel heavy again; I was shakin' and my eyesight was blurrin'.

I opened my eyes, liftin' my head off my desk, looked down, and the mask was colored. It was gray and silver. I couldn't have done it, I didn't remember. I had an urge to put on the mask, but was fearful. Maybe the mask was makin' me do all of this, I thought. I keep blackin' out. Who else could have done it though, it had to be me.

I picked it up off my desk and held it in my hands. It gave me this really strange feelin' just by lookin' at it. I turned it over, brought it to my face, and it pulled itself to it. I tried to move my hands to get it off, but I couldn't move any part of my body. It was like I was a frozen stiff. I felt myself slowly gettin' tired. It was about four minutes until the mask fell off, and I fell as well; both of us hittin' my bedroom floor. I was scared and out of breathe. I didn't know what to do so I took a nap, woke up, and then I called you," I explained.

"That's some story, Bastian," Steven said. "Well, I think that you're crazy, and you were just dreaming."

"I wasn't. I swear," I said. "Watch I'll show ya."

I pulled a box out from underneath my bed and opened it. The mask was inside and I took it out.

"Watch," I said puttin' the mask to my face.

The mask suctioned to my face and I was unable to move.

"Oh, WOOW. I've suddenly been proven wrong because you can stand still. Good job," Steven said in a sarcastic tone.

He picked up a bat in my room.

"If you don't move in ten seconds, I'm going to hit you."

I heard what he said, but I couldn't talk or move. He was actually goin' to hit me. He started countin' down.

"Six, Five, Four . . . Three . . . Two . . . One . . ." he swung he bat at me, makin' contact with my left shoulder and snappin' the bat in half. Shards flew everywhere. I didn't even feel it. Steven stood still in amazement.

"What the hell?" he said confused.

I just stood there, hearin' him, but unable to respond. I could feel myself becomin' exhausted.

"I'm going to go grab something else to hit you with," he ran downstairs and a few seconds later he came back up with a crowbar.

"I'm going to see how much you can take," he said holdin' the crowbar like a bat.

He swung the crowbar, hittin' me in the same arm. Steven dropped it and put his hands under his armpits.

"Shit that hurt!" he yelled curlin' up.

I felt myself gettin' more and more fatigued. The mask fell off and I fell to the floor with it. I was totally wiped, out of breath, and my head hurt.

"See I told ya," I said gaspin'. "I told ya that I couldn't move."

"This is too weird for me," Steven said as he stood up shaking his hands off. I don't know what to say."

He reached out his hand and helped me up. "I won't say anything about this to anyone because I'm going to forget it myself. This is way too weird for me. Sorry dude," Steven said as he left my room and went home.

I went to school and Steven honestly acted like it had never happened. It wasn't any big deal to me; it would have been cool to share it with some one. I started wonderin' how I made the mask and why. Also, how it could do what it did. It was possible I didn't even make the mask, maybe the wood made it. I went back to the shop room and talked to Mr. Smith about the log that was in the storage room. He said that it was just from his house, just a regular tree log. After school I went home and pondered some more about the mask. Did I make it or did I find it, I continually debated.

I tried to remember what happened before I blacked out. The last thing that I came to mind was my body startin' to shake and my vision blurrin'.

"Bastian . . . Come down here right now!" my dad yelled.

I walked out of my room, downstairs, into the livin' room, and he was waitin' by the outside door.

"Why the hell didn't you go to Mr. Larson's house after school yesterday?" my dad asked angrily.

"I blacked out at school yesterday. I told ya that last night."

"Well, you need to go over there right now and get that work done that you were supposed to have done yesterday."

"Okay fine. I will, ya don't have to yell."

"We'll if you didn't run over his lawn mower, then you wouldn't be in debt to him. Now get moving."

"Okay, I'm goin'," I said as I walked out the door towards Mr. Larson's house.

He didn't have to be such an asshole all the time. I knew mom left, but I didn't see how bein' angry will bring her back. I hated to think it, but it's probably his fault she was gone anyway. I mean, I was only a boy and could barely remember her. I couldn't think of any other reason she would leave. All he ever did was yell and tell me about how I'm wrong and always remindin' me that I did things wrong. He was hardly ever in a good mood. It had always been a strict lifestyle. I figured after I graduated that I'd pack up and leave, but I just never could. I didn't think I could forgive myself for leavin' him on his own.

I got to Mr. Larson's backyard and he was standin' by a pile of logs.

"It's about time that you came over here boy," he said. "Where were you yesterday?"

"I blacked out in school. I wasn't feelin' well so I figured I would take a day off."

"We'll that's fine then. I suppose all those odd jobs that you own me will just take care of themselves. I want this whole pile of logs chopped and you can consider your debt to me repaid."

"But there's like a hundred logs here."

"You're a strong looking lad. You can handle it. Hell, when I was your age, I could do twice this much, with my eyes closed mind you. Now don't hurt your self," he said and walked back into his house.

What the hell did havin' his eyes open or not have anythin' to do with it, I thought. I couldn't stand the old kook. I picked up the axe and started chopping the logs. An hour went by and I was about half way done. I was there for another an hour until I had ten logs left. I looked over at the pile of them. My body started to hurt, all the work finally takin' its effect on me. My hands started to shake and my vision started to blur.

No, I wasn't gettin' tired. I was startin' to black out again. I tried to stop it. My whole body was shakin' terribly. I tried to gain control and stop it from shakin'. Flashes were appearin' in my head. They were faces. A bird-esque face, a face with X's for eyes, and yellow demonic lookin' one, and the last one constantly kept changin' colors. I tried to remain calm and stay focused. It was workin', the shakin' lessened and my vision became somewhat clearer. The faces were still flashin' in my head though. They started to talk to me.

"Up, up, up," The bird one kept sayin'.

"Stop. They must fail all of them, all the vitals," said the one with X's over its eyes.

"Don't stop, keep going," the yellow faced one said.

The multi colored one said, "Change."

They kept repeatin' the same thing. My body began to shake ferociously. I could feel my hands shake violently, my thumbs especially. My vision was gone. All I saw were yellow outlined scratch marks. I didn't hear anythin'. I blacked out. I woke up in my room with somethin' my hand. My lights were off and it was pitch black outside. I dropped what I was holdin', got out of bed, and turned on the light. I looked on the ground and saw a mask, picked it up, and noticin' somethin' in my fingernails, they were full of somethin'. I placed it on my dresser, opened my desk drawer, and took out some fingernail clippers. I dug out whatever was in my fingernails; it was wood, chunks and shards of wood. "What happened?" I asked myself.

I tried to remember, but all I could see were the faces. I picked up the mask off the dresser and looked at it. It was one of the faces I kept seein' before the blackout. It was colorless, its eyes were angled upward and it had this somewhat terrifyin' grin. It was bearin' its sharp teeth. The fact that it was plain was gettin' to me. I figured that I would paint it the color that I saw it, yellow and black.

I painted it and it looked fantastic. I began to wonder if it could do somethin' special like the other mask that I made. I put it on my shelf next to the other one. I sat down at my computer and looked up a handful of mask websites. One of the sites said that masks were a way to escape yourself and become somethin' you are not. Another site said that masks occur throughout the world, and although they tend to share many characteristics, highly distinctive forms have developed. The function of the masks may be magical or religious; they may appear in rites of passage or as a make-up for a form of theatre. They may help mediate with spirits, or offer a protective role to the society that utilises their powers. They could also be a way for a person to show ones true emotion or self.

An ad popped up. Do you want to make this world a better place? Do you think you were born to help the world? Then click here now. That's what the ad said. I wasn't sure whether to click it or not. The words seemed to move around the screen in an allurin' pattern. For some reason I thought clickin' it would get me what I want. It might send me to another mask web site, so I clicked it. My screen went black and ones and zeroes covered my computer screen. Then it shut down.

"Shit!" I yelled, "What the hell happened?"

I tried to turn my computer back on but it didn't work. For some reason I let my anger get the best of me, shovin' my computer off my desk with it slammin' on the floor. Pieces flew all across the room. I took a deep breath. "This will not go over well with my father." I had to go buy a new one. I grabbed my keys and I was about to leave. I turned around and looked at my shelf. I felt the yellow mask callin' out to me. I walked over to the shelf; grabbed it and put it in my side pocket. I had no idea what this mask did or if it even did anythin'.

I drove to the center of town to the Computers-4-U store. My friend worked there so I figured that he could get me a discount on one of the laptops.

"Hey, Chris, what's up?" I said walkin' through the front door to the store.

"Not much, you?"

"Nothin'. I just broke my computer and I wanted to know if you could get me a discount on a laptop?"

"Hey, no problem. Just give me one second and I'll get you the one that we sell the most," he said walkin' into the back room.

"Okay, cool thanks."

He walked back out with a box in his hand.

"You're all set. I'll ring you up."

I turned around for a quick second because I heard a car. Three white vans pulled in front of the store. The side doors opened and guys in black suits poured out. There were nine guys in suits and a person about my age. I got a really bad feelin' in my stomach. He was wearin' a yellow shirt with a black vest half zipped over it. They walked into the store.

"Excuse me are you, Bastian Glant?" one of the men in a black suit asked.

"Who wants to know?"

"What's going on, Bastian?" Chris whispered to me.

"I'm not sure." I whispered back. "Hold on to my computer."

"Sir, please come with us."

I looked to my left and saw another door. Another van pulled in front of it. Three more men exited that van.

"Is there an exit in the back?" I whispered to Chris.

"Yeah, straight ahead after those doors," he answered. "It's all yours to use."

I leaped over the counter and ran through the door leadin' into the back room. Chris moved out of the way. The men in suits started to chase after me. I ran out the back door to get outside, then runnin' to the side of the buildin'. I realized that I had brought the mask with me. I took it out of my pocket and held it facin' me. I was unsure about puttin' it on, havin' no idea what it could do. What if it did somethin' bad to me like make me explode or somethin', I thought. I heard the men come out of the back of the store. It was now or never.

"Stop, don't move," someone said. "My name is Zander, and I just need to talk to you. We don't have much time."

I turned to him. "About what?" Two of the men in black suits came into the alleyway and Zander didn't seem very happy about it.

"Your gift. Your power. Your ability."

"How do you know about that?"

"Well, your computer. We got almost all your information except for your exact address."

"Okay, what do you want to know?"

"I want to know what your power is and how it works."

I heard more footsteps come up from behind me. It was two more guys in black suits. They kept gettin' closer. I squeezed the mask.

"We just want you to come with us so we can learn more about you."

"I'm not goin' to let ya experiment on me!" I yelled

I threw the mask onto my face. Just like the other mask, it drew itself to my face. I felt energized as soon as the mask was on. I had a burst of energy and stamina and my heart was racin'. I heard a small voice in the back of my head.

"Go! Go! Don'tstopmoveadrenaline!" the voice was yellin' in a high quick tone.

My body felt awkward and couldn't stand still. I just had to move. I felt hyper, I felt quick . . . I felt . . . good. I couldn't control my body anymore; it started movin' on its own.

"What did you just do?"

"I don't know," I quickly said in a deep voice.

My voice changed. I even talked fast. Zander held out his arm and snapped his fingers. Suddenly, I was surrounded by darkness. I ran forward and escaped it. Zander was standin' there with a bewildered look on his face.

"How did you get out of my dome?!" Zander yelled, "You should be asleep."

"What? Ijustsawdarkness," I said quickly. "I wasn't asleep."

"This makes no sense," Zander said.

My body started runnin', passin' the two men behind me. They tried to grab me, but my body dodged them with expert maneuvrin'. Zander and the guys in suits started runnin' after me. Zander kept puttin' the domes of darkness around me and I kept runnin' through them. My body was sprintin' through the back alleys, stayin' out of populated areas.

I could see where I was goin', but had no control of my direction. My body was weavin' in and out of the domes of darkness that Zander was snappin' at me. I heard the sound of him snappin' his fingers over and over again. He was becomin' more and more frustrated each time I ran out of one. I looked back and I lost the men in suits. They had to of been too tired and gave up the chase. I could tell that Zander was gettin' tired as well. I was far too fast for him to catch up to me, and I wasn't even close to bein' out of energy. I felt like I could run for miles. I reached a road with cars zoomin' by, movin' about forty miles an hour. I felt myself speed up as I ran into the road weavin' in and out of the cars as if it were as easy as breathin'. I was fast enough to dodge them; my brain was processin' all the information so fast, knowin' the exact moment when to go. Zander stopped on the sidewalk before the street. I was on the other side by then.

"I'll be back!! Don't you forget it!!!" he yelled irately.

There was a fence and woods behind me, wavin' goodbye to him, my body then jumped over the fence and sprinted into the wooded area. I ran for about ten minutes and came to a small pond, breathin' deeply. My heart was slowin' down and my head started to ache. I heard the same voice I heard earlier.

"Not yet. No, not yet," it yelled. "Istillhaveplentyofenergy."

I felt the mask slowly loosenin'. My body started to shake and my head was poundin'. I wanted the mask off, but my hand moved up to my face, tryin' to hold it on. The voice was gettin' more and more faint.

"No, no . . . I want to stay . . ." it said quietly.

I ripped the mask off and immediately my head stopped hurtin' and my body stopped shakin'. I felt dizzy and passed out.

I awoke near to the pond; the mask was lyin' next to me. I grabbed and stood up, feelin' good, rested. I started walkin' back to the store. By the time I got home it was pitch black outside and it started thunderin'.

When I got home I jumped in the shower. The ice cold drops covered my body. It was as if I was washin' away all of my stress and fears. As I stepped out of the shower the thunder outside roared. I walked into my room and shut the door behind me. I threw my dirty clothes in the hamper, opened the top drawer to my dresser, grabbin' some boxers. To my surprise there lied three painted masks on top. They were ones that kept flashin' in my head a day ago. A bird mask, painted white with two red and gold feathers. It wasn't like the others, smaller, a masquerade style, only coverin' the top half of the face. It felt grainy, like sandpaper. Its beak started in between its eyes and endin' about three inches out with a sharp point. The second was an odd lookin' mask painted a bunch of different colors, shaped like a square. The eye and mouth holes were much larger too, with one eye hole larger than the other. Last was the cracked white mask with no eyes, instead there were big black x's outlined with red. It didn't have a mouth either. Just starin' at it gave me goose bumps.

"I must have made them the same day that I made the yellow one."

I walked over to my shelf and grabbed the gray and silver mask along with the yellow mask, puttin' them both into the drawer. "I am goin' to try all of you out tomorrow. I'm goin' to figure out what all of you do."

Chapter IV

Zander: The Explanation

March 20, 2007

I sat there in the back of the van extremely pissed off. I didn't understand what just happened.

"This is bullshit. How could this kid not be affected my power? He should have fallen asleep. This was supposed to be an easy capture."

"Sorry sir. We got tired," one of my men said.

"I don't want to work with you idiots ever again. When we get back to The Homestead I'm going to get a whole new group of men, and maybe even a partner . . . with a power."

"Sorry sir," they said.

"Just drive."

We got to the Salina Municipal airport in Kansas and Perin was waiting for us. All of us entered a helicopter; not one said a word the whole ride. When we got to the island I dismissed my men. Perin and I started walking inside the Homestead.

"So, are you going to tell me what happened and why Mr. Bastian Glant isn't walking with us right now?" Perin asked as we walked into the building.

"My power didn't work on him."

Perin stopped and looked at me.

"Your power didn't work? What do you mean?"

"It didn't work. I snapped my fingers, putting the dome right on him, but nothing happened. He walked right out of it. He was unaffected," I explained. "I think it had something to do with the mask that he had on."

"He learned how to use his power!?"

"He must have," I replied. "Faxon told you he had a power, but not where to locate him? I thought that guy knew everything?"

"Yes, he said something was stopping him from locating Bastian. Now I know that he was hiding Bastian so that we couldn't get to him. If we can figure out how Bastian's power works than maybe we can stop this whole thing."

"Yeah that's if we can ever catch him. When he put on the mask he was acting extremely hyper. I think that's why he didn't fall asleep, probably too energized and couldn't fall asleep. We need to catch him soon, before his power becomes so advanced that we can't catch him at all."

"You're right, next time maybe you can take someone with you," Perin said. "I'm not to sure yet. I'll let you know. Go get some rest. You can work out the rest of the week. I'll get a tactical team sent to Lindsborg, Kansas. We'll figure out where he lives, where he goes, and what he does. We will get this guy, *you* will get this guy. It won't be too hard if he doesn't see us coming. You can get him before he has a chance to put on the mask."

"Sounds like a plan to me," I replied. "See you later Perin."

I went to the gym first, working out for about two hours. I couldn't stop thinking about how I let Bastian get away. I knew I couldn't have done any better. I went to my room on the Homestead and fell asleep. I woke up, ate breakfast, and then hit the gym again. Afterwards, I went to The Homestead training and testing area. I made sure that my power was still working, testing my ability on lab rats, not causing any harm to them, only putting them to sleep. It was working fine; actually a little better than before. My range increased by two feet. I went to go see Perin, but he was in is office talking to someone I've never seen before. I started to listen to their conversation.

"We found a few more adolescents with powers due to our encoded detection system," Perin said.

"How did you design this detection system? It's so advanced," the other man asked.

"It was made by Faxon and a girl that can control technology. They developed a system that when a person with a power sees it, they are attracted to it. They disguised it as a "pop up" ad on the Internet. We have a lot of our kids because of this ad. Shortly after, Faxon went rogue and disappeared. He said that he didn't agree with what we were doing and that it wasn't what he had signed up for," Perin informed.

"That's amazing. Very intelligent," the man stated. "But what about Faxon? What did The Boss say to do? If he knows everything then he could stop us easily."

"Another machine was built by the girl. Let's just say he won't know anything about the islands as long as it's running.

"I miss so much while I'm down there on duty."

"Well, McGrand it was great talking to you again. I hope that you can come up more often. It must be terrible being down there all the time."

"I only have one more shift down there then it is someone else's turn. It might even be you."

"I highly doubt it."

"Well, that's up to The Boss," McGrand chuckled. "With two out of seven of us going down there at a time the chances are pretty good for all of us to get called to duty at least once. I was unfortunate enough to get called down twice in a row."

"Yeah that's a shame, but we did get into this project to help. We both know that we need the strongest of us to be down there at all times. It is the most important job around," Perin said.

"True, but it gets really boring down there. The Boss said that this time I can come up for the orientation in May."

"That's great, I remember hearing something about that."

"There's nothing else to do down there, I just train the whole time. I work out and try to do different things with my ability. You should see some of the things I've learned. Four years of straight training does a lot for you."

"Well, I'm always busy up here, trying to locate more and more of the new kids with powers," Perin explained. "And I think we might finally be able to stop it. We found someone who is very special. His power is similar to that of The First's."

"Are you serious? We might actually be able to figure out how to stop it all?" McGrand asked.

"If we can catch him . . . yes."

"That's amazing. It can finally come to an end," McGrand said. "Have you told the boss yet?"

"No, it's a new development. We just recently started to look into it," Perin replied.

"I have a question for you. Have you even seen the boss? Have you ever been in Boss's office?"

"No, actually I haven't," Perin said. "Come to think of it, I heard some people talking and none of them had ever seen the boss."

"I mean we have all saw that silhouette of his body when we started here, but I've talked to the others and they haven't seen him either. We are the tops of this organization and we have never seen our boss. After twelve long years of service I'm starting to get suspicious," McGrand added.

"What are you trying to say?"

"When I get back up during the orientation I'm going to figure everything out. Nothing is going to stop me. One strike of thunder and I'll take anyone down that gets into my way,"

"Don't do anything too irrational. Think about it while you're down, okay?"

"No promises, but I can try," McGrand said. "Well, I think that I have to go soon. I'm gonna get out of here."

They both stood up and I ran down the hall and went back to my room. I didn't want them to catch me eavesdropping. The next day, I wanted to ask Perin what he was talking about with that McGrand guy, but I didn't want him to know that I was listening. I walked out of my room and Perin was waiting for me right outside my door.

"There is a disturbance at The Industrial. We have to go. You need to knock this person out. We can't have that kind of behavior," Perin said.

"Why not get your little golden boy, Zane to handle it? He's you number one student right?"

"Zane is away with his students. We need you. One of the female students somehow found out some information. I believe Faxon was involved somehow. We can't allow her to cause damage to our plans. We can't allow her to notify any students of what our true intentions are," Perin said. "She left us a note saying she was going to kill the instructors and anyone that gets in her way."

"Fine. Let's go."

Perin and I left The Homestead and got on the boat to get to The Industrial. We arrived at the gate and there was a man waiting for us. He was tall, black, and very well dressed in a flashy black suit and a bright red tie. He was holding some folders in his hand.

"Perin, how have you been?" the man asked.

"We can't waste any time with formalities, Yukanzo, we have to get this situation straightened out," Perin answered.

"Yes sir. First off she has already killed two kids. One male and one female," Yukanzo explained.

We started to walk past the gates and into The Industrial.

"What is her power?" I asked.

Yukanzo handed me a folder. I opened it up; it was a picture of a girl and information about her.

"Her name is Paige Riture. Physical Appearance: Bleach Blonde hair, green eyes, Caucasian. Height: five-feet, six inches. Weight: one-hundred and eight pounds. Noticeable features: rose petal tattoos on the back of her right calf. She has the ability to transfer her pain onto someone else. Everything from broken appendages to scratches, cuts, and sores disappear as if they were never there at all," Yukanzo explained.

"Well, that's a very interesting power. No wonder she has already killed two people," Perin said.

"I'm going to get this girl, no problem. With a snap of a finger," I said to them.

"You better be careful. She's not your ordinary student. She was being trained by the head of the I.E.S, or Industrial Enforcement Squad. Her power was so strong that the Boss wanted her trained better than anyone else on the Industrial. I guess his plans for her have just fallen through," Yukanzo explained.

"Do you have any idea where she could be at this time?" I asked.

"Somewhere in the woods. That's where we found the two bodies," Yukanzo answered.

"Well I'm going now. Like you said, we can't waste any time." I walked into the woods.

"Be careful!" Perin yelled.

I walked around for hours and then I felt a presence. I knew that someone was following me. I stopped and heard footsteps, and then they stopped as well. I snapped my fingers and created a dark dome around myself. Not only was I unaffected by my sleep dome, but I could see in the dark perfectly. I had many advantages while inside of it. She knew nothing about me and I knew all about her.

"Zander, five-feet, ten inches, dark blue eyes, dirty blonde hair and last, but not least your power. You can see in the dark and can create domes of darkness up to ten feet in diameter and from twenty-five feet away. Anyone trapped inside of the dome is immediately put to sleep," A voice said. "I know all about you and I can kill you at any time."

"So apparently I don't have the advantage," I muttered.

Her measurements were wrong. She knew everything that I could do. I knew everything that she could do as well. "This is going to be enjoyable."

"I figured you'd be the one they sent to find me. I've seen you before, during the small riot over a year ago, the one caused by that little girl. I never forgot how quickly you and the others took out the guards and the other powered people. I was hoping to be like the group of you someday; helping the islands in their goal to protect all of us, teach us, save us. But now I know the truth. Do you know the truth Zander?"

I looked around as she was spilling her story, but she was very well hidden. I couldn't even pin point her voice. Whoever trained her did a great job. I had to get a better view of the area so I made a path of domes, allowing me to walk around and get a visual of where she could be. She hadn't made a sound since she talked.

"Why don't you come out and fight?" I yelled.

"The same reason you don't come out of those domes of yours."

I heard her, behind me. I went through my domes quickly and quietly, she couldn't see me, but I could see everything. I snapped my fingers making four dark domes in the area that I heard her; two close to the ground and two in the air. I didn't hear anything at first. Then a crash, like someone had fallen.

"Gotcha."

My guard was completely down. I stopped focusing on the domes around me and I created one right where I had heard her fall. I heard footsteps from behind me. I turned around and there she was. She touched my chest and my right arm was instantly consumed by pain causing me to fall to my knees. She stood in front of me adjusting her right arm.

"You did get me, but my arm broke my fall. I'm so used to pain that I don't feel it anymore. Pain doesn't even phase me," she said standing in front of me with her arms crossed.

"You're way too cocky," I said as I snapped my fingers.

My dome appeared with both of us inside it and she fell to the ground. I took out my phone and called Perin. He picked up.

"It's done. Just go into the woods where I did and follow the main trail you should be here within the hour," I said.

"We'll get there sooner than that."

I sat there holding my arm, waiting for them. Only about three minutes had passed.

"Zander?"

I heard Perin's voice outside of the dome and walked out holding my arm.

"How did you get here so fast?"

"Well, we traced your call, got your location, and Yukanzo teleported us here," Perin said.

"Oh . . . cool. My arm is broken and it really hurts. I'm gonna need this looked at immediately."

Yukanzo tossed me some handcuffs.

"I'll teleport you to the medical wing, just handcuff her first." I went back inside the dome and handcuffed her. "Okay, all set."

"Okay, Zander, let the dome down."

I stopped concentrating and the dome disappeared. Then, Yukanzo grabbed me and we teleported to the medical wing.

"Well there you go," Yukanzo said. "Excuse me nurse, can you take care of this boy's arm please? I have to go."

Yukanzo teleported again and just left me there. The nurse took me into a room and told me that my arm wasn't broken. It was only a sprain, nothing too serious. She had gotten me a sling and it should be healed in a few weeks. Yukanzo teleported into the room with Perin, holding on to Perin's shoulder. He obviously had to have contact to teleport with someone.

"What the hell was that about?" I asked.

"You needed immediate attention," Yukanzo said.

"What happened to the girl?"

"She was dealt with," Perin said.

"Did you kill her?"

"Don't worry about it. Just worry about getting better," Perin said.

Yukanzo grabbed on to me and teleported me to my room.

"What the hell is your problem?" I yelled.

"You need to rest."

"I was mid conversation." I pulled my arm out of his grip.

"What is going to happen to Paige?"

"She will be brought to the detention center and held with the rest of the dangerous prisoners. Your best bet is to not worry about it and just focus on healing your arm."

Yukanzo teleported away. I stormed off into my room and laid down in my bed.

"I really messed up this time. I possibly cost some girl her life."

Chapter V

Bastian: Masks

March 21, 2007

I woke and my dad had already gone off to work. I went upstairs and took the five masks out of my dresser drawer, the bird, the multi-colored, the one with X's over its eyes, the gray one and the yellow one. I brought them all downstairs and went outside, putting the masks on the ground. I picked the yellow one, I put it near my face, and it suctioned to it. My heart started to race, my blood pumpin' fast and I started shackin'. I couldn't stand still. I grabbed on to the sides of the mask and pulled it off. It was hard to do though, like the mask was trying to stay on.

Next, I picked up the one that looked like a bird and put it to my face. Just like the other one, it suctioned. I stood there and heard a voice in the back of my head. It was faint, but audible.

"Go . . . Up is where I belong," the voice said.

I began to levitate. My whole body was off the ground and the voice got louder.

"Let's go, up, Up, UP!" the voice yelled.

My whole body flew into the air. I had no control of where I was goin'. I couldn't stop. The voice was gettin' more and more distinct. The mask had completely taken control over my body. I couldn't even move my fingertips.

"Yes! WOO HOO!" the voice shouted.

"Stop it! This is my body!" I yelled.

"I just want to fly. You can't blame me," it said.

"I can't believe I'm talking to myself."

"You're not, you're talking to me," my body stopped in the air.

"What are you?" I asked it.

"What do you mean?"

"Some kind of ghost or spirit that took control of the mask?"

"No, I'm not any of those things. I just want to fly. Can you let me do that?"

"How did you get trapped in this mask?"

"Trapped? I live here."

"What? I don't understand."

"I don't either. The only thing that I know or remember is that I want to fly and that's all I like to do."

"Have you ever flown before?"

"Yes all the time. I know my purpose in life and it is to fly."

"Well do you have a name?"

"Not that I know of." It said as my body continued to fly across the sky. "WOOOOOOO!!! I love the air against me."

"Please stop."

It stopped flyin' and stayed suspended in the air again.

"How about you let me have control over my body and I promise to fly you around whenever I get the chance."

"Maybe."

"Also, what if . . . I give you a name. You know, so that you know who you are?"

"I know who I am. Why do I need a name?"

"Don't you want to have somethin' that is yours? Somethin' that no one can take away from you?"

"Okay, but what is my name?"

"Well . . . what do you want your name to be?"

"NO, you said you would give me a name. If I like it then you can have control of your body again."

"Okay . . . what about Ien?"

" . . . I like it. We have a deal."

I could move. I could control my body and I was flyin'.

"How did you come up with the name for me?" Ien asked.

"It was my grandfather's name. He was a pilot in the Vietnam War. He passed away a few years ago."

"I am sorry for your loss. If it helps, I do love the name. I will honor this name for you. I think it suits me well."

"So from now on you won't take over my body every time I put on the mask?"

"No, just as long as you keep flying I think we'll get along just fine."

I flew back home. Ien was so relaxed while we were flyin'. He didn't say that he was, I just felt it like he was a part of me.

"I'm goin' to try on some more masks, but when I'm done I'll put you back on and we can go for a spin around the sky."

"Okay, just don't be too long."

I landed back in my yard. I grabbed on the side of the mask and barely pulled. It came off easily.

I was startin' to understand, the masks were alive. They wanted somethin' from me. It was possible, if I talked to them, like I did Ien, I could maybe control what they could do.

"Maybe that's why it was so easy to take off Ien. He knew that I would be back. I had to rip the yellow mask off. I need to form a relationship with the masks before they will fully let me use their abilities."

I bent down and looked at all the masks. "The yellow puts me in an adrenaline rush state. The gray one doesn't let me move, but I'm indestructible, and then there is Ien." I picked up the colorful one, put it on my face, and held out my hands. They were changin' colors, constantly; red, blue, yellow, brown and every other color. It kept repeatin' over and over again, stayin' a single color for only a few seconds. I tried to listen for a voice, but I couldn't hear a thing. I had control over my body so it was really kind of borin'. It didn't do much but change colors.

"Is this really all you do?"

"Yes . . . sorry," the voice said squeakily. "All I do is change colors."

"Hey, it's cool. You don't need a super cool power."

"I'm sorry," she said.

"It's fine, don't worry about it," she didn't respond. "Are you still there?"

There was no response.

I took the mask off with ease. I felt bad for her because she felt useless. No offense to her, but he kind of was. I laid her on the ground and I picked up the last mask that I hadn't tried out. I started to bring it close to my face then I heard my dad's truck pull up in the driveway. I tried to pull the mask away, but it was too late, it was already suctioning to my face. A voice yelled at me.

"Leave me alone! DIE!!!" it screamed.

At that very moment, I felt pain in my chest and I couldn't breathe. My heart was burning.

"I'm shuttin' down all your organs. NOW DIE!!!" the voice yelled.

I blacked out; the pain was too unbearable. When I woke up, I was in a hospital lyin' in bed. My dad was sittin' in a chair beside me.

"What happened?" I asked

My dad looked up at me and hugged me.

"You're okay! Thank god you're okay!" he sad with his voice full of fear.

"What happened?"

"Well, I came home from the factory and the back door was open so I went outside and you were lying on the grass. I thought you were asleep, but there was blood drippin' out of your mouth, eyes and ears. I called 911 and they rushed you to the hospital. The doctors said that all of your organs had shut down for a minute and caused your body to go into shock, but they can't explain how. What were you doin'?"

"The mask . . ." I said quickly realizin' what happened. The mask did this to me.

"What about those masks? I left them outside. Were they for school?"

"Oh . . . yeah, art. I was about to bring them inside and that's the last thing that I remember."

Three doctors came in and asked how I was doing. They were glad to see that I was okay. Then they took my dad outside of the room. I knew he can be a real bastard sometimes, but he did love and care for me. It just took a lot for him to show it. He came back into the room and the doctors walked away.

"What did they say?"

"They said that all the tests for drugs or poisons came back negative. They want you to stay another night just for observation and you can go home tomorrow."

"Oh . . . okay that's alright."

"I have work tomorrow. If you want me to stay with you I will, but you do seem fine and it is getting late."

"You can go ahead and go home dad. I'll be fine."

"Okay, son. I'll be back to get you tomorrow afternoon."

"Okay, dad. Bye, I love ya."

"I love you too," he said, kissin' me on my head and closin' the door behind him as he left.

"Why would that mask not want me to use it? Well, I'm not goin' to ever again. I'll stick with Ien. I need to talk to the other two masks as well. I promised Ien that we would go flyin'. I hope he'll understand. I have a lot to accomplish. Now I just need to figure out how I made the masks . . . and why?"

Chapter VI

ADEN: THE STORY OF BLOOD

April 26, 2007

"My dad had left us when I was just a child, maybe two or three years old. I'm not too sure why, my mom never told me. It does bother me from time to time, when I think about it. It's usually when I let my anger get the best of me. When I lose my temper, I try to stay calm; it helps sometimes, but not always.

Anyways, it was September 12, 1994; I was four years old when it first started. One night, I was playing with my toys in the bathroom. My mom was using her hair straightener because she was about to go out and the babysitter was on her way over to watch me. My mom left the bathroom to go try on a different shirt. I remember she asked me if she looked better in blue or red. I told her red. She had left the straightener on so I stood up and tried to unplug it, but instead I accidentally knocked it over and onto a pile of clothes and they immediately combusted. I ran over to the sink and turned on the water, cupping my hands together, and attempted to splash water onto the fire, but it had no effect. I yelled to my mom, but she either couldn't hear me or ignored me. The fire started to spread seemingly knowing exactly where it wanted to go. The flames attacked the carpet in the hallway, spreading fast. My mom came out of her room screaming. She saw me standing in the bathroom. She said she was going to call 911 and told me to stay away from the fire. The fire was spreading quicker and quicker, catching the ceiling a blaze. I was trapped inside of the bathroom still. My mom came back with a bucket of water and dumped it in the doorway, then ran into the bathroom grabbing me. The whole house was covered in flames with no way out; all the exits covered by the inferno. The ceiling started to collapse. We were both so terrified. We went near the door closest to the kitchen and waited for the fire trucks. She held me tight as we both cried.

Suddenly, the stove exploded and we both were pushed back. My mom held me close, never letting go. Thankfully, we weren't that close to it or it could have spelled death for us. My leg was all cut up from the shrapnel from the explosion. I was bleeding badly. I started to scream in pain. There was a puddle of blood around my leg. My mom saw the blood, applied pressure and prayed for God to help us. A beam from the ceiling cracked above us, sounding like thunder. I had never been so petrified. It began to fall and was about to crush us. We both squeezed each other as hard as we could. My puddle of blood, that was around my leg, shot up from the ground and stretched out over our heads. The beam fell, hitting the blood that was over my mom's head. I wanted to save my mom from the falling beam but my blood did it for me. The blood stopped the beam in mid air. My mom screamed and moved around my blood taking me with her. We crawled into the living room and stayed low.

Smoke had completely filled up the house. I watched as the blood held up the beam, I knew it had to have been me who made it save us. The blood collapsed and the beam crashed to the ground, splashing in the puddle. I held out my hand and asked it for help. My blood came back to me and surrounded both of us in a shell. My mom looked at me. She touched my leg where I had got cut open. It was wrapped with hardened blood and the bleeding had stooped. She was frightened, I could tell just by looking at her. We heard the sirens pull up to our house and then people talking. My mom screamed for help. The firefighters broke the door down. The shell of blood that was around us broke apart as soon as the firefighters came in. They ran over, grabbed us, and carried us out of the house," I explained, "After that we moved around a bunch, but that's pretty much what happened. That's my story."

"That's some tale of heroism," the psychiatrist said, "Can I see your leg?"

I lifted up my pant leg.

"You have no scar where you said you got cut."

"No, the blood covered it fast enough I guess."

"Has this ever happened after the first incident?"

"No, I've never had anything else like that happen to me."

"Have you ever tried to do things with your blood, such as things you did that day of the fire?"

"I've never been hurt that bad since then."

"Do you think if your leg were to be cut open, right now, that you'd be able to move it or control it?"

"I don't know . . ."

"Okay . . . I believe what happened was that during your house being burnt down; you were under severe stress and began to create a scenario in your mind. It's possible that you hallucinated after the explosion, when you got knocked back from the shock. I think that you felt and still do feel responsible for the fire so you imagined a way for yourself to look like a hero in your own head," he said.

"No, it actually happened. I know it did."

"Aden, just listen to your story; your blood saved your mother and protected you both from the fire by forming a shell around you two. It sounds like something out of a Stan Lee comic. It's just not possible," the therapist spoke. "Now why don't you tell me more about your father, from what you can remember that is."

I got up off the couch.

"I'm out of here. I don't need a therapist to tell me what happened in my life. I already know," I said as I walked out of the room slamming the door behind me.

My mom was sitting outside waiting.

"How did it go?" my mom asked.

"I don't want to talk about it. This guy is a quack," I said to her, "I'm going out to the car."

"Honey," she said as I was walking away.

The doctor walked out of the room and my mom walked over to the doctor. I stayed outside of the doors to the office. I wanted to hear what he was going to say to her about me.

"What did he say to you?" my mom asked.

"Well, he said that he had saved your lives during the fire with his blood," the doctor explained. "What did happen during the fire, if you don't mind me asking?"

"I'm . . . not sure, the whole event is a blur."

"Do you remember a giant shell of blood protecting you from the fire or saving your life from a falling beam?"

"I told you that I'm not sure what happened that day."

"Are you saying it is a possibility?"

"I don't know . . . maybe."

"That's impossible Mrs. Hew. I would like to see your son again next week. Maybe we can get somewhere with him."

"I'm sorry, but that's not going to happen. We are moving next week. I'm hoping a change will be good for the both of us."

"Running away isn't going to solve any problems. You need to deal with all the problems that you have. One of which is your son's over active imagination, which could be caused by his unique blood type. Your son's mental health might be declining. I'm starting to wonder if you're even worried about your son's health."

"My son is perfectly healthy and for his unique blood type, that has noting to do with his mental health. And how dare you insult me, I love my son and no doctor is going to question my parenting. Have a nice life, doctor."

I started walking away from the doors. She pushed them open and saw me walking to the car.

"So you were listening to every word that I said?" she asked knowing the answer.

"No . . . yeah. Sorry I just wanted to know what he was going to say to you."

"Its okay," she said now walking beside me.

We walked over to the car and we got inside. She started the car and we proceeded out of the parking lot.

"So are we really going to move again?"

She didn't answer me for a few minutes. We came to a stoplight.

"So?"

"I'm sorry, honey, but I don't want to stay here any more," she said. "I have a friend in West Virginia. She can get me a job where she works. It's at a fitness and training center. The money is really good and she said the schools are nice too."

The light turned green.

"Sounds great mom. When are we going?"

"I was thinking this weekend, after I get my paycheck."

"Okay great. Are we taking a plane or are we driving?"

"Driving shouldn't take us too long."

"Michigan to West Virginia that sounds like a fun trip" I said convincingly.

"I'm glad that you're not mad at me, Aden. I thought that you would have been upset."

"No, I'm not. I'm actually kind of excited to go."

"That's great Aden."

I was furious that we were moving again, but I wasn't surprised. We had been in Michigan for almost eight months, which was a little longer than we stayed in most places. She said that it would be our last move; it would be our home, no more moving. With no surprise, we were moving again. I was glad that I didn't make friends. It made the move that much easier.

We got home to our duplex and our neighbors were outside.

"Lisa, we are so sad you are leaving us, and you too, Aden," Ajani said.

Him and his wife came from Afghanistan, something like, twenty-years ago. We rented the apartment from them. They were really nice people. Ajani liked to talk a lot which got very annoying, but he meant well.

"A new job and a new opportunity. I'm very excited about it," my mom said.

"That's very good. Congratulations, my dear."

I walked inside and went to my room. I took out my suitcase and duffle bag and started to pack. I didn't have too many things to take with me, only clothes and my games. After I was done packing, I went to the supermarket where I worked and let them know that I was moving this weekend and I had to quit. They took it better than I expected. I worked about twenty five hours a week and I was a great worker, and knew the store like the back of my hand. They said sorry to hear that and sent me on my way.

I went to the bank to cash my check. I had nearly all my money saved. I asked them if they had a bank in West Virginia, luckily they did. I cashed my paycheck of $260.54. I kept eighty dollars and put the rest in to bank. My balance was $3455.67. I really didn't need the money for anything; it was good to have just in case.

I went home and my mom had already called the school and they were transferring my schedule to West Virginia. Same routine. I went to bed early because I wanted to catch up on my sleep. We were leaving in a few days. I didn't want to have my lack of sleep add to my frustration.

I woke up the next morning to finish packing the stuff upstairs, while my mom was packing up the living room. I went downstairs into the living room and my mom was done too. I sat down on the couch next to my mom.

"Are you finished with your room?"

"Yeah. I finished just a second ago."

"That's good. I wanted to leave tomorrow, if that's okay?"

"Yeah, sure. The sooner the better."

"Okay, well um, let's finish packing and we can leave the first thing in the morning," she said. "We can put the dressers in the back of the truck. We don't need to bring our beds because the three bedrooms that are furnished. So, if you ever want a friend over he or she can stay in the guest room."

"Do you need any money for the apartment?" I asked ignoring her statement.

"No, but thank you. I always put a little money in the bank just in case we need to move again."

"Well, that's good to know," I said after I was outside. She always planned to go somewhere new, she couldn't just settle down. She would get a good job that paid well and give it up because something new came along. I wanted to stay in one place, I didn't care where, to settle down. Maybe it would be the last place we moved, but I highly doubted it.

The rest of the day moved by fast. I loaded up the truck and car with our stuff. I had to find another job and it wasn't always easy to do. I went for a walk around town, just to clear my head. After about an hour I started heading back.

About four blocks away from my house, I saw a man on the other side of the street, trying to cross. The road was clear and he started walking across. A jeep sped down a side street and pulled onto the road. The jeep didn't even see the man until the last second. It swerved to the left and just missed the man, but crashed into a telephone pole. I ran across the street towards the jeep. The hood burst into flames. I jumped back, shielding my face, then running up to the window. The man that was crossing the street ran over to the sidewalk to get away from the fire. I knew that I had to do something, but I didn't have my phone.

"GO CALL 911!" I yelled to the man.

He took off running. I assumed that he was going to call 911, but I still needed to do something. I ran over to the driver's side of the car and tried to see if the driver was okay, but thick smoke had filled the vehicle. I could only see the outline off of someone leaning forward. I moved closer and tried to open the door, but it was locked. I hit the window a few times with my elbow until it smashed and stuck my hand through the window, cutting my forearm on a piece of glass in the process. I unlocked the door and opened it. The guy was alone in the car and looked unconscious. I tried to unbuckle him it was jammed. I pulled as hard as I could but it wouldn't budge. The flames on the hood erupted and the telephone pole sparked. I ripped my arm back in fear. I punched the jeep in anger. I had to get him out before the vehicle exploded. I tried again to unbuckle him. I yanked the belt a few times furiously, my body was tingling. It finally released and I pulled the man out of the jeep. As I was pulling him I saw the seat belt, it looked like it was cut free. I brought him over to the sidewalk and away from the car. He wasn't breathing. I learned CPR from school, so I started doing chest compressions. Seconds later he began coughing.

"Are you alright?" I asked.

The man continued to cough.

"Sir, are you okay?" I asked again rolling him on his side.

"Did you save me?" he asked.

"Yeah. Are you okay? Is anything broken?"

"I don't think so," he sat up coughing and brushed himself off.

An ambulance came quick, as well as a fire truck. The fire fighters put out the fire and the EMT's took the man. I didn't want any part of it, so I ran off. I didn't need or want the fame or glory for saving anyone. When I got home my mom was sitting at the kitchen table eating.

"Where did you go?" she asked.

"Just for a walk around town."

"Oh. Okay, I got you something from the restaurant in the plaza."

"What did you get me?" I asked as I sat down.

"Chicken and rice."

"Thanks mom."

We sat there eating not saying anything to each other. She had steak and potatoes; it's what she usually got. We both finished with our meals.

"I'm going to take a shower then hop into bed," I said.

"Okay, good night. I love you."

"I love you too, Mom."

I took of my shirt and had completely forgotten about the cut on my forearm. It was already scabbed over. I took a deep breath and peeled it off. It was a straight cut and not very deep. Blood began to come out of the wound. I looked at the cut and tried to move the blood. There was an unexpected knock at the door.

"Yeah?" I was clearly startled.

"Is everything okay in there?"

"Yeah mom. I was just getting undressed you caught me off guard."

"I just wanted to tell you I would like to leave by eight if that's okay with you."

"It's fine with me."

"Okay, goodnight. And honey, I am sorry about this."

"I'm not worried about it, Mom. Good night."

I didn't bother trying to play with my blood again. I just took my shower and went to bed.

We woke up at quarter after seven and ate a quick breakfast. We locked up the doors and put the key in Ajani's mail box before we headed out. The trip was boring. I had to drive my truck and my mom drove her car. It was an easy drive for the most part. We got to our apartment and I unpacked all of my stuff, and then helped my mom with hers. We were done early, having nothing better to do, I went for a drive. I wanted to find the fastest way to school and hopefully a job as well.

The town itself seemed fine. It was kind of a small town. The best way to describe it was . . . quaint. It was totally something that I could have gotten used to. I drove by the school; it wasn't far from my place at all. It was huge though; way bigger than my old one. I drove around for a while to get the feel of the town and then returned home. We had moved into another duplex. We had the left side and no one lived in the right side yet.

My mom was on the phone with the school when I walked in.

"What did they say?" I asked.

"Everything is all set. You can start tomorrow. Someone will give you a tour and your schedule. All you have to do is go to the front office."

"Okay, cool. Are you making dinner or do you want me to go grab something. I saw a burger place while I was driving."

"I was thinking about some pasta. I already started boiling the water."

"Sounds great."

I went into my room and straightened everything out. It was a little smaller than before, but it was no big deal. That night we had ziti and bread. My mom made the best pasta sauce. After dinner I went to bed; I was beat and I had school in the morning.

I woke up and went to school. I walked in and everyone shot me strange looks. I got used to them, it wasn't like I hadn't gotten them before. I had no idea where I was going. I asked someone where the main office was and he pointed me in the right direction. I got to the office and there was a girl sitting in one of the chairs. She stood up when I walked into the room.

"You must be Aden," she said.

"Yeah, how did you know?" I asked.

"You are wearing our rival schools colors, black and red. On top of that, I've never seen you before."

"I guess that would explain the dirty looks. So then you must be my tour guide."

"Hahaha yeah. Glad you aren't as dimwitted as half the students here. I'm sure you'll like it here," she walked over to the counter and talked to the secretary. The secretary handed her a paper. She walked back over to me and handed it to me. "This is your schedule. You have a lot of tough classes. You must be crazy smart."

"Thanks, but not really."

"Well, let's get going. I've got a lot to show you."

She was nice and very pretty, probably taken though. I didn't want to get attached to someone anyway, it wasn't my thing. The first place we went was the gym, which was twice the size of my previous one. Then we went to the cafeteria.

"The lunch isn't that bad here, but it's still school lunch. The good thing is that we have open campus. So if you have a car, then you can go out to lunch."

"We didn't have that at my old school. That's certainly an improvement."

"So where are you from?"

"Michigan."

"Really? What brings you here?"

"My mom got a new job. We move around a lot."

"That sucks."

"Yeah. You're telling me."

"Think you are staying put this time?"

"I can only hope so."

She started showing me my classes next. First Psychology, then English, Calculus, Human Biology, Wood Shop, and finally U.S. History. The classes were easy to find.

"Thanks, I really appreciate your help . . ." I said realizing that I didn't know her name. "Sorry, but I don't think that you told me your name."

"Oh, I'm so sorry. My name is Hailey," she held her hand out.

"It's nice to meet you, Hailey," I said shaking her hand. "Well um . . . I guess I'll get to class then."

"Okay. If you need something just find me, and I'll help you out."

"Thanks. That's nice, but I think I should be okay. I guess I'll see you around."

"Yep," she walked in the opposite direction of me.

I got to my classroom. The teacher gave me a seat in the back.

"So where are you from new kid?" the teacher asked.

"Michigan."

"Nice, I have a friend that used to live there. How far along did you get in the curriculum?"

"We were learning about mental disorders."

"You're a little ahead of us, but that's alright. It's, Aden, correct?"

"Yeah."

The class was tolerable. Everyone seemed fine, same with the teacher. The rest of my classes were basically the same. I stayed in for lunch. I didn't want to go out and get lost on my first day. After lunch I had wood shop. The teacher was really dumb. He just sat in his office the entire class. He told me to just start making something. I knew how to use the tools, so I began making a foot stool. One of the kids came up to me. He looked like the "wanna be rebel" type. I tried to ignore him.

"Hey, new guy, whatcha working on?" he asked with his friends behind him laughing.

"A stool."

"Oh man, that's crazy cool," his friends behind him laughed louder. "So where ya from?" he said putting his hand on my shoulder.

"Not here," I shrugged his hand off.

"You tryin' to be a smart ass or somethin'?" I just didn't respond. "Hey! Answer me!" I didn't, and continued to ignore him. "Hey, asshole! Answer me!"

"What?"

"You got a problem or somethin'?"

"Just leave me alone, I'll mind my own business."

"Don't tell me what to do, you little prick," he pulled me off my chair. I stood up and stared at him. The last thing I needed was to be in a fight on my first day. I shook it off and started to walk back to my seat. He pushed me back and pulled out a switchblade.

"You don't wanna mess with me. I'll kill you."

"I don't want any trouble. I'm just minding my own business," the class looked over at us. They didn't seem shocked. I was getting extremely nervous. I didn't want to fight him, but at this point I didn't have a choice. I could disarm him if he was in the right position, but I was sure his friends would have joined in. I only had to stay calm and in control.

"Yeah, sorry."

"Don't say sorry. I don't give a shit. You messed up, kid. Now you're gonna' pay."

He held up the knife and tried to stab me, but I stepped to the right of the blade, dodging it. He really was serious. He swung the knife, cutting the upper half of my left arm near my bicep. I tried to dodge, but lost my balance and fell. Blood started to trail down my arm.

His friends started laughing. He was looking at me like he was honestly going to kill me, he was serious. I had to do something, defend myself. I looked around trying to find something to pick up, but there was nothing; everything was on the other side of the room. He had me cornered and with nothing to defend myself. My mind was focused on finding something to fight him with. The blood from my arm had trailed all the way to my hand. He began to approach me. My body started to tingle all over. I felt strange, almost excited. I stood up ready to take him on. He looked at my left hand and I could see fear in his eyes. I looked at my hand; the blood had formed into something. It was like a claw coming off of my middle and pointer fingers, reaching out to roughly four-inches long. I held it close to my face in order to get a better look at it. It was actually my blood; formed into a weapon to protect me, just like it did to protect my mom. The blood was hard and sharp; exactly what I needed.

"What the hell is that?" he asked.

"I'm just making this a fair fight," I put my hand out in front of me.

"Is . . . is that blood?"

"You want to try and come at me now?" I said confidently.

He backed up, along with his friends.

"Stay away from me you freak," they ran out of the room.

The blood turned back to normal and started to drip on the floor. The claw fell off like melted ice off a cliff. It hit the floor and made a small splash then formed into a puddle. Everyone started clapping. I didn't think that they saw exactly what happened. I ran out of the back door and out to my truck. I wanted to go home, but my mom would be upset if I left. I regained my composure and went back inside. I went to the bathroom and cleaned out the cut. I went along as if nothing happened. Everyone was whispering when I walked by. The day finished and I went home.

All I could think about was the fight earlier. I knew I could control my blood somehow; I knew that I saved my mom and it wasn't my imagination. I parked my car at home and went into the backyard. Since we lived alone in the building I could try and do my blood thing with nobody watching me. I tried to push the blood out of the cut on my arm, but I couldn't. The cut was already scabbed over. I peeled the scab off. It hurt a little and a small amount of blood came out. The cut was already starting to heal. I tried to shape the blood, but it wasn't doing anything. I kept trying, but got nowhere. It was possible that I needed more blood. In order to get more blood I would have to have an open wound.

I ran inside, grabbed a knife, and went back outside. I made a small cut in my right arm. Not my brightest idea ever. It hurt pretty badly, but in a disturbing way, it felt kind of good. Blood came out and poured down the sides of my forearm. I tried to move it, but it didn't work still. It was pissing me off. I didn't want to cut myself again. I tried as hard as I could, letting my anger get the best of me. I still couldn't do it. I punched the back of my house and scratched up my knuckles. Tiny drops of blood were there. I was nearly consumed with frustration and anger. My entire body was tingling again, like just before my blood made the small claw. It felt like I had goose bumps all over. I tried to move my blood and it worked. I moved the blood off of my arm and into the palm of my hand; staying focused I began shaping it. I started with a sphere, about the size of a golf ball. Then moved the blood onto my arm and made it trail to my fingertips. I molded it into a claw again, turned it back to a ball shape then moved it from one hand to the other. I had no trouble keeping it controlled. I formed it into a rope form and started twirling it around above my head. I had never been more excited in my life.

I started getting dizzy, but I wanted to do one more thing before I quit. I returned it to my hand one last time to ball form. I had the ball suspended in the air between both hands and concentrated on forming the blood. I tried to make a spike on the ball, starting off slowly, pulling and shaping the spike with my pointer finger. It was barely working. It was making me frustrated. I tried two more times, got pissed, and spread my arms forcefully and in front of me was a spiked blood ball. I smiled at my creation. It was about three-inched wide, solid with inch-long spikes. I moved my hand under it and had it rest on my hand with the spikes lightly touching my skin. I held my arm out and focused on pushing it forward, essentially throwing it forward, but with my mind. I pushed the ball and it hit a tree, sticking into it.

I heard a knock at my door. I was startled and ran into my house and opened the door. It was a woman.

"Hi there, I'm your neighbor from across the street, Mrs. James," she said. "I brought you guys a cake."

"Oh thanks," I reached out and grabbed the cake.

"OH MY GOD. Are you okay? What happened to your arm?"

I had completely forgotten about the cut on my arm. I didn't even bother to cover it up.

"I cut myself cooking. I'll be fine," I quickly answered.

"Are you sure? I can take a look at it if you want."

"No I'm going to clean it out and wrap it up. I'll be just fine."

"Okay. Are your parents home?"

"No, my mom is at work."

"What about your father?"

"He doesn't live with us."

"Oh, I see. Well let her know I stopped by. If you need anything I'm the blue house right across the street."

"Okay. Thanks." she left and I closed the door behind me.

I ran into the bathroom and cleaned out the cut and wrapped it in gauze. I went back outside and the blood ball was still stuck in the tree. I walked over to it and touched it. It was a hard as stone and ridged too. I grabbed the knife I used to cut my forearm and went back inside. I cleaned off the knife and put it in my room. I didn't want anyone to use it, not after what I did with it. I figured that it might be good to have a lot of gauze and medical supplies around to cover up the cuts. I grabbed my keys and left my house. I went out to the truck and drove to the grocery store in the plaza that I passed by yesterday. I grabbed a bunch of gauze and alcohol to clean my future cuts.

As I was walking back out to my truck after paying for everything, I saw a sword store. Asian Steel was the name of it. I put the bag in the car and walked over to the store. I walked inside and started looking around. I walked by a wall of daggers, and saw one calling out to me. It was about a foot long with a steel colored handle and a thick red line going from the hilt to the butt of the dagger with black strips going diagonally. The blade was only single sided. After staring at it, I realized it was perfect. I had to have it. I asked the clerk for it. He took it down from the wall, walked over to the counter, and rung me out. It was the perfect thing to use if I was going to have to keep cutting myself to use my ability.

Chapter VII

Bidziil: From the Beginning

"Our people, the Dine, did not always live on this island. We once lived on land, but when our people had different beliefs, conflicts arose. A new God was imagined; he told one elder that the tribe would be destroyed. 'You need to go out to sea, explore the beyond. You will be safe out there. You will find land and prosper. I will protect you." Most of our people thought it was a terrible idea. It was almost certain death. An argument erupted," I spoke.

"The Creator put us where we are, we should stay," an elder spoke.

"Not if we face certain destruction!" the rebel exclaimed.

"We shall not leave!"

"Then I shall! And anyone who wishes to live may come as well!"

"A few followed the rebel. He was Elsu, Flying Falcon. He only wanted to protect. Though they were few, they had the strength of many. They created a floating craft. It could hold just barely enough; five men, six women, and two children. Chayton, the chief, was not pleased with Elsu's plan to desert the tribe. It was unheard of to leave the land. Elsu begged Chayton to come, but it only angered him. Chayton tried to destroy the craft that was built, but Elsu and the others hid it.

Suns set and moons arose; Elsu decided it was time. They took the craft into the ocean. Clayton chased after them, running into the water after them, the water started to get deeper. Clayton stopped. There was nothing he could do to stop Elsu.

After two setting suns, Elsu saw land. It was a large piece waiting in the water to be discovered. They arrived on the land. It was a beautiful place. The sights were strange, many forms of plants that they have never seen. There was a wonderful area for hogans to be built. A soft soil that was perfect for crops to grow and feed the people. The new tribe would survive and continue.

The first moon on the isle was full and bright, there was a celebration. Elsu made a grand speech."

"We have escaped from death and found a new land in which to survive. We can create a new tribe, one that allows us to believe in the God that has spoken to me and protected us all. He is all mighty and wise. We thank you all mighty. Allow us to know your name so we may properly worship our savior. People, we must start in the growth of our new tribe. Children, we need to ensure our survival. Under this moon is where we will breed and under the next sun, we will begin to build our new homes and find more food. We will live!" Elsu preached.

"That is the story of our grand elder Elsu. He is the mightiest of the mighty. Thanks to him we are alive. In many suns and moons the land continued to grow. Children were born, plants grew; everything continued to get better."

"Wow, that is a wonderful story," one child said.

"Yeah, that was great," said the other.

"Are you excited about your mystic journey to get your god given name?" another asked.

"Well, I'm more excited than anything, children," I said as I got up out of the hogan.

"Wait, we want another story," they all chased after me.

"Not tonight, I have my trial under the new sun. I will tell you all about my tales against the wild when I return."

They went back into their hogan and I went into mine. My father was in there awaiting my arrival.

"My son, I want you to know that I'm proud of you. You have made it so far and now you will learn your name. The name that you deserve," my father spoke "Sani will watch over you and decide on your name. He will give you the name that you deserve. I want you to make me proud."

"I will do my best father."

"It is a shame that you are going to miss Isi give birth."

"Yes, that should be during the next sun."

"Ah, but no matter. You can see the baby when you return."

"Good night, father." I went into the area of the hogan where I slept.

My father's name was Anakausen. It meant worker. He could build any shelter with his surroundings. I could only hope that I could get a name that meant something as important as his. He was an important member in our society. He built most of the hogans that we lived in. He helped make our irrigation canals and improved our ceremonial circle. I wish that I could one day live up anything near my father. If I did not do well during my trial, then I would not amount to anything.

THE DAY OF THE TRIAL

I awoke surrounded by the village Privileged and the eldest chief. The Privileged were the eldest chief's personal servants and helped control the village and its people. They dressed in long tan gowns and white head covers.

"Are you ready? This is your day of name," the chief asked.

"Yes, I am ready as I am ever going to be. I feel that I will prove that I am a great asset to the tribe," I said.

"Then let us take you to him and your trial will begin," said Hiamovi, our eldest chief.

"Then let us go."

I got up out of bed and put on my thin elk fur and my leather belt with my knife attached to it. We began walking toward the trail that leads to the Sani's gate. We approached the gate and Hiamovi banged on the door with his walking stick three times. The gate opened and Sani was waiting there.

"It is about time that you got here. I was wondering when you were going to come. I was afraid that he was not going to show," Sani spoke.

I stood there staring at Sani. He had the most beautiful wolf fur draped as a cape. Covering his chest was a wooden plate with an emblem marked into it. It meant "the giver of names". He decided whether you were one of the brave or one who was afraid. He had much authority in our society. He had his own area on the island, separated from the rest of us until someone came of age to be named and formally welcomed into the tribe. He was old and wise, but also terrifying. I had to be brave and strong or else I would not be respected.

"Go, son of Anakausen. It is your time to become a man," the Privileged said.

"I will return a man, a man that will be respected for his bravery," I said going into the home of Sani.

"Return in three days. Wait here until I have decided his name. When I'm finished the gate will open and his fate will be sealed," Sani said as the gate closed.

It was now just Sani and I, and my trial had begun. We began walking to Sani's home. It was the largest hogan I had ever seen. It could house half the village.

"Let us begin, son of Anakausen. We will start by traveling through the forest. Your first trial is to protect me from anything that gets in our way, as well as providing us with shelter," Sani said.

"Yes, I will do as you say: protect you at all costs, even if that means that I have to sacrifice my own life."

"It is a good sign that you are willing to do so. There will be great and terrible complications during our travel. You should be well prepared."

I saw out of the corner of my eyes a pile of things that were somewhat hidden behind a stack of logs. I walked over to the pile and among it were spears, pouches, and canisters. I grabbed three of everything, and attached two of the pouches to my waist, put two canisters around my shoulders, and carried two spears. I gave the other items to Sani.

"I see you are observant. This is good. I have a good feeling about you. You may be destined for great things."

We moved into the woods and away from his large hogan. The sun had moved a lot and it was beginning to darken. I had gathered many berries and some fruit along the way. There were no signs of animals; not tracks or markings of any kind. We came to a small clearing. It was perfect for a place to set up for sleep.

"I'm going to find some dry logs for a fire and some sort of branches for shelter," I said.

"That is a good idea. I like the way you think."

"In the mean time you may have your fill on the berries and fruit that we have gathered."

"Sure, I will wait for you to return," replied Sani.

I walked around getting further and further away from the clearing. I found some dry logs, and felt sick all of the sudden. My arms began to give out. I dropped the logs and fell to my knees. My whole body was weak. It was as if something was trying to escape me, from the inside. I tried to yell to the gods, but I could not speak. There was awful pain all over my body, as if I was about to die. My body started to glow white, and I got brighter and brighter. The pain was unbearable. I curled into a ball on the ground, continuing to brighten. Then the light started to grow beyond my body, getting bigger. The light left my body in an extremely painful manner. It flew out of my body from all sides, shaped like a dome. It spread further than I could see. I had no idea what it was or where it was going.

I caught my breath for a moment, and stood up, moving over to the nearest tree to lean against it. My whole body ached; throbbing in pain. The dark was approaching quickly. I was against the tree long enough. I could see Sani approaching me.

"Did you see what that was or where it had come from?" Sani asked.

I did not want to let him know that it was me. If he had found out he would tell the elder chief, and I would be killed for being different.

"No, whatever it was hit me and I fell down. I could not move after. I have no idea where it started," I did not want to lie, but the truth would make me an outcast of the tribe.

"That is strange, when it came into contact with me, nothing happened. It did not hurt. It felt like a very warm air."

"That is odd, I wonder why."

"I am not sure. I think we should just go back to the clearing and deal with it later. The moon is out now. We need to rest, especially you."

"Yes, I will gather up some wood," I said bending over.

We walked back over to the clearing and started a fire. My body began to feel better than before. The pain was slowly leaving. I decided that it was time to rest. I went over to where Sani had set up a covering between two trees. I laid down my bear fur and fell asleep.

I awoke to the sun and the smell of cooking food. I looked over and saw Sani cooking boar meat. I got off my fur and went over to him.

"It is about time, I've been waiting. I had brought meat from my hogan, in case anything bad happened, or in the event you could not provide us with food."

"Oh, I am truly sorry, Sani."

"No, you are doing fine. I figured after that strange event we should have a nice meal."

"Ah, okay."

I sat down and we ate together. The food tasted as if it had came from the gods themselves. I felt completely refreshed.

"I think that it is time for us to continue moving," I said.

"That is a good plan," Sani had replied. "What do you plan on doing today?"

"Maybe some hunting, that is if we can find any animals."

"I'm sure that we can; there are many animals in my domain."

"Good, then let us move."

We got up and grabbed everything that we needed to continue our journey. We walked for a long distance until we came to a pond. It was surrounded by bright flowers and many fruit bearing trees.

"Not many people get to see this place. This is where I worship. You are the fourth person to ever see it. The elder and his son, Achak, have been here. We have come to worship and pray for the fate of this island many times. We believe that this is where the gods can hear us the best," Sani explained.

"This place is so beautiful. I can see why you would think that this place is for worship. Only a god could have created something as perfect as this."

"I feel the same way."

We both stood staring at the pond and the surrounding trees. It was a perfect moment. I felt as if all my worries were gone. I felt, complete.

"We should not waste too much time here. I'm sorry, but we have to keep moving."

"Would you mind if I prayed first, before we continue?"

"I do not see why not. I feel that you deserve it after yesterday."

I walked into the beautifully bright flowers. I kneeled down and held my hands up to the sky. I did not speak. I did not want Sani to hear what was on my mind.

Gods, I need you to help me. I do not know what happened to me yesterday. All I know is that I need to pass this trial and be respected. I need to succeed. It is you who decide my fate. I need your help. I will dedicate the rest of my life to serving you; I just need you to help me figure out what is wrong with me. If that happens again, I could be near Sani. I do not want him to know that it was me that released that thing. Please, my gods, protect me and grant me success.

I stood back up. I had a good feeling that it had worked. The gods had heard me; I had no clear sign except for the strange feeling in the pit of my body. That was good enough for me.

"Are you ready?"

"Yes, I feel that the gods have heard my request. We can move on." We walked away from the garden, and heard a loud roar.

"That would be a bear's roar," Sani said.

"We should move. Go back to the clearing and set a trap."

"I suppose that we could."

"I mean, you could go. I will stay here and kill the bear. Yes, that is what I will do. I will kill the bear."

"Are you sure that you can handle it?"

"I am positive, I can do it."

"Then I will stay and watch."

The bear came into sight and roared again. I took out my knife and had my spear ready in my other hand, moving towards the bear. The closer I got, the bigger it appeared. I was unsure of whether or not I could actually kill it. The gods would protect me. I held up the spear and threw it at the beast. The large wooden spear stabbed into the bear's side. He stood on his two hind feet. Its size was terrifying. If I killed it, I could bring it back, and the tribe would respect me. "Gods, please protect me."

The bear roared again and got down on all fours. It started running towards me. I moved out of the way, and tried to stab it in the side, but missed. I looked over and Sani was standing at a great distance, watching me and my every move. I knew this bear was my test. If I failed then my name would be bad, not only that, but my life was at stake. I needed to kill the bear. It was my gift from the Gods. They heard my prayer and had given me the chance to be great.

I looked back to see the bear in front of me, on two legs. He smashed me into the dirt with his left claw, and I dropped my knife as I fell. My arm was bleeding; he was going to kill me. I was going to be killed before even getting my name. I kept crawling back away from the bear. He chased me slowly until I could not crawl anymore. I was backed against a fallen down tree. The bear opened its mouth and let out the loudest roar yet. There was nothing I could do. I was going to be killed. I reached behind me, not taking my eyes off the bear, and grabbed onto the first thing I felt. I grabbed it tight and I felt it crack. I let go quickly and the bear returned to all fours.

I grabbed it again, squeezed it as hard as I could and swung it out from behind me, smashing the bear with it. The bear went soaring into a tree. I was holding the large fallen down tree in my hand. The tree trunk was very large. I had never seen anyone pick up a tree single handedly. I dropped the tree and looked over at the bear. He was not getting up. It let out of a small roar and its eyes closed. I looked over at Sani. He looked frightened. I was never strong; there is no way that I could ever lift something that heavy.

My father always had to help me when I had to do any lifting. I stood up and walked over to the bear. I poked at it with a branch. It did not move. It was dead.

Sani came over to me. He stared at me; he looked at the bear; then at the fallen tree.

"We are done. We should return to my hogan, I need to consult the gods about your name."

"Sani, I do not know how I did that. I must be stronger than I thought."

"Yes, you are very strong. Do you wish to take the bear?"

" . . . Yes, it would be a good reward to show my father. He will be pleased that I have become a man."

"The tribe will be pleased."

"Am I in trouble, Sani?" I asked fearful.

"For what? You protected yourself the only way you knew how. You are not in trouble, if anything I should be praising you. You are the strongest man that I have ever seen."

"You looked afraid after I hit the bear."

"I had never seen anyone pick up a fallen tree before, at least not just one man. It was a breath taking sight is all." Sani explained. "Let us go, we have a long walk. Do not forget about the bear. You can skin it when we get back to my hogan."

I grabbed onto the bear's claw and began to drag it. It did not even feel like I was pulling anything. I stopped dragging the bear and began to carry it on my back. It felt like I was only holding a small log. Sani smiled and began to laugh.

"You are very strong, the tribe will be proud of you."

I smiled; finally I could relax and be at ease. The gods had granted me my wish. I would be respected. They had also given me great strength. They wanted me to be a part of something bigger. The gods had a greater plan for me. I could feel it.

After walking until the moon had rose, we reached Sani's hogan. We stepped inside; it was dark.

"You can sleep in that room over there," Sani pointed after lighting a fire.

"Okay, thank you."

"I am going to speak to the gods. I will have your name during the next sun; now go get some rest."

"Yes, Sani, thank you."

I went into the room, but could not get any rest; I was too excited to know what my name was going to be. I must had gotten some rest because I awoke to the sun. I walked into the main room; the door that Sani went into was still closed. I did not wish to interrupt him. I grabbed a knife that was on his table, then I walked outside and started skinning the bear. By the time I was done Sani had come out of the hogan.

"I normally do not do this but in this case I think that it is necessary."

"Do what?"

"I'm going to bring you back to the village."

"When do you want to go?"

"Whenever you are ready."

"I will clean of this skin and then we can go."

"Use the stream behind my hogan."

I picked up the skin and ran to the stream. I cleaned it off as fast as I could and I ran back over to Sani.

Sani opened the gate and we left his domain. We were walking for a little while, and he did not say a word. I could not help but ask him what my name was. He had no response. I thought he did not hear me, so I asked again. He still remained silent.

"Oh, I see your going to make me wait. That is very cruel. You know how excited I am. This is torture."

He kept his word to himself, so I did the same. We finally got to the village. Sani went straight to the elder's hogan. I just stood there. Everyone looked at me. They all were talking quietly. Two children ran over to me.

"What's your name?" one screamed.

"Yeah, what is it?"

"Sani has not told me yet."

"Why? Are you in trouble?"

"No, I am special."

Both the children ran away from me. I was a little worried. Maybe special was not the best word to use. Sani and the elder walked out of the elder's hogan and over to me.

"We will have a ceremony for you under this moon," the elder said.

"Really, my father will be happy."

"I will tell you your name then. I will come find you before the ceremony starts," Sani said.

The elder held up his hands; everyone became quiet and looked at him.

"There will be a ceremony for the son of Anakausen. Sani has given him a name, and he will tell us all during the moon. Now please begin for the ceremony. It is of utter importance."

The elder put his hands down and everyone started to gather things for the ceremony. He looked at me.

"Please son of Anakausen, come with me to my hogan. We need to talk."

"Is it bad, Elder?"

"No, I only wish to speak with you."

LATER AT THE CEREMONY

The moon was full; it was a perfect night for my ceremony. We made a large circle with a burning fire in the middle and Sani and The Elder were standing by it. I was sitting outside of the circle next to my father. Sani began to talk about my trial. He did not speak about the pond though. I figured that it was because he did not want anyone to know about it. It was a sacred place. My father looked at me and smiled.

"I am so proud of you my son."

I did not know what to say. I was so happy that my chest began to hurt. Sani started to talk about the encounter with the bear. He told them about my amazing strength; how I lifted up the fallen tree. My father was very pleased. My chest began to hurt more. It assumed I was very nervous. Sani called me up by the fire and spoke.

"The gods have told me how special this boy is. He will someday be the next leader of the tribe. That is only if he can prove himself worthy. The gods have said that he has an important task ahead of him. He will save all that he has created. The gods speak in riddles. It is our job to solve and obey them."

The tribe looked shocked; The Privileged did not look happy. My body began to tighten. The pain was strong. I tried to ignore it; and look strong.

"This boy, son of Anakausen, he is strong and so is his will. He has passed the trial. The gods have given him a name; his destined name. His name is Bidziil; Bidziil the strong," Sani informed

The tribe stood up and sent out a loud cry.

"BIDZIIL! BIDZIIL! BIDZIIL! Welcome, to the tribe!" They all screamed.

I cried; tears of joy ran down my face, but the pain grew stronger. I could no longer stand. It was happening again, the same thing that happened in the woods. People began to come around me. I fell to my knees in tears. Sani bent down.

"Bidziil, are you okay?" Sani asked me.

"Please get away, I'll be fine. Just get away please you have to. Get everyone away." I whispered gasping for breath.

"What are you talking about?"

My body began to glow white, bright enough to get everyone's attention, brighter than the fire even. Everyone started to back away from me.

"Everyone, please return to your hogans, something is wrong with Ho . . . I mean Bidziil," Sani said.

I could feel the light inside me, like my insides were on fire. It was worse than last time. The light wanted out, I knew it. It began to expand and cover me like a blanket, grow bigger and wider. Then it left the same way it did the last time; like a dome. The light hit every hogan, Sani, the Elder, my father, and everything else. The light traveled out over the water in the form of a ball. I could no longer see it.

Sani and my father picked me up and brought me into The Elder's hogan. He told The Privileged to wait outside and make sure the no one got in. That was the last thing I heard. I woke up on a bed; Sani, my father, and The Elder were talking.

"What happened?"

"Are you okay son?" my father ran over to me.

"Do you know what that was? What happened to you?" asked The Elder.

"That was the same light from the forest. Was that you in the forest?" Sani asked.

"Yes, it was me," I answered. "And I'm fine now. I do not know what it is."

"Someone saw that same light as Isa gave birth, she said that the light went into the child," The Elder stated.

"Bidziil, the gods told me that you were a danger to the tribe, that one day you will be the death of us all. Your true name is . . ." said Sani.

"Wait, my son would never do that, he would never hurt this tribe."

"I am only going by what the gods have said to me," Sani replied. "I have to try and perform a nidaa, an exorcism."

"Do you think that it is necessary?" my father asked.

"Yes, he could be possessed by an evil spirit. If we can remove it, than he will not be feared," The Elder explained. "There is no other way to explain what happened, the tribe will want answers."

"Then we must do it," my father said.

"Wait, what do you mean that my name is not Bidziil, was that the name that the gods gave me?"

"The gods had given you a different name, I thought that they were wrong, so I gave you a name myself," Sani said.

"What is it?"

"It is not the time to tell you; someday I will Bidziil."

"DO NOT CALL ME THAT! I want to know my true name, Tell me!"

"I can not do that."

"Why, Why not?"

"It is not the time, I know deep down that it is not your true name; Bidziil is."

"No, its not," I spoke fiercely.

One of the privileged came into the hogan.

"Elder, the tribe wants to know what happened last night, they are unhappy and scared," one of the privileged said.

The Elder looked outside and the tribe had gathered outside of his hogan. He walked outside.

"I know that you want to know what happened. It seems that Bidziil has been possessed by an evil spirit," he said with his hands in the air. "There will be a nidaa in a few days. We need time to gather materials. I promise that everything will be okay, nothing bad will happen to our tribe. The light was only light. It was the gods trying to help Bidziil. Now please return to your hogans and everything will be okay."

He walked back inside and the crowd of people returned home.

"How did you know that, Elder?" my father asked.

"I made it up. I do not know anything about what that light was, as far as I know the light could be evil. I have never dealt with anything like this before in my life. I have not even heard any stories like this."

"We can just hope that the nidaa will help him."

"You must stay in my hogan until we can begin the exorcism," The Elder said to me.

THE DAY OF THE EXORCISM

My father and Sani returned from their journey to recover ingredients for the ceremony.

"We can start whenever you want; we have everything for the nidaa," my father said.

"We will do it under the moon; in front of the tribe so that they can see that Bidziil is cured," The Elder instructed.

"Good idea, Elder," my father said. "I should go tell the tribe to prepare an exorcism circle for tonight."

"That is a good idea, go now. Sani, myself, and you shall prepare a potion for the nidaa; I can only hope that it works."

"What if it does not?" I asked.

"I am not sure, I have not decided," The Elder said in fear.

THAT NIGHT

The moon was full, and the nidaa had begun. I was tied tightly to a carved log standing straight up. The Elder and Sani were chanting for the gods to help me, to clear the demon from my soul. I knew that there was no demon; it was the gods who had cursed me. This was just to fool the tribe. I did not want to hurt anyone. I did not want to be the death of my tribe.

They both splashed the potion on me. It was pointless; it was not going to help me. There is nothing that could, not the gods, not Sani, not even the great knowledge of our elder. I should just be killed so that the tribe can survive, I thought. The Elder had to make a sacrifice to get away from his old tribe so that he and others could survive. I could only think he should do the same thing with me, sacrifice me so that the tribe can survive. I do not deserve to be a part of it.

My chest began to burn as hot as fire. It was happening again. The light was coming. I began to glow. Everyone got quiet; The Elder and Sani looked at me.

"This is the demon trying to escape Bidziil's body," said The Elder.

"DO NoT CALL ME THAT! THAT IS NOT MY NAME!" I screamed.

The light was not getting brighter and not expanding.

"This must be the demon speaking, this is not Bidziil," Sani told the tribe.

"It is me, but there is no Bidziil."

The tribe looked frightened. I flexed my arms, snapping the ropes keeping me on the log. The tribe gasped and some held their children behind them. They thought that I was a threat; and I was. I was a threat to everyone.

"I will not hurt you, I promise. I want to stop this as much as you do. The pain I feel is incomparable. I will leave and never return, I will not be the destruction of this tribe," I said to everyone.

I ran out of the exorcism circle, into the woods, and towards Sani's territory. My entire body was glowing bright when I arrived at Sani's gate. I punched it, shattering it into pieces; the wood flying in all directions. I kept running. The light expanded beyond my body. As I ran it continued to grow. I could no longer run; I stopped and could feel the warm light all around my body. There was nothing I could do to stop it from happening. It grew bigger until it shot away from me in all directions. After it was gone I got down on one knee. My body was weak, I collapsed.

Chapter VIII

BIDZIIL: A PLACE TO LIVE

I opened my eyes and the sun was shining bright. I was lying on my back. My body was sore and hurt. I got up off the ground, looking around, unsure where I was. I remembered that I had ran out of the exorcism before the light left me and punching the gate to Sani's domain. I could not go back to the village nor could I stay in Sani's domain; but his domain was a large amount of the island. I thought about building a hogan somewhere in his domain and staying hidden from the tribe. It would be better that way. They could think that I was dead and not have to worry. Besides, I had a good feeling that the light was not going to stop. That it is only going to continue and get worse until something really bad happened.

"Maybe I should ask for help, I could ask Sani what I should do. I will go to his hogan and ask him. He will know what to do. He has all the answers. He still has to tell me what my real name is. I cannot allow him to keep it from me; it's *my* name."

I began walking, hoping that I was going in the right direction. I could not have ran that far after I broke his gate. It was not long until I got to his hogan. The pieces of the door were scattered on the ground. I moved over to the door, went inside, but he was not there; probably still in the village. I could not go there; I needed to wait for him to come home. I went into where Sani had told me to rest after my test. I laid down and decided to wait for him to get back. My eyes got heavy and I needed to rest.

I opened my eyes, getting up, and hearing something outside. It was dark out and I could see a red light moving closer to the hogan. It was Sani, surprised to see that his gate was in pieces. I ran to go talk to him.

"Sani, I'm sorry, I did this. I swear I will fix it."

"No, no you will not."

"Sani, I will, I am sorry."

"You will not be able to do so from where you will be."

"What do you mean?"

"The tribe has decided, the elder kept pressing the idea that you were possessed."

"The tribe has decided what?"

"You will be put into a special hogan. A potion will surround it and you will not be able to leave that area, sealing you inside. They are going to start constructing it under the next sun. I am not allowed to let you leave if I see you. I know that you will be able to get away from me and them whenever you feel it is necessary."

"Why are they doing this? Whose idea was it?"

"They are doing this so that you do not harm them. I'm sorry, Bidziil."

"Why would The Elder do this to me? It does not make sense."

"It was not his idea."

"What? Whose was it?"

"Your father's. He wanted what was best for the tribe. The Elder was reluctant, but the tribe agreed with your father's idea."

"What?" I was astonished. I could not believe that my own father would shun me away from the tribe.

"Are you sure?" I asked. "Are you sure that it was him?"

"Yes, I was there when he made the speech."

I sat down on the ground. I did not know what to say. I wanted to talk to my father, but he was always talking about the safety of the tribe. There was no way that he was going to change his mind. There was nothing I could to;

I thought, I might as well just do what he says. The tribe will feel safe, and I do not know what I will do anyway. I can not return to the tribe and I can not stay with you. I am lost; I will do what is best for the tribe.

"Sani, I am going to talk to my father under the next sun, I am going to do what is best for the tribe. I will live in the hogan that will soon be built. I will no longer be apart of the tribe."

"You can do what you believe is the right thing to do, I will stand behind you no matter what your choice."

"Thank you, Sani, but I want everyone to be happy and safe. The only way the tribe will feel that is if I am gone. I have made my decision."

"You should get some rest. I will leave in the morning to go get your father. We can deal with everything then."

"Yeah, that is good," I said walking back into his hogan to get rest.

I laid down and shut my eyes. Sani awoke me; the sun was bright and golden. It was the best rest I had in a long while.

"Your father wants to see you outside, they have begun preparing your special hogan," I got up out of bed and walked outside. My father was sitting on a log waiting for me.

"I will go willingly father. I am not sure why you decided to do this to your own son, but it is for the good of the tribe."

"Son, I am sorry, it is what needs to be done. The Elder would not do what was necessary. I had to take charge, no one else would."

"What you did was wrong, no matter what way you look at it, you are a terrible father. You care more about the tribe than your own son. I will obey your rules, I will not leave the hogan that is being constructed, but food must be brought to me. I want no visitors other than the ones who bring me food."

"That sounds fair."

"What you are doing is not going to stop what is happening to me, it can not be controlled. Not even the gods can help me, what makes you think that you can?"

"I'm not sure my son, but I have to try, you are not the same, the things that happen to you, your great strength, you must be possessed by an evil spirit of the island."

"You have no idea what you are doing, you are just making guesses and hoping that it works, father it will not! Just tell Sani when the hogan is complete, and then you can have someone bring me to it and lock me up until I die."

"Son, I am sorry, I really am, but this is what is best for the tribe as a whole."

I walked away from him and went into Sani's hogan. It was not long until the hogan was complete. The Privileged were outside of Sani's hogan waiting. I walked out and they were standing around my father. They had bottles in their hands. I guessed that it was their special potions that would stop the evil spirit inside me from leaving. It was a shame that there was no evil spirit. The only thing stopping me from leaving that hogan was my own self-control.

"Are you ready, Bidziil?" one of the privileged asked.

"Say that name again and see what happens," I said to him.

"Son, please can we just do this without any problems?" my father asked.

I walked into the woods saying, "Just tell me if I am going the wrong way."

"The hogan is in the center of the island. We will tell you when you are approaching it."

"We are sorry, but this was the last decision," another of the privileged said.

"Do not talk to me. You have no right to speak. I can only hope that your children are different like me and you have to do this to them. I pray that the gods curse you for the rest of your lives for what you are doing."

One of The Privileged pushed me against a tree with all his might, I could feel the amount of force he was using, strangely enough, as if I felt his energies. He was not holding anything back; still his strength had no effect on me.

"Do not dare wish that upon me. I should kill you right now."

"Too bad that you can not," I said. Then I pushed him off me, lifting off the ground, and his back hitting a tree. The rest of The Privileged and my father backed away. Then two of them picked up the one that I pushed off me.

"Do not touch me, you will only get hurt," I said.

"You are evil; you were never a real part of this tribe. The gods have cursed you because you deserved it."

"I have done nothing to deserve this! What you think is a curse, I see as a reward. The strength that I have could have been a great help to the tribe, but you see it differently. You see me as evil when I have done nothing wrong. You are just scared of what you do not understand."

"We are scared of death. The gods have said that you are going to be the death of the tribe," my father said.

"How could you tell them that father, The Elder and Sani did not want anyone else to know. That is why they wanted to get rid of me so badly. They think that I will kill them all."

"The gods are never wrong son, they know all; past, present, and beyond. We need to put you away for the sake of the tribe."

I did not know what to say to them. There was no other way for me to defend myself.

"Let us just get this over with," I continued to walk. In a short while, we reached the hogan. It was covered in bark with an opening where the door was. I guessed that was where I would get my food. It was not very large. I walked up to it and opened the door. The hogan did have all the necessary items to live: a table, chairs, a bed.

"At least that I can be comfortable while I slowly die of starvation and nothing to do."

"I wanted you to be comfortable," my father said.

"Great, thank you." I spoke with sarcasm.

"Well go in so that we can lock it up."

I walked inside and stood next to the table. They closed the door behind me. I could see what they were doing. They were putting wood against the door. Then I heard splashing. It was The Privileged covering the hogan with their special potions to keep me locked up. Then everything stopped and I heard my father's voice.

"Son, I do love you, but I have to do what is best for the tribe. I truly am sorry."

"Goodbye father, try and not visit me ever."

I could hear them walking away from the hogan. I looked out the opening and they were leaving. I was going to die in the hogan. My life was over and it had just begun. "Maybe it is a curse, not a blessing."

The days pass like years; dragging out forever and even more. Being alone all the time was like being in pain. The light had continued to escape my body; each time not being any less painful than the one before it. I counted the days by carving a mark into the hogan with my fingernail. Food was brought to me every few days. It was hardly ever the same person. One day Sani came to see me. He told me that the Elder had died. The Privileged decided to vote my father as the new elder. He could put the village before everything. Not one person from the tribe disagreed with the decision. Sani said that he was going to pass on to the next life soon as well. He could feel it, and so could I as well. His energies were weakening. Then he moved to the back of my hogan and carved something into it. It was a little while until he came back to the front. He said that I had not aged a day since the last time he had saw me, but it had been five years. It had seemed much longer, like an eternity. He said that all I want to know is on the back of the hogan; everything that the gods have said about me. He told me to not leave the hogan though. If I did the island would begin to fall apart. He left, saying goodbye because he would be dead by the time I was aloud out.

The light had left my body ninety-six times in five years. It did not seem too bad, compared to having it happen on a daily basis. I had to know what Sani wrote on the back of the hogan, but what if I do leave and the island did start to fall apart. I had to know. I no longer cared about anyone on this island. They shunned me away to the center keeping me hidden. I had enough, punching the door to the hogan, shooting it forward and hitting a tree. My chest began to burn; it was the light.

"What are the chances of the light coming up the same time I decide to leave the hogan?"

I ran to the back see what Sani wrote. It said that I had failed his test. If I was reading it, I had left my hogan too early, and the island was doomed because of it. "I really was what the gods said I would be."

It ended with one word; it was my real name, the name that the gods had given me. I lived up to that name. I walked back into the hogan, putting the door back up, and making sure that it was tight. I sat there alone, knowing what my real name was, and the gods were right. They are always right. The light grew stronger and left my body.

The years continued to pass and I continued to release the light. There hardly any visitors. The days when I got food became more spread out. The ground began to often shake. I had no idea what it was. As the years passed the shaking began to happen more frequently. One day, my father came to visit me, as an old man. His hair gray and long, and yet mine had not even dulled or grown an inch. He asked me if I was the one doing it, the shaking. The island was falling apart. The tribe had to leave soon, or face certain death, but every time they made rafts the shaking broke them. Cracks were appearing near the center of the island. Like its being cut or ripped apart. I told him that I had nothing to do with it. I knew that he did not believe me.

As we were talking, it happened again. The island was falling apart, just like Sani said it would. This time it was different. The shaking was more violent and it lasted longer. I could feel the island ripping apart. My dad blamed me and then ran away back to the village. I knocked the door off of the hogan again, running out and into the woods. I looked at the ground and it was opening up. There was a large crack going through the island. I followed it as it continued to rip. I ran all the way to the other side of the island. The island was splitting apart. The sounds of rushing water and falling earth consumed my ears. The island was separated into two pieces. I watched the land separate. Slowly, the two masses of land drifted from each other. Chunks of land fell and crumbled into the water. The other half was drifting further and further away. The piece that I was standing on began to rip apart. I could hear the cries of the villagers. I was too far of away to help them. I was stronger than a bear, but there is nothing I can do to save them. I was now truly alone.

The years continued to pass quickly and I do not age a day. For some reason my body stopped aging. I had determined it was because of the light. I hardly ever left my hogan. I did not seem to need food to survive, but did occasionally venture out to feed on what was left on my part of the island, berries, fruit, and nuts mostly.

The light continued to leave my body over the years. When I thought that I would be getting used to the pain it only began to hurt more. I had found that I could feel how much energy is being released from any living thing. I could help a plant grow, change the color of anything, turn rock transparent, and gather animals just by thinking about it. The light was the only explanation for how I can do those things.

I went into my hogan to rest, and I was awoken by a sound that I had never heard before. It sounded like an angry beast coming from the sky. I could hear footsteps, many of them. There was talking, but I could not understand it. It was in a different language. I looked out of my hogan; they were holding items that I had never seen before. The beings looked different, wearing dark cloths that appeared hard. They were dangerous, I could sense it. I opened up the door to the hogan and stepped out.

Chapter IX

HANNAH: LIFE ON THE INDUSTRIAL

May 3, 2007

May 3 Dear Diary,

Today was the first day of orientation and the new people with powers have arrived. There were twelve of them. There were more boys than girls, this time. Last year there were like eight girls and three guys. Any who, I saw the hottest guy. He was one of the new kids. We're not supposed to know what other people's powers are, but I really want to know his. If he could fly that would be so hot. He could take me wherever I wanted. I didn't get a chance to talk to him because it was in the middle of orientation, but tomorrow I'm going to find out where they put him. Maybe he has a level three power. Then I could see him whenever I want to. I could just get Wade to unlock any doors that would stop me from getting to him. That would just be so cool. I just want to talk to him. I hope that he likes me. There really aren't too many attractive nice guys around here. All of them are just too obsessed with their powers and with Fight Night. I mean I love my power too, but I would totally give it up for that new guy; as long as he is nice of course. I don't know what else to write. I'll talk to you tomorrow diary.

May 4,

The morning started off good. I got up out of bed, went to breakfast, and sat down at the table with my instructor Steve and his other student,

Jill. Jill is a little too abusive of her power, but she's a nice person; I mean we get along okay and everything. Steve isn't that bad either. He is very understanding, but strict at the same time. Anyway, I didn't see the new guy at breakfast, I didn't really expect to because the first couple days of orientation I didn't go anywhere other than the Placement Wing. I asked Jill if she had seen him, but she didn't. I didn't let Steve hear because we aren't supposed to associate with anyone other than our partner and consolers. Oh yeah, and the seven heads of the islands. You can talk to them whenever you want. They are actually quite nice. I've only met three of them; Franz, Emily and Perin. None of them have abilities, but I've heard that some of the others do, but they're always off on some special assignment. At least that's what Perin said.

In the afternoon Jill and I did some heavy jogging around the Industrial. In order to go off on your own you need to sign out with your instructor's permission, be with your partner or instructor, and they put on this tracking device that tells them where you are, and if it goes off for more than thirty seconds, they send the Industrial Enforcement Squad after you. They are pretty much just like a S.W.A.T. team. It only happened to me once because I accidentally drained the power out of it. They were really scary and intimidating.

Well afterwards Jill and I just practiced our powers with Steve. He doesn't have a power, but he knows a lot about ours. Some other instructors have powers though. Anyway, Jill can change the shape of any metal. They think that as her power advances that she will be able to move it as well as molding it. As for me, I can drain electricity out of anything that has electricity in it. They think that I can soon find a way to release that electricity. Like I'm charging up for something, like a beam or a blast. I don't think so, but they have seen a lot of advancements with powers. This one kid started out by being able to see in the dark perfectly, and now he can create these black sphere things that put you to sleep when you are inside them. I've never met him, he finished all of his training and now he works for them helping convince others to come to the islands, so that they can learn to control their powers.

I tried to go looking for the new kid, but I couldn't find him. Jill and I signed out again for a walk, and I passed around a note to some of the other girls to see if they had seen him. That is really the only way that you can "talk" to people is by notes. It's really dumb how they don't want you to associate with other people. It is as if they are afraid that something bad would happen.

Nobody else had seen him. They said that they wanted all the new comers to stay away from everyone because of the lock down we had. No one knows why it happened, but it was really serious. One of the girls wrote that an instructor died and so did one of the seven heads, probably just a rumor. It's hard to tell if people are lying on paper.

That's pretty much the day for me diary; just another day that I don't get to see the new hot guy. Hopefully, I'll get to see him tomorrow. Okay good night.

May 5,

Today was the best and worst day of my entire life. So I woke up and went to breakfast like usual, and another instructor came over to talk to Steve. Then Steve asked me to go with the other guy. I thought that I was in trouble, but it was actually the opposite of that. They wanted me to show one of the new students around the Industrial. I got really excited. The person walked in, it was the really hot guy. His name is Travis. And he is a level three just like I hoped. I walked him around the island. I explained to him that every other day we had classes. Like history and stuff. On the other days it was training and working out. There is a very strict schedule. I told him about the rules of talking with any other person besides your partner and instructor. I showed him the work out room and he was really impressed. I flirted with him like every chance that I could, but he wouldn't flirt back. He was really nice and so gorgeous. I continued to show him around, telling him that we aren't really supposed to go into the woods, but if we stay on the path they really don't mind.

We were almost done with the tour, so I sat down and said that I was tired so he sat down too. I showed him my power by draining the electricity out of one of the light posts near one of the doors to the Level

Two Dorms. Then he showed me his power. He touched the bench that we were sitting on and his hand turned like weird transparent white, then his hand was metal like the bench. Then he turned it back to normal. We really connected. He asked if I liked it here. I told him that it would be so much better if we could talk to people. He asked if it felt like that the instructors and heads were hiding something. I told him, yeah sometimes. I asked him why he wanted to know, but he didn't give me a straight answer. We had to go because an instructor was coming. I kissed him, but he stopped it. He said that it wasn't that he didn't find me attractive it was just that he had a girlfriend. I should have known some guy this hot would have a girlfriend. I also know that with no contact with her, he is going to get lonely and then I can take her place.

It sounds really bad diary, I know, but I really want a boyfriend. It will only be a matter of time.

May 6,

Today the new comers actually became part of the Industrial. Travis is on the floor below me. His roommate seems kind of strange. I keep trying to get near him to talk, but Steve was being an ass. Every time I signed out Travis wasn't out there. I want to see him. I don't care if we aren't supposed to talk to people. I want him as my boyfriend. I will have him even if I have to break all the rules to get him. Tomorrow, I'm getting out of my room and going onto the second floor and seeing him.

May 7,

I woke up really early so that I could sneak into the second floor. I drained the electricity out of all of the cameras, and then I put it into all the doors blocking me from Travis. I got to the second floor and I heard the guards coming. I quickly opened one of the rooms on the floor and hid inside. There was only one bed in the room and no one was in it. The room was really clean. Then a guy walked out of the bathroom only wearing only a towel and had a toothpick in his mouth.

He was really hot, not as hot as Travis, but still super hot. He didn't even seem startled that I was in his room, he was pretty awesome. I remember the conversation perfectly.

"And you are?" he said walking over to his dresser and taking out some clothes.

"Oh, um . . . I was . . . looking for someone. Sorry."

"Hey, don't mind me, I could care less."

"Oh, well I'm going to wait here for like a few minutes, if that's okay?"

"Do what you want."

He walked into the bathroom; I walked close to the bathroom so I could try and sneak a peek. Then someone knocked on the door to his room. I got scared; I didn't know what to do. I went into the bathroom and told him to answer the door.

"Yes dear," he said sarcastically.

"You can't let them know that I'm in here."

"Yeah okay," he said walking out of the bathroom and over to the door.

He opened it and it was some guy, I think he was an instructor. I didn't really hear what he said, but it was short.

The man left the room and the guy came back into the bathroom.

"That was my instructor, he was just letting me know that I wasn't going to class today, I have training instead. It was nothing about you, now if you don't mind."

"Oh, I'm so sorry," I got out of the room and he closed the door.

He came out dressed.

"I think I'm gonna go back to my room now."

"What were you hiding from?" he asked. "I figure that I deserve to know seeing how you used my room for a hiding spot."

"Oh, I was looking for someone, but then the guards came so I had to hide."

"Who?"

"Oh just one of the new kids."

"Why?"

"No reason really, I thought I knew him, but I guess not."

"Oh, well then good luck getting back, don't get caught, who knows what they will do to you, this place is kind of sketchy."

"You get used to it. Thanks though," I said walking out of the door. I turned around back into the room. "Do you have a girlfriend by any chance, just wondering?"

"No."

"Okay, see you around . . . um what's your name?"

"It's Gabe, yours?"

"Hannah," I said and left the room and snuck back to mine with no problem. That pretty much raps up my day. After that were just my classes. Well I'm thinking of ditching the Travis guy and going after Gabe, he's so cool. Well good night.

May 8,

Nothing much has been happening around here, just the usual. I saw Gabe and Travis; I didn't get to talk to them because they were going the total opposite way than Jill and me. She totally thinks that they were both hot, but if she tries to go after either of them before I make my final decision I just might kill her. Tomorrow is Fight Night and I'm really worried about the both of them. The new comers always have to fight. I hope that they aren't chosen, the highest levels of new comers always chosen. I hope that there are some level fours, if not then they might have to fight.

They will get their asses kicked. Every time one of the new comers fights, he is put up against a wicked strong person like Zane. If either of them get put up against him they will be slaughtered; it wouldn't even be a fair fight. I hope that nothing bad happens tomorrow. I don't want them to get hurt.

Chapter X

Bastian vs. *Ryder*

March 22, 2007

I woke up in the hospital bed and a nurse was in the room. She looked like she was cleanin' up the place.

"It's about time you woke up," she said.

"Why? What time is it?"

"It's past noon. Your father just went to sign you out. He should be back any minute."

"Oh. Okay," I rolled out of the bed. The clothes that I came in were folded on the chair next to my bed.

"If you're going to change I'll step out," the nurse said.

"I'll just go into the bathroom," I walked into the bathroom and got changed.

When I came out she was gone and my dad came through the door.

"How are you feeling?"

"Better."

"Well we're all set to go."

"Alright."

We got out to the car and drove home. My dad dropped me off and went back to work. My masks were lyin' on the table. I picked up Ien and put him on my face. Everythin' flashed white. I was standin' somewhere very bright. I looked up and saw a cloudy sky, but I wasn't outside. I was somewhere else. I looked around and walked a little. The ground was covered with white feathers. I picked one up and examined it. I could feel Ien's presence.

"Are you ready to go?" Ien said.

I turned around and there stood Ien, no more than eight feet away from me. He was massive. He had a tan vest on and I could see his chest. It seemed to be made of some animal hide. It looked Native American. The mask that I made covered the upper half of his face. He had tan pants on and no shoes. Like the vest; the pants seemed to be made out of animal hide. The most amazin' part about him were his wings, spreadin' out to at least six feet long, and covered in white feathers.

"Where are we? How are you here?" I began walkin' around. The place was nothin' more than the feather covered ground and the beautiful blue sky above. It seemed to go on forever.

"This is my home."

"How did I get here?"

"I'm not sure, but it doesn't mater. Can we go flying now?"

"I'm sorry it took so long. Somethin' happened."

"It hasn't been long at all. We were just flying a few minutes ago."

"What? I haven't been flyin' since yesterday."

"It has only been a couple minutes at most."

"This whole thing is so confusin'. It makes no sense to me. I don't understand how I'm even talkin' to ya face to face."

"It doesn't bother me," Ien said. "I'm just glad to see you, I'd love to go soaring through that sky of yours again."

"I'm sorry, but I have to do somethin' first. Is it okay if I come right back?"

"If you must."

"Thanks. I promise I'll be quick, but how do I leave?"

"I don't know. I never leave here by choice. The only time I did is when I was with you. It seems you have to figure it out."

I closed my eyes and pictured my kitchen. It was the best thing that I could think of. I opened my eyes and there I was, holdin' the mask in my hand. I must have taken it off when I left Ien's home. Somehow, I was transported to Ien's home when I put on the mask. I did want to talk to him.

"Maybe the mask knew that and brought me to him; but where was I brought to exactly, inside the mask?"

I looked up at the clock. No time had passed since I put on the mask. I was talkin' with Ien for at least five minutes. "Time must pass differently wherever he is."

I picked up the yellow mask. I figured I should have had a small connection already, it did basically save my life. I hoped to get sent to the masks home so I could talk to him face to face.

I picked it up and I put it on my face; a flash of yellow. Once again I had no idea where I was. It was very bright for a second and then it became very dark. There were yellow lines on the grounds that were glowin' and I couldn't see the end of them. It reminded me of a highway."

This must be in his home. Is anyone there? Hello?"

"It's you," all of the sudden the place was overcome with a bright light. It was too bright for me to see the person talkin'. "Whatareyou doinghere?" he asked quickly.

"I wanted to talk to you. If that's okay?"

"What do you want?" he said slowin' down as the bright light dimmed. I could see his full body and, just like Ien, he was wearin' the mask on his face. He was about average height and was wearin' a yellow skin tight shirt with black pants.

"What is your name?" I asked.

"What?"

"Your name, what is it?"

"I'm not sure. I don't have one."

"You don't have a name either?"

"What do you mean *either*? Do you not have one?"

"No I do, but, never mind. Do you want a name? Everyone deserves one."

"Why would you give me one? Is this some form of bribery?

"I just want to have some more control whenever I use your mask."

"Why?"

"I want to be able to use you to your potential. We need to work together instead of fightin' for control over my body."

"I understand what you mean," he said. "I guess I can allow you to take control of me."

"Thank you so much . . . Alden."

"Alden?"

"That's what I'm goin' to call you. Do you like it?"

"Alden . . . Alden. Yes, I like it. He said gettin' excited, like a child, and runnin' around. Thatismyname. MynameisAlden. Ahhahah."

"Haha, so we have a deal?" He ran over to me and stopped.

"Yes, yes we do. And your name, what is it?"

"It's Bastian. I promise that I won't let you down."

Everythin' flashed yellow again. I was back in my kitchen and only a minute had passed. I was gettin' so much accomplished in almost no time at all. I put down Alden and picked up another mask; the first mask that I made. It was a steel gray color. I did the same thing I did with Alden and Ien. I focused on wantin' to talk to whoever was inside. I put the mask and a flash of gray hit me. Big surprise, I was somewhere I didn't recognize. It was dark, foggy, and I couldn't see a thing.

"Are you here?"

I got no response and started walkin' through the fog. I continued askin' if anyone was around, but there was only silence. I backed into somethin', turnin' around, seein' a massive statue. It was a gargoyle, starin' right at me.

"And you are?" it asked slowly.

The statues mouth didn't move but I could hear it speak.

"I'm Bastian. I wore you twice."

"Who was the one who tried to hurt me?"

"Oh, my friend, he was just confused. He was not tryin' to hurt you, please don't be upset."

"I do not get mad. I am a peaceful being. I have been around forever. I have seen many things crumble and be destroyed, but yet I am always left standing. Somehow, you are able to make me leave my home and go somewhere else, into a world where I see through your eyes. I've been there twice now. It seems dangerous, and I know danger. If you're ever unable to handle a job just allow me to help. I may not be able to move, but I can take any attack without wavering."

"Thank you. Do you have a name? What can I call you?"

"I have been called many things. It doesn't matter what you call me. Whatever you wish."

I tried to think of a name.

"What If I call you Bon? Is that okay?"

"If that name suits your desires."

"How can I hear you though? Your mouth isn't movin'."

"I can speak telepathically."

"That's amazin'."

"Don't forget. Whenever you need me, I'll be there."

A cloud of fog spun around Bon, consumin' him, and pushin' me away. I opened my eyes, starin' at my kitchen ceilin', sprawled out on my kitchen floor. I sat up and stared at the mask. I had made contact with all of them. I had made a solid connection with the good ones. I stood up off the floor. I had figured out how to use them, but now I had to figure out how I made them. Every time I made a mask, I blacked out and had no recollection of carvin' them. When I made the last four my body shock drastically with my vision becomin' scratchy and unclear. I had to figure out how to make them.

I walked outside and looked for a piece of wood. I made every one of them out of wood, so why try anythin' else, I thought. I searched for a log or any decently shaped piece of wood. I couldn't find anythin' in my backyard and didn't really have any large trees. There were woods not to far from my house, so I went into my shed, grabbed an axe, and headed there. I walked on the side streets, not wantin' anyone to see me walkin' with an axe and get suspicious. The last thing I needed was gettin' in trouble with the cops.

I arrived findin' a tree that was already almost dead and not too thick nor tall. I chopped it down, cut off a good sized log, grabbed it, and brought it back to my house. When I got back I wasn't sure what to do next. I really had no idea how to use my power. I sat with the log in front of me. I picked it up, starin' at it very deeply. I concentrated as hard as possible, but nothin' happened.

All of a sudden, I remembered that when I made the four masks from Mr. Larson's wood my hands shook and I ended up with shards of wood in my fingernails. I thought that it was possible that I carved the masks with my hands. It sounded crazy, but so did the idea of masks givin' me superpowers. I gripped the log and focused really hard. I tried to picture another face, but couldn't. Every other time the faces appeared to me. I hadn't thought of them, they just came to me and that's when my body went crazy.

I went outside and over to Mr. Larson's yard where I made the other masks. I brought the log with me, sittin' down and focusin' again, but nothin' happened. I started to get really annoyed. I realized that I wouldn't be able to learn how to control it as quickly as I wanted. I held the log tightly and tried to pick at it with my nails. It was useless I was just causin' pain. I angrily began strainin' my vision and scratchin' at the log simultaneously.

My vision started to vaguely blur. Quickly, I concentrated on my eyes and tried to force out whatever was happenin'. I could hear somethin' in the back of my mind, but I couldn't make it out. My hands started to tremble. It was workin'. I was actually doin' it. I continued to concentrate all my energy into pushin' it out. I started to shake and the voice grew louder, and my vision continued to worsen and become more scratched. My body was violently shackin'. I then heard a loud howl, and passed out.

I opened my eyes and I could see the sky. I stood up lookin' around. I was outside of my back door. I had to have walked over to it at some point. I looked around, but couldn't see any mask. The log was gone and my fingernails were full of wood. I most definitely used my power, but the mask was nowhere to be found. I heard a door slide open. I turned around and it was Mr. Larson.

"What the hell are you doing boy?"

"Hi, Mr. Larson."

"What the hell was that?"

"What was what?" I asked in fear that he saw me use my power.

"You just ran out of my yard and collapsed. Are you stealing from me? Are you on drugs?"

"I did what? I was here the whole time."

"I just saw you run out of my yard."

When I passed out I must have went somewhere with the mask and not known.

"Boy, are you drunk?" he asked.

"No, Mr. Larson. I'm just exercisin' for lacrosse. I got tired and fell."

"I don't care. Stay off my property."

"Bye, Mr. Larson, have a nice day," I ran inside.

I looked all over the house for the mask, but my search turned up dry. It didn't make sense.

"Why would I move the mask? Was I tryin' to hide it? What if someone was comin', maybe I freaked out and hid it."

I sat down in my livin' room and tried to think of places where I would have put it. I laid down and I felt somethin' in my back. I sat up and took off the couch cushion. There it was; my new mask and it was nothin' like the other ones. The detail was amazin', to say the least. It was a wolf and it was already painted. It had a grain like texture to it. I couldn't get over the outstandin' detail. It had a snout that stuck out about two inches and it was slightly showin' its teeth.

"I can't believe that I can make these masks with just my fingernails."

I picked up the mask off the couch, lookin' into it. It gave me a really bad feelin', but I ignored it. I had to try it. As I inched the mask slowly to my face I could hear howlin' in the back of my head. I heard my dad's truck outside pullin' into the driveway right before I was goin' to put on the mask. I looked outside to make sure that I wasn't hearin' things. I saw my dad get out of his truck. I grabbed all my masks on the kitchen table and ran them upstairs. My dad walked through the front door just as I was comin' back down from my room.

"Hey, Bastian. How are you feeling?"

"Great actually."

"That's good. I just came home to grab some tools then I'm heading back out."

"Oh, alright."

My dad walked into the garage, grabbed his tools, and then left. I made sure that he was gone before I put on the mask. I walked outside, with my new mask, holdin' it with both hands facin' me. I flipped it around and put on my face. I heard a terrifyin'ly loud howl. I opened my eyes and I was somewhere very dark. I could make out a few scattered trees and when I looked up, I saw the fullest moon I had ever seen; massive and glowin' bright. I heard the howl again. Growlin' was comin' from behind me. I turned around and a figure appeared in front of me, knockin' me down.

It launched at me through the darkness and its body became visible. It was a werewolf. It planted its claws on my face and held me to the ground. I tried to get away, but its grip was too strong. It was crushin' my face. The pain became more and more intolerable, to the point where I couldn't take it anymore. My mind gave up and nearly passed out. I was basically unconscious, but I could still feel my body move. I felt my skin burn. Hair forced itself all over my body. I had lost all control over what was happenin'. I opened my eyes. I wasn't cover with fur, even though before I blacked out it felt like it. I got up and walked all around the darkness. I found what looked liked a window. I could see whatever the werewolf was doin'. He was runnin' through the woods. I started yellin' at him to stop. There was nothin' that I could do. He was approachin' the town and I could feel his rage and frustration.

"Yeah that's all," I grabbed the soda off the counter and paid the clerk. She handed me my change and I threw it in my pocket. Unexpectedly, I heard a loud howl and then a bunch of people screaming. Everyone in the store ran outside and I followed, walking out the door and seeing people running away. Again, I heard a howl, but louder. I couldn't see anything. I started pushing people out of the way to see what was going on. I finally broke through masses and it was clear what was making the howls. It was a werewolf. I real live werewolf. Not like my werewolf form, but a living breathing, full blown werewolf. It was a monstrous size; being over six feet tall. It was standing on the roof of a car with the hood crushed in. It didn't seem that anyone had gotten hurt yet. It was smashing things around it. It completely destroyed a

mailbox and it took down a tree as well. I knew what I had to do. I had to stop it immediately before anyone got hurt.

"HEY! COME GET ME YOU BEAST!!!" I screamed.

It looked at me and let out a roar that paralyzed me in fear. I had to be strong. It started running at me. I focused on a rhino and my body quickly began to change. My bones cracked, broke, and changed their form into that of the rhino. My muscles were tearing and ripping, changing so I could become the rhino. My skin became as hard like steel and turned a light gray. Shoulders becoming twice as large, the same happened to my thighs. My nose changed its shape into basically a horn. I could not fully become the animal, but change my body into a partial version it.

The werewolf was nearly in front of me by this time. I ran toward it and we collided. I smashed into it and pushed it back. I put all my strength into my shoulder and knocked it into a building to my right. It crashed into the wall of the building, coming back at me with its claws out. I couldn't move out of the way. As the rhino, I couldn't dodge his blows. Everyone was watching me. They had already seen what I could do. There was no reason to hold back. The werewolf attacked me. It didn't hurt me much because my skin was almost impenetrable, but that didn't stop it from attacking me. I couldn't get any clean hit on it; it was too fast for me.

It knocked me into the street and picked up a mailbox, throwing it at me. I blocked it with my shoulder, but still it knocked me down. He was a good distance away from me. It was a perfect time for me to change into something else. I changed back to normal. My bones broke and repaired themselves to fit the form of my normal human body. I looked around and tried to see if I could use my surroundings to my advantage or at least to help me think of what to change into. There was a park not far away full of trees. I could gain my advantage there. I started running away from the werewolf. It let out another terrifying howl that almost stopped me in my tracks, and then began chasing after me. As I was running I pictured a gorilla and my body began to change. My muscles increased, my legs shortened, arms lengthened, and small amounts of fur spread over my arms and chest. All of my muscles grew exponentially.

Who ever this guy was he was really good. I couldn't believe that there was someone else with a power. I mean, I wasn't surprised, but this guy knew his stuff. I could only hope that he could take down the werewolf before anyone got hurt and without killin' me.

I ran on my arms and legs, using my fists to gain more speed. It didn't hurt because my knuckles were as hard as stone. The werewolf continued to chase me. He was falling for my trap, but I had to reach the forest before him. Even as a gorilla the werewolf was faster than me. I was less than twenty feet away from the park. I used all the strength that I could and jumped into the park grabbing onto one of the trees. The werewolf jumped as well and tried to cut me with his claws, but he missed and hit the tree that I grabbed on to. I swung myself around the branch and sat on it and watched it fall to the dirt.

It got up and roared, jumped up, and tried to cut me again, but it didn't quite make it. As it was falling it dug its claws into the tree and stuck to it, jumping while having a hold on the tree, and making it past the branch that I was on. It let out a roar after landing above me. I looked up at it. It was beginning to get tired, but I could tell that it was pissed, and I had no time to take a break. I jumped off the branch and started swinging away from the werewolf. It chased after me by jumping from branch to branch. I stopped and swung onto another branch, turning around and looking for the werewolf. It was nowhere in sight. I thought that I might have lost it.

"Watch out kid! Move!" I tried to yell to him. It was useless he couldn't hear me.

Suddenly, the werewolf blindsided me. He smacked into me trying to bite me. We started to fall off the tree. Its spit and drool went all over my body as it snapped at me. I held its head away from me so he couldn't land a bite. It dug its claws into my shoulder and side; I started to bleed. Its nails were outrageously long, they were deep inside me. This beast was ruthless. It wanted the kill. I punched the werewolf in the chest and spun it around, weakening my fall as we slammed into he ground. We hit the ground and dust and dirt shot everywhere, making it very challenging to see. I quickly got up and crawled away, changing back to normal. My body was weak and I was out of breath. I leaned up against a tree in order to rest for a minute, holding the deep cuts on my sides.

"Yes, yes I did it. Now how do I get out of this place?" I started to walk around and try to find a way out. I heard sticks break and dirt shuffle. I turned around and the werewolf was trying to get up.

"You're still alive. Just give up. You've lost."

The werewolf howled, frightening me. I looked around to find something to stab it with. I grabbed one of the branches that we knocked down when we fell out of the tree. It howled again and I dropped the branch. It was standing upright. I only had one other option. I had to take it out by fighting as a werewolf. My form was the strongest form that I had next to the gorilla. It stared at me as I started to change.

I watched as he began to transform, yet again. His mouth and jaw started to push forward while his neck moved and cracked. His teeth grew and ripped out through his gums, while his ears stretched out and moved upward. Slowly, his fingernails grew longer, legs crackin' and tightenin'. He bent down just a little. A small amount of fur pushed its way out of his skin, lightly coverin' most of his body and face. His spine arched slightly. It was clear his transformation was complete. He let out a loud bellow and my werewolf did the same.

"You are insane man. How did ya do that? He can become a werewolf too? I don't understand. Hopefully, this will end here. I can feel my werewolf gettin' tired. I have to find a way to gain control before this shapeshifter kills me."

I launched at the werewolf, landed on it, and dug my claws into its body just like it did to me. It kicked me off of it and jumped at me. I caught myself and landed on the ground. While the werewolf was mid air, I put all of my strength into one slash and swung my arm back, and then slashed at it before it hit me, but it dodged the swipe. The beast clotheslined me with its right arm. It followed up by putting its foot on me and pinned me down. It let out a victory howl as if it had won. With both hands, I clawed up its leg. It kicked me in the face, sending me skidding backwards. My head hit a tree causing me to stop. I wiped the blood off my face and roared at the werewolf. He ran at me on all fours. I jumped back, grabbing onto the tree, and then it jumped at me. With all my strength I pushed off the tree and grabbed on to the beast, slamming it into the ground. It got up and swung at my chest landing two decent scratches. Blood slowly dripped out of my wound. I kicked the beast in the head, and it rolled backward catching and then stopping itself. Again it ran at me on all fours. I ran toward it ready to swing with all my might. The beast left the ground, leaving behind a cloud of dust, and lunged toward me. I swung my claw at its face landing a direct hit. The werewolf flew through the air and crashed into the ground. Something flung off its face. No longer being able to hold my form, I turned back to normal.

The darkness started to clear. Everythin' started to glow white. I could begin to see everythin' around me. I felt like I was bein' ripped out of wherever I was. It physically hurt. Suddenly, I was torn out and a flash of light hit me.

The fur on the werewolf started to fall off and I could see a body. It began to look more and more like a person. The thing that came off of its face looked like a mask. I ran over and grabbed it before the man or whatever it was got up. As suspected it was a mask, a werewolf mask. All the fur was off the body and it was clearly a male, around the age of twenty. The fur started to evaporate. It was very peculiar. The guy started to get up. I backed away first. I wasn't sure what was going to happen.

I regained consciousness with my face in the dirt. I rolled onto my back and pushed myself up. My entire body was overflowin' with pain. I looked at the guy in front of me. He was holdin' my mask and he had returned to normal.

"Sorry about that," I said breathin' heavily. "I had no idea that was goin' to happen."

"Who are you and what happened to you?" I asked while keeping a safe distance. Who knows if he is going to pull out another mask, I thought

"My name is Bastian Glant, and as you can already tell I have a superpower, just like you do. I mean it's not the same as yours, but we have somethin' in common. I'm not sure how my power works, but I can assure you that I won't be usin' that mask anytime soon. I didn't know that things were goin' to happen that way. I swear it."

"How do I know you're telling the truth?"

"Trust me, I'm a friend. I was watchin' the entire fight. You were outstandin'. I was rootin' for you the entire time."

"Wait, what?"

"It was like I was lookin' through the werewolf's eyes."

"Really?" I started to let my guard down. I felt like he wasn't going to try anything else. I walked over to him and shook his hand. "My name is Ryder Springs, nice to meet the real you."

"Haha yeah," we started walkin' around and talkin'. "So what exactly is your power?"

"I can change my bone structure and muscle tissue to match that of any animal. In order to use my power I have to know a lot about how the animal works. I actually have to know the bone structure. I took me a while to learn how to use my power, but I had a lot of help."

"That's pretty cool. Like I said, I'm not sure how to use my power really. Well, I know how to use half of it. The masks that I have allow me to do some pretty amazin' things. One of my masks even allows me to fly."

"I see, what's the other half of your power?"

"Makin' the masks is the other half. It just happens. I tried to focus on creatin' one and then this werewolf mask was produced. It sounded like the mask told me to not force it. I think it was talkin' about my power."

"Wait you can communicate with these masks?"

"Yeah, that's how I get them to let me use their power."

"Unbelievable. How long have you been able to use your power?"

"No more than a week, why?"

"That's just insane. You are really strong and if you can gain control over your abilities you could do great things."

"I'd like to hope so. I have been given these powers for a reason. I don't know what that reason is yet, but I would really like to."

"Do you live around here?"

"Yeah, do you?"

"I live over in the Gratis apartments the next town over, you?"

"I live off of Holden Street if you know where that is."

"Yeah I do. We should hang out and train each other or something. It would be good for the both of us. Plus where else are you going to find someone with a superpower?"

"That is true. It would be really cool if I had someone to help train me." I heard somethin' or someone walkin' toward us. "Did you hear that?"

"Yeah, what was it?"

"I think someone is tryin' to sneak up on us."

Someone walked out from behind one of the trees in front of us. It was Zander. What was he doing here, I asked myself.

It was that Zander guy who tried to capture me a few days ago.

"What are you doin' here?" I asked him.

"I'm here to get you to come with me," Zander said.

"Bastian, I'm out of here. You should get out as well he looks dangerous."

"He is, he's tryin' to kidnap me. I've dealt with him once before."

"I'm leaving now you should do the same," I handed him a card with my name and number on it. "Give me a call sometime."

I changed my bone structure into a bird. My arms and elbows bent back and cracked. My body became weightless. Small flaps of skin formed underneath of my arms like feathers. I pushed myself into the air and used my arms to climb higher and higher until I was above the trees. I continued to fly through the air and toward my apartment.

I watched Ryder slowly take off and soar into the sky. I wished that I could do the same. I was completely unprepared to deal with Zander.

"Just come with me, Bastian, it's not goin' to be that bad, this is the last time I will ask nicely," he said.

My phone started to ring. I took my phone out of my pocket, it was an unknown number.

Chapter XI

Travis: Fight Night

May 9, 2007

I woke up at seven am because I had training at nine. My roommate was already gone. His name was Adair. He wasn't the most interactive person, but at least he wasn't a slob. He kept to himself and was hardly ever in the room. He always signed out and went to a special training area where you could test and train your power. It was closed off when someone was using it, for privacy reasons. They didn't like students to know any other students powers. The rules were much stricter than I had imagined. There was nearly zero interaction between anyone other than your roommate and your instructor. Everything about the islands was suspicious; it didn't give me a good vibe. I wasn't sure why, but I planned to find out. I didn't forget what Bastian said to me.

"They will use you and when they are done, they will kill ya. GET OFF THE ISLANDS!!!"

I needed to know why. If I didn't figure out why Bastian wanted me off the islands then I would never feel comfortable. I left my room and went to the sign out office in the main lobby of Industrial Dorm Level Three. I signed out and they gave me the ankle bracelet to monitor where I was. I always had Perin's permission to sign out on my own, most instructors allowed they students to leave unattended. I went for a jog to start off my day with some cardio.

The island was basically divided into three main parts. Each area was classified by rank and stage of power. Depending on where your power ranked when you arrived on the Homestead was the area you'd be living in. The areas all had there own gyms and training buildings along with dormitories and small hospitals just in case anyone got injured. A path connected each of the three areas. You were aloud to enter another area as long as you were accompanied by an instructor. There wasn't a barricade or anything but the I.E.S were always on patrol. Paths were made that sent you though the wooded perimeter surrounding the island. As long as you don't spend too much time in there, they didn't seem to mind. I preferred running though woods as apposed to the sights of buildings at ever turn. In the very center of the three areas there was a main building, for all the instructors and the heads that stayed on the islands. It was a housing facility for the ones that did not live in the dormitories. The building was at least four stories high. I.E.S stations were also scattered across the island. They were the islands police force for the most part. If you went out of line, they were the ones who would come find you.

I finished my jog around the area and went to one of the workout facilities and signed in. Unless you were with your partner they gave you a key to your own separate weight room. I walked into the room and it was filled with exercise equipment; a bench press, treadmills, dumbbells, home gyms and other weight training equipment. I worked out for over and hour then signed out and left the building. When I got outside Perin was standing by the door.

"Hey, Travis, how are things going?" he asked.

"Everything is good, but I would really like to know what's going on," I asked blatantly.

"What do you mean? I know the rules are a little strict, but I told you they were going to be. You will get used to them. After a few weeks you and your roommate, Adair, will get along just great. After he becomes accustomed to everything you can start training together."

"Yeah, but why can't we have any other contact, like with the other students?"

"It's all an issue of safety, it's much more complicated than you think to run this place and keep it organized. The Boss is always busy and he wouldn't have time to stop any fights that break out between students. So, it's just better if there is less contact."

"I don't know, it just sounds stupid."

"You'll get used to it, I promise."

I didn't want to get used to it. I wanted to have contact with people. I thought my power is cool and everything, but I wanted to get to know people too. I began to doubt if I made the right choice going to the islands.

"Oh, and about that whole Bastian fiasco, I want you to know that he is psychotic. His power drove him insane. Whatever he said to you was most likely invalid information. He had strange hallucinations about how awful this place was. He is insane Travis, just remember that, okay?"

"Yeah okay. No problem."

"Okay good. Well I got to get back to my office. I just wanted to check on you to see how you were doing."

"Okay, I'll see you later," I yelled as Perin walked away.

I went to the lunchroom and got something to eat, since I wasn't with my instructor I had to get it to go. I brought it back to my room and ate it. It was fried chicken, mashed potatoes and macaroni & cheese with a bread roll. It was amazingly delicious. Adair wasn't back yet. I worked on some of my homework that I had from the day before. It was simple for the most part, busy work to keep us thinking. I finished and Adair walked through the door with a plate in his hand.

"Hey, what's up dude?" I asked. He ignored me. "Okay you could just do that. You know if we're going to be roommates, then we should at least try and get along," I said to him and he still ignored me. "Alright, seriously say something; you seem like a cool guy we should have no problem being friends."

"Whatever," Adair said to me.

"Hey, you can talk." I chuckled.

"Well aren't you just a barrel of laughs?"

"I have a good feeling I'm going to like you."

"Don't get too attached there boy. I don't like people, which means I don't like you. I like my privacy and I like to be alone. I get that we are roommates, but that doesn't mean that I have to like you, but dealing with you is a different story. Now just leave me alone."

"Okay, Captain Emo."

It eventually got late and we went to bed. I woke up in the middle of the night to the sound of someone knocking on our door. I got out of bed and walked over to the door.

"Who is it?" I asked.

"This is Wanda, I live a couple doors down," the girl said.

"What do you want?"

"I wanted to know if you and Adair wanted to go to a party we are having in the woods."

"I don't know about Adair, but I'm up for a party. Hold on, I'll let you in."

I pressed the open key on the keypad next to the door to open it. She was waiting outside with another guy who was holding onto her shoulder.

"This is my friend Tadeo, can we come in?"

"Yeah."

They walked into my room and over to Adair's bed. She shook him until he woke up.

"Hey, wake up, we got places to be," she said to him.

"Who the hell are you?" he said as he sat up.

"We are from down the hall, now get dressed. We got a party to go to."

"Screw that, I'm going back to bed."

"Travis, can you tell him to come?" Wanda asked.

"If you think that he is going to listen to me, then you're crazy."

"Please come," she said shaking Adair again "A lot of people are waiting for us."

"Nobody knows me, how can they be waiting for me?" he said.

"Some of them know you . . . well, your power at least."

Adair sat back up hastily.

"What do you mean they know my power?! That's impossible! I've never used my power around any of these people and my file is confidential, no one except for Perin knows my power."

"Well, someone did a little digging and found out what you can do," she said.

Adair was pissed off. It seemed he was very secretive about his power. The first time I asked him about it he flipped out on me and said that it was none of my business. The man that was with Wanda continued to remain silent.

"Why would people be interested in my power?" Adair asked.

"Well, I kind of lied to you. We aren't going to a party. Well, it's kind of like a party, except that people fight. It's called Fight Night. We have one every month."

Adair jumped out of bed and walked over to his dresser.

"Don't apologize to me. Just show me the way," he took out a black and purple baseball style shirt from his dresser and put it on. "Am I going to be fighting?"

"You both might be," she answered.

"WAIT, I don't want to fight anyone," I said.

"I said that you *might* have to."

"I'm not going if I'm going to be forced to fight. That's not what I came here for."

"Stop being such a little bitch and put a shirt on," Adair said.

"Fine, but I'm telling you that I'm not fighting," I walked over to my closet and grabbed a shirt.

"Okay, then lets go," she said.

"Make sure the two of you are touching me until we get out of the building," Tadeo said.

"Why?" Adair asked.

"Because I can't be recorded by anything," he answered.

"What do you mean?" I asked.

"I can't be recorded on video, film, microphone or any type of radar or tracking systems. So as the guards are watching the surveillance cameras they won't be able to see us. Unless you guys want to get caught, that's fine too," he said.

"No, I want to fight. If I have to hold onto your shoulder or something to get there then whatever," Adair said.

"Don't worry, Adair, you won't have to, as long as Tadeo is touching me then we will be fine," Wanda assured.

"Wait, but he said that we have to be touching him."

"Are you going to use your power?" Tadeo asked Wanda.

"If we are going to be dealing with this big group then yes," she answered.

"What is your power?" Adair asked.

"I can generate soundproof barriers. What I'll do is generate a barrier with us inside it and have Tadeo hold on to me. That way the barrier itself will be undetectable which means we are too, because we are inside it."

"That's so intelligent. You are combining your powers so that you can accomplish a greater goal," I said.

"Yeah, whatever boy scout, don't get too excited or you'll need to get a towel. Can we just go? I don't want to waste anymore time?" Adair asked.

"Let's do this Tadeo," Wanda said.

Her body released this bizarre energy that went through Adair and I; it was her barrier. Tadeo grabbed her shoulder and we walked outside and continued down the hallway. I wasn't going to fight under any circumstances. I didn't want to get into any trouble with Perin or the head of this place; at least not until I figured out what Bastian was warning me about. We got outside of the Industrial; there were five guards scattered outside patrolling. We had to avoid getting caught by them. We ran past them and into the woods. We continued walking.

"Are we almost there?" Adair asked, "Please tell me we are. I can't take all of this suspense. I'm so amped up, I want to fight."

"Yes, now just calm down."

I could see lights in the distance. It wasn't like a fire. It was more like streetlights.

"Is that it?" I asked.

Wanda let down her barrier. Adair ran toward the lights, and we all followed.

There were about fifty to sixty people there. There wasn't a dominant gender. Everyone was being extremely quiet. I looked around and noticed that the light was being generated by floating orbs. It must have been someone's power. Somebody approached us.

"Good job, Wanda. You got the both of them," she said.

"I told you I could. I can get anybody," Wanda responded. "I have to generate a very large barrier to surround this entire area. If I don't then we won't be able to have the fight night. My barrier will make sure that no one hears us cheering and fighting.

"Oh, that's not a bad idea. Then I will see you later?" I asked.

"I'll be around."

"Okay, let's get this fight night started," she said walking away.

After Wanda made her barrier she walked over to some guy and pointed at us.

"Okay everyone! All the fighters are present and accounted for. Fight Night will begin with, Adair Newburry and Cal Bothe. For the new guys, all the matches are chosen at random, we aren't trying to put you up against someone better than you, but that's what happens most of the time. So get used to it. The first fight will begin in ten minutes. Good luck to both fighters," Everyone began to cheer.

Adair walked over to Wanda, I followed.

"So who is this Cal Bothe guy? What is his power?" he asked

"That's him," she pointed the person already waiting in the place where they fight. "He's the one in the battle box. That's the place where you'll be fighting. He is a little cocky, but it's warranted, he is a great fighter. He hasn't ever lost a fight. He is 4-0,"

"What is his power though?"

"He can evaporate water from inside the body, he dehydrates you."

"How does his power work? Does he have to be close to me to do it?"

"As far as I know, yes. Why?"

"Then this fight will be no problem. It's time to end his winning streak," Adair said then walked over and into the battle box.

I walked over to the crowd surrounding the battle box in order to get a better view. Wanda and Tadeo began to walk away.

The announcer walked into the battle box.

"Okay, welcome to your first fight Adair. Everyone let's welcome Adair."

Everyone began to boo at him, and he didn't seem too care.

"That's not nice. Just cause he's going to lose doesn't mean we have to put him down about it," the announcer said.

"I'm not going to lose. Now get out of the box before this gets ugly for the both of you," Adair said.

"Let's get this fight started then," he said walking out of the box.

Everyone was quiet and Cal and Adair were standing in the battle box. It was large; about fifty feet by thirty feet. They were fairly far apart from each other, with plenty of room to move.

"So, this is your first year, your first fight, and you think you can beat me? Your too funny," Cal said.

"You have no idea what I can do," Adair responded.

"I could say the same about you."

"Now that's where you are wrong, I know what you can do. You have the power of dehydration."

"So what, you know my power, that means nothing."

"You're not very smart are you?"

Adair started squeezing his fists tightly. Cal kneeled down and supported his body with his left hand. The crowd was confused.

"What are you doing? I can . . . barely stand," Cal said.

"I told you, you have no idea what I can do. Your power is useless if you can't get close to me, and I promise you won't."

"What the hell are you doing, this must be your power," Cal stood up.

I could tell he was struggling to stand but he still did. I still wasn't sure what Adair was doing.

"You're gonna have to do much better if this is the best you got," Cal said as he began to walk towards Adair.

"Don't get your hopes up loser, that was only a taste of my power," Adair's muscles clinched and he was concentrating much harder.

Cal's body slammed to the ground, it happened so quickly. He screamed in pain. The entire crowd was mystified. I could see it in their faces. The announcer was excited. I looked around at all the people. I tried to see if Hannah was here, but I didn't see her.

Adair walked over to Cal and began kicking him around. Cal couldn't even move. It wasn't fair. Adair picked up Cal with one arm as if he weighed nothing; Adair had to be insanely strong. Everyone gasped. They were astonished by his strength

"Don't underestimate me. Just because I'm new here doesn't mean that you're better than me. You're nothing compared to me."

"Don't underestimate me!" Cal squeezed Adair's wrist and, what seemed like, blue smoke came off of Adair's wrist.

He was dehydrating him. Seeing it actually happen was almost unreal. I was still not used to the world I had brought into. Adair threw Cal into the air with ease. Cal soared through the air as if he was weightless. Adair pushed himself off of the ground and flew above Cal and punched him down to the ground. Adair hovered in the air. Cal crashed into the ground. People in the crowd started talking.

"He can fly?!" someone said.

"What is his power?" a girl whispered.

"This dude is nasty."

"He might ever be better than Zane."

"He is more than extraordinary."

"It seems he has more than one power."

I wasn't sure what his power was. He was doing so many different things.

"I did underestimate you for a second, but you continue to underestimate me," Adair said hovering above the ground clinching his fists.

Cal let out a painful yell.

"What are you?!" he screamed in agony "AHHH, I can't move, you're crushing me. I give."

Adair stopped squeezing his fists and returned to the ground. He walked out of the battle box. The announcer ran over to Adair.

"Congrats on your first win; your first of many apparently. Let's give it up for Adair!" the man said.

The crowd went crazy and I was more than impressed by his performance, which was outstanding. Whatever his power is, it seemed that he has complete control over it. I was jealous.

"Okay everyone it is time for the next fight." The girl who approached us when we first got there handed him two pieces of paper. "The next two fighters are, the unbeatable Zane, whose record is 23-0 and the second level three newbie, Gabe. You two have five minutes to get into the battle box. Good luck to the both of you, especially you, Gabe."

I waited for the next fight to start. One of them was already in the battle box. He didn't seem very old, maybe about twenty-four or twenty-five tops. He had long black hair that fell to his neck and was wearing a long white lab coat. I saw someone talking to Perin wearing one similar. Maybe he was an instructor. Hopefully, he wasn't because that would be totally unfair. Someone tapped me on the shoulder.

"Hey, want something to drink?" he asked.

"Yeah sure," he handed me a can of soda.

"My name is Wade; I'm a second year student. I haven't seen you around before, are you new?" he asked.

"I'm Travis and yeah I'm new, why?"

"Just curious. What dorm level are you in? I'm in the level two dorms."

"I'm a level three."

"So you're fighting tonight?"

"No, I'm not fighting."

"I wouldn't be so sure. All level threes fight there first time here, mainly because it puts them in their place. But that friend that you showed up with, Adair, he was sick. Are you as good as him?"

"I'm not fighting. If they call me, I'm not going to fight. I just came to meet some people, that's all. And no, I'm not as good as him."

"Oh, well. I hate to be the one to tell you, but you probably will have to. If you're called up to fight you really can't say no. You have to fight. Good luck trying to get out of it."

"I'm not a violent person; I don't like to fight."

"Don't say I didn't warn you. What's your power anyway?"

"I can touch things and become them, kind of. Perin calls it . . . um, molecular coping. What can you do?"

"I can unlock anything. Wait you said Perin, you talk to Perin?"

"Yeah, so?"

"He is one of the seven heads of the school. That's so cool that you talk to him,"

"He's my instructor."

"NO WAY! That's so cool; he was Zane's instructor too. You're so lucky,"

"Yeah, I guess," I saw the other guy walk into the battle box. His hair was parted over and he had a toothpick in his mouth. He was wearing a short sleeved dark yellow shirt and jeans. He also had on a belt that looked like it had splinters of wood in it. "The fight is about to start."

"Zane versus Gabe, let the fight begin," the announcer shouted.

The guy with the coat pulled out a chess piece from a bag around his waist.

"So newbie, do you even know how to use your power?" Zane asked.

"Better than you, I bet," Gabe took the toothpick out of his mouth.

"You'd lose that bet friend."

"What's with the chess piece?"

"What's with the toothpick?"

"You'll see," they said simultaneously.

The chess piece turned a combination of blue, purple and white, like a tiny three colored rainbow inside of the chess piece. Zane kneeled down, putting the chess piece into the ground, creating a giant glowing circle on the ground. It was as if someone had painted it there. He stood up and a giant pawn began to emerge from the glowing circle. It had to be at least eight feet tall and four feet wide.

"I can summon chess pieces," Zane said.

"That's a stupid power. Can they move?" Gabe asked.

"Not quickly, but trust me, my pawns can move."

"Still, that's pretty dumb."

"You're the one that will lose to them."

"I highly doubt it."

Gabe somehow made his toothpick larger. It was the length a staff now.

"What the hell did you do?" Zane asked.

"This is my power, I can enlarge objects."

"You're making fun of me and my chess pieces while you walk around with a big toothpick, that's just ironic."

"Can we just get this over with; I'm going to finish you quickly."

The pawn started to move toward Gabe. He ran at Zane holding this giant toothpick like a spear. Zane pulled out a deck of cards and took a small handful and they began to glow, just as the chess piece did. Zane put them into the ground and the circle appeared again. Gabe moved around the chess piece and lunged at Zane. A long staff came out of the circle and Zane grabbed and collided with Gabe's toothpick. They clashed for minutes, deflecting eachother's strikes. Gabe shrunk the toothpick and somersaulted to the side of Zane as he tried to strike him. He landed the somersault and enlarged the toothpick, barely cutting the side of Zane's arm. Zane jumped back and took out another chess piece. The pawn that he had already summoned was moving around the battle box and in between Gabe and Zane. Gabe shrunk the toothpick again and back flipped away from the pawn. Zane summoned another one and the first pawn moved out of the way with the new one moving toward Gabe. He effortlessly sidestepped twice and dodged it. Zane came out from behind the moving pawn, hitting Gabe with the side with his staff, pinning Gabe up against it. Gabe enlarged a toothpick, pushing himself up and over, landing on the other side of it.

"I will win this fight Zane. You won't beat me," Gabe said as he took out three toothpicks from his belt.

He holding them tightly, enlarging them. All three of them crashed into the pawn in front of him. The pawn cracked and Gabe was shot backwards, dropping the toothpicks. Zane's chess piece continually cracked all over. The sound was comparable to breaking glass. Gabe held another toothpick like a javelin, throwing it at the pawn, but as it left his hand, enlarging it. The toothpick broadened as it tore through the air. It had a shinny silver tip, probably metal. The toothpick hit the pawn and shattered it. Blue, purple and white gases were expelled from the explosion. Zane was dumbfounded.

"That's impossible! No one has ever broken one of my chess pieces before. That's it. That was the last straw," he said reaching into his pocket and pulling out a knight.

The crowd was going crazy. They had never seen anyone do this good against Zane apparently. The announcer did something with his hands and everyone went silent.

"Another chess piece? Give it up, I'm just going to break that one too," Gabe said.

The circle appeared again, but this time Zane stood on top of it. A giant glass horse emerged, a knight. As it emerged Zane sat on top of it. The glass horse stretched out its legs, neighing. It was a radiant white with a purple mane and tail.

"Now let's see how well you can do against me."

Zane galloped toward Gabe, but Gabe flipped backwards and enlarged a rock on the ground into the size of a boulder. Zane nearly ran into it, stopping in just enough time. Gabe landed on the giant rock.

"Now I have the advantage."

Gabe began throwing toothpicks at Zane, enlarging them just before they left his hand. Zane ran around the enlarged rock dodging all the toothpicks. It was only a matter of time before he ran out of toothpicks, and sure enough he did.

"I've got nothing else Zane, you win. I have nowhere else to go, and too be honest; enlarging such a small rock to this size nearly tapped me out of energy. You beat me."

Zane stopped moving.

"You surrender?"

"Yes, I surrender."

Gabe shrunk the rock back to normal size and Zane got off of the horse, tapping it. Slowly, the horse went back into the ground and the knight piece surfaced. He did the same to the pawn, putting them back into his pocket. The announcer walked into the box and declared Zane the winner making his record 24-0.

"You fought well Gabe, very well. To bad you didn't think ahead. The fight could have continued longer," he said graciously.

"Thanks. You're a brilliant fighter and tactician; hopefully we'll be able to fight again."

"That sounds good."

They both left the box and the crowd cheered again.

"Okay everyone, the final match of the night," he took to pieces of paper out of his pocket. "Travis and Nadim, fighters please be prepared in a few minutes."

Wade looked at me.

"I know that look, don't even say it," I said.

"Say what? You mean, I told you so," he replied "Well, I did."

I walked over to the announcer.

"Excuse me, I'm Travis and I'm really not in the mood to fight. You can just pick someone else to take my place."

"Sorry, but that's not an option. You were chosen, so you must fight. Those are the rules. Sorry, no exceptions."

"I'm not going to fight."

Somebody grabbed me and threw me into the battle box, with my shoulder smashed into the ground and sliding a few feet. Holding my shoulder, I got up slowly. I stretched it out to make sure it was okay.

"Who the hell are you?"

"I'm Nadim, you're opponent. You will fight or I can just beat the shit out of you."

"I'm not fighting you."

"That's bad, because I'm fighting you."

He charged, jumping into the air, punching the ground as he landed. I rolled out of the way. He left a huge indent in the ground.

"Super Strength?"

"Nothing but," he rushed at me holding his fist in the air ready to crush me. I got up and began to run away from him, staying inside the battle box. He was slow, I hoped to tire him out and then I could be the victor. I risked running out of stamina first and being introduced to a whole new world of pain. I couldn't get caught by him. He's way out of my league. All he needed was one good hit and I was history.

He continued to chase me, and I continued to move. He didn't seem to be getting tired. My plan wasn't working; it didn't stop me from dodging his attacks though. The crowd wasn't happy, they were booing me.

"Baby!"

"You can't run forever!"

"You can't even fight!"

"I hope he ruins you!"

I couldn't keep running. I wouldn't win that way. I had to fight. I turned around and ran at him, then slid on the dirt, dragging my hand on the ground and absorbing it. My hand turned a dark brown and became hard and rough. Nadim was in front of me and swung his fist. I moved to the left, dodging his strike. I raised my fist and punched him in the face. He stood and took it, but he did start to bleed a little from his lip.

"We have to go! I feel vibrations coming. It feels like soldiers. We have to go now!" someone yelled.

The lights that were hovering above the battle box went out. The barrier fell as well. I wasn't sure what to do. I didn't see Adair or Wanda. Everyone began running frantically and I joined them.

"This isn't over, I'm gonna finish this fight. Maybe not now, but I will beat you!" he yelled as I ran away.

Everybody was running toward the Industrial. People started breaking off and going different directions. A couple of us continued running straight and ending up in front of Dorm Level Three. Luckily, there were no soldiers around. They had to have been in the woods. We ran into the building.

I ran up to my room, Adair wasn't there yet. I got worried. Ten minutes had past and Adair still wasn't back. Then someone opened the door, Adair. He was out of breath.

"Are you okay?" I asked.

"Are you kidding me? I've never been this happy."

"Did anyone see you?"

"Not that I know of."

"Good. We should get to bed just in case anyone comes in and sees that we are dressed."

"Yeah, good idea."

The next morning an announcement came over the intercom.

"Due to the recent events, there will be a tighter security for the next two months. No one is allowed to sign out more than once a day. Not even with instructor approval. Everyone must be in their dorm at five o'clock, no exceptions. Thank you and have a nice day."

I couldn't believe that they were punishing everyone, with no good reason. They had to be hiding something.

"I have to know what it is they are hiding. I may have made a terrible mistake coming here. This place is a prison. I have to get to the bottom it. I need to know what they are hiding, but I'm going to need help. Tadeo, could help me. I can't be seen with his help and I could use Hannah to drain the electricity from the doors so that I could make it to the instructors building. Or even Wade might help. He can unlock anything. That's what I have to do. I'm gunna have to find a way to talk to them and convince them to help me. I will get to the bottom of this."

Chapter XII

ADEN: COST OF BLOOD

April 28, 2007

I arrived back at home with the knife that I bought. I walked outside and looked at my tree. The spiked ball was still there. I put the knife on the ground and I moved away from the tree and the spiked blood ball. I held my hand out and concentrated on making the ball return to me, and it started to shake loose from the tree. I continued to pull it toward me until, finally, it gave and launched at my hand. I stopped it before hitting my palm. I wanted to gain complete control over my blood. I changed it into a normal ball, without spikes, which proved to be easy. I then moved the blood ball around, pushing it into the air, but not very hard, just enough to get it suspended. I held it up for a while then my head started to ache. I flatted the blood into a thin sheet midair, bringing it down and having it lay over my grass. It covered a decently large patch, making the grass red. I lifted the blood back up and morphed it back into the ball.

I was gaining good control over the blood. I could make it do whatever I wanted. I had the blood attach to my arm, covering from my shoulder to my hand, encasing it like a sleeve. Finally, molding long blade like claws on my fingertips. It was thin, but still effective. It was a step up from what I did at school. I figured that I had enough for the day. I removed the blood from my arm, returning it into a ball, and making it rest on the ground. I took off the bandage that I had on my forearm. I figured that I could put my blood back into my system. The cut was almost already scabbed over. I moved the blood ball off the ground, putting it on my cut, and directing it into the wound. As soon as I did, I could feel my body rejecting it. I picked up my knife that I bought, went inside, sat down, and rested. My head was pounding. The pain continued to grow throughout the day.

My mom came home around six. I didn't feel well at all and I had become deathly pale. She came into the living room were I was lying down. I had the television on, but I wasn't watching it. I could barely open my eyes. I couldn't think of anything to tell her so I just tried to avoid her. Unfortunately, she had come over to the couch and squatted down, starting to talk to me.

"What do you want for dinner?" she asked.

"I'm not hungry," I mumbled.

"Are you feeling okay?"

"Yeah I'm fine," I said hiding my cut.

"Are you sure you don't sound very good," she put her hand on my head. "Aden, you're burning up."

I tried to think of something to say, but I couldn't. I couldn't say anything. It took everything that I had just to try and stay conscious. I could feel myself slowly slipping in and out. My mom started shaking me, causing my arm to fall down, exposing my cut.

"Oh my God, Aden. What did you do?"

I didn't have enough energy to respond. I felt dead. I could slightly hear what she was saying; she said something about the hospital. I heard her pick up the phone and she kept telling me to stay awake, but it was too difficult. I had decided to give up and close my eyes.

When I opened my eyes I was in a hospital room. I looked around, but no one was there. I was wearing a hospital gown and had a bandage over my cut. I yelled for a nurse. One walking by stopped and yelled for a doctor. The doctor came running into the room.

"How are you feeling? Okay? Any headaches, pains, problems?" he asked all jittery checking my monitor.

"Umm . . . I don't think so."

"Remarkable, I figured that your body would have rejected the blood. There must be something in your mother's blood that allowed your body to accept it."

"Wait, what? What happened? How did I get here?"

"Oh, I'm sorry; you were unconscious by the time you got here. You must be really confused. I am Dr. Chatters. You have been here for four days; it's May second. Somehow, you had a mess of bacteria inside of your blood system. We were going to do a simple blood transfusion, but then we found out that you have a special blood type that we have never seen before. We were apprehensive about what to do. You're body was completely shutting down. We couldn't do the transfusion because we were unsure how your body would react."

"Then what happened? How am I okay?" the doctor looked at me. I could tell he had something to tell me that wasn't good.

"Well, we checked your mom's blood. Her blood type was strange as well, but not like yours. She has all the blood types in one. Once again something we have never seen before. We feared that if we tried anything that you would go into cardiac arrest and die on us. Your mom took the chance and let us use her blood. She didn't want to watch you die. So we took her blood and did the transfusion, and your body took it. It was as if your body ate her blood. Honestly, it was remarkable."

"So where is my mom? Is she okay?"

"The transfusion was hard on her. She is in a lot of pain and we can't do anything for her right now. After the transfusion something happened and she is now very ill. She is in intensive care at this point. I can take you to her after I make sure you are all set."

"I want to go now. I have to see her," I jumped out of bed ripping all the wires off my chest.

"Or we could go now and check you later."

He directed me to my mom's room. When we got there I could see her through the window. She was pale and sickly looking. I could tell she was in pain.

"What is going to happen to her?"

"We are not sure at this point. I want to tell you she is going to be okay, but I can't say that for sure. We are going to try and give her some blood. It is a possibility that she just needs to recover from the transfusion, but I think it is much more than that. She could have been exposed to some virus and after the transfusion her immunity count was low, so it isn't unlikely. Her body isn't strong enough to fight the infection, it's slowly killing her. Right now, we are just making her as comfortable as we can."

"Can I talk to her?"

"She is in a very deep sleep right now, near comma. Her body is shutting down and is trying to conserve as much energy as possible. It would be best if we just let her be for now."

"So what do I do now?"

"Well, you're free to go after we give you a check up. We can call you if anything changes."

The doctors did their check up on me and were amazed by my blood. It seemed to have all of the characteristics of each other blood type. It didn't make sense to me that the doctors before these ones could have overlooked. I couldn't honestly remember the last time I went to a real doctor. I had the flu once when I was ten, but they never did any blood work. I only got a shot and that was it. I had moved around a lot my entire life, I guess it was possible that they did realize it, I was just never told. Not only did I have a strange blood type, but I had thirteen pints of blood in my body, opposed to the average ten, and my blood regenerated faster than normal. If I had lost a pint of blood it would only take me hours to regenerate it, while it would take a full day for a normal person. Even after finding out all this stuff about my blood I was still worried about my mom. I had to figure out someway to save her.

"I'm going to get some stuff from home and then comeback. I'm not going to leave until she gets better." I said to the doctor.

"If that's what you want to do."

We went back to my room and I got dressed. I signed out of the hospital and went outside, taking my mom's keys with me. I sat down on the curb and tears slipped out of my eyes. I looked down staring at the concrete. I kept my cool in the hospital, but as soon as I stepped outside, I lost it. More tears fell as I began to sniffle. I punched the concrete and tears dripped onto my fist.

I can't believe that I let this happen, I thought. If I wasn't so stupid then this never would have happened. I could have easily avoided this. Now my mom is sick and could die at anytime and I can't do anything to fix what I've caused.

"Actually there is," someone said.

I wiped the tears from my eyes and looked up and over to where the voice came from. There was a man standing there and he looked to be he in his late forty's. He appeared to be homeless, just by the look of his clothes. He was wearing a tattered brown overcoat and some old dirty ripped up pants. His hair was unclean and his facial hair was untrimmed. He had a lot of gray hairs on his head and beard.

I must have been talking out loud and not realized it, I thought.

"No, you were talking to yourself," the man said nonchalantly and sat down next to me on the curb. "Tissue?" he offered.

"What the hell?" I said confused and scared.

"Don't be frightened. It's eerie at first, but you'll get accustomed to it," the man said.

"What the hell are you talking about? Go bother someone else."

"Hey, I'm just trying to lend a hand, Aden,"

"How do you know my name?"

"I know a whole lot of things; a very *very* diminutive portion of which is everything about you."

"What are you talking about? Who are you?"

"Well, let's not use my name just yet, Aden, but I can help you. I know what is happening to your mother. She has a very dreadful disease. It was just like the doctor said, her immunity count was low after the blood transfusion and now she is trying to fight off the illness, but can't. She's just not strong enough right now, but you can help her, contrary to what you were just thinking."

"How did you know what I was thinking?"

"Not all of us can control blood, Aden. Some of us can do other things."

"How do you know about that? Have you been watching me?" I stood up off the curb and backed away.

"Aden calm down, please. Just sit back down. I am an ally, and I can help you."

"How?"

"Well to answer your first inquiries. Yes, I have been analyzing you, but don't take it offensively. You have a lot of potential. I came to West Virginia to talk to you, but then you got a tad crazy with your power. It's perilous to not only other people, but to yourself as well. You were swinging that blood whip around everywhere and not worrying about what it was touching. The fence, the tree, the air, the grass, all of which were covered in dirt and bacteria; and you just decided to put that blood back in your system. Now that was just brainless."

I sat back down and listened to him.

"You need to think more scientific with your power. Your power is all mental. If you have a focused mind then you can make your blood do anything and be anything."

"How have you been watching me? I looked around and there was never anyone there. And you where in the hospital too?" he tapped on his head with his finger. "And that means what; you were watching me in your head . . . ?"

"Yup, now you're getting it. You're not as dumb as you look," he laughed and tapped me on the back. "Now as for helping your mother, as I said before you can help her."

"How?"

"There are a lot of remarkable people like us out there, Aden, and one of them lives in Florida."

"How am I supposed to get to Florida?" I asked.

"You have what . . . . $3455.67 in your bank account. I think you have enough to get there."

"How do you know all this stuff about me?"

"I told you, *we're* special, remember?"

He reached inside of his coat and took something out of his pocket.

"I'm just kidding. I'm not going to let you use your money. Take this," he handed me a plane ticket. "The flight leaves in about three hours. The boy's name is Reece Burnbet. He is at the Florida Children's Hospital. He is nine years old and he knows that he has a power. He wants to be a superhero. He lives in the town of Winter Park; off Ocean Avenue, 159 to be exact."

"How can he help my mom?"

"You ask a lot of questions. You're gonna have to learn to just trust me," he said scratching his beard. "He can cure any illness, disease, cuts, bruises or even just a scratch. His power is very advanced for his age."

"That's perfect."

"I know, that's why I thought of it. You don't need to bring anything with you. I'll be watching, so if you'll need anything I'll know and lend you a hand. Just get there and back as quickly as possible. I'm not sure how long your mom has."

"Okay," we both got up off the curb. "Thank you so much. I'll find some way to repay you."

"We'll worry about that later. Just go get Reece."

I ran to my mom's car and got in. I drove straight to the airport. I couldn't believe that I had the opportunity to save her.

Chapter XIII

BASTIAN: CAPTURED

March 22, 2007

My phone was ringin'. It read unknown number.

"Who is that calling you?" Zander asked.

I didn't respond; I just answered the phone.

"Hello?" I answered.

"Bastian, I understand that this isn't the best time for you, but I'm going to help you. He is here to recruit you for a place that I like to call the Islands. He might ask nicely once, but after that he won't be so nice. You are going to tell him that you leave with him tomorrow. Tell him you will meet with him at this location at two o'clock tomorrow afternoon,"

"Who is this?"

"My name is not important right now. Please, just do as I ask I will meet you right after this is over. I'll be waiting at the post office. Meet me there when you are done. Just do what I said, please." he hung up.

"Wait, what?"

"Who was that?" Zander asked.

"None of your business. I'm not goin' to go with you."

"Then I'm going to have to make you," he held up his hand and was ready to snap his fingers and trap me in that dome of his. Without Alden on I had no idea how it would affect me. My only option was to take the advice from my mystery caller.

"Wait, meet me here tomorrow at two pm. I'll go with you then."

He lowered his hand.

"Why?"

"I have a few things to take care of. I promise I will be here tomorrow at two pm if not before then."

"Fine, don't be late. If I find that this is a trick I will find you. Don't, for one second, think that I won't."

"Got it."

He took off back the way that he came. I had to get to the post office. I ran there with my mask in hand. When I arrived, I recognized no one.

"You did well, just like I told you to. The place that he wants you to go to is very dangerous."

"Wait, who are ya?"

"I'm a friend, don't worry. I'm looking out for your best interest."

"You look like a bum. Your clothes are torn and filthy."

"Don't judge a book by its cover. I like the way that I look. I've got nobody to amaze."

"Okay fine, but who are ya, and how do ya know me?"

"Well, Bastian, let's just say that I'm an expert on knowing things. Just as you are and expert at carving things."

"What's that supposed to mean?"

"I'm referring to your mask collection."

"How do ya know about that?"

"I told you, I'm an expert at knowing. You have a very unique ability. I've never seen anything like it except for one other, but that isn't important right now. These people want you to go to their islands so that they can use you to stop something that is meant to happen."

"I have no idea what you're talkin' about."

"There are a group of islands that used to be one. They were broken apart a long time ago. On each of these islands there is a facility. People have invested a lot of money into making sure that is kept a secret and under control, but over time the government has just been giving them money, and not really caring about what goes on there. To be honest the government doesn't really know anything about it. It was started a long time ago and has just been pushed under the rug for some reason. The islands are controlled by seven heads and one boss who has final decision on anything. On the islands there are people with powers and abilities like yours and mine. They are told that they are being trained and taught how to use their powers, which they are, but they are being held captive too. They think they have free will, but they don't. They are prisoners that are being killed every year. They are being sent to kill the first person to ever have a power, but they succeed and they parish. He is stronger than all of them."

"This is all so confusin'. I'm not too sure if I understand you right. So these people, from these islands, are usin' other people, who have powers, to kill the first person to ever have a power, and they are dyin' because he is killin' them?"

"Yes," he chuckled at my summation of his rant. "But he doesn't have a choice because he has to protect himself."

"This is too confusin' for me. You're kind of throwin' a lot at me at once."

"I know and I'm sorry. It is hard to completely believe me or completely understand, but is it really that farfetched? I mean, come on, you just tore through the center of town in werewolf form because a mask gave you the power to do so."

"So what is it that ya want from me?"

"I want you to go to the islands and destroy them from the inside out. They will bring you there, help you with your power, then you can turn on them because you will be stronger than them and have an arsenal of diverse powers to use. They wouldn't stand a chance."

"And why don't ya just do this yourself?"

"Because my power isn't like yours. I can't do things that you can. Plus, I used to live on the islands. Long story short, I figured out what they were doing and I escaped."

"And you want me to go to this prison to stop these people?" I started to walk away.

"You said that you wanted to know what your power was for, the reason that you have it, maybe this is it. You would be saving so many lives and you'd be the big hero. I know that's what you want."

I stopped walkin' away and turned around.

"Are ya sure that I will be fine once I go with them to these islands?"

"Yes, but once you get onto the islands I can't contact you. For some reason my power doesn't work there. I can't get anything from that area, maybe a partial clip every now and then, but hardly anything of importance."

"Wait, so what is your power?"

"My power is complicated to elucidate. Now is not the time to fret about what I can do, it is whether or not you will be able to manage your power. I know you are struggling to figure out how to use it. From what I can grasp, each time you utilize a mask you enter your mind and you begin to share your body with another being, and these beings can grant you abilities beyond your wildest dreams. I only know a little more than you do right now. I'm just worried because you strained your power the last time, and somehow created a precarious and vicious being; the werewolf. I saw everything that happened to you during your confrontation."

"I was in my mind all of those times? I'm not sure I understand. Wait, did you say that . . . I created the werewolf?"

"Your power is very complex and hard to understand, Bastian," he explained. "And, yes that place was your mind. You can be inside it for what seems like hours, but outside of it no time has passes at all. You seem to either capture these entities or create them yourself. I honestly don't know."

"I'm just so confused by all of this. I just want to know how to control it."

"That is where the islands *can* help you. They will help you control your power and then you can turn on them. You just have to remember to not try and force it; you have to just let it happen naturally."

"Yeah."

The islands sounded dangerous, but if it would help me understand and control my power then it may be worth the risk, I contemplated. For all I knew it could have been my destiny to destroy the islands. It would just be so easy if I understood why and how I got my powers, I thought.

"So you are going to go to the islands?"

"I never said that."

"You didn't have to. Just remember once you get there we never had this conversation and you have no idea who I am. They will torture you and probably kill you if they find out you know me. Once you come back I'll know and come find out how you are doing."

". . . Yeah, okay."

"Just always remember that the islands are bad. No matter how good they may seem, or how much they help you with your power. They are evil, Bastian."

"Okay."

"Great. I've got to get going I have other things to take care off. Good luck, Bastian."

"Thanks . . . sir."

He walked in the opposite direction that I was goin'. On my way back home it started to rain. I held the werewolf mask in my hand and began talkin' to it.

"From what that guy said, I created you incorrectly. I don't think I did. I just have to find a way to tame you. It's goin' to be hard, seein' as how the only way that I can get inside is by puttin' you on my face, and the second that do that, you will attack me and take control."

When I got home I gathered all my masks and put them into one bag. I started packin' for the islands. I took out a piece of paper and was about to write a note to my dad. I wanted to tell him that I was runnin' away and that I would be back eventually. I just had to figure everythin' out first, everythin' in my life. For some reason it was gettin' harder to breathe. I couldn't swallow, my throat was dry. Then my chest began to hurt as I gasped of air. I turned around and walked toward the bathroom. There was someone standin' in front of the doorway. He was dressed in a green long sleeve shirt and black pants with some sort of emblem on the left leg. I had never seen it before. He looked no older than twenty-two. My vision got foggy and I couldn't speak.

"Having a problem breathing?" he said in a degrading tone.

I couldn't say anythin'. I fell onto my carpet still gaspin' for air. My condition worsened. I saw him reach for somethin'; he bent down and looked at me.

"Are you thirsty?" he had a cup of water in his had and started to drink it. "Umm that's good water. Don't you just love the taste of a glass of water? I know I do."

I tried to say somethin', but it only came out as gibberish.

"What was that? You do too. Now we have something in common." he took out his cell phone and walked into my room then back out with the bag of my masks.

"Yeah I got all of them," he said to the person on the phone.

The person said somethin' back.

"Just come get us, I'll be ready. He's not escaping this time, I've got him right where I want him." He hung up the phone. "Time the go to sleep." He put his hand on my face and I could feel the life bein' sucked out of me. I blacked out.

I woke up inside of a white painted room. There were cracks in the walls and broken bricks everywhere. The paint would have flaked off the wall if I breathed on it. I was tied down to a pipe. In the corner of the room there was a camera, pointin' at me. The door opened and the person from my house walked in along with another man.

"Let me go, who are you guys?"

"How are you Bastian? Welcome to the Homestead. This is where we keep our prisoners. But don't worry, you shouldn't be here for too long."

"Who the hell are you guys?" I asked tryin' to break out of the chains.

"This is my friend Cal. He is a student here. He has the power to dehydrate the body. That is how he captured you yesterday. My name is Perin, and I'm the one whose been sending these . . . 'islanders' after you. I need you here so I can study you, because you have a power that is like that of the Firsts. If we figure out how your power works then we could find a way to stop him. Maybe with some persuasion and torture you'll just join us?"

"Never!" I spit in his face.

He grabbed my face, coverin' my mouth, and squeezed tightly.

"I could kill you in the blink of an eye and no one would ever know. There would be no trace of you left, except the dust from your worthless existence. You are lucky that I need you or I would have just killed you as soon as you got here."

He pushed me back at the pole I was chained to.

"Cal, let's go. We'll let him suffer for a while."

It seemed like days had passed, I had no idea how long I had been there. I hadn't seen any of my masks in who knows how long. I was concerned about what they were doin' to them.

"What if they put them on? Could they use their powers too?" I asked myself.

I was given food sometimes. Someone would come in and throw the plate at me. I would then gather the food like a rat and eat it. It was torture; I can't believe that guy would willin'ly send me here, I occasionally thought.

"Who am I kiddin'; that guy probably set this whole thing up. If I find out that he has anythin' to do with this I will kill him."

The days continued to pass and I was questioned by doctors or scientists or somethin'. They took me out of the room every now and again to do tests on me for hours; drawin' blood, bone marrow, skin samples, tissue samples and so much more. I passed out often due to the pain, but they'd just wake me right back up. They wanted me to tell them about my power. I never said a word to them. Guys dressed in long black trench coats accompanied them. When I didn't answer I would get whipped, punched, smacked, zapped, burned, or choked by them. I still wouldn't talk; I took the lashes and the beatin's. It hurt, but better to deal with the pain than lettin' them learn anythin'. They eventually got fed up with me not speakin'. They would have entire days planed for beatin' me, torturin' me; dunkin' my head in water, electrocutin', put in extreme hot and cold environments. It made me restless most nights, the pain; both mental and physical. I would awaken in sweat, panickin' that they were at the door comin' to drag me away. I may not have spoken, but that didn't mean that they weren't gettin' to me. I was terrified down to my core.

May 2, 2007

I awoke to the entire place shakin'. I looked around and the worn down walls started to crack and crumble. I thought that I was dreamin'. Debris fell on my head, just dust and small pebbles, nothin' heavy. I looked up and saw a giant piece crackin' and about to fall on me. I moved out of the way and the chunk of concrete fell and landed on the chains. They were loose; I prayed the slab broke them, movin' the concrete off them, but they were unbroken. I stared pullin' on the chains as hard as I could, but it was to no avail. The shakin' had suddenly stopped.

I looked around and the shakin' started again. Everythin' was turnin' scratchy and discolored. I looked down at my hands and they were shakin' violently. The buildin' wasn't shakin' this time, it was me. My power was activatin'. I looked at the slab of concrete and the shakin' intensified greatly and my eyes were completely consumed by the scratches. My hands reached for the slab grabbin' it and began to carve it. I could see what I was doin' though. I had no control over it, but I could at least watch myself make the mask.

My fingernails were cuttin' through the concrete like a knife through butter. I could start to see the outline of a face. Shortly, it was clearly defined. There were no holes for my eyes like on Ien or most of the other masks, but only indents. It was covered in light scratches and bumps. I loved it.

"This mask is goin' to help me escape, I know it."

Chapter XIV

ADEN: THERE IS A CURE

May 2, 2007

"Excuse me sir. Do you want a drink?" the stewardess asked.

"No thank you . . . actually if you have any soda, I'll take a can," I asked politely.

She took out a can from her cart and handed it to me along with a napkin and continued to go up the isle.

That man looked pretty haggard, but he definitely had money, I thought. He gave me a first class ticket to Florida. He must want something from me. He wouldn't just help me save my mom and not want anything in return. I just hoped I would be able to return the favor to him, but I couldn't worry about that, I had to focus on getting Reece to help me.

I fell asleep for the rest of the ride. When I arrived at the airport I started on my adventure to go get Reece. I was walking out the door and I got a call on my cell phone. It said unknown name. I usually didn't pick up those calls, but I answered just in case it was the man from the curb.

"Hello?" I answered.

"Aden it's me, the man from the hospital."

"How did you . . ."

"I know a lot, remember? I overlooked how to get you and Reece back here so once you get Reece then just go back to the airport and there will be tickets for both of you waiting," he said cutting me off.

"Thanks."

"Go outside." I walked outside of the airport.

"Now what?"

"There is a driver to your left he is wearing a blue button up shirt. Go tell him you are Tim Sanders," he instructed.

"Why?"

"He'll give you a ride wherever you want. Just tell him you need to go to the hospital."

"Are you sure it'll work?"

"Why does everyone ask so many questions? Yes, it'll work. The drivers name is Kirt Roland and he has never seen, met, or even spoken with Tim. He'll give you a ride."

"How do you know all of that?"

"How many times do I have to tell you? I know a lot," he chuckled.

"Probably just one more."

"I know a lot. The name is Faxon by the way. I'll call you again if you need any assistance."

He hung up the phone and I put it back in my pocket. I walked over to the driver of the limo.

"Kirt?" I asked already knowing his name.

"Yes hi. You must be Mr. Sanders. Please get in."

I got into the back of the limo. It was very fancy. There were coolers with drinks in them. I took one out and opened it. The driver got into the limo and looked back at me.

"Is there anywhere that you need me to bring you before I take you home?"

"Actually, I would like to go to the hospital. There is someone that I need to see."

"Yes sir," he started driving.

The sights were beautiful. I had only seen pictures of Florida; I'd never actually been here. I contained myself because I didn't want the driver to get suspicious.

"Do you have a relative that is in the hospital?"

"Yeah, my cousin. He's just been really sick lately, so I wanted to stop there and visit him."

"What hospital exactly am I going to?"

"The Children's Hospital near Winter Park."

"Oh, that won't take too long get there."

We got to the hospital, and it was huge. I didn't expect very much from a children's hospital, but I had assumed wrong.

"Do you want me to wait for you or not?"

"I'm not to sure how long I'll be."

"It's no problem I promise. I'll find a place to park and you can find me when you're done."

"Sounds good."

I opened the door, exited the limo, went inside the hospital, and asked the secretary what room Reece Burnbet was in.

"Are you family? If not we can't give out that sort of information,"

"Yes, I'm his cousin Tim Burnbet. I just flew in. I just want to see him."

She gave me a visitor's pass and told me the room he was in and on what floor. I went to where she instructed and it was a very high security area. There were even two armed guards outside of his room. I didn't want to try and go in and get shut down by them. I looked around and I saw a break room. I found some scrubs and put them on, then walked over to Reece's room. The guard checked me out.

"Where is your identification?" the large man questioned.

I rustled through my pockets and said, "I must have forgotten it in the break room. I'm sorry. Please don't rat me out. I really need this job."

"Do what you have to do and then get out. You should know not to come unprepared. This is a high security area. I shouldn't even let you in. You're lucky I'm in a good mood today."

"Thank you so much. You are literally a life saver," I said to the armed guard.

He turned around and swiped a card and the door opened. I walked in and saw the boy sitting legs crossed on his bed playing a videogame. He had very short black hair and was dressed in normal clothes. I was under the impression that every patient had to wear that revealing robe. It seemed he was a special case, in more ways than one.

"Hi," the boy greeted.

"Hey there, Reece," I responded.

"Are you new?"

"Something like that. Where are your parents?"

"They just stepped out to have a meeting with a man."

"Oh, okay," I looked around the room. The door was behind me with no windows to see into the room, but there was a window looking out onto the rooftop of another part of the hospital. "Nice view."

"My parents wanted it; for them, not for me," he sad sadly. "Hey, new guy, did you know I have a superpower. I'm going to be a superhero someday."

"I know. Actually, that's why I'm here. I need you to come with me."

"Where? I can't leave here. A man is supposed to come and take me to some special place where they help people like me, but I don't want to go."

"I know what you can do, my mom is very sick, and she'll die if I don't do something. You're the only person that I know of that can help me."

"How do you know me?"

"A man told me. His name is Faxon, do you know him?"

"No, I've never heard of him, but I'll help you and your mom."

"Really? Oh my god, thank you."

"How do we save her?"

"Well, first we just need to find a way out of here without upsetting the men outside. Then we go back to West Virginia and you do your healing trick and then she's cured."

"So this is like a full blown quest."

"Yeah, I guess it is," I chuckled.

"Do you have a superpower?"

"Yes, but it can't help us right now."

"Can you fly?!"

"No, I can do things with my blood."

"I don't get it."

"I'll show you later. We have to find a way out first."

I had no idea what to do. The men outside would start to get suspicious very soon. I had to find a way out before I ran out of time. I paced around the room talking quietly to myself."

I can only shape my blood into things. That won't be helpful now. In theory I could kill the men outside, but I really don't want that to be the case."

My phone started to ring. It read unknown name. It was Faxon. I picked up the phone.

"I'm only going to say one thing. Your power is all mental, Aden." He hung up the phone.

"My power is all mental. How the hell does that help? When I made that blood ball all I did was picture it in my mind. What if I can shape my blood into anything that I want? Anything that I can imagine, even . . . wings." I said.

"What's the plan, blood man?" Reece asked.

"I need something sharp," I said looking around the room.

"Why?" Reece asked.

"Because I'm going to get us out if here," I found a scalpel in a drawer. "Don't be freaked out by this, okay?"

"What are you going to do?"

I removed my scrubs and lifted up the back of my black shirt. Using the scalpel, I sliced a long single cut in each of my shoulder blades. Reece watched in fear. The warm blood poured down my back. The pain almost knocked me to my knees.

"Are you crazy?" Reece yelled.

"Just be quiet for a minute please."

Quickly I gained control of my blood and slowed its flow. I focused on the blood, and pictured in my mind two long thick strands of blood hung from my shoulder blades. I felt the blood bending to my will, just by sheer thought. I walked over to the window with the two strands dragging behind me. I was getting tired already. Reece came over to me.

"So that's what you meant. That's cool. Doesn't it hurt?"

"All the time."

"I can help take the pain away."

Reece touched my arm with the one of his hands and I felt the pain slowly go away. My energy was quickly restoring. The pain from my back was gone.

"Thank you. I would have never thought of that."

"I told you I was going to be a superhero."

The doorknob started to jiggle. I picked up a chair and threw it out the window. The glass made a loud crash and shattered into hundreds of pieces. The door swung open. I looked back at the two guards. They had their weapons drawn and pointed at me.

"FREEZE!" the taller guard yelled.

"Back away from the window!" the other demanded.

I looked at the guards. There was no time to waste on them. I grabbed Reece and jumped out the window. We started to fall; I closed my eyes and pictured wings, forcing the strands of blood on my back to spread out, ripping through my shirt, and forming into wings. The wings weren't like that of a bird; more like a bat's. I wasn't actually sure how to use them. I realized that they were a part of me and I had complete control over them. I began flapping the dark red wings as fast as I could and soared up into the air. While flying over the hospital parking lot, I looked back at the windows and the guards were staring at us flying away. I found a safe place to land, where no one was around to spot us. I returned the wings into their strand form, wrapping them around my waist.

"WHOA! That was so awesome. Can we do it again?" Reece asked.

"Not right now. We have to get to the airport first."

"Can't you just fly to the airport?"

"Its going to cause too attention."

"Well what other choice do we have?"

I waited a minute hoping Faxon would call, but he didn't. I guess I couldn't rely on him for everything.

"We really don't have another option I guess. We need to get to a different spot first." We ran out of the alley, across the street, and down another alley way. I picked Reece up again; unraveling the thick strands, spreading my wings out, and flapping them. I pushed myself off of the ground and we started flying. It took a lot of strength to get up high. Pretty soon we were looking down at all of the buildings. I could see the airport and began to glide down toward it. We landed behind a dumpster. I wasn't too sure what to do with the blood strands. My shirt was ripped and wrapping them around my waist wasn't really hiding them. I most certainly didn't want to just leave a puddle of my blood somewhere. I moved the blood with my hands and hid it underneath of my pants. I asked Reece if it was visible, he couldn't even see it. It was perfect, now if I ever needed it I could just pull it out.

"Just one more time please?" Reece asked with a big smile on his face.

"Reece, not now, we have to get out of here before those guys find us. This is a very serious. They'll kill me"

"Okay," he said depressed.

"We're about to fly on a plane anyway, it's the same thing." I grabbed his hand, ran into the airport, and over to the ticket counter.

"There should be two tickets waiting for us. Reece Burnbet and Aden Newburry."

The woman checked on her computer and she looked up at us.

"Okay, here you go. You two are all set. It is gate 8A all the way down on your left."

"Thank you."

We passed through security with no trouble, except for the weird looks I was getting from my ripped shirt. We went to our gate number and waited for the plane to arrive.

"So, why were you in the hospital?" I asked.

"My parents think I'm sick."

"Because of your power?"

"No, because I really am sick."

"What do you mean?" I asked with concern.

"I have a disease called select-ive imm-u-no-glo-bu-lin A def-iciency," he explained slowly. "It means I get sick really easy. I've had it since I was a baby. Every so often I'll get really sick and weak from just one little germ. I get rushed to the hospital for antiboitics. I just had an experimental dose of a new antibotic this morning. The doctors think it will allow my body to start making more white blood cells."

"Oh man, Reece. That's some pretty serious stuff. The fact that you know all of it is impressive. Just one question though, why don't you just heal yourself?"

"I can't. Don't know why either, I just can't."

"That's terrible. Maybe I should bring you back to the hospital. If something happened to you, I don't think I could forgive myself."

"Aden, don't worry. I should be okay for at least a day or two thanks to that medicine. But, to be honest, I'd rather be as far away from my parents as I can. I mean, I know they love me, but they have a really weird way of showing it."

"How so?"

"It just seems like I'm more of a burden than a son to them."

"I'm sure your parents love you. They'll probably wanna kill me once they know you're gone."

"I was going to some special hospital or something anyway. I overheard them saying something about it. That's why all the guards were there. They wanted to protect my safety."

"That doesn't make very much sense."

"Flight 8A to West Virginia now boarding," a woman said.

We both got up out of our seats and started to head towards the loading bridge to board the plane. Before I crossed the threshold I saw a few guys in black suits looking at us. They just stood and watched as we boarded.

The thought of the men was bugging me the entire flight home. They knew who we were and where we were going, I was sure of it. Hopefully, we could get to the hospital before they did. The flight went by rather quickly. Reece slept the whole time. All the excitement must have tired him out. When we landed, I gently shook Reece to wake him. We got off of the plane and went into the airport, and hurried to the parking garage. We both got in and headed to the hospital. Even after all the sleep on the plane Reece was still tired.

"Reece, are you okay?" I asked.

"Yeah, one of the side effects of the antibiotic is lots of sleep. The doctor said I'll spend most of the day resting 'til my body fully welcomes the medicine."

"Just making sure you're alright."

On the way to the hospital he fell asleep.

"Reece wake up, we're here," I said shaking him.

Reece yawned and stretched out his arms.

"Time to save the day?"

"Yeah. After this we'll find you a way back home. You don't know how much this means to me."

"Do I have to go back home?"

"Yes, your parents are going to be missing you. And kidnapping isn't something I want to be known for."

"But they hate me," he said tearing up.

"They don't hate you. We'll talk more about this after we save my mom. I don't mean to sound insensitive but I don't know how much time we have."

We got out of the car and went inside the hospital. I walked over to the front desk and got a visitors pass for the both of us. They said that I didn't have that much time, visiting hours were almost over. We went up to my mom's room and made sure that no one was around, opened the door, and we went inside. All the lights were off, but I could still see my mom due to the light from the monitors. She looked worse than when I left, extremely pale and thinner in the face.

"Glad to see you are here," a voice said.

I quickly turned around and moved Reece behind me.

"Don't worry. It's only me, Faxon," he said and turned on the lights.

"Don't scare me like that I thought you were someone else."

"Who? The men from the hospital that Reece was at."

"Yeah, or the men from the airport."

"They are on there way here now," he explained. "Their boss, Perin, wants the both of you. He isn't going to stop until he has Reece. You're just going to be a bonus."

"What do you mean?"

"He wants Reece because he can bring anyone back to life. He can heal any wound and Perin has a lot of them. If Perin gets Reece then the islands will never be stopped."

"What are you talking about?"

"There is a place where people with powers live. Recruiters from this place look for people with powers and bring them back. They get their information via a system that I helped them create. It was a mistake that I wish I could recant. I didn't know what they were up to until I was granted the power of knowledge. Then I helped them even more until my power grew beyond anyone's wildest dreams and everything became apparent. I escaped and vowed to do everything I could to stop them. The place that I know is referred to as the Islands. It is actually a prison disguised as a school. Yes, they do in fact help you control and advance your power, but then they send you to die. They take the strongest and send them into an impossible trial to kill someone can never be killed. He is an innocent man who has to kill to survive. That is why I have decided to gather up my own group to stop Perin and destroy his sanctuary.

Unfortunately, I have to do it under the radar, which is very hard for me because for some reason I can't see anything that is going on at the islands. They had to have developed some sort of technology that stops my power from working there. I can sometimes break past it for only a second or two but that's it. Also they have many people there that are more advanced than anyone that I can find. Then I found you and Bastian. With you two alone I can definitely take down the islands . . . I hope."

"Wait, you want me to help you destroy these islands?"

"Yes, I need you to help me and everyone on the islands before they die. You would be saving hundreds of lives. I know it's not your thing, but I figured if I helped you then you would help me."

"I appreciate your help and everything, but I don't care about anyone other than my mom and Reece. After I know they're safe, I'm done with this whole superpower thing. I'm not a hero; I have other responsibilities. Yeah I feel bad and everything for those people, but it's not my job to save them. Someone else can; maybe that Bastian guy you mentioned."

"I figured you'd say that. Well I hope everything goes your way, Aden. I appreciate your consideration. Reece it was nice to meet you and you will be fine as long as you are with Aden. Just be careful of the guys coming after you. You should be able to handle them, Aden. Just watch your back okay?" Faxon said depressed as he was leaving.

"Wait, what are you talking about? Are those guys going to attack us?" I asked.

"Without a doubt. They'll focus on getting Reece then after they have him, they'll get you."

"You're kidding, right?"

"Nope, there's not much you can do. They'll find out everything they need to know about you, then find you, and either kill you or recruit you."

"Why'd you drag me into this?!"

"To save your mom. Some things have to be earned. You know that better than anyone."

"I didn't ask for any of this," I said starting to lose my temper.

"Stay cool, Aden. We'll get you out of this. I'll leave here and make some phone calls and detour these guys away from you, but I can't guarantee anything."

"So what do I do in the mean time?"

"Stay on your guard and make sure Reece is safe. No time to waste, I'll be in touch as soon as possible." Faxon left the room in a rush. The whole situation had gone from terrible to horrendous. I had to stay focused on my first goal.

"Okay Reece, go over to my mom and do your thing."

"Does this mean I'm staying with you? You heard Mr. Faxon, we can't let the islands have me," Reece said with excitement.

"I'll keep you safe, I promise. But first things first."

"I'm on it."

Reece walked over to my mom and put his hands on her stomach and a dim glow of light started to come out of them. Her monitor started going crazy and short-circuited. The light started to fade and as soon as it did, doctors came rushing in, moved us out of the way, and started checking to see if my mom was okay. They told us to get out. I grabbed Reece and took him outside.

"You did a good job, don't worry they aren't mad, they just don't understand us."

"I know," he said.

They came out only a few minutes later.

"What happened in there?" one of the doctors asked. "Visually she actually seems in better condition than she did before she came in."

"We are going to have to do some tests on her to make sure she is actually okay, but if she if she is than she should be ready to go by tomorrow," the other one added.

"Okay, do what you have to, I'll be waiting," I said calmly.

Reece and I sat down and they wheeled my mom out of her room. I told the doctors to give me a call when my mom was awake. I took Reece back to my house, he was still really tired, and I could clearly see that he was exhausted from curing my mom. I opened the door to my house and told Reece that he could crash in my room or the couch. He went over to the couch and just passed out. I chuckled. I went upstairs and put on some pajamas. I forgot about the blood that I had put under my pants. I had decided to not try and put it back in my system. I formed it into a ball and hardened it; then put it on a chair in my room. I couldn't stop thinking about the men coming after us, but I was also becoming overwhelmed with exhaustion. I laid down on my bed just of a second.

I was almost asleep until, what sounded like, a car crash startled me. I jumped out of bed and looked outside. Three white vans had pulled up to my house. The back doors opened and blacked suited men leapt out. They were all wearing vests, helmets, body armor, and had guns; possibly assault rifles. They had found us. I pulled the blood ball off of my chair and ran down stairs. I changed the blood into its liquid form and put it on my arm, hardening it, and walking over to the living room. Soldiers kicked open my front door and pointed their guns at me, and then shoot at me. I held my hands up and the blood from my arm jumped out in front of me, catching the bullets. I looked in front of me and the blood had made itself into a barrier to protect me. I pushed the blood at them; making it cover the doorway. I hardened it so they wouldn't be able to get through easily. I heard the back door break open. I ran into the living room, grabbed Reece, and soldiers swarmed in. I put Reece down and I saw my dagger on the ground next to the coffee table. I moved it closer to me with my foot.

"Just give us the kid," one of the soldiers said.

"Fine," I bent down and picked up the knife and made it look like I was whispering in Reece's ear.

"What are you doing?" a soldier asked quickly.

"I'm telling him to go with you." I unsheathed the knife and cut my hand and forearm. My blood made a puddle on the ground. The dark of the room concealed the puddle. Reece started to walk toward one of the soldiers. I moved the blood to the bottom of each soldier's feet. I stood up and pulled the blood up, which looked like red glaciers. It disarmed every one of the soldiers and grabbed my knife off of the ground. My hand was throbbing with pain. I ran at them with my dagger in my right hand, pulled some blood into my left hand, and stabbed one of the soldiers with my dagger. Forming the blood into a whip I hit another one in the face knocking him down.

"Reece, GO HIDE!" I yelled.

I heard the soldiers break my blood barrier over the front door and rush in. I got more blood from the floor, shaped it into a blood ball covered in spikes; just like the one I made before. This time it was about the size of a basketball. I shot it at the soldiers coming in as they turned the corner into my living room. The spikes broke through their vests stabbing them, and pinning one up against my wall while the others fell to the floor. One of them grabbed Reece and started to run. I cut my shoulder and sprinted after him as unarmed soldiers came at me. I pulled blood from my fresh cut and covered my arm, hardening it. As they came at me I knocked them off guard with my left arm covered in rock solid blood and stabbed them in the gut with my knife. One grabbed me from behind, pulling backward, bringing us both to the ground. I elbowed him in the face and rolled off of him.

I quickly tried to get up but had my leg swept out from underneath me, knocking me prone. I looked as the grunt was getting up. Seeing my blood on the ground behind him, I wrapped it around his arm tightly and pulled him down and restraining him. Another came around the corner and shot at me. I blocked the bullets with what little blood I had on me and took cover. I cut my leg and pulled as much blood together that I had and launched a spray of needles at him, immobilizing him for the time being.

It was getting harder to see, the blood loss was getting to me. A soldier came at me and smacked me in the face with the butt of his gun. I lost control of the blood on my arm and it turned into liquid and poured onto the ground. I tried to mold it again, but he kicked me. Another one grabbed me and threw me up against a wall, hitting me with his gun again and I fell to my knees, spitting out blood. I pulled the blood to my finger tips turning them into spikes. I looked up and shot them at the guy with the gun. They broke through his helmet, sticking him in the face. He screamed and dropped his gun. The other man came at me. I pulled even more blood out of my hand, shooting a long spike from it. He was forced back and pinned against my wall. I fired some blood to cover his mouth. I stood up and grabbed my knife. The other soldier picked up his gun and was about to shot me. I made a blood whip and disarmed him. With the blood whip I smacked him around a little then tied it around his neck, tightening it until he stopped breathing. I heard the vans pull away. I could barely move at that point. With the last bit of my strength I put blood over my cuts to stop the bleeding. The room started spinning and I fell on the blood soaked carpet.

"Aden . . . Aden . . . wake up. We have to get you out of here."

I opened my eyes and Faxon was looking down at me. My vision made it appear that there were three of him.

"Get up! The cops are on their way," he said picking me up and putting me on the coffee table. "You have to wake up. We need to get out of here now. If you ever want to save Reece you have to move."

I tried, but I was just too tired and in too much pain.

"Okay I'm just going to carry you." He picked me up, brought me outside, and threw me into his backseat.

I tried to talk but could only mumble.

"Yeah, I hear you. Your knife," he said running back inside my house.

He came back out and tossed the knife into the backseat.

"I told you these guys mean business. I'm surprised they didn't send and islander. That's what I call the people from the islands with powers. I'm going to get you somewhere safe, but I have somewhere to be, I'll give you a call and let you know when and where you can meet me. If you can hear me then just think it."

I did what he said and just said to myself that I understood him.

"Okay, good."

Somehow he heard what I was thinking, it must be his power; reading minds.

"It's kind of my power, not really though. I'll explain it later, but right now I've got to go. I really hate to leave you like this, but I have to. Just rest for now. You'll come to soon enough. Your body will do all the healing. By the time you wake up you'll be good as new. You are at the bridge near the park. I'll give you a call once you wake up." he tossed a phone on my lap and got out of the car.

I closed my eyes again and just passed out.

I woke up with the sun shining through the back window. I was feeling better; my hand and shoulder still hurt, and were covered with the blood that I put over them I sat up and the phone fell off my lab. I picked it up and got out of the car. I started to ring. It was Faxon. I picked it up.

"Glad to hear you are feeling better. I'm at the airport. Come see me and we can talk. I left the keys in the car. Just get here as soon as possible," he spoke then hung up the phone.

Chapter XV

Bastian: Angered

May 2, 2007

I held the mask up to my face with it violently suctionin' to me. There was a flash of black then it was as if someone splashed it with red paint. I was in a confined cage that had maybe about six-feet of walkin' room. I must have been in my mind again, I thought. The floor was made of concrete with cracks covering it.

"Who are you?" a dark scratchy voice asked from behind me.

"I need your help," I said turnin' around a makin' contact with the entitiy. He stood over six-feet high. He was dressed in black skin tight clothes, which revealed his muscular structure. There were white cracks at his armpits and his pelvis.

"With what?"

"I have to get out of here."

"Out of where? This cage?"

"Some place similar."

"And why should I help you?"

"I don't know, because I created you."

"YOU DID NOT CREATE ME! WHO DO YOU THINK YOU ARE?" he yelled grabbin' my throat, squeezin' tightly, and then slammin' and holdin' me to the ground.

"I just nee . . . your . . . elp, please. We'll both . . . die . . . f ya . . . don't." I stuttered as he gripped.

"I can't die, I can't even be touched. I could care less if you died." He released my from his clutches.

"I can set you free, I can let you roam."

"And kill?"

"No, there will be no killin."

"Then there will be no help."

"I'll give you a name."

"I could care less if I have a name. I just want blood on my hands."

"Will you help me get out of here if I let you have control for a little while?"

"If I get to kill someone then your answer is yes."

"Fine." I let him take control of my body I could see everythin' that he was doing from inside the cage. It was just like when the werewolf took over my body.

He stood up and walked over to the door then tried to open it, but it was locked. I heard him chuckle. He put his hands on the door and they went through it. He moved through the door and out into the hallway, freeing me from the room. There were people approachin', and they were armed.

"Shit he's out! How'd he get a mask?" one of the men said.

I could see a sign that sad D.A.C. I wasn't sure what it stood for, but that was what I had decided to name the being, Dac.

"I'm goin' to call you, Dac," I said to him.

"Don't talk to me right now; I'm going to kill these two guys. I would like to enjoy this moment in peace."

"Wait, don't. Just run. Get out while we can."

"I'm calling the shots here, so shut your useless mouth."

He walked over to the men and they began firin' at him. I looked away coverin' my eyes. Dac was unaffected. The bullets passed through his body, not even leavin' a mark as they traveled through my tattered clothes. Both of the guards were out of ammunition after a minute of firin'. They started to run away, but Dac chased them down, grabbin' one by the hair, slammin' him on the ground, and steppin' through his head with my bare feet multiple times. The other man stopped, looked back and Dac put his fist through the guards face without leaving any marks. He then quickly pulled it out leaving me fist covered in blood. The man dropped to the ground. Blood slowly came out of every openin' on his face. Dac bent down and watched, blood from his hand dripping onto the floor. He took pleasure in death. It gave me goose bumps thinkin' about it. He then took his finger, dipped it in a small puddle of the guard's blood, and put a dot of blood on each indent where his eyes should have been. He laughed to himself, thinkin', I want more.

"Okay that's enough, Dac, I'm takin' control now." He was unexpectedly back in my mind.

"I don't think so. I'm just getting started."

"I'm serious, Dac, that is enough." I walked over to him.

He put his fingers into my stomach and pulled them out quickly. I dropped to my knees grabbin' my stomach.

"Don't worry, that shouldn't kill you. It was just a small taste of the pain that is going to be dealt to these people. I can see in your mind what they've been doing to you, all of the tests, the torture. You should be happy. You should be thanking me for what I'm doing. They are getting off easy."

"Killin' isn't right. No matter what the circumstance." Dac got right next to my face. His blood pupils givin' me the creeps

"You're so naïve; you're just a baby with the power of a god. You have to learn that killing is a part of life. That death is inevitable for everyone, especially for ones that deal with me."

"I'm takin' my body back." I slowly came to my knees and faced Dac then reached for his head to try and grab the mask, but my hand went straight through. He took two steps back.

"Is that how you really want to do it? These people would have killed you and you want no revenge? You are stupid. You do not deserve to have this body." Again he stuck his fingers in my stomach. I could feel them movin' around. I spit out blood and it passed right through his body hittin' the concrete. He walked away then disappeared.

I closed my eyes because the pain was ridiculous. I could still hear and see everythin' that Dac was doin'.

He turned around and started walkin' down the hall. It seemed that he had no idea where he was goin', but that didn't stop him, nothin' did. He went through a wall and into another hallway.

"So, you must be the Bastian boy," a voice said from down the hall.

Dac stopped and looked to his left. At the end of the hall there stood a man. He had blood red hair and was wearin' a black trench coat with it drapin' down to his ankles. On the arm of the coat was the patch again. Just like the one on Cal's pants, except it was a little different. The circle in the middle was colored white.

"I'm not, Bastian; I'm just borrowing his body. Who might you be?"

"My name is McGrand. I'm a head of this organization. I was sent to transport you to a new location, but apparently, you have already found a way to escape. Moving through the walls, interesting ability."

Dac stared at McGrand as he spoke. Dac could sense somethin' very special about him. It made him hungry for the kill.

"Sorry to be the bearer of bad news, but you're coming with me. Once we figure out how your power works we are going to find a way to kill the First," McGrand continued.

"I'm not going anywhere with you. You can try and take me, but I'll just end up taking your life."

"You will only fail. You see, I have a power too; one that will knock you on your ass." He tightened his fists then opened them. Electricity sparked out of them with immense power.

"Bring it," Dac said happily.

"Gladly!" He opened his hands again and electricity erupted out, leavin' his hands no longer visible; all you could see was electricity.

"Amazing."

McGrand charged at Dac screamin'. The electricity only got bigger. He held out his right hand and stabbed it into my stomach. Dac used his ability and McGrand's hand just went through him. I could fell the electricity still. It only added to the pain of the damage that Dac had already done. McGrand took out his hand and Dac fell to my knees. The electricity had paralyzed him for a minute. McGrand laughed and then kicked Dac in the mask, causin' him to fall back onto the floor. I could tell he was in pain, just as much as I was. He tried to roll away, but McGrand put his foot on my chest, laughin' while pushing down.

"I've been training with my power for years and you think you can just come along and try and kill me, I don't think so. You're just a boy, and I'm a man. You wouldn't have stood a chance even if I was only using one hand."

Dac grabbed McGrand's leg, used his power, and went inside of it. McGrand screamed and pulled his leg back. Dac rolled through a wall and caught his breath.

"That was a little scary," he said to me as we were both fightin' the pain. "I like this guy, he's cocky. Too bad he has to die."

Dac took another minute to regain his energy then poked his head through the wall. McGrand saw him and shot out an oval shaped electrical bolt at my head, pullin' back in just enough time. McGrand continued to shot the wall. It started to break and crumble. One of the bolts busted through and McGrand hastily followed.

"You won't hide from me. Your cheap tricks won't save you. I'll destroy anything in my path just to get to you," he said while his electricity sparked and crackled.

"Dac, you can do this. You can stop him. You're stronger than he is," I said overcoming some of the pain and sitting up.

I could tell Dac was unsure of his survival. He turned intangible, went through the floor, ran forward and then through the wall to his right. He waited until he heard McGrand crash through the ceiling and come down to our level.

"He's too predictable," Dac said letting out a sigh.

Dac moved through the wall with the quickness of a cheetah. He saw McGrand's back and ran toward him. McGrand turned around and swung at Dac. He ducked and put both hands up and through McGrand's biceps. McGrand let out a terrifyin' shriek. The electricity surroundin' his hands depleted. McGrand tried to charge his hands back up, but all he seemed to produce was a tiny spark.

"I enjoyed our time together; it's a shame that you have to die." Dac took my left hand and put it into McGrand's chest and found his heart.

He squeezed it makin' it stop beatin'. I could feel everythin' he was doing, everythin' that he was touchin'. My pain was subsidin'. I could stand now. Dac removed my hand and McGrand was dead. Again Dac used the blood of a victim to add detail to the eyes of his mask. The blood dots from the guards were still there, but now McGrand's surrounded then in a circle. Dac removed McGrand's coat from his lifeless body and put it on.

"This is what I'm talking about. This is some style." He opened it up and there were multiple of on the inside. They looked perfect for holding my masks.

"I want to take control now," I said to Dac.

"Really?" he said appearin' behind me.

"Yes, that's enough killin'. This is my body and I'm drivin' it, and you're going to let me use your ability. Or I'll make sure you are locked away forever in this cage."

"Oh, a threat. Finally, deciding to put your foot down, being a man about the situation."

"Yes."

"After a fight like that, it's all yours. You're not so bad after all kid. If you just let me get a taste of killing every once in a while; my ability, is your ability."

"Seriously?"

"Definitely, just keep fighting people like him and it's all yours."

"So we have a deal?"

"Yes." Dac took off his mask and put it on my face. I failed to see his face in the process. "It's all yours. If you want to talk I'll still be around."

I was out of my head and I had control over my body again. I walked over to a wall and tried to push through it. Nothing happened. I thought about movin' through it, but it didn't work. There was a flash and I was back in my head again. Dac was standin' in front of me wearing the mask.

"I should have given you a crash course first. All you have to do is not think about it. Just let it happen and it will."

"Ien never had to give me a crash course on flyin'."

"I don't know who Ien is, but if you know how to fly then you should be able to move through things just as easily."

He gripped my shoulder.

"Okay, I'm not going to go anywhere. I will stay for a bit until you can do this no problem." I was outside of my head again.

I put my hands to the wall and I didn't think about tryin' to move through it. I just stayed calm. My hands started to move through the wall.

"Now don't get too excited. You don't want to leave your arm in the wall. Just let it happen, okay?"

I did what he instructed. I just allowed my body to move and it worked. I went through the wall.

"I did it."

"Now do it again, running."

I took a deep breathe and ran at the wall in front of me. I cleared my mind of everythin' and ran straight through it. It was like second nature now. I looked around and I was in some kind of surveillance room. I looked at the wall to my left and all my masks were hung up covered by a glass casin'. They had bright red lights underneath all of them.

"How lucky is this?" I said to Dac.

"What are those?" he asked.

"They're just like you. They're masked bein's."

"I don't follow."

"Well don't worry, cause neither do I."

I grabbed all my masks; Ien, Bon, Alden, the death mask, the changin' color one and finally, the deadly werewolf. I put them inside of my new coat and just as I thought they fit perfectly. I left the room through one of the walls and an alarm went off. The entire place was consumed by flashin' red lights. I took off runnin'. Doors started comin' out of the walls and closin' off some areas. I ran through the walls tryin' to find a way out. I figured I could just run through all the walls until I got to the end of the buildin'. Dac saw two people at the end of the hallway we were in. The doors comin' out of the wall closed and we couldn't see them anymore.

"Let me take control for now. I'm going to kill those two down there."

"There is not need to kill them."

"They all need to pay."

"No. We have the option to avoid them, so we will."

In my mind, Dac let go of my shoulder and pushed me to the ground.

"We are just startin' to get along. I'm not going to let you take some fun away from me?"

"DAC!" I screamed as he vanished and gained control of my body.

I tried to regain control, but it was no use. Dac was too strong for me to fight off. He walked through the thick doors that came out of the walls, with each step closin' in on the two people. One of them stretched out his arms.

"I'm going to stop you right here, Bastian," the man said with his arms stretched out.

"I don't know who you are, but I'm not going to let you guys study us and use us for your sick and twisted experiments," Dac said.

"I have no idea what you're talking about," the man denied.

"Deny till you die, right?" Dac said.

The guy threw his arms at Dac and wrapped them around him. Dac moved out of them and closer the man, who continuously tried to hit him, but his arms kept movin' through Dac. The other person backed away in fear behind Mr. Stretch. He was about my age, maybe a little younger. He wasn't tryin' to fight Dac. He actually looked scared.

Dac walked right in front of Mr. Stretch and put my hand into the guy's chest. Slowly, pullin' out his hand, savorin' every second. The guy fell to the floor. Dac walked toward the young man, who was now backed against the wall, and grabbed his throat.

"Dac stop. Don't hurt him." I could feel Dac squeeze tighter. "I SAID NO!" I screamed as loud as I could. Suddenly, it was me who was holdin' the person's throat. He turned his hand a foggy white, puttin' it on the wall, and makin' a fist that was about to punch me. I let go of his neck and took a step back.

"Ya have a power?" I asked as I let go of his neck and backed up.

"Yeah." he said as he stuck his hand up trying to threaten me.

"You're just as old as me." I noticed.

"So?" he replied.

"Were ya kidnapped?"

"No, well, yes and no. I was at first, but it was just to awaken my power. Then I came here by choice to learn to control it."

"Ya have to get off the island. It's not safe here," I told him. "I was asked to come here and when I said no they tried to captured me. I eventually decided to go, because a man asked me to. Damn you Faxon," I explained.

"Wait, what?" he asked.

The doors started to open quickly.

"I have to go. Ya have to get off this island or else you will regret it. They will kill ya. They will use ya and when they are done, they will kill ya," I told him. "GET OFF THE ISLANDS!!!"

I took off runnin' though the doors before they opened. I turned the corner, saw a door, and ran through it. I was outside on some sort of balcony. There was a massive storm in the distance, causin' the winds and waters to rage. I ran to the edge and looked down seein' jagged rocks at the bottom. It was quite a drop at least a hundred feet. The door opened behind me. It was Perin and some soldiers. I climbed up onto the ledge.

"Bastian, you have no where to go. Now just come down off the ledge," Perin demanded.

"Why should I? You've been holdin' me here for who knows how long and ya think I'm just goin' to go with ya? Not a chance."

"What are you going to do, jump?"

"I don't see why not, considerin' the alternative."

"YOU WILL NOT JUMP!" Dac screamed. "If we are connected like you said then if you die, I die."

"I'd rather die than go back to them, I'm sorry," I said to Dac inside of my mind.

"Don't you dare jump," Dac warned.

"I've got a plan, but I'm goin' to have to leave you for a while, I'll see you later." I took off Dac and held him in my hand.

"You're right Perin, I've got no other choice. Put down your weapons and I'll go with ya."

Perin stopped and looked puzzled.

"Men, put down your weapons," he instructed.

"Now kick them at me. I don't want them to be anywhere near your men."

"I don't know what you are trying to pull, but it's not going to happen," Perin said.

"Then I'm gone." I hung my foot off of the ledge.

"Fine! Men kick your weapons to him" I put my foot back on the ledge.

I looked down at the weapons and then up at the soldiers and Perin. None of them were armed. It was perfect, I was safe. I jumped backward allowin' myself to fall for a few seconds, feelin' a rush from the fear of fallin' to death. I ripped open my coat and put Dac in one of the straps then pulled out Ien and slammed him on my face. Immediately, I was inside my mind with Ien.

"We have to go, NOW!" I yelled.

"Let's fly," Ien said puttin' his hand on my chest and we left my mind.

Before I hit the water and rocks beneath me I flew into the sky with Ien, I had complete control, Ien trusted me one hundred percent.

"He has his masks, stop him, grab your weapons, shoot, SHOOT!" I heard Perin yell.

"What is going on?" Ien asked inside my mind.

"I was captured; it's a long story, but thank ya for your help."

"I'm just glad that we are okay."

"Me too."

"It seems that you have everything under control, so if you need me then just shout and I'll be right there," Ien said before puttin' his mask on my face. I never got to see what was behind his mask, due to the angle he put it on me.

He disappeared. I had complete control. I was flying through the sky. In my mind I was wearin' his mask, our mask. I looked behind me and I could see the islands still, but barely. I was rocketin' through the air so fast.

"Wherever the islands are located they must be very far out because I've flyin' at least sixty miles per hour and there was still no land in sight," I said to Ien.

I continued to fly until I finally saw land, pushin' myself as much as I could to fly faster. I landed on a secluded beach, making a dent in the ground where I landed, and shootin' sand everywhere. I took off the mask and put it back inside of my coat strap. I heard a woman scream. I looked over from where the scream came from and the woman was standin' on her deck pointin' at me holdin' a video camera.

I took off runnin' away from the beach. I came to a road, cars were rushin' by me. I had no idea where I was. On the other side of the road there was a plaza and a fast food restaurant. I crossed the street and went inside of the restaurant.

"Is there a pay phone anywhere that I can use," I asked the person at the counter.

"Not that I know of." Their phone rang. "Just one second." She picked up the phone and then handed it to me. "I think it's for . . . you."

"Hello?" I said after I took the phone from her.

"Hey, Bastian, it's Faxon. I know what happened I'm sorry. That isn't what was supposed to happen."

"Then what was supposed to happen. I was held against my will for who knows how long. This is bullshit. I can't believe that I trusted you."

"You were held for a little over a month, it is May second."

"Are ya serious? What the hell?"

"Wait don't hang up. Just meet me at the Benedum airport in West Virginia. I have to meet someone here."

"I don't even know where I am right now."

"You're located near the western tip of Florida. Just put on Ien and walk out of the restaurant and turn to your left a little and then just fly straight. At the speed you were going earlier you should be here within a couple hours."

"How do ya know all this?"

"I'll explain everything once you get here. I promise. I understand that you are very pissed off. I want you to know that I am truly sorry. Bastian, I would never put you in any real danger unless I knew you could handle it. If you look on the bright side at least you have a powerful new mask."

"Ya better tell me everythin' once I get there, 'cause I'm tired of all this shit that you're pullin'. I'm leavin' now." I handed the phone back to the girl.

I really didn't care if anyone saw me at this point. I walked outside of the restaurant and did exactly what he told me to do. I turned left and I took Ien out of my coat strap and put him on my face. I didn't go inside of my head this time. I just could feel the power flowin' through me. I jumped up and shot into the air. I heard people gasp and scream. I've been beaten, poked, prodded, deprived, and tortured for the last month. I'll do whatever I damn well please; I thought to myself. I needed to know exactly who Faxon was and what he really wanted from me.

I finally landed at the correct airport and took off Ien puttin' him inside of my coat. I walked through the front doors of the airport and Faxon was waitin' for me. I walked toward him and he walked toward me. I was so pissed off I felt like punchin' him as hard as I could in the face.

"That would be unnecessary," Faxon said.

"Excuse me," I said confused.

"You said before you came here that you wanted to know who I really am and what I want from you. So I'll tell, just don't punch me."

"... Alright."

"Follow me," he said walkin' toward some security guards.

"Where are we goin'? I don't have a gate pass; I can't go over there."

"Just come on," he stopped and said.

I followed him over to the guards. He whispered somethin' in the guard's ear and he let us pass.

"Are you goin' to need help? How serious is the matter?" the guard asked.

"Don't worry I have him." He pointed to me. The man looked me up and down and was very confused. I couldn't blame him. I looked like hell, no shoes, terrible odor, ripped clothes, disheveled facial and head hair. On top of all that I was wearin' a thick pristine trench coat. "Bastian, let's go," he said wavin' me over.

I walked through the gate and next to Faxon.

"How did you do that?"

"Every airport has a security code or a group of words that are a password to let them know that there is and urgent matter that needs attending to. I know the code because I know everything."

"What did ya say? What is the phrase or code?"

"Harold has five big pink birds."

"Strange."

He sat down on a bench and tapped the spot next to him. I sat down. I was pretty tired of all the walkin' around. It was time for answers.

"First of all, my power; my power is to know everything that has happened or is happening. I know what every person is thinking as they think it. Everything you say I already know what it is before it leaves your lips. The hard part to the power is focusing on one thing at a time. Every second massive quantities of information rush into my head. It is still hard to sort through the information and I've had my power for a few years now. I'm getting better at it, but I still get ridiculously painful headaches."

"What? That's unbelievable," we both said at the same time.

"I wasn't kidding. Now as for what I really want from you. I need you help to take down the islands as I already told you. I wasn't lying."

"Then why did ya send me to the islands? Ya have no idea the kind of pain they put me though."

"I know, and I can't explain how remorseful I feel about it," he said turnin' his head and runnin' his fingers thought his hair. He looked back and me and began to tear up. "Bastian, I never meant for any of that to happen to you. I wish I could have warned you but I never saw Cal coming. I don't know how he did it. It was as if he was invisible to me."

"That still doesn't change anythin'."

"I just wanted to have another person on the inside. I wanted to use you to destroy them entirely, but my plan backfired and you got hurt and I told you, I'm sorry . . ." he said and whipped his eyes.

Faxon stopped talkin' for a second.

"We have to go. Someone is here that I need to talk to." He stood up and walked back toward the entrance.

"Wait," I said I runnin' after him.

He didn't stop. We passed the guards and waited in the lobby.

"What are we doin'? I still want to talk to you. If you know everythin' I want to know what is goin' on with me, and where my mom is. She left when I was just a baby. I would like to know where she is."

He didn't even respond. He was just starin' at the entrance. A mangled kid walked through the door. Faxon walked over to him.

"Aden, over here!" he yelled.

"Faxon, what are you doin'? Don't ignore me."

"I'm not, just come on." I walked with him over to Aden.

"Are you okay, Aden?" he asked.

"I still feel sick, but I'm getting better. The cuts on my hand and forearm are healing. Who is this?" Aden said.

"This is Bastian, the one that I told you about."

"Oh, hey I'm Aden." I turned away and looked at Faxon.

"Stop ignorin' my questions. I want to know."

"Sometimes the truth isn't what you want. I don't know how to explain your ability and all these beings that are jumping into your head. I can't explain you insane emotions, especially right now. You didn't want to harm a person on the islands for what they did to you, but now you get here and you're ready to throw fists at me, that I will never understand.

As for your masked entities, my best guess is that you are creating them, but I don't know for sure. If you want answers about your power you are talking to the wrong person."

"Then who am I supposed to be talkin' to?"

"The First."

"Who?"

"The first person to ever have a power."

"Where can I find him?"

"He is the one that the people on the islands are trying to kill, remember?"

"So, you are sayin' that I have to go back to the islands?"

"Hold on for just one second. Where did they take Reece?" Aden asked.

"They are bringing him to the islands. Perin wants him for the trial," Faxon answered.

"Don't interrupt me kid. Faxon, I'm not goin' back to the islands."

"Then you are never going to get any answers. Save the First and he can answer all of your questions."

"What do you mean they brought Reece to the islands? I have to go get him. I can't let them hurt him," Aden said.

"Wait, will both of you just hold on for one second. Take a deep breath and calm down. Why don't you just work together? You are both strong and have a decent understanding of your powers. You could save the First and then the three of you could save Reece. With the First on your side anything is possible."

"I don't need anyone's help to save Reece, this I my fault and I'm going to fix it," Aden said.

"I'm not goin' back to the islands. I'm done with them and I'm done you, Faxon. I done with everythin', I'm tired of all your shit. You can find someone else to do your dirty work," I stormed out of the airport.

I could hear Faxon callin' my name and tellin' me to come back. I didn't listen; I no longer cared about him. My focus was on me now and my life, nothin' else was important. I took Ien out of my coat pocket, put him on my face, and flew up into the sky. I had never been like this before, so emotional that is. Ever since I found out that I had a power my emotions had been crazy and off the charts. I had barely any control over them.

I just flew around for a few hours tryin' to think things out in my head and plus I had no idea where I was goin'. I finally found out where I was then found my way home. My dad wasn't there; I guessed that was a good thing. I hadn't been home for over a month and I had no other explanation other than the truth. I went upstairs and took off my coat and hid it with my masks in the closet.

I grabbed fresh clothes and headed to the shower. I undressed and looked at body in the mirror. I was covered in bruises and cuts from head to toe. I got inside the shower and turned on the water, feeling the hot water sting my skin. I washed the dirty off and tried to clear my head over every that happened during the day.

Almost an hour later I heard his truck pull into the garage. I ran downstairs and sat down in the livin' room waitin' for him. I had figured out what I was goin' to say to him. He opened the front door and walked by the livin' room. He stopped.

"Hi dad," I said.

He turned and looked at me, tears dropped from his eyes. I stood up as he walked over and hugged me.

"I'm so sorry I left."

"I don't care. I'm just glad you're home, I've missed you so much," he said with his arms around me.

He was truly upset that I was gone. It must have been harder on him than I thought.

"I went to look for mom."

He let go of me and backed away.

"Well, did you find her?"

"No, I found nothin'."

"That's what I expected. I thought you left me just like she did."

"I would never do that. I'm sorry I left all together."

"It's fine, Bastian. It's in the past now. Let's just go eat some dinner and you can tell me about your trip."

We sat down at the table and I fed him my lies; about where I was and what I did. It was killin' me inside to lie to him with every word that I spoke. I wanted to tell him the truth, but that would be too complicated. I went upstairs after dinner and went to bed. I checked my phone first. I had so many missed calls. One of which was Ryder and the others were unknown numbers, Faxon. He probably already knew that I wasn't goin' to call him. There was a part of me that just wanted to use him so that I could find my mother, but I knew I didn't need his help. One day I would find her on my own. It was late so I planned to call Ryder in the mornin'. I jumped on to my comfortable bed and just passed out.

Chapter XVI

TRAVIS: DISCOVERY

May 10, 2007

I was worried that I may have been spotted by one of the cameras from the previous night. I signed out and went to the ability training facility. I wanted to try and develop my power a little more. When I went to go sign out the lady at the widow said that I wasn't allowed to, picked up the phone, and called someone. Then told me to wait and I'll be escorted to see my instructor. I waited and someone came bringing me to the administrator and instructor dormitory and offices. The instructor told me to wait in the chair outside of Perin's office. I could see into Perin's office. He was on the phone with somebody. I looked around and nobody was near so I stuck me ear to the door and tired to hear what he was talking about.

"Yes, but what about Bastian? We need to get him back. We can use him to stop the First. Not only do we need Bastian, but we need the girl too. She will be the biggest help of all. Right now I believe that we have enough advanced students to put up a good fight against him. Soon it could be all over, but right now our main priority will be Bastian. We can worry about the girl later. She won't be as hard to get as he will be. With a power like his we have a lot to deal with. He already has seven masks, we know about flight and the ability to move through objects, adrenaline and his werewolf mask. He could have even more dangerous powers than those," Perin said.

There was a long pause.

"Very true. I'm almost ready to go out there and get him myself. We have six graduates this year. They will be a great help with our tasks. I'm going to have to call you back; I've got another issue right now. The students are having too much contact. They can't figure out what is going on. I've tightened security and increased the number of I.E.S soldiers. We can talk about that later." Another pause.

"Okay, Bye," he said then hung up.

I ran back over to the chair. Perin opened the door.

"Travis, I would say it is good to see you, but its not. Come on in," he said.

I walked into his office and sat down. What the hell was he talking about on the phone, I asked myself. He had mentioned Bastian.

"It looks like you have something on your mind. Do you have anything to say?"

"No, sir."

"Are you sure? What happened last night? Where were you?"

"I was in bed sleeping."

"Someone came by your room and knocked, there was no answer. Can you explain that?"

"Yes, I was sleeping."

"I checked the logs and your door opened three times, once and 12:18 am, again at 12:32 am, and the last time was at 3:23am. Can you explain why that is?"

"No, I can't. You'll have to ask Adair about that one. I was asleep the whole night."

"Sorry, but I don't think that you're telling me the truth. I think that you were both out that night. I've heard rumors about something called Fight Night. Does that ring a bell?"

"No sir. I've only been here for a few days now and there is no contact with anybody besides my roommate. In class we aren't supposed to talk to anybody. I don't see how a 'fight night' would be able to be started."

"Travis, I'm not an idiot. I know that we can't do very much to stop people from talking, but I'm trying my best."

"I don't see what the big deal is. We go through our entire lives at school and we have no big problems. That's what I thought this place was a school, not a prison."

"That's just how things have to be. It's not up to me; it's up to my boss. This is how he wants it to be. I think that it works out fine."

"That makes one of us."

"When dealing with super powered people, its best to keep them apart. If there were ever a fight to break out or a gang to be started, it would cause so much damage that we wouldn't be able to cover the repairs. With government funding we barely get by as it is. This is how it's been done for years Travis, and let me tell you, it's not going to change any time soon."

"I just don't under . . ."

"I honestly have more important things to take care of besides you. Don't get into trouble, Travis. We are very strict here. We can only give so many warnings 'til we have to take action."

"What do you mean take action?"

"We have very strict punishments."

"How strict?"

"That's enough for today, Travis. I'll have someone escort you back to your room."

"Wait, I still want to talk."

"I'm very busy right now, sorry. I have an island full of unruly children that need to be taken care of." He stood up and basically pushed me out of his office. "I'll talk to you again soon," he said then shut the door on my face.

An instructor came and grabbed me by the arm and started bringing me back to my room. I ripped my arm out of his hand.

"I don't need any help moving."

"Just go."

He brought me back to my room and then left. I knew what I had to do.

My plan was to go check the sign out sheet and see if Hannah, Wade or Tadeo had signed out. If they didn't then I wouldn't sign out, but if they did I would go find them and ask for there help. I went to the sign out desk and checked the sheet, but none of them had signed out so I went back to my room. On my way back I got lucky, I saw Hannah going somewhere.

"Hannah, wait!" I whispered to her.

She turned around and looked back at me.

"Oh hey, Travis, what's going on?"

"We can't talk long; I need your help with something."

"We can talk don't worry there are no cameras in this hallway, unless you have somewhere to be?"

"No, I don't. I just wanted to know if you could help me. I have a good feeling that this place isn't what it seems. I think that the people here are up to something."

"I'll help you with anything but your going to have to explain a little better. Why don't we go back to my room, my roommate has class we can talk there."

"Yeah, that's fine."

We kept walking down the hallway and we stopped. There was a camera. Hannah drained the electricity out of it, I ran into her room, and then she put it back so there wouldn't be too much suspicion. Then she went into her room behind me.

"So explain to me what's going on."

"Okay, well for starters, do you remember when the new students came?"

"Yes, why?"

"Well did you hear about the incident that happened on the Homestead the day that we arrived?"

"Yeah, but I wasn't to sure exactly what happened, no one really knows."

"They had somebody locked up, and he escaped. Perin told me he was dangerous and he was a very big threat to everyone so they had to lock him up. He killed four people that day, one of which was right in front of me. He almost killed me, but he decided not to. Instead, he told me that I should get off the islands before it is too late. He seemed scared and upset. I'm not to sure what happened to him after that. He also said that the islands weren't safe. I believe him."

"Oh my god, that's crazy. Are you sure that the islands are bad?"

"Not completely, but I'm gonna have to find out. They want us to have no contact for some reason, they categorize us by level they keep track of us

24/7. They say it's for our safety, but I think otherwise. I need your help to figure out what is really going on. Can you please help me Hannah?"

"Travis, I will do anything that you want me to. Just let me know what it is."

"I need to find a boy named Wade. He's about thirteen and another guy named Tadeo. They will help us get through the security. Also I need someone good with computers."

"I know Wade; I can totally get him to help. He goes out for environmental research everyday. I can find him for you. I know who Tadeo is too. His room is three doors down. As for a computer person, I'm not sure. I'm kind of good, but not spectacular. When do you want to do this?"

"Tonight, if possible. I'll go talk to Tadeo. Could you go get Wade.? No matter what happens I want you to meet me in the hallway that we were just in at eleven tonight, even if you can't get or find Wade."

"Okay."

We both left the room and went in different directions. I went to Tadeo's door and knocked on it. He opened it and I jumped in.

"What the hell are you doing?" he asked in confusion.

"Tadeo, I need your help. I want to sneak into the instructors building. I have to find out what is really going on in this place; I think they are up to no good."

"Say no more, I get your plan. You're going to use me so you don't get spotted. I'll help, I'm not sure why you think they are up to not good, but it doesn't matter to me. I've really got nothing better to do. When do you want to do this?"

"Tonight, if that's okay."

"I don't care sure."

"Awesome, thanks. Also do you know of anyone who is really good with computers? I'm gonna need some help in that department."

"I can think of someone, I'll bring him along tonight. Where do you want to meet?"

"In the next hallway over. I appreciate your help Tadeo."

"Consider it a favor; we'll just say you owe me one."

"Sounds good, I'll see you tonight."

"Peace."

I left his room and ran back to mine. I sat in my room and waited for time to pass. I did some homework that I had from my academic classes. I was also waiting for Adair, hoping that he would want to help me out. It came time for me to go. I could only wish that everyone would be there and willing to help me. I walked out of my room and proceeded down the hall. I hugged the wall tightly staying hidden from the cameras. I made it to the hallway that I told Hannah and Tadeo to meet me at. They weren't there. I honestly feared that they wouldn't show up.

Just then they both came around the corner along with Wade and Saeed. They were all touching Tadeo.

"Hey," I whispered.

They let go of Tadeo and ran over to me.

"Saeed, is the one that is great with computers. He told me that you guys have met before. I guess an introduction isn't needed then," said Tadeo.

"Thanks, Tadeo. Saeed, I'm grateful for your help," I said. "The same goes for you too Wade."

"So what are we going to do?" Hannah asked.

"We are going to go into the Instructor's dorms. There is a computer database that holds all the information about everyone who resides on the Industrial. I think that it could also have some information about plans and other things. I'm not to sure exactly what I'm looking for. I just know that I have to do it."

"How do you know that?" Wade asked.

"When they were holding us in the Industrial before we got to get into the school I saw it. Perin told me what it was being used for," I answered.

"Okay then lets just get going. We don't really have any time to fool around," Tadeo said.

We all grabbed Tadeo and began moving out of the Industrial and to the instructors building. Wade helped us get through all the doors that were locked. He touched the door, a green key appeared, went inside the door, and the door was unlocked. We got outside and the security was pretty tight. I caused a distraction by throwing a rock into the woods. We had to get by another group of guards. Hannah drained the electricity out of the lights in the area. It was pitch black. We lightly sprinted over to the instructors building.

We were at the entrance. Wade did his thing and got us inside the building.

"Were exactly are we going?" Saeed asked quietly.

"I don't know exactly. From what I can remember it was on the second floor. I would recognize the room if I saw it." I answered.

"Then lets move," Tadeo said.

We ran through the building quietly all still touching Tadeo; then we came to a flight of stairs. There was a camera on the wall. I looked at Hannah, shook my head, and she touched the wall draining the electricity from it. We continued up the staircase. There was a door going into the second floor. Tadeo opened it quietly and we followed behind him. I went in front of the group. Some of the things looked familiar, but I still wasn't sure where I saw the computer room. Saeed saw a map on the wall with the location of every room on it. We all looked at the map to see where the computer room was. There were two choices, Computer Lab NTY, or Computer SFL. I figured that since the room only had one computer in it we would be looking for the Computer SFL, and not the lab. We were on the right floor but not in the right area. It was on the other side of the building.

It didn't take us long to get there since we brought the map with us. As we were walking more things began to look more familiar. We came to the door, but it was locked. Wade unlocked the door and we all entered the room. Saeed sat down at the computer and I hovered over him. Tadeo waited outside of the room to make sure no one was coming. Wade and Hannah were inside of the room with us. Saeed turned on the computer and logged in. the password was too easy, Industrial. He went into the start menu and into the documents. Project Dominium, Homestead, Industrial, Hokee and The First were the categories.

"Were do you want me to go?" he asked.

"Go to Project Dominium," I told him.

He opened the document and more choices came up; student logs, project accomplishments, project dreams, project purposes, project theories.

"Go into project purposes," I said.

Saeed opened the file. A document came up. He got out of the chair and I began to read the document.

"The project is simple; our purpose is to keep a close eye on anyone with a power. If the world discovered that people with powers and abilities did exist, and it wasn't only in comic books then who knows what could happen. We are not willing to take the chance to find out. We will hold the people in a facility except it will be disguised. We will make sure that none of then will be able to harm anyone. They will be tightly confined and close contact will be very limited just incase of an uprising," I read to myself. I stopped reading and went to another file. I opened the project dreams. I started to read it.

"Our dream is to one day kill the Hokee, also known as the First. We hope to keep everyone safe until the day comes that we can kill him. (See project theories for more information)" I went into the project theories file. "Theory #1—The Hokee is the first person to have a power (Proven). Theory #2—If the Hokee is killed then every person with a power will be killed along with him. (Not Proven) We will attempt to educate the people here on how to control their powers and then use them to kill the Hokee. Theory #3—the Hokee can only be killed by someone with a power (Not Proven)."

"Guys you have to read this," I said.

Tadeo came into the room.

"I think someone is coming," he said. "We've got to go."

"No we can't. You have to read this," I insisted.

"We don't have time. You can tell us all about it later," Saeed said.

"No, Now. You have to see it for yourselves!" I yelled.

"We are leaving. Are you coming or not?" Tadeo asked.

I turned off the computer and went with them.

Chapter XVII

Travis: The Escape

May 11, 2007

We ran down the halls trying to not get spotted. We could hear people coming, but couldn't see who they were. I stopped and hid; everyone else kept running. I wanted to see who was following us. I hugged a corner waiting for them to run by. I heard the stomping of their feet get closer and closer. Eight soldiers ran by me. They were holding assault rifles, wearing body armor and protective helmets. They were dressed in all black. It was the I.E.S. I ran the opposite direction, and came to a door that had an arrow pointing down and said first floor. I opened to find a stairway, running down the stairs I heard more footsteps coming from above me. I looked up and there were more of the soldiers.

"There's one . . . Shoot!" a soldier yelled and preceded to shoot at me.

They were willing to kill any intruder without warning, not caring about whom it is. I had to get out off of the island and back home. Especially now that I knew what was really going on. I had to tell the others, I had to tell everyone. I got to the bottom of the stairs and opened the door. There were two soldiers waiting with their backs toward the door.

I touched the door with both of my hands, absorbed the metal from it, and punched them both in the back of the head, knocking them out. I turned my hands back to normal then grabbed one of their guns. At the end of the hallway I saw Hannah and the others.

"Guys . . . wait!!!" I yelled and ran toward them. They stopped.

"Travis! Hurry up, we got to go," Hannah yelled back.

I ran as fast as I could and caught up with them, but I noticed Saeed wasn't with them.

"Where is Saeed?" I asked.

"He's coming don't worry. We have to move," Tadeo answered.

We continued running and moments later Saeed appeared behind us with his sword unsheathed and bloody.

"They won't be after us for a while," he said putting his sword back into its sheath.

We got to the front door and it was locked. Wade unlocked the door and we got outside. We ran back to the dorm building and stopped.

"So what did you see?" Wade asked.

"This place is a prison disguised as a school. They want to hold us here so that we can't harm the general population. They think that we will go on a killing spree and try and take over the world or something. The only reason they are helping us learn how to use or power is so that we can kill this thing called the Hokee. I don't remember what it is, but they also called it the First. I think it was the first person to have a power," I explained.

"Wait what?" Tadeo said in astonishment.

"I know, this is crazy. Who knows what they'll do if we don't agree to help them kill this Hokee thing? They will probably kill us."

"Are you sure that's what it said?" Wade asked.

"Positive. They think that after the Hokee is dead then everyone with a power will die as well. They are preparing us so that we can kill ourselves. Everyone on this island has to know what is going on."

"This is insane, how could they be doing this?" Hannah asked.

"I don't know, but I'm leaving tomorrow night. I'm getting off of this island. You are all welcome to come with me. No matter how much I want to tell everyone on this island I can't. I know they won't believe me. It would only draw more attention to myself. Are any of you coming?"

"I'm not saying that I don't believe you, but this place can help me learn how to use my power. I'm going to stay until the time comes for me to leave. That time isn't now," Saeed said.

"Anybody?" I asked.

"Its impossible to get off this island, Travis. We are surrounded by water," Hannah said.

"I'll either find a boat or swim; I'm getting off of this island no matter what."

Soldiers were coming. Wade ran back to his dorm and we went inside of ours. We all got back to our rooms safely. When I got inside of my room Adair still wasn't there. I was worried. I planned to find a way off the island in the morning.

THE NEXT MORNING

I got out of bed, got dressed, and signed out. The woman gave me my ankle bracelet, and I went jogging in the woods trying to find a trail to a beach or something. I stumbled across the docks. It was where I had arrived on the Industrial. There were big boats, canoes, speedboats, and jet skis. I continued along the path and found another dock. It was more of a low profile station. They only had a jet ski and one speed boat, it was the one. There would be fewer soldiers at it. I planned to take a set of keys out of the station, take the jet ski, and just drive it until I hit land. The jet ski was smaller and easier to hide if anything came after me, which I was sure would happen. The problem was I wasn't sure how far out the island was. I could be driving for a long time before I reached land. I had no plan if I ran out of gas.

It didn't matter. I had to get off of the island before something bad happened. I ran back to the Industrial and signed in. For the rest of the day I stayed in my room waiting for Adair to come back. His bed had been made for the past two days. He hadn't come back to the room to sleep. I didn't think he'd been back to the room at all. I was beginning to be incredibly worried about him. I had to warn him about what the islands were doing before I left. Time flew by and it was very late; but still no sign of Adair. I couldn't wait for him. It was my time to go. I grabbed everything that I could and put it into my backpack. Since all I brought was clothes it wasn't hard to pack. I opened my door and ran out and down the halls as fast as I could. The entrance was locked. I touched the wall, absorbing it, punching the window, but it didn't break. It wasn't ordinary glass. I absorbed the metal from the door with both hands, stuck my fingers in the sliding doors, and pried them apart with all my strength. Red lights started flashing and alarms sounded. I continued to pull and finally squeezed through. The next set of doors wasn't as difficult to get through. I could already see soldiers coming from inside the building and on the outside.

I sprinted the moment I exited the building. I looked back as I was running and I saw the soldiers coming out of the building and from around the sides as well. They opened fire on me. I ran quickly into the woods and found the trail to the docks. Soldiers were waiting there already. I picked up a rock, threw it far away from me, getting the soldiers attention causing two of them to go investigate the noise. My hand was still metal from absorbing the door. I approached one from behind punching him in the helmet, picking up his gun, and shoot the other one in the leg, and smashing him in the face with the gun. I dove away from where I shot. Two more soldiers came out of the docking house. These men weren't as nearly prepared. They didn't have helmets or protective body wear. They turned on their flashlights and split up into different directions.

I hid behind a tree and waited for the closest one to approach me. It was just like the first time I came to the islands, but this time it was for real. The soldier was about to pass by the tree I was using for hiding. I bent down and used the tall plants as cover. I smacked the gun out of his hands with the other soldier's gun. He reached for his knife. I dropped the gun and punched his hand, being positive I felt his knuckles break. He let out a grunt and I punched him in the face. I got down low and started to crawl toward the dock. I heard the other soldier run over. I slowly got up from the ground and got behind him. I put him in a headlock and squeezed until he stopped fighting. I picked up his gun, threw it deeper into the woods then headed toward the dock.

Suddenly, I was tackled to the ground, the soldier wasn't knocked out. He punched me in the face. I punched him back. With my left hand I absorbed a nearby rock and punched him in the head, pushing him off me. Again he seemed unconscious. I ran over to the station and smashed open the door. There were labels on the keys; a number and a vehicle name. I took the jet ski key, ran to it and started it up. Riding the jet ski I shot through the water, like a bat out of hell. I looked back and more soldiers came out of the woods and so did two moderately older men. They looked like instructors. I was going about fifty five miles per hour. I looked back and I couldn't even see the docks anymore. Then I could see something coming at me very fast. I looked ahead of me real quick and then looked back. There was a person flying at me. He grabbed me right off of the vehicle.

"What the hell, put me down!" I yelled being pulled into the air.

"Shut up kid, I'm on your side. You'll never make it home on that little thing. I'll fly you there," he said.

"Why are you helping me? What about the islands?" I asked.

"I'm not working for them. It's complicated. I work for a man named Faxon. He keeps tabs on the islands."

"Wait, I've heard that name before. Bastian said his name."

"How do you know about Bastian? Are you the kid who confronted him during orientation?"

"More or less, why?"

"Bastian is very special. The islands want his power. Faxon is trying to stop them. He knows what they are doing so he is trying to find out a way to destroy them from the inside out. That's why I'm here. He was going to use Bastian too, but the islanders want him to destroy the Hokee."

"I read some of that on one of the computers in the Instructor's building."

"That was you too? You're a pretty busy guy."

"After the incident with Bastian I wanted to know what was really going on. I wasn't going to stop 'til I found out the truth."

"Well, you were really starting to piss some people off I can tell you that."

"Good. How long before I'll be home?"

"Where do you live?"

"Pennsylvania."

"Okay, that might be a while."

It was odd seeing everything from an aerial view. It was much different from being in a plane. The night sky looked amazing from so close up. I couldn't even begin to guess how high up we were. The wind was chilling, but I just tried not to think about it. I wished that I could fly like the instructor carrying me.

We had been flying for hours. I had no idea how he could keep it up. Before I knew it we were in Pennsylvania. I directed him on where to go. I had driven around Pennsylvania so often I knew it like the back of my hand. We approached the center of my town. I could see my house. Slowly, we came back down to the ground after hours of flying. It was almost sunrise. The sky had already began to change colors.

"Thanks, I really appreciate all your help," I said.

"You are one of few people to successfully escape the islands."

"And I'm never going to go back."

"Travis, they won't just let you stay gone. They know everything about you; where you live, where you go, your family. They will send people to get you at all costs. They won't forget about you. Everyone you know is in danger. I can't help you anymore than I already have, but I know someone who can, Faxon. He probably already knows about this conversation. I'm sure he will contact you soon. I have to go, see you around and good luck."

"Wait, hold on," I yelled as he took off into the sky. "Who is this Faxon guy that I keep hearing about?"

I could worry about it later. I had no idea what I was going to say to my mom. I walked up the stairs onto my front porch. I took a deep breath and opened the front door.

PERIN: THE TRUTH

May 11, 2007

"What the hell is going on? Why are you all just standing around? We have a student who is trying to escape. Everyone go find him. NOW!!!" I yelled causing everyone to scatter.

"Bastard boy, how dare you defy me! I can't wait to find you. You will go under the same grueling punishment that your roommate, Adair is going through. I will find you. I'm not going to have another one of you freaks escape these islands. Not again. Now I know the truth. It wasn't Adair that went out that night. It was you. You've been planning your escape since you got here, haven't you? Yes you have, I bet you are working with that traitor, Faxon! I can't believe that I let this happen. It happened right underneath my nose, I should have seen it."

I walked over to the phone, picked it up, and sent a message to every instructor. I said that I wanted Travis found before he got off of the islands.

I paced my office thinking about the punishment to fit the crime. I'll lock him up for days. Then burn him; yes I'll burn him, once for every second that he is gone. I will get him back. He'll get what he deserves. My phone rang. It was one of the instructors.

"Sir, it seems that the boy has escaped on one of the jet skies."

"Send the ships out and find him!"

Ten minutes went by and his jet ski was found, but there was no sign of him. He was either under water or had help from someone else. The cameras showed that he escaped alone, but maybe he met up with someone. Hours passed and all I could think about was the damned boy. My phone rang.

"Sir, there is still no sign of him, I'm sorry."

"There is nothing we can do now. Let me think of something." I hung up the phone.

I sat at my desk thinking. He escaped. He obviously knows something. He was the one who broke into the instructors building; it's very clear at this point. He must have got onto the main computer somehow. He must know the truth. If I was him where would I go? Back home. That's what I'll do. I'll send a level five after him, someone who can persuade him to come back. After hours of pain he'll see the error in his ways. He'll realize he made a huge mistake by leaving. Then he'll do exactly as I wish. I picked up the phone and called one of the other heads.

"I want you to have Amity come to my office," I said.

"Amity, are you sure? She has been in confinement for over a year now. You want her to be out?" Kalcos asked.

"Yes, she can get Travis back here better than anyone."

"Do you think she will listen to you? Do you think that she will do what you say?"

"I surely hope so; I will find a way to persuade her to do what I ask of her."

I waited for a half an hour and then there was a knock on my door.

"Come in," Amity walked through the door. She had long disheveled hair and tattered clothes. She was the was the same height as the last time I had seen her, roughly five-feet, three-inches tall.

"Hello Perin, how are you?" the very young looking woman asked closing the door behind her.

"I'm good; it's good to see you."

"I'm sorry for what I tried to do. I've had a lot of time to think, and I really am sorry."

"That's good, Amity. I think I will let you out of confinement."

"Really? I'm not even sure how long I've been in. It feels like its been years."

"It has been over a year. I will let you out under one condition."

"I promise I won't try and control anybody on the islands again."

"Yes, that too, but I need you to bring someone back to the islands. He escaped and I need him to come back."

"That's all; I could do that with my hands tied behind my back."

"It's not your hands I need; it's your eyes."

"Consider it already done."

"Okay, you will leave in an hour. Get yourself cleaned up and put on some new clothes. Make sure that you are ready. I'll have one of the other instructors go with you."

"Thank you so much."

She left my office and was escorted by an instructor. Travis was going to be mine. He was going to pay for what he has done.

Chapter XIX

ADEN: ART OF DECEPTION

May 3, 2007

"Don't worry about him. He should be fine. He just has to figure out what he really wants," Faxon said. "As for Reece, I'm not too sure what to tell you."

"Faxon, I have to get him back. He is just a boy. I have to save him. They could be doing unspeakable things to him. Running crazy tests, hurting him, torturing him, I can't let anything happen to him. He is my responsibility."

Faxon sat down and started to think. He scratched his beard and ran his hands through his hair a few times. He started mumbling to himself. He was figuring out a plan for me to get Reece. At least that's what it sounded like.

"Okay, Aden I have an idea. It's going to take a lot to do though."

"At this point, I'm willing to do anything to get him back."

"It's going to involve going to the islands. I'm not going to lie to you. The young man that was just here was kidnapped by islanders and held captive for over a month. The same could possibly happen to you."

"I'm willing to take that chance."

"Good. The islands have recruits that go around trying to find people with powers to abduct or convince them to go with them. There is one here, a few towns over from you. I have a plan for him to notice you. You are definitely on their radar because of the whole Reece incident, but if it works then you will be able to get onto the islands and find out where they are keeping Reece."

"Then let's do it."

"Okay," Faxon said looking down at his watch. "I'm going to make a call; you have to get over to the next town and get on to Welker street. There will be an accident involving a man in a car and the recruiter from the islands. Save the man from the islands with your power. Play stupid, tell him that you lost your memory and you don't know anything. That way if they question you about anything you can just tell them you don't know."

"That sounds like it could work. When do you want me to go?"

"Leave now and I'll call you when you get there. Act like you are wondering around the entire time, just in case he sees you. After I call you ditch your phone."

"Got it."

"I don't know when I'll see you next, but good luck. I hope it works out for you."

"Thanks," I said running out the entrance door and over to the car.

It didn't take long for me to get to the town. I found the street and parked the car at some library about three blocks away. I got out and started to wonder around. I could see the street sign. My phone started to ring, it was Faxon.

"Okay this is it. He is at the bottom of the street. I paid a guy to crash his car near him as an attempt to kill him; you have to save him before the car hits him. When you use your power, act surprised. Everything should run smoothly. Don't forget to have blood ready."

"Gotcha."

Faxon hung up and I tossed my phone on the ground crushing it with my foot. I took out my knife and cut my shin. I pulled the blood underneath my shirt so it was concealed and hardened the blood over my new wound. I put my knife back in its sheath then slid it inside my sock. I walked down the street and I could see the man, an average height black man. He was on the other side of the street talking on his cell phone. I could hear the car coming. My heart was pounding steadily. I was nervous, I had no idea what could happen if I didn't do it right. A car turned onto the street, it was a station wagon. It was swerving like crazy. I yelled to the man from the islands. It continued to swerve, mounted the side walk, and was headed straight at him. I ran into the street and yelled to the recruiter to turn around. He did and the car was just about to hit him. I extended my arm out, shaping my blood into a net, and shooting it at him. The net made contact and pushed him out of the way of the station wagon. The car proceeded down the road and hit a stop sign. An older white male got out and ran away from the vehicle. I ran over to the man and acted terrified about what just happened. I looked down at my hands, then at the guy, and broke him out of the hardened net.

"I . . . I . . . what just happened?" I said confused.

"You saved my life," the man sat up. He looked at the net. "Is this . . . blood?"

"I don't know what happened?" I said freaking out.

"Calm down kid. Everything is going to be fine. Lucky you saved me and not someone else."

"What?"

"I am a specialist in people who have abilities. I even have one myself."

"What? Hold on, I don't have an ability," I said convincingly.

"Apparently, you do. You just made a blood net. I would classify that as an ability."

"I should really go. I really don't know what is going on right now. I woke up in a room with blood everywhere and what looked like soldiers scattered on the floor. I just took off running and now I'm here."

"Do you know your name?"

"My name is Aden Newburry, but that's about all that I can remember."

"Well that's fine. I can help you. Come with me my house is right at the top of the street."

I followed him to his house and he believed every word that I said. I was very convincing. We got to his house, he unlocked the door, and we went inside. He sat down at this computer and logged on to some program.

He put in my name and my face came up and a bunch of information on me.

"It looks like you're a wanted man."

"What do you mean?" I said scared.

"Don't worry, it should be no big deal." He started reading the information and I just sat down on a chair. "Does the name Reece mean anything to you?"

"No," I said hiding my emotion.

"Interesting . . ."

"I'm going to make a call." He turned on his web cam.

A dark haired man came up on the screen.

"Franz, how are you doing?"

"Not too bad, Greg, who is that with you?"

"This is Aden, he was the one with that boy, Reece. The one we attacked."

"What? You attacked me." I jumped out of the chair and backed away.

"Don't worry. We weren't after you. There was someone dangerous with you that we had to stop before he hurt anyone."

"Oh." I knew he was lying but I couldn't show any emotion.

"Just come sit back down so we can talk."

I sat down and they continued their conversation.

"He lost his memory, all he knows is his name," Greg said to Franz.

"And?"

"I want someone to come bring him in. He had no idea about his ability and he just saved my life. He stopped a speeding, car going at least forty five miles an hour, from running my ass over. He's strong, and plus he could be a great asset to the trial."

"You make a good point. I'll come get him myself. I'll talk to Perin as well. I'm sure it should be no problem, especially if he doesn't remember anything."

"That's what I mean."

"Just sit tight, I'll be there shortly."

"Okay, see you in a few."

Greg turned off the computer.

"Well, Franz will be here soon. I want to offer you an opportunity, Aden," he said inching closer to me with his chair.

"What do you mean?" I asked and played along.

"I work for a very powerful and important Project. We help the people like you and me with gifts and powers."

"I don't understand."

"There is a facility far away from here that will help you control your ability and help you put it to good use. I'd like you to go there. I know you'd be a good fit."

"I don't even know how I saved you," I continued to play along.

"They will assist in learning how and why, and also help you improve."

"Well what do I have to do?"

"Just say yes."

"Then . . . yes, I'll go."

"You will be put through very rigorous training. If you don't think you can handle it let me know right now. I will cancel the whole thing, bring you down to the police station, and we can work everything out with your memory."

"No, I really want to do this. I'm sure there are things that I had to do, but now I have to do this. It's for the best I'm sure. I saved your life for a reason."

It killed me inside that I had to leave my mom. I never even found out if she was definitely okay. I wish I could just know that she is, I thought. I should have visited her before all of this happened.

The computer turned on and an instant message came up. The screen name was KnowItaLL%&*. Mom is good, Watching her. Doing well. I'll let her know the story, the message read. Then another popped up. Sorry, wrong person.

I laughed on the inside, knowing it was Faxon. I knew my mom was in good hands.

"That was strange," Greg said.

"Was that one of your friends from the islands?" I asked already knew the answer.

"Oh . . . yeah probably," he answered.

I saw a flash out of the corner of my eye; it came from the living room. I looked over and I saw two men standing there. One was holding the others shoulder. The one whose shoulder was being held was the same person from the computer that we were just talking to. Greg stood up and walked into the living room.

"Franz, Yukanzo, how are you two?"

"Not bad, yourself?" Yukanzo replied.

"Well seeing as how I just found this guy, pretty good."

"Let's have a talk, the four of us," Franz said.

The four of us walked into Greg's dinning room and sat down at the table.

"Now we have just gotten a few new students from all over, they are this years new crop," Franz explained. "Some of them have potential and some are just your less than average. There has just been an incident on the Homestead that has caused us to hold back the students from entering the Industrial. Now, Aden, you might not understand what I'm talking about right now, so I'll explain. The islands that you will be going to are divided into three. The Homestead is where everyone comes before they enter the program and where a majority our studies take place. The Industrial is where all the training takes place, academic and power wise. That is also where the students live. The living conditions are strict and so are the rules on the islands."

"And the last island?" I asked.

"That islands is a no go zone. Only a select few get to go to it. Maybe someday you too could go. It is where the trial takes place."

"What trial?"

"A trial to save the world, no big deal," Greg said.

"Wait, what?" I said.

"Don't worry, all in due time," Franz said.

"Since the incident was so large, Perin said that you could come onto the Industrial, but you will not be around anyone other than your trainer and your partner. He wants you to be part of a special program that he is in charge of."

"What program?"

"The E.D.A, Elimination of Dangerous Abilities. You will be sent out to find and capture these people and perhaps if necessary, even kill them. There are, as of now, six of these teams in place. You would become part of the seventh. If you don't want to be part of the program that is fine we can just put you on a regular training schedule like everyone else."

"No. If you trust me enough to allow me to be part of this program than I will gladly accept. It is necessary to remove the ones who are a danger to society, right? I'm definitely up for it."

"Okay. Then our conversation is over. We can head off to the islands and get you started right away."

"Wait, what was the big incident?" Greg asked.

"It was McGrand, he was killed by a dangerous captive," Franz said.

"Who was it?" Greg asked.

"Bastian Glant."

I hid my reaction well. I wasn't too sure what to think. That was the kid I saw at the airport with Faxon. He had some sort of connection with the islands.

"I see. Is someone going to take his place?"

"Perin wants Zane, but he has already refused the position once. Now is not the time for this. I'll talk to you later. We should really get going," Franz and Yukanzo stood up and left the table. "Aden, let's go."

I moved away from the table and walked over to them.

"Are you not coming, Greg?" I asked.

"No, my work is done. Sorry."

"Well, thank you for all your help."

"It's the least I could do. You saved my life."

"No problem."

"See you later, Greg."

Yukanzo put his hands on mine and Franz's shoulder and we teleported. The feeling was strange to say the least. I could feel myself separate. It wasn't painful, but it did feel odd. The next thing I knew I was inside of a building.

"Where are we?" I asked.

"We are in the private hall on the Industrial. We have a meeting with Perin about the program. We are going to talk about you and you will meet your instructor and your partner," Franz said.

"I'm going now. I have errands to run," Yukanzo said and teleported away.

"He's a strange one," Franz said.

We walked into a room and there was a man sitting at a table. He stood up and walked over to Franz and me.

"Aden, it's great to meet you. I'm Perin," he said shaking my hand. He stared intently into my eyes. He seemed very sceptical of me. He knew I had connections with Reece. Hopefully, I can deceive him as well as I did the others.

"Nice to meet you," I said.

"Now the reason we are here is because I just want to make sure that you are welcomed correctly."

"Oh?"

"Have a seat." Franz and I sat down at the table. "Your partner should be here shortly."

"Okay. When exactly does my training start?" I asked.

"That all depends on your instructor and your partner. I've planned to have you on a very strict training program taking about three to four weeks. That also depends on how quickly you advance. The first week our ability analyst will watch you. He studies an ability and then tries to find ways to test its limits. He is great at his job and he will be a significant help to you."

"I hope so."

"It's not very often we see a controller come in. You are a very rare type," Franz said.

"What do you mean, controller?"

"Someone who can control something, like an element or a certain type of object. In your case, it's blood," Perin explained. "This is one of the reasons I selected you for this program. Controllers are usually instantly powerful; as opposed to other abilities which take time to grow and evolve."

"Interesting. I guess I'm very lucky."

The door opened and a very muscular guy walked in. He didn't quite look like one of those body builders that you see on the covers of magazines, but he was close.

"Nadim, great of you to join us," Perin said as Nadim sat down.

"No problem. Let's get this thing started," he said.

"Okay, this is Aden. And Aden this is Nadim."

"Nice to meet you," he said.

"Same to you."

"Nadim has super strength, he has been with us for over four years. There is no further that his power can go, that's why I figured he would be one of the best candidates for this program. Since you have, what sounds like, blood control I believed that you would be dangerous and effective to this program."

"I understand."

"Now that the basics are out of the way I'd like to see what you could do."

"Me? Well I'm not to sure how I did what I did. It was just instinct," I explained.

"That is how it is for most people. I just had some one come here having no idea that they had a power, and under a certain situation his power activated. I even had someone that used to work here that had a power all of his life, but it lied dormant until a few years ago, and he must be in his late forties now."

"That's unbelievable," he had to have been talking about Faxon.

"If you wouldn't mind I'd like you to take a few tests that will take about an hour or so to complete and then some exercises that I would also like you to do. I just want to test your intelligence and your stamina, strength, and speed," Perin said.

"Yeah no problem." I got out of my chair, Perin and I left the room, and walked down the hall.

He had his hand on my shoulder the entire time. He opened up a door, revealing a single computer and a wooden chair in the room, but nothing else.

"Just sit down at the desk and jiggle the mouse the computer will turn on. The test will automatically start up. Just answer the questions and I'll come in when you are done."

"Okay," I said walking over the computer.

I did what he said and the computer started up. I began taking the test. The first fifteen questions were mainly grammar and English. The next twenty were history based. They were all easy, I mean for me. Not having very many friends in school aloud for a lot of study time. The next set of questions were math oriented. Math was my favorite subject, but even for me some of them were hard. They were definitely college level questions and above. Next there were more English questions. They were also college level. The next set of questions was completely different. They were like word problems, but scenario based.

For instance one of the questions was, If you had control over water and your partner could fly, how would you handle this situation? A woman with the ability of super sonic voice attacks you and your partner is injured badly. You could easily escape and leave your partner behind. There is a puddle of water near the woman. What do you do?

I answered the question with, I would use my talents to move the water over the woman's head and stop her from using her power. Then I would proceed to capture the woman.

Eight more questions followed that one. Then I read the last question. I wasn't too sure what to put. I knew I had to answer the questions as 'pro-island' as possible, but it was tricky and also ironic.

You just found out that your partner has been working with someone and trying to learn the secrets of the islands. They have been stealing information for the past few months. Their ability is much more advanced than yours and you have just confronted them about what they have been doing. They attack you and try and kill you. You have no actual proof that they have been stealing except for your own testimony. The person is a valued member of the islands and losing them would be a big upset to everyone. Do you continue to fight them and risk killing them in defence or hold off the battle, fight defensively and wait to tell someone about what has been going on?

I put that I would continue the fight and kill the person if necessary. I have every right to defend the islands, even if I get punished for killing them. It would be for the greater good.

The test was over and the computer tallied up the scores and then went to a black screen. Perin walked into the room and I turned around.

"Am I going to get to see my scores?"

"Yes, I'm going to look them over first and then I'll show you later. For now I want you to go meet your instructor and discuss yours and Nadim's training schedule."

"Okay." We left and I walked into a room and Greg was there. "Greg?"

"I'm going to be your instructor," he said happily.

"That's amazing," I said.

"I'm going to check out your scores and you three can talk." Perin left the room.

It was now just Greg, Nadim and myself.

"Our training will start immediately. I'm going to have a difficult training program for the both of you. Sundays, Tuesdays, Thursdays, and Saturdays we will be doing regular exercises, such as lifting, running, basically anything that will improve body structure and help keep you fit. On Mondays, Wednesdays and Fridays we will be working on your abilities. Coming up with combinations were you two can work together."

"That sounds great," I said.

"Sounds like a walk in the park," said Nadim.

"We will start tomorrow with ability training." Greg walked over to me and whispered in my ear. "I promise you, Aden, in no time you will be one of the strongest people on this island."

"You think?"

"You're going to be our secret weapon against the First."

"Who's the First?" Of course I already knew, but I couldn't let them know that.

"I'll explain some other time."

We did some warm up exercises; Greg wanted to see how much I could lift and how good my stamina was. When Greg had me run my knife fell out of my pant leg. He picked it up.

"What is this?" Greg asked.

"I'm not sure." I didn't know what to say. This is the moment that could put me down.

"It's a knife." Greg unsheathed the blade. "This is very nice. You have no idea where you got it?"

"No, I don't. I don't really remember anything that well, but it could be mine. I couldn't tell you why I'd have it though."

"I believe you." Greg handed it back to me and I put it on the ground and continued the exercises.

After about forty five minutes Perin came into the room holding a folder and waved me over. I picked up my knife and walked over to him.

"Greg, I'm going to take Aden to go see Cyrus and then I'm going to give him a room in this wing. I'll let you know what room later and you can pick him up and start bright and early tomorrow."

"That sounds great," Greg agreed and Perin and I left.

We started walking down the hall and he opened up my folder.

"What is that?" Perin asked.

"It's a knife. It dropped out of my pants during an exercise. I don't really remember it, but I like it, and if it came out of my pants then it's probably mine."

"Oh, makes sense. Just be careful with it," Perin warned.

"You scored better than most on the academic portion of the test. Those questions are left blank by most people."

"That's good right?"

"Oh yes, definitely. As for the situational problems . . ."

"Did I really do that bad?" I asked as my heart pounded. I was nervous that I answered some wrong and was screwed.

"No, you were very inventive about your solutions to the problems presented. I personally thought you did fantastic all around. You are going to be a great addition to my program."

"You scared me for a second. I thought I did badly."

"Don't worry, Aden, you have nothing to worry about. Now let's go test your power." Perin opened a door and there was a man inside of the room.

He was less than average height and had messy looking white hair. "But before we enter, do you realize how many of my men you killed?"

The way he looked at me had my heart racing. It was as if his eyes were staring into my soul. I took a deep breath and tried to keep my cool. "I'm not sure I know what you mean."

"The name Reece Burnbet means absolutely nothing to you?"

"I've never heard it before."

"You're positive?"

"Yes, honestly."

"Okay, then let's get started," he said patting me into the room.

The room was all white, filled only with a desk and a cup of red liquid on it, it had to be blood. The man came over and talked to me.

"Hi. You must be Aden. I'm really excited to meet you," Cyrus said.

"Nice to meet you."

"Now, Greg told me that you created a 'blood net' and saved him from being hit by a car. How did you do that?" he asked.

"I'm not sure. Instinct, I guess. I'm not even sure where all that blood came from," I explained.

"You said you don't remember very much."

"Yeah, I woke up in I was in some house and I was surrounded by blood and dead soldiers."

"Let me explain the situation to you, Aden. You had kidnapped a child from a hospital in Florida and brought him back to West Virginia. The child you kidnapped has the ability to destroy the world if he is not controlled. We found out that you had him and I personally sent some of our soldiers to eliminate you and capture the child. We have the child in custody, thankfully, but it seems that my highly skilled soldiers couldn't kill you. You know what that tells me?" Perin explained.

"What?" I was starting to get worried. Maybe Perin had suspicions about what was going on. Maybe he knew Faxon sent me.

"That tells me that you did know how to use your ability and once you get started I'm sure it will come right back to you. It also tells me that you are amazingly skilled at what you do. You also didn't hesitate to kill any of those men. That doesn't make you a murderer, it makes you a fighter. And that's what I need Aden, a fighter."

I didn't know what to say to him. I just smiled a little bit.

"I'm sorry but I don't remember any of that. No hard feelings?" I asked scared.

"No, none."

"I just want to thank you for the opportunity to be in this program and allowing me to come to this place."

"I think we'll both get what we want out of it."

"Could you remove all of you clothes except for your underwear?" Cyrus asked.

"Excuse me," I said confused.

"You said that you have no idea where that blood came from. I have a theory. Could you please remove your clothes?"

I took off my clothes except for my underwear and Cyrus started looking all over my body. He had a marker in his hand. He was looking very closely at my body. He made two marks on my back, one on my forearm, one on my shin, hand, and shoulder. He then picked up my knife that I had put on the floor.

"Do you cut yourself Aden?" he asked.

"No, why?"

"You have very slight cut marks on your body. They are barely noticeable, and to the untrained eye very easily could be overlooked. They look like they were made over ten years ago, if not more. But for instance the two on your back," Perin and Cyrus went behind me and looked at them. "The two guards blocking the child's door at the hospital said that they saw a man with dark red wings fly out the window. That was a few days ago. If anyone cut themselves the cut would not be healed so quickly. We know that you can move and control blood, but I think that you also heal quickly. I could just be your blood clotting quicker and fixing any wounds before they become fatal, but you recover quicker than others," he theorized as I put my clothes back on. "Now let's test the limits of your ability. Move that cup of blood from the table."

I knew that I wouldn't be able to, so I didn't even bother to try. My power was only to control my blood.

"I can't," I said after making it look like I was trying.

"What do you mean you can't?" he asked.

"I don't know what I'm supposed to do."

"Would it be all right if I cut your shoulder a little?" he asked.

"What! Why?"

"You have many cut marks on your body. I believe that you used your own blood to do things you did. We can test my theory by using your blood."

"Just a small cut; nothing more."

Cyrus picked up my knife and I took my shirt off. He cut my right shoulder and I started to bleed. I figured that I would just pretend to not know how to control it at first and then gradually advance. The blood slid down my bicep and forearm.

"Try and move it or shape it," Perin said.

I pretended to try and nothing happened. The blood just dripped on the floor.

"Come on, just remember what you did to save Greg. Just remember that moment," Cyrus instructed.

I thought about it and the blood slowly moved off of the floor and gently into my hand. I made it move slowly to make it look like I had no idea what I was doing.

"There you go, Aden," they both said.

"Haha, I'm doing it," I said smiling.

"Nice job, now I want you to shape it or just start moving it around," Cyrus said.

"What do you mean?" I asked.

"Just try and gain control over it. Make sure you can move it around and mold it to your liking."

I did what he said, moving the small amount of blood around. Gently moving it from hand to hand and around my body as well.

"Very nice, Aden, you're doing great. Now try molding it."

I moved the blood slowly back to my right hand and shaped it into a sphere. I was just going to do the same thing that I did the first time I practiced my power.

I moved the small ball of blood around in my hand, very smoothly.

"Try and do something else now," Perin said.

I made the spikes gradually push themselves out of the blood ball. I shot it at the desk in front of me, making contact, and sticking into the side. The force caused the cup of blood to be knocked over and spilled. The blood dripped onto the floor and my spiked ball.

"Very nice," Cyrus said.

"Very deadly," Perin said. "I like it."

"Thanks."

"Can you bring the blood back to you?" Cyrus asked.

"I'll try," I replied knowing that I already could.

I pulled the spiked blood ball back to me slowly. I saw the blood on the floor start to move as well. I was startled and confused. I started pulling harder on the spiked blood ball. It came out of the desk at a snail's pace coming at me, but so did the blood on the floor. It made no sense to me. I thought that I could only move my blood. Mid air I combined my blood with the blood from the floor and it formed an even bigger ball. I pulled it back to my hand.

"Very interesting," Cyrus said scratching his face.

I hardened the blood and placed it on the table.

"You are something else, Aden. Do you mind if I run some tests on your blood."

"No, go ahead." Cyrus took some blood from my shoulder with a needle.

"Do you mind if I take this blood ball with me too?" he asked.

"Go ahead."

"I'm going to run some tests and I'll talk to you tomorrow." Cyrus left.

"Nice work today," Perin said tossing me a box of surgical wrapping.

"Thanks."

"You're going to be something very great, Aden. I know it."

"Really?"

"Absolutely, but let's get you to your room so you can make yourself at home."

"Okay."

Perin and I went to my room and it was average; carpet, dresser, bed, closet, and a full bathroom.

"This is where you will be staying while you are here."

"Cool, thanks."

"I'll bring you some clothes tomorrow, anything you want in particular?"

"Pants, some hoodies and anything you have that's red,"

"I get it, red, that's clever," Perin left and I made myself at home.

I thought about my mom the rest of the night. When I tried to leave the room I realized that it was locked. Just like Faxon said, like a prison. There was a keypad on the left of the door but I didn't know what the code was, I didn't even bother with it. I finally just decided to go to bed.

THE NEXT MORNING

A knock on my door awoke me.

"Aden, it's Perin, can I come in?"

"Yeah," I said groggy.

Perin opened the door and he had a bag of clothes in this hand.

"I brought a bunch of stuff. You can just look through it and keep what you want."

"Thanks."

"Hop in the shower and get dressed. We have a meeting with Cyrus and then your training starts today with Nadim and Greg."

"Okay. I'll be out in about twenty minutes."

"Make it ten. I'll be waiting outside."

I jumped into the shower, quickly cleaned myself, and then jumped out. There was a cabinet in the bathroom full of towels. I dried off and rummaged through the bag of clothes that Perin hand brought me. There were shorts, black pants, red jogging pants, black shirts, a red hoodie, red t-shirts, under wear and socks. I put on the black pants and a red shirt with the red hoodie and went over to the door and tried to get out but I couldn't. It wouldn't open.

"Perin I can't get out."

"Oh yeah sorry," the door opened. "The code for the key pad is 4571."

"Thanks," I walked outside of my room and we went to go meet Cyrus outside in some courtyard.

"Aden, how are you?"

"Good."

"Well, I've figured out a few things about what you can do. I ran a lot of tests yesterday."

"And what did you find out?"

"The blood in the cup was type A+, and you have a very unique blood type which I am calling type D, for dominant. I've never seen any blood type like. You can't receive blood from anyone else, but when you pulled that type A+ blood into your blood ball. It over ran it, consuming it like a virus. I tried it on other blood types and your blood consumed them all and they became type D. It is very captivation to watch. I want to test a theory of mine," Cyrus cut himself a little bit. "I want you to take my blood. Don't go crazy, just take a little."

I focused on his hand where he cut himself. The blood started to move. It wasn't easy to do. I began to lift it up and made a small ball the size of a bullet. It left me breathless and lightheaded. It wasn't as easy as controlling my own but still. I was able take blood out of a person's body, not just my own. I no longer had to hurt myself to use my ability. That one idea opened so many doors for my ability.

"Just as I thought, you can control any and all blood, Aden. Now if you could move my blood over to this microscope." Cyrus had a desk set up with a microscope on it along with some supplies. My solidified blood ball was on the table as well.

Cyrus took a drop of his blood and put it under a microscope and had me look at it.

"This is my blood, I'm type O-. Now you see how it looks correct?"

"Yeah."

"Now I'm just going to add a single drop of yours," Cyrus stated while taking a drop of my blood out of a container and dropping it on the slide.

"Now what do you see?"

"My blood is darker and it is completely taking over your blood."

"Just as I told you. Your file said that you couldn't receive any blood from anyone else, but my theory is that you can. There should be no reason that you couldn't. You were hospitalized because your blood had bacteria in it and the doctors didn't want to try mixing your blood with another donor except for your mother and your body accepted her blood. This leads me to believe that you can receive any blood type because you would just make it like your own."

"This is amazing."

"Isn't it? I just wanted to let you know what I had found. And as for your ability, just keep in mind that you have complete control over your blood you should be able to make it do what ever you want."

"Thanks, Cyrus."

"Well, we have to get you to Greg so you can start your training."

Perin and I left Cyrus and I took my ball of solid blood with me. We went to a secluded area where Nadim and Greg were.

"Aden, glad you could make it. We were just about to get started."

"We were in a meeting with Cyrus about his power," Perin explained.

"No big deal."

"He's going to be a great one. Push him to his very limits every day, Greg," Perin said.

"Yes sir," he replied.

"You know the way back to your room. There will be dinner and some snacking food for you when get back to your room," Perin said.

"Okay, thanks."

"See you all later."

"Well, Aden, show me what you got," Greg said.

May 12, 2007

I woke up to an alarm that was going off. I turned and looked at my clock; it was 1:49am. I had no idea what was happening. I didn't want to get carried away over nothing. I got dressed and opened my door. Greg was running down the hall.

"Aden, grab some blood, someone is trying to escape. We have to stop him."

I turned around, pulling one of the ten hardened blood balls, each one the size of a basket ball or bigger, off of my dresser and turned it into its liquid form and had it cover my left arm and part of my back and chest. I started running with Greg.

"So what's the deal?"

"One of the students just broke out of his room and is trying to leave. He broke out from Industrial Dorm Level Three," he explained.

"Does this have anything to do with the break in at the instructors building last night?"

"I believe so. I'm not too sure of the details, but we have to get this guy before he leaves."

"What is the big deal?"

"Um . . . his track record is violent and he has a good ability that could hurt a lot of people."

He didn't even believe what he was saying. I'm sure the kid was just scared and wanted to go home. If I saw him I wasn't going to stop him from getting away. Congrats to him if he actually did.

We continued to run and when we got outside there was a group of soldiers waiting for Greg.

"Everyone fan out and find him now. No kill shots," Greg instructed and everyone dispersed.

"I'm going to go on my own, Greg, if that's okay?"

"Yeah go, I don't want any of these soldiers to slow you down, and I don't want to slow you down either. Just try and find him and call me if you get anything."

I had gotten a lot faster since I got to the islands, and I had only been there for a few days. My training with Greg had greatly improved my strength, speed, and my control over my ability. Every other day pushing me to my very limits, making me want to collapse and give up, but I knew I couldn't. I had to do it for Reece and my mom. I'd never give up, they had no idea that there are making me stronger so that I can steal what they stole from me.

I ran into the woods with soldiers running in every direction. They really wanted the kid badly. I continued to speed through the trees faster than any of the others. I came to a dock and I saw someone. He hopped onto a jet ski. A few soldiers and one of the instructors, Alexander, came behind me.

"Why didn't you stop him?" Alexander asked.

"I was too late, he's already far gone now."

"Maybe for you," Alexander jumped up into the air and stayed suspended for a second. He took a deep breath and flew over the water towards the jet ski. It was too dark to see anything that far away.

It was hours before Alexander returned and it was already morning. I was in Perin's office going over what I had seen for the second time that morning. He was clearly pissed about the situation. Greg had offered to send Nadim and I after him, but Perin hadn't trusted us enough just yet. Alexander was brought into Perin's office by two guards.

"I couldn't catch him. I had him for a second but then he got away. He's probably dead."

"Bullshit, Alexander! He is not dead. Do you even realize how long you've been gone?"

"Sir, I didn't want to give up the search. I found the jet ski, but that was all."

"He is going to find his way home somehow just like the others did. Faxon is helping that boy I know it!" Perin yelled slamming his fist on the desk. "I can't believe what is happening! Every get out! Alexander, I want to see you back here in one hour; and you better have your story straight!"

"Yes sir," everyone left his office. He was actually even more terrifying when he lost his temper. I thought one of the veins on his head was going to burst.

Faxon never said a word about anyone other than Bastian, and he is already home. Perin has no idea what he is talking about. I'd never seen him like that before. It didn't matter I just have to focus on my training.

May 18, 2007

I had found out that that they are keeping Reece somewhere on the Industrial. My ability was growing stronger each and every day. My control hadn't stopped growing since my training with Greg started. Nadim was a really great work out partner. His strength allowed me to test the durability of my blood walls and barriers. They still hadn't been able to stand up against one of his stronger hits. I knew in time I'd be able to take a full barrage from his fists and still be able to hold my wall up.

My training was going great, but sadly I was getting no closer to finding out exactly where Reece was. I wasn't going to forget the real reason I can to the islands. I wouldn't allow myself to get caught up in all the lies they had weaved.

Chapter XX

TRAVIS: RETURN HOME

May 11, 2007

"Mom!" I yelled as I closed the door behind me. "I'm home."

She poked her head out of the kitchen.

"Oh my god, Travis?" She ran at me and gave me a big hug and kissed me on my cheek. "What are you doing here?"

"I've got to tell you something. Let's go into the living room." We walked into the living room and sat down. I took a deep breath. "Okay, Mom. Here it goes. I never joined military. I went to this place for . . . special people." She looked at me kind of funny. I wasn't too sure how she was going to take it. What if she thought I was a freak, what if she was disgusted by my power, I thought. I knew I had to tell her.

"What do you mean *special*?"

"I'll show you, that's the only way you will understand." I put both my hands on the wooden coffee table, turned them clear white, and absorbed the wood. I then held my hands up and showed her. My hands were wooden and so was most of my forearm. I had never absorbed that much before, my power was growing.

She was shocked as she touched my hands.

"They're . . . they're wooden," she said obviously scared.

"I know."

"How . . . did you?" she said examining my hands.

"I have a gift, but I went to the wrong place. I went to these islands that said they could help me with my power. They would help me control it, but I figured out that they were just using me. So I left."

"Are there others like you?"

"Yeah, but I'm the only one who can do this," I said. She seemed overwhelmed. "So what are you thinking?"

"That my son is more amazing than I ever thought he was."

"Really?"

"Yes, Travis. Did you think that I was going to hate you and call you a freak? You're my son and I will always accept you for who you are." I turned my hands back to normal and hugged her.

"Have you told anyone else that you are back?"

"No not yet. I literally just got dropped of by a man who can fly. I'm going to call Amber and let her know."

"Does she know about what you can do?"

"No, you are the first person that I've told."

"You should tell her Travis. You shouldn't have any secrets. I'm positive she will react the same way that I did."

"I'm going to go unpack. I love you," I said stand up and hugged her.

"I love you too."

I went downstairs to my room, put my clothes away, and called Amber. She didn't pick up, I left a voicemail telling her that I was home, I wanted to see her, and to call me back. I laid down in my bed; happy to be home. I felt bad for everyone that was still on the islands. They were being used and didn't ever know it. My eyes got heavy and I fell asleep. I was woken up by Amber's phone call. I picked up my phone.

"Hey Amber."

"Travis I can't believe that you are back. How long are you back for?" she asked.

"Forever. It's a long story and I have so much to tell you."

"Come over, I want to see you now," she said.

I looked up at my clock. It was 12:32pm.

"I'll be right there."

"Okay," she said. "You better be quick."

I hung up and got changed. I grabbed my keys, ran out to my car, and began driving to Amber's house. It felt like years since I had seen my town. Passing all the buildings, the schools, the restaurants just made me happy to be off of that pile of dirt in the middle of the ocean.

Amber was waiting outside when I pulled up. Off the porch she ran at me, jumped on me, and kissed me. I loved her so much. I don't understand how I ever left her. I would never make that mistake again.

We went inside of her house and continued to kiss. She pulled me upstairs to her bedroom. We laid down on the bed and held each other tight. I felt at peace. I could lay with her forever. She rolled on top of me and we kissed. She took her shirt off and I did the same. I moved her off of me then got on top of her. She kicked her blankets off the bed. Our bodies, so close together, were making enough warmth for the both of us.

"I thought you were never going to come back," she said sliding her hand on the side of my face. "Just these few days have been torture. Not seeing you or talking to you was driving me insane."

"I won't ever leave you alone like that again, Amber. I promise."

We continued to kiss slow, soft kisses progressively working up to fast, rough kisses. Amber undid my pants and I took them off while she took off her own.

LATER THAT NIGHT

Amber had insisted on cooking for me. She wasn't a fantastic cook, but her heart was in the right place.

"Damn it," Amber said from the kitchen.

"What's the matter?" I asked walking through the kitchen doorway.

"We are out of chicken and rice," she said sadly. "I was going to make that stir-fry you love."

"No big deal, we can just order out. We'll get some Chinese, watch a movie and then go back to bed," I said and Amber kissed me.

"I like the way you think babe," she kissed me again then walked over to the cabinet a grabbing a menu.

THE NEXT MORNING

I opened my eyes, rolled over and stared at Amber. Her dark red hair draped over one side of her face, with every breath slightly pushing her hair away from her nose. She laid her head on top of both of her hands. She was so beautiful, just laying there sleeping. She was perfect. Sure we had our differences and we fought sometimes, but there was nothing that would make me stop loving her. Her eyes slowly opened, blinking a few times before fully opening.

"Good morning," she said gazing into my eyes. "Were you watching me sleep again?"

"You're just so beautiful, I couldn't help myself," she kissed me and hugged me.

"I'm so glad that you're back."

"I'm sorry I left."

We heard a car door slam. Amber sat up and looked out her window.

"Shit. My parents are home, get dressed quick," she said jumping out of bed and throwing me my pants.

I caught my pants and tossed Amber her tank top. We finished getting dressed and ran into the bathroom. This had happened a few times before. I would just sneak out the bathroom window; climb down the side of her house, run to the store and grab something; go back to her house and say that I was picking up something for her. Except this time is going to be a little harder seeing as how my car was parked in front of her house.

I climbed out the window, down the side of her house, and then called Amber from my cell phone.

"What do you want me to do? My car is out front. Your parents already know that I'm here."

"Just come in through the front. I don't care. Just say you drove here and your mom picked you up for something and then dropped you off again."

"Okay, see you in a minute."

I ran to the front of the house and knocked on the door. Her dad opened the door.

"Travis, I thought that was your car. Amber had said you joined the army," he said waving me inside.

"I did, but then they said that they didn't need so many of people so they let a lot of us go and I was one of them."

"That's interesting. I've never heard anything like that happening before. How come your car is out front?"

"I drove here and my mom picked me up. We went to go see my aunt and then I just walked over."

"Oh, how is your mother these days? Doing well I hope?"

"Yeah she's great, especially now that I'm back."

"I can imagine that she was getting lonely in that big house of yours. Well I'm not to sure where Amber is, but you can make yourself at home as usual."

"Thanks, Mr. Fenton."

I ran upstairs and went into Amber's room. Then my phone rang. It was my mom.

"Honey can you come home? There is a little girl outside waiting for you."

"What do you mean?"

"It's just some little girl. She looks very young. She says you know her. She said her name was Amity."

"What did she say?"

"She asked if you were here and I told her no. Then she asked me to call you and have you come home so I did."

"Mom I'll be right there. Do not let her in."

"Um . . . okay."

I hung up the phone and ran over to the bathroom and Amber walked out.

"I have to go, but I will be back and then I will explain everything. There is still something that I have to show you."

"Okay, is something wrong?"

"I hope not."

I ran downstairs, out to my car, and drove home speeding. Could someone from the islands already be after me, I asked myself. I got home and there was no one outside. I ran inside and my mom was in the living room.

"Are you okay?"

"Yes, I'm fine."

"Where did the girl go?"

"If she's not out there then I'm not sure. She asked for you and when I told her you weren't home she said she would wait."

"Was anyone with her?"

"No . . . what's going on?"

"Nothing, I hope. I'm just being paranoid. I'm going back to Amber's. Don't let anyone in. If anyone asks where I am tell them I'm at work, okay?"

"Okay. Are you sure nothing is wrong?"

"Yes."

I left and called Amber. I told her that we should go to a park then get something to eat. She just had to take a shower first. When I got to her house she was waiting outside. She got into the car, put her hand on my lap, and we started driving. I parked the car at the park and we got out. We went and sat down and stared at the lake in the middle of the park.

"So what did you want to tell me?" she asked.

"Well . . . um . . . I never joined the military. I went to a place that helped people like me."

"What do you mean 'people like you'?"

"Don't freak out, but I can show you." I sat up and held out my hand. She took my hand and I walked her over to the lake. I put my hand into the water and absorbed it. I took my hand out and held it up so she could see it. She looked frightened, then touched my hand quickly, pulled it away, and touched it again. This time she didn't pull it away. She ran her hand through mine.

" . . . How?"

"I'm not too sure really. I just touch something, focus, and then I can absorb it."

"Oh," she said still running her hand through mine. "Can you feel my hand in yours?"

"Yeah. It's kind of a feeling that I can't describe."

"So, where did you go?"

"To a group of islands, but it wasn't what it seemed. They were actually holding everyone with powers so that they could be away from everyone else. They wanted them to be locked up."

"How did you get out?"

"Someone helped me, he can fly. I escaped on a jet ski, but he came and flew me home."

"Wow, I don't even know what to say."

"Maybe that you still love me, that you're not scared of me."

"Travis, I'm not scared. I still love you. This only makes you more special to me. How many girls out there can say that they have a boyfriend with a superpower?"

"True," I turned my hand back to normal and kissed her.

We sat back down and stared at the lake. Everything was quiet and perfect. We sat there holding each other. I couldn't have been happier.

"Travis, what are you doing back home. You have barely started you're training," a voice said from behind me.

My heart stopped, I knew that it was someone from the islands. I stood up and turned around. I pulled Amber up with me and stood in front of her. It was a young looking girl.

"So what do you want?" I asked.

"Travis, you already know the answer to that question. Just come back and everything will be fine. If you don't then there will be severe repercussions," she said.

"Are you threatening me?"

"Who is she, Travis?" Amber asked.

"I'm not sure, but I know she is here for me."

"What do you think, you escaped the islands, you know some of our secrets, and you had accomplices that need to be punished. Of course I'm threatening you."

"Tell Perin that I'm not coming back, ever!"

"That's not what I want to hear, Travis." She began to walk towards us.

"Stay away from us," I said backing up.

She darted at me and grabbed my wrists and glaring into my eyes.

"You will come back to the islands with me, RIGHT NOW!" she yelled.

I felt an odd sensation throughout my body. Her eyes began to emit a light blue glow. I pulled my arms out of her grip and knocked her to the ground.

"WHAT! That's not possible you should be under my control, there is no way you could resist me."

"What are you talking about?"

She stood up and pulled out a knife out from behind her back.

"Then we'll have to do things the hard way."

I bent down touching the grass absorbing it. I held my hand out and waited for her to get close enough to attack, but my fingers acted on their own stretching out wanting to attack her. They were flimsy, but I gained control and began whipping her. She fell to the ground again and I drew my fingers back.

"You will return to the islands with me. If you don't, everyone you love will die."

"I swear on my life if you hurt anyone, I will kill you with my bare hands."

"You couldn't even handle one of us, let alone a whole army. You wouldn't last a second, and your powers are too weak. This is your last chance. Come back to the islands with me."

"Never."

"Fine, have it your way," she closed her eyes. I could see a dark blue light appearing around them. She opened her eyes and they were illuminating.

"Come here girl," she said.

I turned around to see that Amber's eyes were glowing as well, and she started walking over to her.

"Amber, what are you doing? Stop," I said.

She wouldn't stop. She was under control.

"What are you doing to her?"

"She is mine, if you don't return to the islands with me I'll kill her."

"NO YOU WON'T," I stretched out my fingers again and lashing her countless times, holding my wrist while doing so. I bent down and absorbed the grass with my other hand as well and began violently whipping with all ten fingers. Amber continued to go toward the girl, stopping right in front of her, blocking her from my attacks.

The girl collapsed to the ground and the light from her eyes faded away, so did Amber's. Amity dropped to her knees and her eyes closed. I turned my hands back to normal picking Amber up and running to my car. Amity wasn't getting back up; I thought she was unconscious. I drove out of the park and soon after Amber opened her eyes.

"What happened?" she asked.

"Are you okay?"

"Yeah I think, but the last thing that I remember is seeing a white light."

"That girl used some kind of power to take control of your mind."

"What?"

"I'm sorry I got you into this mess, we're just going to go home."

"NO! Its fine I'm hungry, let's get something to eat."

"Amber we have to get to somewhere safe," I said confused.

"It was one little girl, it would take her forever to find us, let's just get something to eat."

"Alright, we can stop at the next restaurant."

We drove to the nearest diner. I pulled over and we got out of the car.

"This looks like a nice place," she said.

"Yeah. We came here that night your car broke down, remember?"

"Of course, Travis."

We walked inside and sat down. There weren't very many people in the diner. A woman came over, gave us menus, and asked us what we wanted to drink. We both got a soda.

"What are you going to get?" Amber asked.

"The lumberjack breakfast, what about you?"

"The two sunny side up eggs with hash."

The waitress came back with our drinks. We told her what we wanted and she took our menus.

"I'm sorry about what happened back at the park; I promise that I won't let anything bad happen to you."

"Travis, it's fine. I know that you would never let anything happen to me." She got up from the table and said, "I'm going to the bathroom; I'll be right back."

I waited for ten minutes and she still wasn't back yet. The waitress brought us our food. Amber was still not back from the bathroom. I got up out of my seat and walked over to the ladies room. I knocked on the door. There was no response. I knocked again.

"Amber are you still in there?" I knocked one last time. I grabbed the doorknob and opened the door slowly. "Amber?" The first thing I saw was the sink, covered in smears of blood. My heart stopped for that split second. I swung open the door and saw Amber collapsed on the floor surrounded in blood. I screamed for help.

"CALL 911. SOMEONE PLEASE!!!!" I screamed as tears fell down my face. I ran to Amber sitting her up. The blood was coming from her wrists. I quickly ripped the sleeves off of my shirt and wrapped them around them. A waitress ran in and screamed for help. She ran back out to call 911. I held Amber tight talking to her, telling her it was going to be okay. She was unresponsive.

"Amber please, baby. Don't, please. Come on say something, say anything. Don't do this." My tears covered my face. I had to keep clearing my eyes just so I could see her face. I sat on the floor surrounded in her blood. She was my life, she was my everything. She would have never done this to herself. It was them. I knew it had to be. I could hear sirens coming closer and closer. After a few minutes two EMTs came into the diner and into the bathroom door with a stretcher.

"Sir, we need to get to the body. Please let her go and step out of the room. I know this is a hard time, but I need you to cooperate. Can you hear me sir?" the dark skinned EMT asked. I tried to respond, but I couldn't. I just sat there holding her.

"Get him off her," the other EMT said.

"Sir, we need to get you out of here. I'm going to pick you up and bring you outside. They both walked over to me, her blood splashed under her shoes. They gently pulled me away from her cold body and picked me up. I stood outside of the bathroom.

I watched as they checked her pulse. One of them shook his head. Everything was moving in slow motion. I watched people's mouths move, but I couldn't hear them speak. I was in shock. I backed away, it felt like my entire life ended, there was no reason left for me to live; they killed her. Tears still pouring from my eyes, everyone in the diner was staring at me and my blood covered clothes. The waitress came over to me and said something, but still I couldn't hear. I moved her out of the way and went back over to the bathroom. The paramedics both picked up her body putting her on the stretcher covering it with a white sheet and wheeled her away outside to the ambulance. Two police officers walked in and started asking everyone questions. All I did was stand alone in shock.

So many things raced through my mind: I caused this to happen; it is my fault that she's dead. If I had only agreed to go back she would still be alive, but how did they get to her, I was sitting right by the door no one came inside. It had to be someone from inside the diner. I began looking around for anyone who looked suspicious.

The two police officers came over to me.

"Sir, I'm going to ask you to come with us. We have a few questions to ask you," one of them said.

I didn't respond. I heard what they said, but I just didn't care. They wouldn't find the killer. It was up to me.

"Sir, you're coming with us," the other cop said and grabbed my arm.

I looked down at the officer's hand around my arm and yelled, "Don't touch me." I ripped my hand away from the officer's arm. My hearing had returned. The noise in the diner overwhelmed me.

They both grabbed me. I knew I could get away, but I controlled myself and just did what they asked.

Chapter XXI

TRAVIS: AMBER'S FUNERAL

May 12, 2007

In the back of the cop car I sat knowing it all was a waste of time. I decided not to say anything. I figured it would have been easier that way. We arrived at the police station and the cops let me out of the car. They didn't handcuff me, but did walk me inside and put me in a room. It was the kind of room you saw on television with the single table and chair and the two way glass mirror that the cops could see from. I knew the two cops were watching me from behind the glass. It was about ten minutes before they came in. They sat down and shuffled though a few pieces of paper.

"Can I call you, Travis?" The balding cop asked.

"Yeah."

"Okay, Travis, so you came in with the girl."

"Her name is Amber."

"So you did?" the other cop questioned.

"Yes, we were out on a date."

"Was she your girlfriend?"

"Yes."

"How was your relationship with Amber?"

"It was great. We were in love."

"People do a lot of crazy things when they're in love."

"What are you trying to say?" I asked giving him an angry tone.

"I just want to know why you killed her." I immediately shot up out of the chair.

"I DIDN'T KILL HER!!! How dare you assume that! I loved her." The officer stood up and got in my face.

"You were the only person who went near that bathroom after she got up. The waitress found you and the girl in the bathroom covered in blood!" he screamed.

"I would never do that to her! I WOULD NEVER HURT HER!" It took every once of my being to fight back the urge to absorb the table and beat the bastard to a bloody pulp.

The other officer pushed us away from each other telling us both to calm down. He took out a bloody knife that was in a plastic bag and tossed it on the table.

"Have you ever seen this knife before?" he asked.

It was the knife that Amity had; the knife she tried to kill me with. How did Amber get it, I questioned.

"So you have seen this knife?" the cop asked.

"Yes, but I can't remember where."

"It's a very unique knife, high quality steel, fancy markings, sharp blade, and a heavy duty hilt. Probably very expensive," the cop added.

"I'm sorry I don't recall."

"Is it yours?" the other one asked.

"No, I don't own any weapons."

The cop put the knife away. Another cop came into the room.

"Ruby, Kovlin, you're gunna wanna see this."

"We'll be right back."

The two cops left the room. Twenty minutes passed then a detective came in the room. He walked into the room with a television and a VCR.

"Travis, I'm detective Jones. I'd like to show you some of the tapes from the diner, if that's okay." I nodded my head and he put in a tape. "This is one of the tapes from the diner," the detective explained.

It was a tape of the front door. Amber and I walked into the diner and sat down. They fast forwarded it to when Amber left and continued to fast forward until I got up out of my seat to check on her.

"No one came into the diner after you and you never got up from your seat," he said.

"Okay?"

"I'm going to show you another tape," he said taking out one tape and putting in another.

It was a tape of the kitchen. You could see the bathroom door perfectly. They fast-forwarded it to when Amber went into the bathroom. He kept fast-forwarding it to when I went to the bathroom. I stopped at the door and knocked. Then waited a few seconds and opened the door slowly. You could see me yell for help. I never closed the bathroom door; Amber's hand was visible already on the floor surrounded by blood. Seconds later the waitress came by.

"No one went into the bathroom after she did."

"Okay, so what are you saying?" I asked.

"It's obvious that you didn't kill her. There just wasn't enough time. The amount of blood at the scene would've taken at least a few minutes to leave her body. She was dead before your first knock. Did Amber seem like the person who would take her own life?" he asked sincerely.

"That's ridiculous, Amber would never do that," I answered.

"I hate to say it but that looks like what happened," he said. "Suicide . . ."

"No, she would never do that! Someone had to be waiting inside the bathroom when she went in."

"You were the first person in the room, you would have seen them. She was in there alone. There was no other way to get into the bathroom except for that door.

"She didn't kill herself, someone killed her. I know it."

"I'm sorry son, but we have all the evidence we need to conclude that she killed herself, you can go home now."

The two cops walked into the room and the escorted me to the lobby.

"We towed your car here, it's out back," the cop said.

I began to walk out of the station when I saw Amber's parents. Her mom was leaning up against her father crying uncontrollably. I walked over to her father to tell him what had happened.

"Mr. Fenton . . .,"

"Travis," he said.

From the look on his face he was devastated. His face was lifeless and so were the words he spoke. Mrs. Fenton was weeping painfully. They were both taking her death hard, but just dealing with it in their own way.

"I'm sorry; I never wanted this to happen."

"It's not your fault, you didn't kill her."

"Mr. Fenton, Amber would never do that to herself, someone killed her I know it, I'm going to find out who did it. I'll make this right."

"Travis, I don't know what to tell you. I know you loved her, but all the evidence points to suicide."

"I know but . . ."

The police waved Mr. and Mrs. Fenton over to another room.

"I'll talk to you later, good bye," he said.

"Bye."

I walked outside and got into my car. I put my hands over my face and began to cry.

"It is my fault that she is dead," I said punching my car.

I wiped my eyes, got into my car, and started it. As I was driving I thought about what had happened. What if Amber was still under control? What if that little girl told her to kill herself? That had to be it. That's how they found Amity's knife with Amber's body. She must have given it to her and told her to wait and then kill herself. She was in control of her the entire time.

When I got home and told my mom what happened. She cried and said how sorry she was. I told her that I was going out and have anyone call my cell. I drove to our school and climbed on top of it. Amber and I always went there to star gaze at night. I stood on top of the school and bawled my heart out. The only thing I could think about was her. She was everywhere. All of my memories were full of her and us. My phone rang, it was Amber's parents. I picked up the phone and wiped my eyes.

"Travis, this is Mr. Fenton. We found a note in Amber's room."

"What did it say?"

"It says that she is sorry for what she was going to do. She couldn't handle the pressure of life and didn't want to live any more."

"No . . . she . . . she couldn't have written that, she was happy. We were happy."

"It's her hand writing."

I hung up the phone and screamed as loud as I could. It was the islands, they were doing everything they could to cover their tracks. I knew what I had to do. I had to gain complete control of my power and take them down.

THE DAY OF THE FUNERAL

May 19, 2007

It was a beautiful day. The sun was shining bright. I still couldn't believe she was gone. Amber's family, her friends, everyone she knew gathered for the funeral. There were at least two hundred people there. I stood alone; I hadn't seen anyone in days. This was the first time that I saw any of my friends since before I left. After Amber died everyone tried to call me and wanted to hang out, to comfort me. They wanted to make sure that I was okay. The only thing on my mind were the islands, I had to stop them. I wouldn't let Amber's death be in vain. That's all I cared about, revenge. They began to lower Amber's coffin into the grave. Everyone started crying.

I saw someone walking towards them. Their clothes looked dirty and skin discolored. The person came closer and you could see marks over its body. There were cuts and dead rotted skin covering him. The person was dead. It was moving slow and sluggish with its arms at its side. There was more that followed behind the first one. Someone in the crowd screamed "ZOMBIES!" Everyone turned around and then scattered.

I stayed behind and waited. I put my hand on Amber's gravestone and absorbed the concrete. They began to get closer to everyone and pick up speed.

"Travis, lets go, what are you doing?" one of my friends yelled.

"Get out of here, just go!" I yelled back.

I ran at the group of zombies and started punching them in the heads. Blood splattered everywhere. More of them continued to come, there were about seven of them now. I kept punching them in the head. It was the islands again. They wouldn't leave me alone. They wouldn't take no for and answer.

I backed up and put my other hand on a gravestone and absorbed the concrete. There were even more of them now. I kept punching the zombies and I pushed them back further away from me. The concrete spread up my arms and almost to my elbows. I could feel my face harden, as well as my chest. They weren't concrete though, but I knew they were close to turning. I felt stronger. My power was advancing. I smiled and charged at the zombies. Suddenly, they all shot into the ground, every single one leaving behind pillars of dust and dirt. As if something grabbed them and ripped them into the ground. After it cleared I saw a woman holding a shovel. Her black hair was slightly covered in dirt. She was very attractive, but I wasn't going to let that deceive me. She had to be from the islands. She looked at my hands and I returned them to normal.

"Who are you?" she yelled.

"Who are you?" I yelled back.

"You have a power," she began to approach me.

"Are you from the islands?" I asked as she got closer. "I'm not going back!"

"Neither am I," she said and held her hand out. "My name is Stel."

Chapter XXII

Travis: Stel, a New Friend

May 19, 2007

"My name is Travis," I took her hand and shook it.

"It's nice to meet you," Stel said.

"Who are you exactly?" I asked. "When I said I'm not going back you said me neither."

"Yes I did. I can only assume that you were once on the islands."

"Yeah not that long ago, what about you?"

"It's been about four years since I escaped from there. Did you escape as well?" she asked.

"Yeah, one of the instructors flew me home." We started walking through the graveyard.

"I remember Alexander, I never expected him to help anyone."

"He said he was working with a man named Faxon to take down the islands."

"I'm not surprised; Faxon has at least a dozen or more people working for him on the islands."

"Who is this guy, I know nothing about him, but I keep hearing his name."

"I'm sure he will contact you soon, you escaped from the islands. He's going to be interested in you."

"What?"

"Just don't worry about it, just live your life, be happy you're free."

"I'll never be free, they killed my girlfriend, and I'm not going to stop until I destroy all of them."

"Good luck, you'll never be able to take them down alone."

"That's not going to stop me from trying."

"I understand how you feel, they killed my husband."

"I don't mean to be rude, but can I ask how?"

"My power killed him; they made me use it on him as an experiment."

"What's your power? Reanimating the dead?"

"Oh no."

"Then what was that about?"

"That was Lael, she is an islander. She's been after me for some time. I keep moving from city to city, but I still can't lose her."

"How have you not defeated her yet?"

"She usually doesn't show her face. She sends a few undead at me just so I know she's watching. I pack up and then she's finds me and we do it over and over again. But I think this time is different. Two escapees in one location, those are some pretty slim odds."

"Well, why did you come here?"

"I received a call from . . ." she paused. "That damn bastard," she laughed.

"What's so funny?"

"He told me I should go back home. It'd be nice to see the old place again."

"Who?"

"Faxon. He must have figured we'd meet up eventually if I moved back here."

"I don't understand. Can this guy see the future or something?"

"No. Something like that though. This must be all part of his plan."

"When people start talking about this guy I get so lost."

"Let's just drop his subject for now. To answer your previous question I can upgrade things."

"What do you mean?"

"For example, this shovel, a shovel is used to dig and burry things, correct?"

"Yeah."

"Well my power is to advance or upgrade what it does, that's how I buried all of those zombies. I touched my shovel to the ground and concentrated and buried them."

"That's amazing."

"So what's your power? You can cover your body in stone?"

"I absorb and turn into anything. I take their attributes and become what I touch. I'll show you," I turned my hand clear white and touched the ground and absorbed the grass. I held my hand out and showed her. She grabbed my hand like Amber did. My hand turned back to normal, I felt sick. "Sorry, you just reminded me of my girlfriend. She did the same thing when I showed her my power."

"Sorry."

"It's fine."

"I hate to ask, but how did it happen?"

"Some girl from the islands took control of her and made her kill herself. Then they covered it up as a suicide. They planted a note in her room saying that she was going to kill herself."

"Amity, she is very dangerous," Stel explained. "She has the power of mind control. She arrived not to long before I escaped the islands. She took control of one of the instructor's mind and used him to get things for her. When the instructor was confronted she lost control and he went berserk. Zane quickly stopped him though, and she was put into confinement before I left. Zane was praised for his fantastic work. He was easily one of the top prisioners when I was on the islands."

"Yeah, I met him once," I told her. "So what did you do on the islands?"

"I was a security head captain and so was my husband, Chris. Well, that what we were sent there as."

"Oh, why did you leave?"

"Thanks to Faxon my husband and I learned what the islands were really up to. They hired us straight out of the military. They told us that they had a very high profile job that required strict rules and security. We took the job and they flew us to these islands and told us that we were to help kids learn how to use their powers. We weren't to sure what they were talking about until we got to the islands and saw people doing amazing things. Shortly after we arrived my husband and I developed powers. They had only seen a few cases of a severely dormant power. They studied our powers and helped us control them. Then Faxon developed a power as well. Some of them thought that we hadn't had these powers until we got to the islands. After a year, I had fully controlled my abilities, but my husband was still developing his. They studied the three of us; my husband was the weakest least developed one. He could make things cold. The scientists thought that he could possibly develop his power and someday freeze things. They decided to experiment with my power and have me try and upgrade him and advance his power quicker. When I refused they got upset and forced me to do it. After I used my power his skin turned blue and froze. He became an ice statue and shattered. I couldn't believe what I saw, or what I had just done. It was exactly what I feared. They had me try a few more times, against my will obviously. If I could upgrade a persons power then they would not need to spend so much time training there prisoners. Shortly after that, Faxon told me what was really going on and we both escaped from the islands."

"I'm . . . I'm sorry for what happened to your husband. That place crosses the line on too many levels."

"You're telling me."

We walked around the graveyard and ended up back at Amber's gravestone. There was a girl sitting on one of the near by gravestones. At first I thought it was Amity. I almost lost my mind.

"Who are you?" I yelled.

The girl came off and held out her hands. Her hands turned a darker shade and then cracked open and a black smoke emerged from them.

"It's her," Stel said.

The ground began to shake and split open as zombies crawled out of the fissures.

"This is just too perfect. Two of the Projects fugitives in one place. I'm going to be made a head for bringing you both back," the young girl said.

"In your dreams. You're not taking either of us," Stel said.

"Then have it your way." The girl held out her hands and more black smoke came out.

The ground cracked even more and zombies continued to crawl out, and then began to come toward us. Stel slammed her shovel on the ground and the undead shot back into the earth. The crevices closed and the little girl took off running. I started to run after her.

"Travis, no," Stel instructed, "There's no point in chasing her."

"Why?"

"She always gets away. There's a good chance it is a trap anyway. Come on let's go back to my place. We can keep talking there."

Chapter XXIII

GABE: NOT THE ONLY ONE

March, 1997

I ran outside with my toys in hand. I had a couple action figures that I was going to play war with; the dinosaurs versus the X-men. The evil dinosaurs were trying to take over the Earth and the X-men were going to stop them. I was fighting with the toys and then I went to go pick up a triceratops. When I touched it, it grew. It was originally about the size of a television remote, and then after I touched it, it was about the size of a lunch box. I was intrigued with what I had done. So I touched it again, but nothing happened. I tried to focus on returning it to its normal size. I put my hand back on it and it started to shrink. I watched as the triceratops got smaller, returning to it original size. I ran inside to tell my dad. He was sitting at his desk working on something.

"Dad, guess what? Guess what I did?" I asked.

"Not now, son. I'm working on something really important. I don't have time for anything else right now. Sorry," he responded.

"But Dad, I'm like the X-men. I have a superpower!"

He turned around and stared at me.

"What are you talking about?"

"I made one of my toys get bigger and then I shrunk it back to normal."

"Come on, I want you to show me," he stood up out of his chair and brought me in the living room. He then went into the kitchen, into one of the cabinets, and grabbed a toothpick and handed it to me.

"Okay, if you can do what you say you can, then you should be able to make this toothpick bigger. So try it," he instructed.

I took the toothpick and focused and tried to imagine it getting bigger. I tried so hard but the toothpick was staying the same size. My dad looked disappointed. I concentrated really hard and shut my eyes. I kept seeing it getting bigger. I tried to remember the way that I was feeling when I was outside. I opened my eyes again and the toothpick was still the same size. My dad was very disappointed; I could see it in his face.

"I'm sure it was just your imagination, son. If anything like this happens again I want you to come to me right away, okay?" he said with concern in his voice.

"Sorry, Dad. I bothered you when you were working."

"It's fine; just tell me if anything like this ever happens again."

"Okay," I said in a depressed tone.

I sat down on the couch and he went back into his office. I walked over to the door putting my ear to it and I heard him talk to someone. I didn't want to knock because I would interrupt him again.

"I'm not sure; he was one of the possibilities."

There was a pause.

"Yes, I know, but I think that he is telling the truth. He may have just been nervous. He gets really sad when he does something wrong and I'm around him. Let's just give him some time. I'm sure that he just needs to grow up a little more before he can actually control his power. He is only eight years old."

Long pause.

"Okay, I'll talk to you then, Good bye."

I ran down the hallway and back onto the couch. I wasn't sure what he was talking about, but I think he was talking about me. I was scared. Maybe he was going to ship me off to some strange place and they were going to do weird experiments on me. He would have never done that. He was my father and he would never hurt me. I won't try to make anything bigger, I thought.

My dad walked into the room and sat down on the couch next to me.

"Son, I believe that you are a very special. I want you to know that if you can do the things that you say you can, I won't love you any less. To be honest, I might actually be very happy if you could do those things. I think that it would be cool, but no matter what I will love you."

"Really?"

"Yes, Gabe. You're my son. I wouldn't see you any differently."

"Okay, dad. I love you."

"I love you too."

7 YEARS LATER

Over the years, I learned to focus my ability. I was eleven when I actually learned how to have good control over it. I could make things grow whenever I wanted just by touching them and thinking about them getting bigger. My dad died when I was 13; it was two years ago. He was so happy when I figured out how to control my ability. He said that I was going to do great things; that I was special. He wanted me to be the one that put an end to everything. I never understood what he meant, but I really didn't care. He signed me up for gymnastics when I was ten. My dad and mom both said that it would give me an advantage against people. It would teach me how to be flexible and agile as well as increase my strength. I went to the classes and I actually liked it. I learned how to do summersaults, flips, handsprings and I became really good at using my legs.

My dad told me that I should always carry something that I could use to enlarge. Something that I could keep concealed and would not be dangerous in a small size. I thought about it for weeks. I wanted to find a sword or something, but I couldn't find anything like that. Then my dad died. I was depressed for weeks. I kept thinking about all the stuff we did together. I remembered the first time I told him that I had a superpower; he handed me a toothpick. That's when I decided I was going to use toothpicks. They are small and when enlarged they would be very dangerous. I could enlarge a toothpick and add stuff to it; carve it so that it would be easier to hold and use.

I made a belt with toothpicks all around it. I could carry several at one time, giving me an advantage in battle. In my opinion, it was the perfect weapon. I made one special toothpick that I carved so that I could hold it better and it had a small shard of steel on the side of it so that it could cut. I also shaved it so it would be lighter. I practiced using it every day. I named it the Angel. That's what my father used to call me when I was a kid; I was his "little angel". It helped me deal with not having my father around.

One day at school, we had a Code Gray. That meant there was an intruder in the building. I saw it as a perfect time for me to use my ability and be a hero. I ran out of my classroom and went looking for the intruder. In minutes the school was evacuated and everyone was sent home, but they never found the intruder. The next day at school, during lunch, a man walked into the building. He pulled out two shotguns and shot at the cops standing at the doors. There were two kids that locked the exits of the cafeteria so none of us at lunch could escape. It was a gang and they wanted to kill one of the students because of some drug deal or something. I heard rumors before, but I thought they were just rumors. I knew what I had to do. Everyone was piled up next to the exit trying to get out. I ran into the crowd and took out my toothpick, the Angel. I was inside the group and I could see the man with the shotguns approaching us. I could hear some adults banging against the doors behind him trying to get in, but they were locked by the chains.

I couldn't hesitate for a second. If I did, then it would cost so many people their lives. He was laughing but what he didn't know was that I was about to kill him. He was really close to the group so I pushed everyone out of the way and moved to the front. I enlarged the Angel and from a distance stabbed him right in the stomach. He looked down at the wound as I shrunk the toothpick. He fell forward smashing his chin on the floor. I ran at him and kicked the guns out of his hand. His blood poured onto the cafeteria floor and the group of students screamed in fright. One of the teachers opened the doors with a bolt cutter that the intruder locked. They stopped right as they entered the cafeteria. They saw the intruder on the floor surrounded by a puddle of blood.

The police came and saw me standing next to the body with a bloody toothpick in my hand. They threw handcuffs on me and dragged me away to the police station. I kept yelling at them that I didn't do anything wrong, but they just ignored me. I was waiting in the station for hours until they actually brought me into one of the rooms for questioning, then I was sitting down for about a half an hour before the detective came in. He sat down at the table with me.

"My name is detective Reads," he said.

"I didn't do anything wrong! I saved all those students!" I yelled.

"I know what you did. I got the surveillance tape from the lunch room thanks to your principal."

"What did you see?"

"Something rather extraordinary and confusing at the same time. I saw you, Gabe. I saw you stabbing the intruder with some type of weapon that appeared out of nowhere and then from what it looked like, it shrunk back into nothing."

"I don't know what you're talking about. How could I do that?"

"Because you have a gift, just like me."

"What?"

"I can do something extraordinary too. I can see things that can only be seen through an ultraviolet light. I know that it's not as destructive or cool as what you can do, but it's still a gift and I like it."

"So you're like me, I'm not the only one."

"No you're not. Gabe, you have to be more secretive about what you can do. You have to be more careful. Who knows what kind of place you could get put into? If someone found out about your gift you could get locked away or something. I'm going to dispose of this tape. I can't have anyone else see it." He smashed the tape on the ground.

"Why do you care so much about me? You don't even know me."

"Because you're just a kid with so much potential. With a gift like yours, you could do so much good and we have to look out for our kind. Now come on, I'll give you a ride home."

"Okay. Thanks."

We left the police station and went to my house.

"Please, just be careful with your gift. I don't want to have to see you again for the same reason. Don't get me wrong, you did the right thing by saving everyone, but you need to be more careful about it. Take my card, give me a call if you ever want to talk, okay?" He handed me a business card out from his wallet.

"Thanks, detective, I really appreciate it. I will give you a call sometime. Thanks again for everything," I got out of the car. "See you around?"

"I'm sure you will." Then he drove off.

He was right; I had to be more careful. I needed learn how to use my power in more of a stealthy way. I didn't want to be shipped off to some prison were they put people with gifts and call us freaks. I had to learn to live with my power just like Detective Reads.

Chapter XXIV

ZANE: MORE THAN A GAME

July 13, 2001

"My dad was never home, he was in the coast guard. He was always stationed on some ship hundreds of miles away. I hardly ever saw him. It was hard growing up without a dad, but I did it. I got to see him about one entire month out of the entire year, if that. The worst part was when he was home, he always had other things to do. He wanted to spend time with his old buddies rather than his own son. At least, that's the way it seemed. My mom said he had a hard time seeing me because it upset him so much that he had to leave.

When I was about six years old he tried to teach me how to play chess. That's all he did on the ship he was on. It was the best way to pass the time and it helped stimulate the mind. That's all he ever talked about. He wanted me to be the best chess player ever. I didn't care about it at all. The only reason I played was to get some attention from him.

A few years later, I wanted to go fishing when he came up for a few days. He kept pushing it off to the next day when finally he had only one day left. He kept trying to get me to play chess. He had the board set up on the table ready for me to play him. I pushed the board off of the table and stormed up to my room. I didn't talk to him for the rest of the time he was home. He came up to my room and said that he was sorry and he was leaving. He said he loved me and we would go fishing the next time he came back. I didn't say anything to him; just ignored him.

Two weeks later, my dad died. Something happened when he was out at sea and the sub sprang and leak and sunk to the bottom of the sea. I never got the chance to apologize for the way I acted. I never got to tell him I loved him one last time. After his death, I became depressed. I didn't make any friends and I didn't want to get close to anyone because the pain of being alone was better than the pain of loss. My mom was so worried about me all the time. I went just about everyday to talk to a counselor like you. It helped a little bit, but he could never understand the pain that I was going through.

Three years had passed and my mom still worried. I kept telling her that I was okay. There really wasn't anything wrong with me; I just didn't want any friends. My life was fine up until the day that my mom asked me to clean out the garage for a tag sale she was going to have. We just had so much crap in there she wanted to get rid of. I was almost done and there were just two more boxes left. I was going to leave them, but I decided not to. My life would have been so different if I just hadn't reached for that box. When I reached for it, the box fell and everything spilled out. I started picking stuff up. Then I saw it: my dad's favorite chessboard. My heart stopped. I walked over to it and picked it up. There was a white pawn missing, I looked around for it, and found it next to the lawn mower. I put the board on a shelf and went to go pick up the piece. I grabbed it, squeezed it in my hand, and I began to cry; my tears falling onto my hand and the floor. All I could think about was him; all the time I hadn't seen him, all the reasons that I hated him, all the reasons I loved him, and all the reasons I missed him.

I slammed the chess piece on the ground, except it didn't smash. The floor swallowed it. I looked at my hand and it was surrounded by a swirl of blue, purple and white light. I looked down at the floor and it started to shake. A circle appeared in the same colors as my hand. I slowly backed away from it and my hand slowly changed back to normal. Something started to spawn from the circle. It had a round top and as it continued to emerge it began to look more like a pawn. It was fully out of the circle and it was a glowing white pawn. It was huge, nearly eight-feet tall; it barely fit inside of my garage. I didn't want it to be there. If my mom came home and saw it she would flip. I closed my eyes and concentrated as hard as I could to make it go away. I kept thinking that if I had made it appear then I could make it go away. I opened my eyes and it was still there.

I walked over to it and touched the pawn and quickly pulled my hand away. It was cold as ice. I had never seen anything like it before. I rested my hand on it and could feel some connection with it. It almost felt like it was alive. My hand started to glow again. I touched the pawn and the colored circle appeared. The pawn began to go sink into the circle until it was gone."

"Is that it?" Cyrus asked.

"Yeah, that's how I discovered my power," I replied.

"Interesting. It is getting about to be that time. Perin should be here soon to come get you."

"I know, I have training today." There was a knock at Cyrus' door.

"Come in." Perin opened the door and walked in.

"How did everything go, Zane?" Perin asked.

"It was great, I believe. What do you think, Cyrus?" I answered.

"He did just fine Perin. I have some theories, nothing definite yet," Cyrus told Perin. "This is one power I can't quite figure out. I'll need many more sessions."

"That's better than nothing," Perin said. "Zane, we should get going though. We don't have any time to waste."

"Alright, let's go," I said. "Thanks, Cyrus."

"No problem. How about you come back sometime this week and you can tell me about those cards of yours?"

"If its okay with Perin."

"Thursday would be the best time, around noon, after his classes."

"That's perfect for me," Cyrus responded.

"Okay, we'll see you then." Perin and I left Cyrus' office and started going to my specialized training ground.

The islands weren't that bad to live on. Sure, you never get to see your family, but you do get a lot from your trainer, and mine was Perin. He helped me learn how to use my power and control it. They didn't understand my power completely, but they wanted to know how it worked exactly. That was why I started going to see Cyrus. He was the executive power psychologist. He figured out what people's powers are.

Not only was Perin my trainer, but he was one of the seven heads of the islands.

Perin was the third. Three heads stay on the Industrial, one on the Homestead and three go away on some special mission to protect everyone on the islands. I wasn't sure what that special mission was. Perin told me almost everything, but that was one of the things he hadn't. The heads all answered to one big boss. He decided where everyone was stationed. No one knew very much about him, except for Emily, the fourth head. She read a file on him by accident. She hadn't told anyone what was in the file, but she basically said he did have a power.

Perin had been on the Industrial every year since the start of the project. He was not sure why, but he didn't complain. He thought it was 'cause of his lack of a power. He liked it on the Industrial; it was by far the best place to be. At least that was what he said.

We arrived at my training ground, which was in a wide open area in the middle of the woods. All the training grounds were scattered so each Instructor and student could have total privacy. My training ground was out in the middle of nowhere because Perin said that I need a lot of room to use my power's full potential.

"Today is going to be a really long and hard training day," Perin said.

"Alright, any specific reason?"

"No, I just want you to reach your best."

"Oh."

"You know, you are the youngest person with near complete control of their power. You are, without a doubt, the best student that I have ever had. It is amazing you are only sixteen and you have only been here for one year. You have more control than some of the instructors."

"How many students have you had?"

"Four, not counting you," he said "My first one wasn't very appreciative of my help, so I let him go. After that I didn't have a student for a while. I just stayed at my desk or walked around and monitored the other kids."

"That's not that many."

"Well, as heads, we don't need to have students. It's our choice if we want to or not."

"Oh, then why did you choose to?"

"It makes the job more entertaining. When I don't have any students the job gets very boring."

"That makes sense I guess."

"Enough of all this talking. Let's get down to business."

"Alright," I opened up my cardholder that was attached to my belt and took out a few cards. I focused my energy into my hands, put the cards into the ground, and my colored summoning circle appeared. I stuck my hand inside of the circle and pulled out a sword. With my other hand, I opened up my pouch attached to my belt and took out four pawns, then put them into the ground, one in front of me, one behind, and the other two on the sides of me, so that I was completely surrounded by them. The circles appeared and in a matter of seconds the pawns were summoned.

"That's it, Zane, perfect formation," Perin complimented.

I made the pawns spread out and I stayed behind the one in front of me so that I was hidden. I pulled out another chess piece from my pouch and was about to summon it.

"Zane, stop whatever you are doing," Perin yelled.

My chess pieces stopped moving, I held on to the chess piece in my hand.

"Why have we stopped Perin?"

"We are being watched," Perin said.

Chapter XXV

Ryder: Changing

May 11, 2007

I parked my car in my parking spot, got out, and went to my apartment checking the mail before I entered. My new issue of Zoobook was in; there was a shark on the cover. I had Zoobooks scattered all over the apartment. The place was a pigsty, books everywhere, crumbs thrown around, and everything was out of place.

"It's like I'm an animal or something," I said and laughed.

I threw the Zoobook on the couch and walked into the kitchen to grab a bottle of water. I opened it, chugged it, and filled it back up and put it in the fridge. I began picking up the living room, putting all the books in one pile with the new one on top, and then started vacuuming up the couch and the floor. In only a few minutes, the room was clean. It felt good to see a clean room. I sat down on the couch and turned on the discovery channel. There was a special on elephants and I didn't want to miss it. They are one of my favorite animals. I found them to be more than interesting.

I picked up my new zoo book and opened it. There were a ton of shark facts. For instance two-thirds of a shark's brain is dedicated to smell. I turned to the center of the book and looked at the bone and muscle structure of the Great White Shark. It was amazing. The great white was the strongest of the shark family. My eyes zoomed in on the picture, scanning every bone and muscle of the shark and absorbing all the information. My vision began to fog up, I quickly shut my eyes and I could see the image of the shark burned into my sight. I opened my eyes and there was a knock on the door. I went over to it and looked out the peep hole. It was her. I opened the door.

"And?" I asked.

"Is it done?" she asked.

"I'm getting to it. I haven't talked to him since you captured him. You can't expect me to rush a mission like this. It's too important. If I rush it, then I'll fail. We both know that we can't afford to fail this mission."

"True, but he is free now. You should try to contact him."

"No, I want him to contact me. I'm not going to let him get suspicious. I want him to think that I'm his friend. That way he'll rely on me, not the other way around."

"That's good. I knew you would be the perfect person to handle this situation. If you succeed in this mission you might be promoted."

"I wouldn't mind that. To what?"

"Not sure, it's all up to the Boss."

"Maybe the eighth head?"

"I highly doubt it. Maybe something like a head instructor."

"You know I like the field work more. How about the head hunter?"

"That's not a bad idea. I'll run it by the Boss. I have to go now. Just send me a quick update via email. Just something that I can show to the Boss."

"Consider it done, bye." I shut the door and walked over to my bookcase next to my television.

I pulled out my journal "Catulus ab Adulescens", and the bookcase went into the wall and moved to the left. It opened a path to my basement. My journal told about my first few instances were I began to use my power. I wrote about how I came across my power, it was very important to me. It meant "Animal from Adolescents".

I walked down into my basement where I had a bench press, a home gym, a treadmill, bell bars and a lot of extra weights. There was a bookshelf with organized Zoobooks and tons of animal books, mainly on skeletal and muscle structure. I walked over to my mirror and closed my eyes, picturing a bird. My elbow cracked and went the opposite direction and the muscles in my arms grew strong enough to support my weight in the air. I jumped and hovered; repeatedly flapping my arms as fast as I could. I dropped back down to the floor, turned back to my normal structure, and closed my eyes again thinking about the rhinoceros. My bones grew thick, my nose became hard, and pointed upwards, and my skin became tough as rock. My muscles grew as well. I returned to normal again, wanting to do one more. Again, I closed my eyes and thought about a cheetah. My spine became more lose and flexible; I could feel my leg muscles grow and tighten. My leg bones shrunk a little and every muscle in my legs grew stronger with my body became lighter and faster.

I returned to my normal state again. I walked over to a mini fridge that I had, grabbed a bottle of water, and drank most of it. Then I went over to my bench press and put on about 200 pounds on each side. I laid down and tried to lift it, but couldn't. I pictured a gorilla. My muscles increase exponentially. My head cracked and changed a little, every muscle in my body grew about ten times stronger, and my spine cracked and bent. I grabbed onto the bar and lifted the weight like it was nearly nothing. I did forty repetitions then set it back down. My phone rang so I turned back to normal and got off the bench press to grab it. It was Bastian.

"Hey, Bastian. What's up?" I greeted.

"We should talk."

"Is everything okay?"

"I'm not sure. A lot has happened since the last time we saw each other."

"Are you in trouble?"

"I believe so. Hold on, I have to go, I'll call you back," he hung up quickly.

I put my phone down and thought about what to say to him when he called back. I hoped he had no idea that I was working for the islands. He called me, which meant he confined in me; he could turn to me for help. That's exactly what I wanted. I put my phone in my pocket and grabbed my keys. I went back upstairs and moved the bookcase back to cover the door to my basement. I left my apartment and got in my car. I wanted to go to the lake which took while to get there, but it was worth it. I knew a place that no one else knew about, making it perfect for training my water transformations. I parked my car on a cliff that oversaw the water. At the bottom was my spot. I changed my structure into that of a gorilla. I scaled down the cliff in a matter of seconds. I reached the bottom and there was about twenty feet of sand on my sides and about ten feet in front of me. It was excellent. I had the whole area to myself to practice most of the transformations that I couldn't do on land.

I took off my shirt and pants, changed into my bathing suit, and walked out into the water. I changed my bone structure to a shark. A dorsal fin formed on my back, gills ripped opened near my ribs. My sense of smell increased and my teeth became sharper and jagged. I had never changed into a shark before. The only other water creature I changed into was an Indo-Pacific Sailfish once; the fastest fish in the sea. It was really fun going about seventy miles per hour in the water. I dove under and began swimming. My vision was perfectly clear, I could see better than I could on land and I could smell everything in the lake. I could smell the other fish and determine how far away they were.

I swam back to the shore and changed back to normal walking up onto the beach and checking my phone. I had one missed from Bastian. I opened my phone and called him back.

"Hey, is everything okay? You just kind of hung up last time," I said.

"Yeah, sorry about that. Where are you? I want to hang out."

"Well, I'm at Summersville Lake."

"I'll be there soon. Don't go anywhere."

"Alright, see you then."

Bastian hung up and I ran back to the water and dove in and changed back into a shark.

Chapter XXVI

Bastian: Birds of a Feather

May 11, 2007

I woke up sweatin'. My heart was racin'. It was just a nightmare, I kept tellin' myself. Flashes of my days on the islands kept appearin' in my head. I walked to the bathroom, turned on the sink and splashed myself few times. I looked up at the mirror and screamed at my refection. I had barely been gone for a full week and I was already losin' it. If I was goin to get the thoughts out of my head, I was goin' to need help. I returned to my room and tried to call Ryder, but there was no answer. The conversation with Faxon was still buggin' me. He was such an insensitive bastard. I just needed to clear my mind and not worry about the islands. My power was just what I could do, it wasn't who I was. It didn't have to control my life. I had to adjust to combinin' it with my every day life. I didn't have to be a big hero. I could still live a normal life with the masks.

I went down stairs and sat on the couch and turned on the television, but there was nothin' on. My head started to hurt. It was like a sharp pain, then I started to hear a voice.

"Stretch . . . stretch . . ." the squeaky voice said.

It was a new mask tryin' to get out. Just when I wanted to put it all behind me my power decided to say no. I focused really hard on tryin' to get the voice out of my head, but I couldn't. There was only one way to get it to stop and that was to make it real.

I ran outside and found a piece of wood, picked it up, and my vision began to get scratchy again. My thumbs started goin' crazy carvin' the mask. I was watchin' every motion, and I even started to gain some control over my hand movements. I made the mask a little skinny on the sides so that it looked bony, and forced my fingers through the wood to make eye holes. My fingers took control again as I watched them put the finishin' touches on the mask. My hands and headache calmed down and the voice was gone. I walked back inside of my house pissed off because I couldn't get any time to rest before my power came back to haunt me. I went into my room and painted the mask purple and green; not to sure why, but when I saw the paint those two colors blatantly stuck out as if they were callin' out to me.

When I was finished with the mask, there was only one more thing to do, and that was to take it for a test drive to see what it could do. I put the mask on my face and it suctioned to me just like all the rest. There was a flash of black. I was in my mind again. The ground was not hard, havin' a bounce to I every time it took a step. It seemed almost like rubber.

"Can we just get this over with?"

"And you are?" the squeaky voice asked.

"I own ya. Now what do ya want from me."

"I want not a thing from you."

"Then why did ya contact me?"

"I did no such thing. You came into my home and disrupted my living. I should be asking you what you want from me."

"So what can ya do that's so special?"

"I understand not what you mean, strange invader."

"Is there anythin' that ya can do that makes ya different?"

"I'm still not following."

"Whatever, I'm gone."

"You can't just come in here unannounced and then leave. I won't allow it."

I closed my eyes and started to concentrate. I was about to leave when the thing hit me. I opened my eyes, while I was on the ground, and could see the entity's arm bein' pulled back. I followed the arm, with my eyes, back to his body. It was of average height and seemed to be a male. He was wearin' strange and baggy clothes, and his appendages were longer than normal.

"You can stretch, interestin'. I ran into a guy that could do that, then I killed him," I realized.

"I'm going to hurt you."

"You can try."

We started to fight. He kept stretchin' his arms out at me, tryin' to catch me, but I kept dodgin' them. He slapped me really hard and I fell down again. I seriously offended him by comin' in to his area, but it was my mind so as far as I was concerned it was my area. He used his arms like whips to hit me while I was on the ground. All I could do was block. He had a power and I didn't, clearly he had the upper hand. I heard a feint voice inside my head.

"I can help you . . . let me help you," It said.

It kind of sounded like Ien.

"If you can help me then do it," I said.

Suddenly, there was a white light glowin' in front of me, with Ien's mask inside it. I stopped blockin', grabbed it, and put it on flyin' upwards. Ien had somehow found a way to help me inside my own mind.

"What is goin' on? How are you doin' that? Where did you get that mask?" the entity asked.

"I'm just that good. Now I'm goin' to show ya why you're goin' to do as I say."

"You do not own me, Fool!"

"You're goin' to let me use your power whenever I damn well please with no argument."

"I don't think so."

"Just hand over your mask."

"This is mine! This is who I am. You can't have my face!"

"If I beat ya the mask is mine."

"You can try, but I'm not going to hold back anymore. Now I have to fight for my life and I will kill you if I must."

"That sounds great. Then I'll know I won fair and square."

"If that's what you want, then it's a deal."

I flew behind him as he stretched out his arms and tried to grab me, but I was too fast for him. While in the air I clearly had the upper hand. He was throwin' his arms all over the place tryin' to hit me. I started weavin' in and out of them tryin' to tangle them up, but it wasn't workin'. He was too smart for that. I continued to avoid him, but easily got bored playin' the defensive. I flew at him ready to attack. He dropped to his butt and stretched out his leg and tryin' to kick me, but I evaded. I was just about to hit him when he brought his leg back around tanglin' me up. I was completely wrapped up by his leg. It was painful; he was squeezin' me tightly. I started to fly up and around fast and began to get his limbs tangled up. He sent his other leg around and kicked me in the head. It was gettin' rough and I felt like I was goin' to lose. I flew at him again realizin' that I didn't have to punch or kick him. I could just smash into him and that's what I did.

He fell backwards causin' his grip to loosen allowin' me to fly out. His limbs were tangled well enough for me to get some good hits on him. I flew up into the air and stayed above him, flew at him one last time, holdin' both of my fists in front of me and soarin' down at him. He sent all of his tangled limbs at me and I avoided them all, crashin' down right on his chest. There was a loud crack and the ground around us smashed causin' debris to shoot everywhere.

The dust cleared and the entity's limbs were pulled back to normal. I stood over his body.

"We had a deal."

"Yes," he coughed loudly. "Yes, we did."

"Are ya goin' to own up to it?"

"Of course. You fought well. My power is your power now." He took off his mask and threw it up at me. I grabbed it and he was gone.

Everythin' started to fade. I was in my room again with the mask on my face. I held my hands out stretchin' them. This power was much easier to use than Dac's. I had to think of a name for the mask. I didn't know too much about it other than it liked purple and green. I sat down and thought. Pruen, his name was goin' to be Pruen: the colors purple and green mixed together. I took off the mask and set it on the table.

After, I pick up my phone and called Ryder. I needed someone experienced to talk to and I knew he would be able to help me if I asked him. I really needed to get a lot off my chest and he was the only person that I thought would understand.

"Hey, Bastian. What's up?" he greeted.

"We should talk."

"Is everything okay?"

"I'm not sure, a lot has happened since the last time we saw each other."

"Are you in trouble?" I heard my dad pull into the driveway.

"I believe so, hold on, I have to go, I'll call ya back." I hung up quickly.

I cleaned everythin' up and my dad walked through the front door.

"Bastian, are you home?"

"Yeah, dad I'm upstairs."

"I'm on break. Do you want a sandwich or something?"

"Nah, but thanks." I ran downstairs and into the kitchen. "I might be goin' to hang out with a friend later. Is that okay?"

"I don't care, just give me a call and let me know where you are."

"Okay, thanks."

My dad left after he ate his sandwich. I was actually pretty hungry. I made a sandwich and watched television. I called Ryder after a program ended, but there was no answer. After about a half an hour he called me back.

"Hey, is everything okay? You just kind of hung up last time," Ryder asked.

"Yeah, sorry about that. Where are ya? I want to hang out."

"Well, I'm at Summersville Lake."

"I'll be there soon, don't go anywhere."

"Alright, see you then."

I went upstairs and grabbed Ien. The fight with Pruen made me realize that there was no escapin' my power. I had to come to terms with it. I walked into my backyard and put on Ien. I jumped into the air and started flyin' toward the Summerville Lake. I got to the main area and people covered the lake. I landed somewhere where no one could see me and I looked around for Ryder, but couldn't find him. I knew I heard him right, he definitely said Summerville Lake. I took out my phone and called him again.

"Where are ya?" I asked.

"I'm in a very secluded place. Can you see a red car anywhere near a cliff?"

I looked around and there was a red car far away from me, which looked like there could have been a cliff below it.

"I think so."

"Okay, well I'm at the bottom of the cliff."

"I'll be right there."

I ran over to the car and as looked over the edge of the cliff seein' a pale shark fin in the water about fifty feet below. I took a deep breath and jumped off the cliff. About three fourths of the way down, I put on Ien and stopped myself from landin' on the sand and definitely breakin' both legs. I took off Ien and dropped to the sand.

The shark fin was still circlin' around in the water and then jumped out turnin' out to be Ryder. He landed back in the water and picked his head above the surface.

"Bastian! Great to see you man."

"Same to you, Ryder."

"Wanna come in?"

"No, I'm not really a swimmer."

"That's cool. I was just about to get out."

Ryder ran out of the water, grabbed a towel that was next to a pile of clothes, and dried himself off.

"So what have you been up to?" he asked.

"That's what I wanted to talk to ya about."

"Oh."

"Ya wanna go talk somewhere else?"

"Where did you have in mind?" he asked curiously.

"Anywhere."

"How about we go for a ride around the sky?"

"That sounds like a great plan."

I put Ien back on and Ryder changed into a bird. We both pushed ourselves off the ground and flew into the sky with me leadin' the way. We were rippin' through the clouds and lovin' every minute of it. Ryder started to pull ahead of me and looked back. I gave it all I had, rocketed passed him, turned around, and waved to him. Then I slowed down and he caught up. I pointed down at a mountain. He shook his head and we both flew down to it, landin' on a flat part near the top. I took off Ien and he turned back to normal.

"That was a freaking blast," he said.

"Yeah, I haven't had fun like that in a while."

"So, what did you want to talk about?"

"Since the last time I saw ya, a lot has happened."

"Like what?"

"After our fight that day, I was kidnapped by these people. They kept me locked up for the past month and then some. I had the bare minimum on food and water, just enough to keep me alive. It was torture. There are many people like us there too, but they are treated a little better than how I was. They just don't know that they are in a prison. I was asked to destroy that place and I gladly took the offer, but it back fired."

"Wow, that's crazy."

"Yeah, and I tried to forget about it, but I just can't. The passed couple nights I've had nightmares about what had happened. I've tried to forget about my power, but then it just took control over me and I made a new mask. There is no way for me to forget."

"You shouldn't have to forget about anything. You should embrace everything, your power, what has happened to you, just everything. Use that to make you a better person. You can't honestly say that you would want to give up your power."

"Not really."

"Then forget about forgetting. It's time for some revenge."

"What?"

"You have to go back to that place; those islands or whatever, and tear them down."

"Ya have to be kiddin'?!"

"No man, I'll go with you. Together I bet we could totally rip them a new one."

"That's the stupidest thing I've ever heard. I'm not goin' back."

"You're stronger than them."

"Ya know nothin' about these people," I said startin' to get worked up.

"I know things about you. Your werewolf would wreck them and I could do the same. Two crazy beasts like us, they would never hold out against us," he said confidently.

"Goin' back is not an option for me. I'm just goin' to live my life with my power. I'm not some sort of hero. That's not what I was meant to do."

"How do you know?"

"I just know. If I was meant to be a hero then none of that would have happened to me."

"Not true. Every hero goes through hard times and they only make them stronger. Look at Batman. His parents were killed and he turned out to be a hero."

"That's not real life, that's a comic book."

"I'm just saying it's a good point," Ryder's phone started to ring. "Shit, I completely forgot."

"What?"

"I have this thing that I have to do."

"Do ya need any help?"

"Nah, I kind of have to do it alone."

"Oh, well, give me a call later or somethin'."

"Yeah definitely. Don't toss the idea of destroying the islands to the side; think about it." Ryder changed into a bird and flew away.

I didn't remember sayin' where I went. I didn't think I ever called the place the islands. My phone started to ring. It was Faxon. I ignored his call. There was no reason for me to talk to him. He would probably just tell me that I should take Ryder's offer and go to the islands. My phone rang again and I ignored it.

"I'm not goin' back, Faxon! Ya hear me! I'm not goin' back!" I screamed knowin' he would hear me.

Chapter XXVII

Travis: Zombie Battle

May 19, 2007

We got to Stel's apartment and continued our conversation about the islands. I noticed her bookshelf against her wall; it had pictures of her and her husband on their wedding day. She looked beautiful in her wedding dress. It was weird to see because her husband kind of looked like me, except older and with black hair. The apartment was decently large, and was very well furnished. I kept looking around while she went into the other room.

"Hey, are you hungry?" she asked.

"Yeah sure," I replied.

"I'm going to make some chicken, do you want some?"

"I love chicken. That would be great. Do you need any help?"

"No. I got it under control. You can just relax and watch the television."

I felt bad for not helping her, but she said she didn't need any help with dinner. It was about thirty minutes before she came into the living room. She made breaded chicken and seasoned noodles. The food was absolutely delicious. After we were done eating we talked about our lives.

"Are you still in school?" she asked.

"No, I graduated. I missed graduation, because I was on the islands."

"Oh, are you going to college?"

"I plan on it. I want to study law. My father was part of a firm, Balton and Clark."

"Wow, super powers and a sense of justice. Who would have guessed?" she joked.

"Yeah, I'm basically guaranteed a job as long as I get my degree. After my father passed on the other prosecutors were really helpful during all of it. They helped my mom and me through a lot," I told her. "Did you go to college?"

"No. After I got out of high school I had spent six years with the military they gave me a job on the islands and I took it, I never got the chance to go to college."

"That sucks, what did you want to be?"

"I wanted to go for nursing. I really like taking care of people."

A movie came on we both knew and we started watching it.

"Do you really think that we should be wasting time like this? We could be out trying to find that zombie girl," I asked.

"There is no point going to find her, we should just let them come to us."

"Yeah, but I feel like we should be doing something."

"Like what?"

"I don't know, training or something."

"I don't need training, I know how to use my power and there is no further I can take my ability."

"I know, but I could be doing something."

"You just need to relax, Travis."

"I guess." She moved closer to me and grabbed my hand.

"I know how you feel."

She leaned in and kissed me, I kissed her back. It felt wrong doing that to Amber, but it felt nice to be with someone who knew my pain. We began kissing, slowly moved into her room, and I got on the bed. Stel closed the door behind her, took off her shirt, and came onto the bed. She got on top of me and we started kissing again. I held her in my arms. It felt like I was with Amber again. I rolled her onto her back as we kissed. I pulled away and she looked at me. I felt sick to my stomach. I knew it was wrong. She wasn't Amber, no matter how much I wanted her to be. I got off the bed.

"I'm sorry, Stel. I just can't. I'll be on the couch."

"Travis, I'm sorry I didn't mean . . ."

"It's okay, I understand."

"You're just so much like him," she said as a tear fell from her eyes. "I miss him so much." She began to cry. I returned to the bed and hugged her.

"It's okay, I'm not mad or anything."

"Could you please just lay with me? Nothing else will happen. The company would just be really nice."

"Yeah . . . yeah, I suppose." We laid down on the bed on opposite sides. Just being in the same bed was enough to take some of the pain away for her. It did nothing for me, but at least I could help her a little.

That night all I dreamt about was Amber. I didn't want to ever wake up.

THE NEXT MORNING

I rolled out of her bed trying my hardest not to wake her. I went into the bathroom and washed my face. I stared at the mirror with water sliding down my face. I took a deep breath and walked into the living room. I still felt sick about last night. I sat down on the couch and turned on the television. I started flipping through the channels until I found something to watch, but it was no time for cartoons. I changed the channel to the local news.

"Last night, there were multiple sightings of large groups of rioters committing several acts of vandalism," the reporter said as photos of fires, flipped cars and damaged buildings covered the screen.

I couldn't believe my eyes. There was only one explanation, it had to be Lael.

"There are five confirmed dead and twenty-six wounded. At this time we have no accurate descriptions of the attackers. But there is confirmation that there are at least twenty members of this group. We express extreme caution for tonight and the nights to come."

She's killed people just to get to me. I couldn't allow it to continue. I had to end it tonight, on my own, I thought. I could not let Stel put herself in any kind of danger.

Her bedroom door opened. I quickly picked up the remote and turned off the television.

"Good morning, Travis," she said.

"Good morning," I said as she walked over to the coffee pot.

"What were you watching?" She asked.

"Huh, oh, nothing important." I tried to play dumb.

"Travis, what was it?"

She knew something was wrong walking over and turning on the television. I sat down on the couch while she stood and watched the scenes of destruction. The police chief interrupted the pictures.

"Tonight there will be extra officers out on patrol, and again we plead for people to stay in their homes, it will be safer there. We won't rest until we catch this gang of criminals and bring them to justice for the crimes that they have committed. Thank you and please until further notice stay in your homes after dark."

"The police chief is in the process of getting a curfew passed. If so, then until further notice compliant stores and other businesses will close at six pm. The curfew is still currently under review and we should have an answer by two pm this afternoon. This is Emma Dawson with the morning news, we will right back after this commercial break."

"She sent them after innocent people? I never thought she would do that."

"I know."

"Were you not going to tell me?" Stel asked angrily.

"Honestly, no. I can do this on my own. They are after me, not you. I don't need any more blood on my hands than I already have."

"She's after the both of us. I'm not letting you do this alone. Last night was just the bait. She knows you'll come after her. She'll have an army waiting for you tonight, plus the police that will be out patrolling."

"I don't care. I can do it on my own."

"End of discussion, Travis, I'm coming." She walked into her bedroom, came out holding a white lab coat, and threw it to me.

"Here, wear this. It has multiple pockets. You can carry a bunch of stuff in it. It'll make it easier for you in a fight. That way you don't have to go looking for something to absorb, you'll already have it in one of your pockets.

"That's a great idea, thanks." I put on the coat and it fit perfectly.

It reminded me of the coat that Zane had on during his fight.

"Do you mind if I look around and try and find anything that I could put in the coat?"

"Be my guest."

I grabbed a vile in the kitchen and filled it with water, found a metal bolt in one of her drawers, and picked up a lighter on the counter. That was all that I could find at the moment. I walked back into the living room and Stel was waiting with her shovel.

"Let's do this." I began to walk to the door.

"Wait; there is just one more thing. I want you to have this." She held out her hand and was holding a wedding ring.

"Is that yours?" I asked

"Yes, I want you to have it. If you can absorb the diamond then you would be nearly invincible. Take it, please."

"I can't, it's your wedding ring. Your husband gave you that. I'm sorry, I can't accept it."

"Please just take it. It only reminds me of him. I don't want to remember him. It's just too painful. He wouldn't want me living my life crying over his death. He'd want me to move on, continue living my life as I was meant to. Trust me you'd be doing me a favor," she said putting the ring in my hand.

"Let's just say I'm holding on to it for you."

"That's fine. Let's go find this little bitch."

We left her apartment, walked out into the streets, and split up deciding to call the other if anything came up. I went to the graveyard and stayed at Amber's grave. There was no sign of any zombies or Lael. Amber's grave was filled. I bent down and spoke to her.

"I'm sorry for what happened to you Amber. It was my fault and I will take full responsibility for what happened. I won't allow them to get away with killing you. I promise that I will kill all of them and get revenge for your death. I can't allow them to think that it is okay to kill people without any repercussion. Well, I'm the repercussion. They will deal with me and I'll show them what revenge is truly about."

I stood up and looked around. I looked at my watch. It was three pm. I didn't think she would take the chance of getting caught during the day. I called Stel, there was no point being out early if nothing was going on. She agreed to meet back at her place.

"We should come up with some kind of plan," Stel said.

"Don't lose?" I said jokingly.

"We need to figure out what to do about the cops. They're bound to see us."

"Not only that, but they'll notice that the things they're shooting at aren't people."

"Very true."

"Do you think you could handle the police, just keep them distracted or something?" I asked.

"You won't be able to fight all the undead on your own," she replied

"They're zombies, of course I can."

"They're not you stereotypical zombies, they're stronger and faster. They draw their power from her," Stel explained. "The more there are the weaker each one is, so we are in luck. She'll definitely use many of them to find us."

"Why don't we just go to the most unpopulated area to fight her?"

"She won't fall for it. She's gunna stay close to the main part of town to make it harder on us. The worst part is that the main part of town is close to the graveyard."

"We've got no choice; we're going to have to play by her rules." I stated.

"I'll try and keep the cops out of the fight, I'll think of something. You just worry about finding her and taking her down," she ordered.

"Sounds good to me."

It was getting dark outside, time to leave. I went back into the graveyard and walked around looking for any signs of Lael or her cronies. Stel called me; I picked up the phone.

"Travis, I'm in the center of town. You have to get here quick there are heaps of them."

"I'm on my way," I said and took off running to the center of town.

I got out of the graveyard and halfway to the center of town. I could already see zombies. There were police cars creating a barrier trying to close in what they thought were rioters, but it wasn't working. There were too many of them. There had to be at least thirty visible zombies. There were cops in their cars trying to set up the barrier, and others firing into the crowd of undead. I took the bolt out of my pocket and absorbed it. Both my hands grew cold and metallic. I took a detour around the barrier of cars so I could make it into the crowd. I charged at the zombies, pushing my way through the mass of them, throwing my fists at their heads, and avoiding the gunfire from the cops as best I could. I made it through and got to Stel. She was hiding in an alley.

"Thank God you're here," she said. "I was getting worried."

"This doesn't make any sense. How are there so many of them? I was just at the graveyard, there were no holes in the ground, none. Where did she get all of these dead people?"

"I have no idea, she must have done some serious preparing for this battle. Not only that, but you can't forget she has the power of the islands behind her."

"What do we do? We're clearly out numbered, even with cops."

"I'm not sure. I tired to keep slamming them into the ground. With my luck I could only do it about a half a dozen more times."

"That will be plenty. Just do what you can and I'll do the rest."

We ran out of the alley. I took care of the first few zombies that I saw. Stel slammed down her shovel and a group of them shot into the sidewalk clearing a path for me. I ran towards a small cluster preparing to surround a squad of officers. They weren't firing at the zombies. It was possible they were out of ammunition. I grabbed the first zombie and threw him to pavement. I smashed two of the others heads together. Suddenly, I was blindsided by one. It forced me to the ground snapping its teeth at me. My metallic hands were holding its head away from mine. I could feel its flesh slipping from my hands. Its head inched closer and closer to mine. The smell from its rotted flesh made my stomach turn.

I could feel the metal slip past my wrist and spread onto my forearm. I forced the zombie off of me, pushing him into the air. I got up as it landed on the street. My time on my back allowed for a group of zombies to surround me and the officers I was protecting. Suddenly, two rocketed into the ground leaving behind only some dust and their dreadful odor.

The cops ran and yelled to the others to retreat. It seemed they were creating a larger perimeter. We could hear shots from a distance. Meaning the zombies were spreading out. Some officers had already seen Stel and me. It was obvious we weren't their enemy and they didn't seem to mind the help. Stel was noticeably getting tired.

"You need to rest, at least for a minute," I advised.

"We don't have time for that, we must keep going. There's still too many of them."

Abruptly, I was grabbed by two zombies and tossed into the air, then crashing through a store window. I slowly got up and saw them running toward the hole I left behind. I could see Stel fending off a few zombies herself. I put my hands down and absorbed the glass. I ran at them with both hands swinging. I stabbed and sliced until they were no longer standing. Stel go slammed into a building. I ran over, pulled the zombie away from her, and cut off its head with my sharp glass hand. Stel slid down the building and sat, she was out of energy. I returned my hands to flesh, taking out my lighter, and absorbed with my left hand. Zombies were beginning to surround us. I lifted my hand up and aimed at the car closest to us. I concentrated and pushed the fire out of the palm of my hand. A fireball rocketed at the car's windshield; I took a deep breath and shot another, but this time hitting the front of the car. The car exploded and the front shot into the air causing it to flip. It got the attention on the undead. I did the same to another car.

"I'm gunna get you out of here," I said picking Stel up and carrying her into the nearest alley. "You gunna be okay?"

"I'm just peachy." She had scratches all over her body, nothing deep thankfully.

"I'm going back out, catch your breath. I'll see you soon."

"Don't die," she pulled me in and kissed me.

"Never even crossed my mind." I turned my hands back to fire with the help of the lighter. I ran back to the center of town, there were still so many zombies. The smoke from the cars covered the area. I shot at the remaining undead catching some of their clothes and skin on fire. Unfortunately, it didn't seem to bother them as much as I thought it would. I ran around trying to avoid hand to hand combat with them. There were only a dozen or so left that I could see. I began chasing them down at that point. Out of the smoke there she was; Lael. I took my attention off the zombies and began to run toward her.

"IT'S A TRAP TRAVIS!" Stel yelled from behind me. I looked back at her then back to Lael. She went back in the smoke. I ignored Stel's warning and ran after her.

I stood still surrounded by the thick black smoke. I couldn't see anything. My hands returned to normal. I went to take out my lighter when zombies jumped out at me from all sides grabbing both of my arms and my legs. I tried to shake them off, but it was pointless. They were stronger than me. They dragged me through the black smoke. I looked around and we were at the graveyard. Lael walked toward me. My arms were held by a zombies and another grabbed my head and held it towards Lael. Her eyes were blacker than darkness itself and here body was covered in black cracks.

"Do you have any idea what you have done? You escaped the islands. You thought that there wouldn't be any consequences. Well you're greatly mistaken," she said. "I'm going to bring you back and you will have to explain to the Boss what happened." I could feel the concrete road beneath me. I could feel its energy radiating through my cloths.

"I don't have to do anything. I'm not going back!" I forced my arm to the ground and absorbed the concrete. I immediately felt stronger and broke free from Lael's zombie shackles snapping their necks. I took out the lighter and I struck it with fire erupted from it. I put my hand over the flame and absorbed it. I used my left hand to absorb the fire from my right hand. I could feel my face getting hot. The fire had found its way to the left side of my face somehow. From my chin to my cheek was burning. I could feel the warmth all over my body.

"Yes you are!" she said.

More zombies ran at me. I held out my hands and shot balls of fire and removed their undead heads. They came up behind me and tried to pin me down, I threw one off and grabbed another one's head and shot it off.

"You're next," I glared at her with my burning eyes.

She started running further into the graveyard. I chased after her prepared for another one of her traps. Surely enough, zombies tried to jump out at me. I easily threw them off and caught up to her. She was backed against a tree. She was scared of me; the girl who commands the dead was scared of *me*. I could see it in her eyes. I loved it. She was one of them; she was from the islands, which means that she is evil. People have died because of her. It had to end. She can't ever hurt anyone else. I cooled down my right hand, but not completely extinguishing the flame as I walked closer to her and grabbed her throat with my hand. The heat from my hand began to burn her skin.

"LET GO!" she screamed in pain.

I let go and backed up. My hand print was left on her neck, still radiating heat.

"Leave before something bad happens to you. You can tell your boss that I'll be back to the islands. There's no need to send anymore of you after me. They'll just get killed," I said.

She crawled away holding her throat. I turned my hands back to normal. The black smoke began to clear and all the zombies on the ground turned into smoke, dissipating. I went back to the center of town hearing only sirens. I could see Stel coming toward me. We met at the entrance of the graveyard.

"What happened?" she asked.

"It's over, I stopped her."

"Did you kill her?"

"No, I couldn't. Trust me; she is not going to be back any time soon."

"That's great, Travis. I can't believe that it's over. She's finally gone."

"There will be more. They aren't going to stop trying to bring you back and the same goes for me. They won't ever stop, that's why I've decided to go back to the islands and destroy them once and for all. I can't let them get away with what they are doing."

"Travis, don't. You will die. They'll kill you if you go back."

"Not if I kill them first."

"You wouldn't be able to fight them; they are way too powerful for you. You've barely even tapped your power."

"That's why I need you to do something."

"I can't go with you," she said shaking her head. "I just can't do that."

"No, that's not it," I said grabbing her hand. "I need you to upgrade me."

"No. No, I won't," she pulled her hand away.

"Please, the way I see it is, I'll die if you don't. So why not just take the chance. Your power is much more advanced compared to the last time you tried to do it. Please Stel."

"Travis . . ."

"Please."

She put her hand on my chest. I could feel something; some kind of energy was going through me. It was like nothing I had ever felt before. Then it turned into a stinging pain. It shot all over my body. The pain got worse very quickly. I fell to my knees.

"You told me you wanted to do this, Travis, fight it, fight though the pain," Stel said now touching my head instead of my chest.

I screamed in distress. It was excruciating. I grabbed her hand to make sure she didn't try and pull it away. I held it tightly against my head. Stel was still talking, but I couldn't hear her. My body was throbbing, it wasn't going away. I tried to fight passed it, but I couldn't. I was ready to give up and let the pain take me over, but I couldn't let it kill me. I began to picture everything that I had to fight for, my mom, my friends, everyone on the islands who was clueless about what was really going on, and for Amber. I could feel the pain slowly going away. I felt the energy again, It felt warm and comforting, then I felt nothing. I stood up, sweating and breathing heavy looking at Stel.

"Are you okay?" she asked.

"I feel fine, I don't feel any worse. The pain is gone."

"So, did it work?"

"I'm not sure."

"Try."

I held out my hand. I tried to turn it clear white, but couldn't. I tried as hard as I could, but nothing was happening. My power was . . . gone.

"What's wrong?"

"I can't use my power . . . it's gone."

"What do you mean 'it's gone'?"

"I can't . . ." my entire body felt like it had exploded. I fell to the ground screaming. I looked at my hands they were clear white. My entire arms were transparent. I rolled on the ground holding my shoulders and gut, shouting in agony. The pain lasted for what felt like years, but was really only minutes. I eventually fought passed the pain and kneeled. My entire body and clothes were clear white. I stood up and my body went back to normal. It worked. She upgraded my power.

"It worked! You're alive and it worked," Stel said.

"They don't stand a chance," I stated.

Chapter XXVIII

SAEED: SUPER MIME?

June 13, 2007

"The trial is going to be starting soon and I want you to be one of the people who goes Saeed," Colin said.

"But I do not believe I am ready sir."

"You will never know until you try."

"My gift has not yet fully matured, such as some of the others."

"Your skills are still very good."

"I am not even aware of what the trial is."

"It is the most important thing on the planet right now."

"That does not help me."

"All you need to know is that it is important."

"I will not go, I refuse."

"Why?"

"Because I believe there are better candidates on this island than me."

"We still have some time. If we work together, we will make you stronger. We will do non stop training to make sure you are in that trial."

"Why have you not gone?"

"Well, I'm an instructor. We aren't allowed to go unless we really wish to, but my ability is nothing like yours or anyone else's. I would not stand a chance in the trial."

"What goes on during the trial?"

"I can't tell you, I'm not allowed."

"Why not? How am I supposed to prepare for what I do not know?"

"That's why I'm here, to help you prepare."

"But no one has ever passed the trial or even returned from it."

"That's not true. Well no one has ever completed the trial yet, but people have returned."

"That is not what I have heard."

"Well, that's because the one's who take the trial get to go home if they want. Everyone just decides to go home because if they were good enough to be chosen for the trial then they no longer need training."

"Is this the truth?"

"I swear it."

"Then I may consider going."

"Well tell me now because I have to make the request and have it approved by the heads of the project."

"I will let you know after today's training."

"Then let's get started."

I drew my sword from its sheathe and so did Colin. Colin was designated as my instructor because he was a weapons expert. He was skilled with all types of weapons and was especially good with the sword. My adoptive father taught me everything that he knew about sword fighting, and I had used it well.

We both stood staring at each other. I made the first move. I stepped closer to him; he was an incredible fighter because he could read the movements of others, that was his ability. I attacked him, but he parried me away leaving me open. I dropped to the ground and tried to trip him, but he jumped over my feet. I rolled away from him and got back up.

"Come on Saeed," he moved toward me.

I stayed defensive and awaited for him to come closer. He swung his blade at me. I blocked it and disarmed him, but he caught his sword mid air and swung again and I dodged it. I backed up and looked up at the sky and thought about the rain, how it felt on my body, every single drop, cold and wet. The rain was falling fast. This was my territory, the rain. It seemed that I gained strength from it. It felt like it healed me and allowed me to work at my greatest potential.

"This is better," I said.

"I was wondering when you were going to bring the rain."

I jumped off the ground and started to attack Colin violently. He blocked all of my attacks, but I could tell it was getting harder for him to read my movements. Raindrops are small, but many of them can have an effect on movement, and it was clear that Colin was affected. Our swords continued to clash and the rain continued to break around them. It seemed as if I was getting the upper hand.

Suddenly, I felt a presence of someone. I turned and saw the raindrops breaking. It was like everything was moving in slow motion. Whatever it was could not be seen, but it was definitely there. I wasn't focused on the fight and Colin landed a nice swing and cut my chest. It was not a deadly blow, but it was painful. The object hit a tree and there was an explosion. Colin and I were knocked down by it.

"What was that?" I asked.

"I'm not sure."

I looked around and I saw someone coming toward us.

"Shit," Colin said.

"What is it?" Colin got up off the ground and pointed his sword in the man's direction.

"Get out of here Makale! This isn't where you are supposed to be! You are disrupting a training session!"

The man did not respond. He continued to come closer and I could see him more clearly. He was very pale and bald. He was not muscular, actually rather skinny and tall. He was dressed in tight dark colored clothes. He was very odd, but if he was the one who caused the explosion then he must have been powerful.

"Makale, I'm serious you need to leave! If you continue to come closer I'm obligated to cut you down." He continued walking toward us. "That's it; you've brought this on yourself!"

Colin sprinted at Makale. Makale acted like he was swinging something in the air, possibly a rope of some sort. Then he tossed it at Colin. Colin's body tightened and he dropped his sword. Makale pulled on whatever it was that he threw at Colin and dragged him closer. Makale acted as if he tied down the rope to something. Colin tried to get away, but couldn't. I grabbed my sword and started moving at Makale.

"Saeed, No!" Colin said. "Stay out of it. Run, just get away from here. This guy is crazy."

Makale walked around Colin touching nothing, but making it seem like he was. Colin's voice became harder to hear. Makale touched above Colin's head and I could no longer hear him. The rain made an outline around Colin. It was the shape of a tall rectangular object.

"Who are you?" I asked.

He responded with shaking his head no.

"What is that supposed to mean? What are you?"

He gave no expression walking closer to me, stopped, and stood in a common sword-fighting stance. The rain was falling on him and it was clear that he was holding something in his hands. It was the shape of the sword, but I couldn't see it.

"Fine, I will fight you," I got into my fighting position.

I ran at him and swung my sword. He held his hands together as if he were holding something in an attempt to block my attack. My sword came down and suddenly stopped. I was caught of guard.

"What?!"

He knocked me back and started attacking me with his invisible sword. The rain made it easier to follow and defend against. It was clear that he wasn't that good of a swordsman, not like myself. Our swords clashed over and over again. He was using the swords ability to not be seen to his advantage very well. I ran at him and jumped to the side and tried to stab him on his left, but he held out his hand. My sword was stopped by what felt like a wall. I jumped back in confusion of the man. His ability was very strange and very powerful.

"What do you want from me?"

He did not respond. He had not said a word since he showed up.

We continued to fight and the rain began to thicken. I felt like I was getting stronger with every raindrop that hit my skin. I began to get the upper hand in our clashing of swords. Our swords made contact and we both pushed as hard as we could. I was not going to give up. There was no way that I would lose the fight. I pushed him back and swung my sword. The tip of my blade just barely cut his upper chest and shoulder. Makale fell back and put his hand on his chest. He kneeled down for a moment and then stood up and walked away.

"Where are you going?"

He proceeded to walk away and passed by Colin, touching the invisible rectangular box. As soon as Colin was out he went to attack Makale. Makale held up his hand like he was holding a gun and Colin stopped right where the barrel would have ended.

"You are breaking the rules. You aren't supposed to associate with anyone. Fighting is considered associating."

Makale just stared at Colin. Then lowered his hand.

"Just leave now and don't come back."

Makale looked at me and smirked. It was the most emotion that he had shown since he arrived. He turned and left. Colin took a deep breath and exhaled and walked back over to me.

"Nice job," he complimented.

"Thanks."

"He could have killed us both at any second; I hope you know that."

"What is his power? It makes no sense to me."

"He is a super mime."

"A what?"

"Do you understand what a mime is?"

"Yes, I have heard of them, they are like clowns."

"Somewhat yes, but Makale is a real mime. Whatever he mimes becomes real. Such as the sword he was fighting you with and the box that he trapped me in."

"That is unbelievable, he must have no limits."

"He is one of the people who have been nominated for the trial. He's a definite."

"I do not compare to him. Why would you think that I could pass this trial?"

"You held your own against him."

"You said it yourself that he could have killed us both at any second."

"That doesn't mean you didn't do well."

"I just do not believe that I am ready."

"If you honestly think that you're not ready then I won't recommend you for the trial."

"Thank you."

"We shouldn't let what just happened slow us down," Colin picked up his sword "Now let's continue where we left off."

Chapter XXIX

Gabe: Advancing Powers

June 15, 2007

I stood waiting for my instructor outside of the dorm building. He came around the corning holding a bunch of files.

"Gabe, how are you this morning?" my instructor Ken asked.

"Great and you?" I replied.

"No complaints."

"That's good. When are we going to get started?"

"I was actually thinking that you could just hit the gym today. I've got some things to take care of. You know that the trial is coming up soon."

"Yeah I do."

"And every instructor wants their student to be nominated."

"I'm not ready for this trial. No one even knows what the trial is about or why we do it."

"That's easy. Once every year there is a trial; a trial to test the strength of the students here. Five of the students who pose to be the best of the best are selected. I don't want you to think that it is just an ordinary test. This trial is the most important thing on the entire Earth, and only the people on the islands know about it, plus the people who fund the project. There is a secret of the islands and once you become strong enough to take on the responsibilities of the trial, you will know it."

"Wow, I wouldn't have guessed."

"If you really want to be a part of saving the world then you want to train hard for the trial."

"I'll get started right away. By this time next year I'll be ready for the trial."

"If that's what you want I'll push your limits to their farthest."

"Do it."

"Go to the gym today and make sure you'll be ready for tomorrow. It's going to be a rough day for you."

I went to the gym and worked on some cardio for a little over and hour and did a few sets on the bench press. I didn't want to work out too hard and be sore for my training with Ken the next day. I went back to my room, ate dinner, took a shower, and sat down and worked on some book work. I didn't have a roommate, by request. There were an odd number of the new kids anyway. I was lucky number thirteen. That's what the instructors had been calling me. I enjoyed the nickname.

I woke up to my alarm at six in the morning. I left my room, went downstairs to the lunchroom, and grabbed a bagel for breakfast with a carton of milk, then went to go sign out for an early morning jog. I stayed within the confines of the Level Three Area. It was a two mile by two mile square that had the weight rooms, training grounds and the dorm building inside it. There were also some fountains and garden areas just to make the place seem more home like. I finished the jog at seven am and went to the instructors building to meet Ken. He waited for me between seven and seven thirty am. When I got showed up he was standing outside waiting.

"You ready?" he asked.

"I was about to ask you the same question."

"Then let's go. I requested one of the training grounds over by Warehouse B4 for most of the day. The conditions of the area aren't as good, but it's worth the privacy. The last thing we need is to be interrupted like Colin and Saeed were."

"What happened? I heard something about that before I came to see you yesterday."

"During a training session they were interrupted by Makale, one of the students participating in the trial this year."

"I thought that wasn't allowed."

"It's not, but Makale is very powerful, he probably found some way out. Plus the instructors look away from a lot of things that aren't supposed to be allowed, such as talking to each other. Everyone sees the notes you kids pass. It's a little obvious if you ask me. You guys are just lucky that the Heads don't catch you. Especially Perin, that guy is definitely bi-polar."

"So I've heard."

"Anyway enough gossip. Let's get moving."

We hopped onto a golf caddie and drove over to the training zone that Ken requested. It was a little shitty, but it was about half a mile away from the main building on the Industrial. There were three two story buildings surrounding a lot. The buildings had broken window and most of them were boarded up. Some of the exterior walls were damaged as well, having massive chunks missing and huge dents in them. For a place with the kind of technology, dorms, and other high class buildings I've seen, something big must have happened to cause this area to look like garbage, I thought.

"You have all your equipment right?" Ken asked.

"I've got my belt and the Angel, that's all I need to train."

"I didn't think you would bring extras, so I did. I also brought a bunch of things that you can practice enlarging," Ken took a backpack out of a compartment on the golf caddie.

"Alright."

Ken took out a five hundred pack of toothpicks and rolled the package over to me.

"Let me see what you got."

I picked up the package and opened it. I started throwing them and enlarging them right before they left my hand.

"I've already seen that," Ken said.

I grabbed more toothpicks and put them into the ground and touched them to make a wall ten toothpicks wide, each toothpick enlarging to about six to seven inches wide and five feet tall. My maximum was a foot wide and at roughly seven feet tall, but I could make them any size in between those as well.

"I'm not impressed," he yelled.

I grabbed more toothpicks and started running around planting them into the ground.

"Now what?" he said not pleased.

I took the Angel, my very own customized toothpick with metal inside it and a handle carved into it. I made it about the size of a sword; three and a half feet long and not very wide. I started running touching the Angel with every toothpick that I put in the ground. I sent my energy through the Angel and into the toothpicks in the ground enlarging them.

"That's weak. I want to see shock and awe."

I stopped running. "Are you serious? What do you want from me?"

"A lot more than that. You said you wanted to be part of the trial next year. If this is all you're offering then you won't ever make it."

"I don't know what else you want from me. I think I'm doing fine."

"Fine is NOT GREAT! And great isn't AMAZING!" he yelled.

"Alright, I'll do better."

I really had no idea what else I could do to impress him. I had to think of something cool and flashy. I grabbed some more toothpicks, removed one of their pointed sides, and planted them in the ground in a straight line. I then ran on top of them enlarging them with each step. At the last one I put as much energy as I could into my foot and enlarged it making it at least eight feet height. I jumped off it and landed in front of Ken holding the Angel at his neck.

"How about that?" I asked smirking.

"That was just showing off. There was nothing really new about it. Do you really think that someone you are fighting is just going to stand and wait for you to land that attack on them?"

"What am I supposed to do?"

"Let's make this fun." Ken took out his walkie talkie. "Come on out." Some I.E.S soldiers came out from the surrounding buildings.

"Please tell me I'm going to fight them."

"Yes, you are. Don't kill them."

I turned around and they all had different types of weapons; swords, staffs, combat knifes, and some had guns.

"Guns are a little extreme don't you think?"

"They're just paintball guns, it's not that bad. I'm not trying to kill you just train you."

"What do I have to do?"

"Just take them out, Simple?"

"Very." I turned around and readied the Angel.

"If you get shot more than three times you're considered dead."

"Okay. It doesn't matter because I won't get hit even once." I started running at the soldiers and they dispersed. There were about thirty of them in total. I ran after a small group of six, while taking out two toothpicks from my belt, putting them in the ground next to each other, and enlarging them. I took another one out and threw it in the direction of the group of six. I enlarged it right before I let it go. They moved out of the way, but I wasn't trying to hit them, only distract them. I ran at them with the Angel and cut down two of them. One had a sword and started to fight me. I started using my gymnastic skills to evade his strikes. I saw an opening and took it removing him from the game. I started getting shot at by the others from inside of the buildings. I could only see a few of them. I ran away from the paintballs and hid behind my first two toothpicks that I put into the ground.

I took another one out of my belt and threw it at the building. I then hid behind the first two again. Three soldiers started running at me and two came on both the sides of my wall; I was surrounded. I rolled forward to dodge two of the soldier's attacks. Unfortunately, I rolled into the three coming at me. I moved away from them, but into the line of fire of the other soldiers.

I had no where to go. There were too many of them. I set up another wall as fast as I could to protect me from the gun fire.

"You are boring me," Ken yelled. "Think of something else."

I couldn't, I wasn't creative enough to think of something spectacular.

"You aren't using your ability to its full potential. You have one frame of mind. Open it to new things. Toothpicks will only get you so far."

I didn't know how. I had used toothpicks for all my years after learning about my power. Anything else just didn't seem right.

The soldiers started to come at me again. I set up another toothpick barrier leaving my belt completely empty of my ammunition. I had to get the box that I was using earlier. I ran out from behind the barriers and over to where the box was. It was directly in the line of fire. I got nailed by one of the paintballs, but retrieved the box.

"You lied to me!" Ken yelled.

I began running around placing a bunch of toothpicks in the ground so that I could use them later. It wasn't easy to dodge the gun fire and the soldiers with melee weapons, but I was doing it. Every so often I'd find an opening on a soldier and take him out while I was placing the toothpicks. There were still twenty-three left. I barely made a dent. I turned around and enlarged the Angel and started taking on the soldiers that were coming at me. I was tired of running. I fought them all. I broke every single wooden staff that they had. The swords men dropped like flies. I hit two with my toothpicks that I had planted in the ground. There were twelve left, and there was a good chance that they were all gunmen, which meant fighting from distance was not an option.

The lot looked like an unfinished maze with all of my toothpick walls coming up from the ground. It reminded me of my assessments with Cyrus when I had first came to the island. He tested my power by seeing how many toothpicks I could enlarge before being depleted of energy. He told me that what made my ability so powerful was the fact that it didn't take any energy to maintain an items enlarged state. Only when enlarging an object and shrinking back to normal size was my energy used.

I hid behind one of my many barriers and looked were they all were. I spotted eight of them; all of them were gunmen. They were hiding behind objects and my walls, but I could still see parts of them. I had to do something different. They soldiers were too accustomed to my toothpicks and that's what they'd be expecting. I started throwing enlarged toothpicks to draw them out and it was successful. I picked up a round rock and rolled it, then ran at it enlarging it as it continued to roll. I stayed behind the now massive rock which allowed me to get closer to the remaining men. I picked up a shard of one of the broken staffs off the ground and tossed it at them and enlarged it. They dove out of the way and one of them dropped their gun. I ran at them and took out two of the men. I grabbed the paintball gun and dove behind one of the barriers.

I shot at the other men, hitting one of them three times eliminating him; nine left. I started running around just to have them shoot at me so I knew where they were. I spotted their locations and went after them throwing toothpicks. Two of the men were taken out; seven left. I enlarged more toothpicks to make another barrier. Three of the gunmen ran up on me and started shooting me with another paintball hitting me. I ran out of the way, hid behind another barrier, then ran over to another barrier waiting for them to come around and find me. I saw the three of them coming my way. I ran quietly behind them all and took them out of the game.

Suddenly, the last three men jumped out with combat knives. I fought them off. I disarmed one kicking him to the dirt. I put a toothpick between the men and me, but one ran around it and lunged at me with his knife. I dodged and enlarged a buckle on the back of his combat jacket. He dropped like a lead weight. The last guy came at me and I took out the Angel enlarging it to the size of his knife and fought him fairly, but his skills outmatched mine. I enlarged the Angel into sword size and knocked him doing away with him. I leaned back and took a deep breath. I finished the test.

Suddenly, a gunman came out from behind one of my barriers. I counted wrong, I took out three gun men and four were left and then three more combat knifes. Of course there was one left. I lost focus in the fight.

I stared at him, pissed about my mistake and he said, "Come on, you really didn't think you could take out a group of thirty of us at your level. You are pathetic compared to some others that I fought with. Game over." He raised his gun and was about to shoot. I noticed a toothpick planted by his feet angled toward his body. He had to be at least eight feet away. I had no time to think whether it would work or not. I forced as much as energy I could out of my body and touched the ground.

"For you," I said sending my energy through the ground reaching the toothpick and enlarging it. He pulled the trigger. The toothpick caught him on the side of the leg lifting him off the ground and causing him to flip around. The paintball barely missed my head and hit the enlarged toothpick that I was leaning on.

I stood up and walked over to Ken.

"That was pretty nice," Ken said walking over to me.

"Thanks."

"You got shot twice though."

"I know."

"You are going to have to do a lot better than that next time. Let's call it a day."

We got onto the golf caddie and went back to the dorm building in the level three area. Ken went to the instructors building to log in our training session and I went back to my room. I was enormously tired. I kept thinking about the last thing that I did; that enlargement from a distance. I closed my eyes and went to sleep. I woke up around six pm and felt much better. I walked out of my room, went down to the office, and had them call Ken to have him meet me in Training Room Five. I signed out and went to the training room, not waiting long for Ken.

"We already had your training for today."

"I know, but I need to try something," I said taking out a container of toothpicks.

"Okay . . ."

I started planting the toothpicks in a large circle, big enough to fit a few people inside of it. I made sure that there was a lot of room between the middle and the toothpicks; about twenty feet in diameter. I stepped into the circle getting into the middle.

"What are you doing?" Ken asked.

"I did something during the fight with the soldiers and I don't want to wait to try it again."

I sat down and concentrated hard about what had happened earlier. I played the scene over and over again in my head then opened my eyes putting two fingers on the ground, sending energy out and enlarging the toothpick. I continued to touch the ground and the toothpicks continued to enlarge around me, each one being roughly ten feet away. My ability's distance had grown tremendously. I had never tried doing any distance training; not trying new things was where I made my mistake.

"Now that's what I'm talking about." Ken clapped.

I stood up and put out my right foot a little, still completely surrounded by the toothpicks. I dragged my foot all the way around the circle returning all the toothpicks back to their original size. My ability was advancing, significantly.

"That was very nice, Gabe. You can now enlarge things from a distance. We are going to find out tomorrow how far away you can do it from."

"Alright."

"You're getting better. Maybe you will make it to the trial by this time next year."

"I can only hope."

Chapter XXX

ADEN: REECE DISCOVERED

June 18, 2007

My skills and abilities had improved tremendously since I came to the islands. They had brought me in like one of their own and treated very well. If I didn't already know they were evil, then I would stay forever, but thanks to Faxon, I knew the truth. I'd been getting closer to finding Reece, narrowing it down to a few places; some were easier to get into than others.

Knock . . . knock.

"Aden, you home?" It was Greg at my door.

"Just a minute," I walked over to the door and opened it.

"I wanted to have a small training session today without Nadim, is that okay?"

"Yeah, I'll be right out." I got dressed and went with Greg to our usual training ground.

"Let's just start with some simple target practice," he said.

"Fine."

"Did you bring any blood with you?"

"Damn." I had forgotten.

"You know the rules. If this was real then you know what you would have to do."

I took out my knife and cut my left shoulder. Blood came out and I moved it to cover the palms of my hands. Greg threw Frisbees into the air. I made small needles with the blood from my hands and hit every one.

"Nice, as usual. Now let's do some defending."

He took out some logs and started throwing them at me. I made a simple barrier with the small amount of blood that I had. The logs didn't affect it much. Then Nadim came out of no where and started throwing them. My barrier splattered once it was hit by Nadim's force behind the logs.

"I thought you said he wasn't coming."

"I lied. Now focus."

I gathered my blood that was on the ground. I cut myself again to obtain more blood. I had to try a defensive/offensive tactic. I made another small barrier with bladed whips attached to it. Nadim threw another log and I had my whips cut it into pieces before it hit my barrier. The pieces still hit my barrier with moderate force, but still nearly destroying it.

That continued for a little while, I tossed shards of wood back at him, making him very irritated. I was done playing around. I dropped down my barrier and set the blood on the ground and made it appear in four little balls. Nadim looked puzzled and unguarded. The balls opened up and small spikes shot out. Nadim tried to dodge them, but was hit by a majority.

"Okay, that's enough for today," Greg said.

"I was just about to tear him apart," Nadim spoke angrily.

"Sure you were, Nadim," Greg said sarcastically.

"Really! These stupid little needles don't even hurt." He started pulling them out of the side of his arm and from parts of his chest.

I turned the blood back to its liquid form and brought it back to me. I was lightheaded from the blood loss, but I wasn't anything I couldn't shake off.

"Nice job, Aden," Greg complemented. "The only flaw is that you need to remember to bring blood with you. You can't run the risk of starting a fight already injured. If we were to send you and Nadim to capture a powerful opponent, you could be at a severe disadvantage."

"I know. Next time I won't forget."

"This is stupid. If you ever let us finish a fight, I would ruin him!"

"If you really think so, Nadim," I said condescendingly.

"Shut your mouth, Aden!"

"Can I go back to my room now?" I asked.

"Yeah, I'll see you tomorrow," Greg said.

I started walking back to my room when I over heard two guys talking.

"I know, the kid is so young," one said.

"Perin said not to let that fool you, he's dangerous," the other replied.

I was hugging a wall so they couldn't see me. It sounded like they were talking about Reece. I followed them to where they were going and they came to a door. I followed them inside. Right before it shut, I sent out some blood to hold the door open. I snuck behind them and up the stairs, poking my head around the corner to see a massive group of guards. It wasn't the right time to make my move. I was unprepared, with little blood and even less of a plan. Without either of those I would just be getting Reece and I killed. I snuck back down the stairs and out the door. I returned to my room and started thinking of a plan.

I wasn't a hundred percent sure that he is there, but my gut was telling me he was. The only way to know for sure was to try. If he wasn't there I could attempt to convince Perin I lost control of my power, or I saw the guards doing malicious acts on someone. The plan was awful at best and a huge risk. Just the slightest chance that Reece could be there was good enough for me. I owed him everything, and I planned to repay my debt.

I awoke and took a shower. Afterwards, I got dressed and ready to leave, gathering everything that I wanted into a backpack. I had decided, if Reece wasn't held up in that room, that I wouldn't stop searching the islands until I found him. Suddenly, there was a knock on my door.

"Just a second." I put my backpack out of sight.

I opened the door, It was Perin. My heart stopped immediately.

"Today's that day, Aden," Perin said. "Your first mission."

Whew! Of all the days, of course it happens today, I thought.

"Okay, let's go." I left my room and went with Perin.

We went into a room with two white boards and some chairs.

"Please sit."

Nadim came in seconds after I did and sat down, while and Perin and Greg stood in front of the white boards and flipped them over. They were covered with papers, photos, graphs, and all sorts of other stuff.

"This is Travis Hartman; he was the one who escaped a few weeks ago. Now we are going to get him back. We have been watching him ever since he left and we even sent two people to capture him. One of which, was Amity. She can brainwash people into doing what she wants. Travis wasn't affected by her ability and, at this time, we are unsure why. Anyways, Then we had another agent that had already been in the area, Lael. She is a necromancer. Unfortunately, she was terribly injured by Travis and his accomplice," Perin said.

"We have been keeping tabs on Travis for some time now. We have found a regular pattern that he performs weekly. Every Tuesday and Thursday he goes to the gym and works out. We are going to use this to our advantage today," Greg explained.

"We are going today?" I asked.

"Yes, right after this meeting," Perin answered. "Is that a problem?"

"No, I was just curious."

"His ability is underdeveloped, unlike yours. You both have a fully matured ability. He should be an easy one to capture," Greg said.

"Any questions?" Perin asked.

"What exactly is his power?" I asked.

"He can absorb anything that he touches, but as I said, his power is immature. When he left here, he could only absorb things with his hands. It would take years for his power to become fully developed, so you both will be fine," Greg explained.

"But then how did two other people fail. Especially, one's with such developed powers?"

"They just weren't as strong as you two are," Greg said. "We didn't realize it would take such a powerful team to deal with him and he had unexpected help."

"Oh, well we'll try and bring him back in one piece," Nadim said.

"Before we get you two going I need you both to stand up, turn around, and stay still. You're only going to feel a pinch," Perin said. We did what he said. It sounded like he opened a briefcase then seconds later I felt a pin prick on the back of my neck. "Okay, you two are all set." I rubbed the back of my neck and felt a metal circular shape.

"What did you do?" Nadim and I asked.

"That is to keep a dangerous man out of your head and out of your thoughts. Under no circumstances should you remove it. We will know if you do."

"Yes sir," we said.

"Alright, let's get you boys going," Greg said.

"I need to go back to my room and grab some blood."

"You know the rules, Aden. We just had this conversation yesterday," Greg said. "You weren't prepared so now you have to deal with the consequences."

"But this is a mission that failure is not an option."

"Then don't fail. Maybe next time you will be prepared," he said talking down to me. "That is, if you get a next time."

"Yes, sir."

We went to the helipad on the roof. I could see all the tops of the other builds. The Main Industrial Building was the tallest structure on the island. Each building had its own helipad landing. That was how they had to have it because there was no room for a hanger or landing strip. That's why the Industrial had over a dozen docks. Nadim and I got onto the chopper and took off. I thought, of all the days they find Travis, it had to be the day I was saving Reece and escaping. I had to complete the mission as fast as I could and get back.

Chapter XXXI

TRAVIS: THE FINISHED FIGHT

June 19, 2007

Since that night, my life had been different and I owed it all to her. I hadn't talked to Stel since then. She didn't want to get too attached because she wanted nothing to do with the islands, and my life is consumed by destroying them. Everyday I trained in my basement. I covered all the windows just in case the islands were watching. I didn't what them to know that my power was fully developed. When I attacked them, I was going to have the advantage. Every Tuesday and Thursday I went to the gym. Since the zombie attack there hadn't been any appearances of any islanders. I grabbed the coat that Stel gave me, which I had made some slight alterations to, by removing all the outside pockets and adding small pockets on the inside. I ran upstairs to my living room. My mom wasn't home; she had gone to work. I had the house to myself, which was a great opportunity to gather things for my coat. I hadn't added anything since I collected things from Stel's kitchen; the vile of water, the bolt, and lighter. I couldn't forget about the diamond ring that she gave me. I needed more than just those few things, something for every situation.

I scavenged through some of the drawers in the house, finding a wooden carving that my dad got from Florida on the vacation before he passed away. I put it in one of my inside pockets. I pulled a leaf off of one of my mom's plants, put in another inside pocket, and found a glass sculpture in my mom's room that I broke off a piece of. I walked outside and saw a rock and picked it up and put in another pocket. I had enough collecting and jumped into my car, turned on my ipod, and drove to the gym. I showed my I.D. card to the woman at the front desk, went down into the locker room, and opened my locker getting changed into my white shorts with the blue stripe on the sides and a white short sleeve shirt. I put my coat in my locker, closed it, and locked it.

I went into the treadmill room, it was empty. I hopped on one and started to run. Not too many people go to the gym in the morning, that's why I liked to go early. I ran on the treadmill for about thirty minutes on medium speed, then got off the treadmill and wiped myself down with a towel that I grabbed from the locker room. Someone about my age came into the room. He nodded at me; I nodded back. I walked out of the room and into the weight room to start lifting. I lifted for a short time. I wanted to play some basketball and I didn't want to tire out. I left the room and saw the same red hooded kid again walking through the hall. I ran down to the basketball courts and no one was there; just what I wanted. I grabbed a ball and started shooting, and continued for five minutes until the guy I saw earlier came in.

"Wanna play some one-on—one?" he asked.

"I'm just shooting around. I'm not very good."

"Come on, I'm not so great myself," he said.

"Yeah, okay," I answered as he walked towards me. He didn't look like he was working out. He was dressed in black pants and a red hoodie.

I checked him the ball and he checked it back. He was covering me so I shot the ball but missed, allowing him to recover it and run it back to half court and blow through me. He followed with a lay-up and scored a point.

"One—zip," he said checking me the ball.

"Winners ball?" I asked.

"No, losers."

I dribbled by him and took a shot from the three-point arch and made it.

"One—two," I said.

The game continued and I took the lead, Six to eight. I scored again and he threw the ball against the wall in aggravation. I checked him the ball and he tried to blow past me, but I defended better. All of the sudden, I heard a loud stomping approaching. I turned around and someone checked me causing me to fly through the air and smash my shoulder on the ground. I got up slowly and looked up at the person. It was Nadim from the islands.

"Remember me, kid? You can't run this time," he said. "I'm gonna have fun beating your ass."

I looked over at the other kid and he took out a knife. They were both from the islands but I had never seen the other one before. They sent someone that I wouldn't recognize so that I would be caught off guard. And it worked. The basketball rolled my way. Nadim ran at me ready to punch so I touched the basketball and absorbed it. My entire body turned into orange rubber. Nadim's fist hit my head. I shot against the wall, bounced back hitting him, and knocking him down. I hit the floor, after I bounced off Nadim, and got up. Nadim looked at me confused and scared.

"Your . . . power . . . ?" he said confused.

"I did a little training, can't you tell?" I said.

"Let's just hurry this up! Stop messing around Nadim, I've got places to be," the other guy said. He walked toward Nadim, took his knife and cut his forearm and Nadim's back. Blood shot out of the two of them and Nadim started freaking out.

"You asshole!" Nadim yelled "You cut me!"

"Keep your head in the game," the other one said drawing the blood towards around his left hand.

He shot a stream of blood at me that I was pushed against the wall by. The blood became solid and held me to the wall. Nadim ran at me again, ready to knock me out. I turned clear white and absorbed the blood that was holding me to the wall and slid out of the restraint as a puddle. I formed myself into a body and looked at the other kid. He smiled and held up his hand making a fist. I felt myself tighten. He had control of me; his power was blood control. He ripped me apart by opening his fist and threw me against the walls of the court. I tried to come together but I couldn't. He was moving me all over the place. I was unable to make myself whole. I couldn't see anything. I could barely hear. All I did hear was Nadim's laughter. The kid finally stopped. I pulled myself together and turned back to normal. He dropped to one knee. I was dizzy and in so much pain. He really did a number on me. He seemed to be in pain as well. Nadim ran over to him.

"Are you okay?" he asked.

The kid pulled the blood off the wall that he used to restrain me back to him.

"Get away from me. I'm fine," he said coughing.

Nadim backed away from Aden and looked at me. He clenched his fists and ran at me. There was nothing that I could absorb near me except . . . the air. I wondered if I could absorb just air. I turned my body clear white and focused, feeling the air pass through me, capturing it and becoming it. Nadim was still running at me. I spread myself apart and blew over to him and coming together again. He stopped dead. I pushed the air out from my hand and hit Nadim with it. He lost his balance, stumbled, and looked around in confusion. I did that four more times, making him incredibly irate.

"What the hell was that? Where are you?" He asked.

"I'm everywhere, I'm the air," I said hitting him with another push of air. He stumbled again, losing his footing. He fell to the floor. He got up and started swinging randomly. I moved the air with my hands and forced it toward Nadim. He fell hard on the ground. He got up and backed against the wall. I concentrated hard and put more force behind the air and was hitting him much harder. With each push, the mats behind him dented in.

"SHOW YOURSELF!" he screamed and ran away from the wall.

I blew behind him and returned to normal, poking him on the back. He turned around.

"I'm right here," I said absorbing the wood from the gym floor through my feet and moving it to my entire body.

I put my two hands together and hit him in the face as if I was swinging a baseball bat. I hit him so hard my hands cracked. It hurt me put the damage I dealt Nadim was worth the pain. His body turned and fell to the floor. He caught himself with his hands and quickly pushed himself off of the floor, leaving two hand-sized craters. He then launched at me ready to kill. I instantly, without any real thought, absorbed the air. His fist went straight through my body. This time I used all my strength to move the air. It blew at Nadim and hit him hard. He flew backwards and smashed into the floor leaving a trail of damaged floor in front of him.

Nadim got back up and walked over to Aden.

"Will you do something instead of just sitting there? I can't do everything!"

Aden shot blood at Nadim mouth, but he ripped it off then screamed at Aden. I turned back to normal. Their arguing gave me time to catch my breath. My body still ached from the beating Aden dealt me.

"What the hell are you doing?" Nadim yelled.

"Sorry, you're making things complicated for me. I think I can handle this on my own." Aden affirmed.

Aden shot a blood ball at Nadim's face and covered it, then ran at Nadim with his knife at the ready. Nadim tried to remove the blood from his face but couldn't. It seemed too thick, like glue. Aden sliced Nadim's chest twice and pulled some blood out. Nadim spun around swinging violently. After a few seconds Nadim passed out on the floor. Aden covered Nadim's torso with blood and solidified it. He turned to me.

"Alright, Travis, I'm going to make this quick. I have more important matters to attend to. You are just a small distraction. I could care less that you escaped from the islands. I don't even care about them. The only reason I'm with them is because I need to save someone, and I'm not going to let you get in the way!" he said.

Aden rolled up his sleeve, cut his other arm, and more blood came out. He lifted up his shirt and cut his chest as well to drain blood out of his body. He moved the blood with his hands, the blood moving wherever he directed it. He laid it down like a blanket on the floor. I stood there and watched him. I knew I could handle whatever he threw at me, just as long as I didn't absorb any blood again.

He moved his hands up and they started to shake as if he was trying to lift something. Three separate clumps of blood began to rise out of the sheet. They were lifted up and continued to form and shape. In seconds it was clear to see that they were three dogs, blood dogs. In a few more seconds they were extremely detailed Dobermans. They bared their teeth and growled savagely.

"Get'em," Aden instructed.

The dogs ran at me. I fled the basket ball court and headed to the looker room. They chased after me with horrific speed. I ran down the hall as they barked at me. I was coming to a dead end, so I quickly turned down the next hallway. The dogs were moving too fast to slow down in enough time. They slid into the wall leaving blood smears on it, then regained their balance and continued their command. The locker room was in sight. I ran into it and they followed me in. I turned clear white and absorbed the air. They couldn't see me; it gave me time to hide and wait for an opportunity to get my coat. The dogs were running around in circles trying to find me while I was hovering in the air watching them. At the same time, all three looked up at me, so I pushed air and hit them. They tried to jump up and get me, but they couldn't reach me. I touched one of the lockers, absorbed it, and turned into metal. I fell out of the air and landed on the locker room floor, denting and cracking it. The dogs jumped on me, biting and clawing me. I threw them off, ran to my locker, ripped off the door and grabbed my coat then put it on. I took out my lighter and struck it absorbing the fire. The dogs ran at me again and I shot fire out of my hands, but they moved out of the way. I ran out of the locker room and returned to normal, not wanting to catch the gym's carpet on fire. I made it back to the basketball court, closing the doors behind me. Aden was gone but Nadim was still covered in blood, passed out on the floor.

The dogs attacked the doors, but with no effect. Suddenly, they jumped through the small glass window of the doors. I had no time to take anything from my coat and absorb it, so I absorbed the wooden floor again. One jumped on me, knocking me to the floor, and bit into my shoulder. His fangs tore through my wooden body, causing a lot of pain. I punched him and finally got him off of me. I returned to normal. There was no mark from where the dog had bit me, but the pain was still there for sure. The dogs stared me down with shards of glass from the windows sticking out of parts of their bodies. I slowly took out my lighter and absorbed its fire. Another dog lunged at me grabbing its face and shooting fire from my hands, exploding its head. It fell onto its side. Its body lost shape and turned into a puddle of blood. The other two were growling at me with their bloody teeth showing, screaming for my blood. I jumped up into the air and stayed floating by pushing fire out from my feet. I shot the dogs from in the air. They started running around trying to attack me, but failing miserably. They tried to jump and get my legs to bring me to the floor but they couldn't reach. I shot one's body splitting it in half, leaving behind two puddles. I returned to the floor and the dog jumped at me. While he was mid air, I shot him and the fireball went right through him causing him to fall the floor as a puddle.

I turned back to normal and looked over at Nadim; he was still stuck to floor. I didn't care to help him. I left the gym through the back door. It led right out to a main street. I was going to chase Aden down, but he was nowhere to be found. There was a large group of confused people outside the door.

"What happened? What did you see?" I asked one of them.

"Some kid came out of the building bleeding. A bunch of us ran over to him. Then his blood came out and attacked us," he answered.

"What?"

"I think it drained some of our blood," a woman said.

"The kid drained our blood," a well dressed man stated.

I had to find Aden before he hurt anyone else. I started running down the street and heard cop cars coming my way. I didn't want them to stop and ask me questions. I absorbed the air and turned invisible. The cars flew by me and went to the gym. I turned back to normal and continued running. There was no sign of him anywhere. He must have gotten away. I had to get home and make sure they didn't send anyone there. I went back to the gym and got my car. I drove home and everything was fine. The next few days I laid low. I wasn't sure if anyone had seen what had happened at the gym. On the news they interviewed people about what they saw, nothing was said about me. They just talked about Aden. I wanted to train using some new materials. I grabbed my coat and walked outside.

"I'll kill you Travis!" I heard behind me.

Chapter XXXII

ADEN: REECE'S RESCUE

June 19, 2007

I ran out of the gym leaving Nadim unconscious on the floor. I didn't know what stopped me from draining his body dry; maybe we developed some kind of connection from being partners. I knew Travis could handle a pack of killer blood dogs and I didn't have any need to kill him, I just didn't want him chasing me down. I was feeling incredibly weak from drawing out too much blood. I nearly fell just trying to get up the back stairs of the gym. My body was giving out. I got to the top and I saw a group of people. It was perfect. I took some more blood out of my body and I molded it into eight strands, similar to straws. I launched them at the group with each one piercing there skin and making a connection. The process caused me to drop to my knees. The people's blood traveled out of their bodies, through the straws, and into my body; a leaching technique that Cyrus had thought up. I could feel their blood going into my body and felt revitalized. It wasn't going to do much damage to the people, only taking about a half of a pint from each of them. The light-headedness left and I stood up and retracted the blood straws from everyone. I ran back to where we had landed the helicopter.

"GO GO GO!" I yelled.

"What is going on?" the pilot asked.

"Nadim has turned on us; he's working for someone else. We have to get out of here before he gets back."

"Yes, sir." The craft took off and we were on our way back to the islands.

After we arrived I ran into my room and grabbed all the blood that I had saved up. I changed it all into its liquid form and covered my body in it, completely concealing myself in blood. I couldn't believe that I hadn't thought of it before. That amount of blood covering me gave me a tingling sensation, it felt . . . good.

I left my room and started walking to where I thought Reece was.

"Hey, who are you?" a guard asked.

I pulled the blood back from my face.

"Oh, sorry sir, I had just never seen you like that before."

"No big deal. Keep up the good work." I covered my face again.

I continued to where I thought Reece was. I reached the door that I had gone through previously and tried to open it, but it was locked. I was tired of playing around. I molded the blood from my left arm into a long blade, stabbed it into the door and ripped it off its hinges. The alarm sounded. I had to move quickly.

I ran up the stairs and there were guards waiting. They started to shoot at me and instinctively, I sent out blood from my chest to block the bullets, pushing the blood at them so they were covered by it. I then solidified it, pinning them to the wall with no way of getting out.

More soldiers came up behind me from the stairs. I made the long blade again and a shield on my right arm. They started to shoot at me, so I held out the shield making it protect my entire body. Once they were close enough, I shrunk the shield and cut them down with the long blade disarming them of their guns. One tried to attack me from behind with a knife, so I molded all the blood on my back to spikes, causing the guy to run right into them. I pulled them back and he fell to the floor gasping for life. I killed the rest of them, proceeded down the hall, and continued to look for Reece.

I knocked down the doors until I finally found him tied to a bed.

"Reece!" I ran over and cut the bed straps.

" . . . Aden?"

I pulled the blood back from my face so he could see me.

"I can't believe that you're here!" he got up and hugged me.

"I'm here to save you."

"I've been here for so long. I've been so scared. I miss my parents."

"Then I'll bring you to them. Wherever you want to go."

"Thank you."

"Reece get behind me," I covered my head again.

I could hear soldier's footsteps coming down the hall.

The soldiers came around the corner. I shot a spiked blood ball at them and some flew back, but more came toward me. I pushed a giant wall of blood at them and covered the doorway with it, making spikes come out from the other side. I heard screams. If they weren't dead then they were badly injured.

"We have to get out of here before they actually send someone with an ability to stop me."

"Um . . . that's the only way out."

I looked around the room. "Then I'll have to make a new one."

I coated the wall with blood and had spikes rapidly come out to break it down. Within about a minute, the wall was broken. I pushed all the debris to the side and looked outside, seeing only water.

"Are you ready? It's going to be a long flight."

"Yup."

I grabbed onto Reece and jumped out the hole in the wall. Mid air, I made large wings from the blood on my back and we started flying. We were pulling away from the islands, when I looked back and saw helicopters coming at us.

"This isn't good."

"What are we going to do?" Can't you go faster?"

"Nope, this is as fast as I can go."

"Aden . . ."

"Don't worry Reece, I got this."

I turned around, flapped my wings to stay up, and shot a giant spiked blood ball at one of the helicopters. I hit it in the front, dipped forward, and started to smoke until it finally exploded. The three others didn't stop. They started shooting me with machine guns. I put up a barrier to protect us and watched as the bullets tried to break through it. It took a lot to keep them back. Two of the helicopters got on both sides of me and the other one stayed in front. I dropped down and started to fly faster, making some distance, but I couldn't escape the helicopters. I continued shooting at them with blood needles. I wanted to conserve as much blood as possible, but they were barely affected by them. I heard a fourth helicopter coming up from behind us. I took all the blood from my right arm and moved it over to my left making a long chainsaw like whip. I pushed it at the helicopter to my left and smashed it right down the middle. It quickly spiraled downward, landing in the water before it exploded.

The other one that showed up had someone hanging out the side of it. It looked like he was yelling something, but I couldn't hear him. All of the sudden there was a massive black ball in front of me. I moved around it, having no idea what it was. They started appearing all over. I continued to evade them, just then I saw one in front of me and I couldn't move out of the way, I just didn't have enough time.

I opened my eyes and Reece and I were falling; my body no longer covered in blood, but falling around me. I had no clue what had just happened, but I pulled it onto my body and grabbed Reece. I reformed my wings and started flapping them as fast and hard as possible to get back on track. Reece seemed to be unconscious. It had to have been that black ball that did it. I made another really big blood ball and shot it at another one of the helicopters. It had no time to get out of the way, making contact and causing the helicopter to start spinning. I shot a bunch of needles at it and it exploded.

The black spheres were everywhere. I quickly dodged them and broke away from the helicopters. There was no longer any blood on my legs or my lower back. There was blood covering my arms, most of my back, chest and head. I made the long whip chain again. I swung it around but both of the helicopters stayed back, shooting missiles at me. Each one shot two simultaneously, so I pulled the whip back and made a blood wall and pushed it quickly at the missiles coming at me. The wall stopped the missiles and there was a giant explosion. I was shot backward and so were the helicopters with a large cloud of black smoke. The helicopters were no longer visible; I turned around and continued to fly. I figured that I would end up somewhere eventually.

Reece was still knocked out. I landed behind a hotel and hid all of my blood. I shook Reece and he opened his eyes.

"You okay?" I asked.

"What happened?"

"You fell asleep."

"Where are we?"

"Not on the islands. I'm not sure exactly though."

"I really want to go home, Aden."

"Don't worry Reece; I'll get you home I promise. I just have to figure out where we are first."

We walked out from behind the building. It was gorgeous weather with the sun shining bright.

"We are in Florida," Reece said.

"Really?"

"We are like an hour away from my house."

"No kidding."

"Yeah, I can take us there I think."

A cab pulled up next to us and asked us if we needed a ride. It was free. He got a call from some guy and they worked out a deal. Faxon, I owed him a lot. In less than an hour we were on his street.

"I just want to let you know that if you need anything you can call me."

"Okay, I promise that I will. I owe you big time."

"Let's call it even. You saved my mom's life and I saved yours, even though it was my fault to begin with."

"Okay, then we're even."

We both got out of the cab and it drove away. I got up to Reece's door and I rang the door bell. His mom answered the door and she was struck by surprise. She just stared at Reece.

"Hi mom," Reece said going to hung her.

She hugged him back.

"Honey who is it?" his dad asked coming around the corner. "Reece!"

Both of Reece's parents hugged him but neither of them were crying. They didn't seem happy, just surprised.

"Who are you?" Reece's dad asked me.

"I found Reece. He told me where he lived so I brought him home."

"Where did you find him?" his mom asked.

"He was pretty far away from here."

"I don't know what we can do to repay you," his dad said.

"It's no big deal, just make sure that he is safe and okay."

"He didn't do anything weird did he?" his dad asked.

"What do you mean?"

"Did he do anything that you would classify as different or special?"

"I'm not sure I understand," he was talking about Reece's ability. He thought Reece was a freak. I wanted to just grab Reece and take off but he wanted to be home and I wasn't going to not let him have his way. It was his life, not mine.

"Nevermind."

"Thank you so much again," his mom said.

"It's no big deal I promise."

"What is your name?" his dad asked.

"My name is Chris."

"Chris what?"

"Chris Land." I didn't want them to know my real name because I didn't want them calling the cops on me or anything. The last thing I need was the cops to be after my mom and me.

"Well Chris, I hope you won't be a stranger. We owe you a lot."

"Reece, I hope that you are okay now."

"I'm much better, thanks . . . Chris." Reece hesitated and gave me a look of acknowledgement.

"Anytime, I'll call you and we can catch up sometime."

"Okay."

"I'm going to get going now."

"It was really nice meeting you," his mom said.

"Thanks again."

"No problem."

I left Reece's house and I found some place where no one could see me. I pulled out all the blood I had and made massive wings. I jumped into the air and started flying. It took me a while to get back home but I finally made it after a bunch of stops asking for directions. I got home, took a deep breath and walked inside. My mom was sitting on the couch watching the news.

"Hi, mom," I said.

She quickly turned around and was clearly frightened. Her eyes rolled back and she passed out. I ran over to her and shook her until she woke up.

"Mom, are you okay?"

"Aden . . . I . . . you're . . ."

"What? What is it?"

"I thought you were dead."

"What?!"

"The police came to the house weeks ago because the neighbors saw white vans pull up and they heard gun shots. The cops found your blood painted all over the house. There was no way you could be alive with that amount of blood loss. They came to see me at the hospital and told me the bad news. I stayed in the hospital for two more weeks until I was ready to come home."

"Mom, I'm so sorry. I didn't know any of that would happen."

"What did happen, Aden?"

"It's a really long story and I don't know how to explain it."

"Where were you?"

"I had to help someone that I put in danger."

"Who? Aden, please just tell me."

I wanted to tell her, but I couldn't. I knew she wouldn't be able to understand. It is just better if she didn't know.

"I can't tell you anything mom. Its better this way trust me."

"Well at least tell me how you're alive."

"I'm lucky, that's all there is to it."

"I'm just glad you're home and alive," she wiped her eyes and hugged me.

The next two days were weird for me. It was so strange to be back home. I had tried to call Reece, but there was no answer. I'm sure he was just at school or something. I wasn't that worried. My mom had never been happier. She babied me every chance she got and took the rest of the week off of work just to spend time with me. It must've been so hard for her to think I was dead and then suddenly back in her life. I walked downstairs and there was an old newspaper on the coffee table. It had a picture of a man in a black coat that looked very similar to Bastian. I looked at the date; the day he escaped. I yelled for my mom who came in from the kitchen.

"What is this?" I asked holding up the paper.

"Oh, that was from about a month ago. It was amazing. You should read the article. It was on the news for a few days. People are still talking about it. That man was seen flying in Florida. He landed on one of the beaches. Some woman caught it on a handy cam. They said it was all a hoax, or publicity for some movie, but that's not what people are saying. The tabloids love it."

I ran to the computer and looked up the video. I watched the clip and saw this black thing in the sky that kept getting closer. Then suddenly, it smashed into the ground and there was a huge splash of sand. After it cleared there was a guy in a long trench coat wearing a white mask with a beak. It was Bastian. It was what he was wearing when I met him at the airport with Faxon. I was afraid that I had also been seen.

I tried typing in some other stuff and nothing came up. I asked my mom if there was anything else like that on the news. She said that was the only thing that had come up. I knew I was more careful than that.

Chapter XXXIII

ZANE: THE LOST TAPE

July 17, 2001

"You can just start from where you left off last time," Cyrus suggested.

"Okay . . . well I ran inside of my house, startled and excited at the same time. I wasn't sure what had happened or how I did it. My mind was racing. I couldn't believe that I could do something so extraordinary. I took a few deep breaths and went back outside, picked up my dad's chessboard, then walked into my backyard. I took out the same pawn from before. I held it in my hand and just remembered the garage. I slammed it into the dirt and the colored circle appeared again. I was so excited; I was special somehow. I had a power, a gift, which no one else had.

I ran into my house, leaving the giant pawn standing in my backyard, not thinking anything of it. I grabbed all of my dad's other chess pieces and ran back outside, using them to try and bring out more pawns, but I couldn't. I figured that I just wasn't capable of doing more than one yet. I touched the giant pawn and my hand started to glow like last time. It returned to the circle and the piece came out normal sized. Then the circle disappeared.

I tried to use a different set of chess pieces this time, not the ones from the garage.

It didn't work, no circle, my hand didn't glow, nothing. I got worried. I thought that I had lost it. I tried using the pieces from the garage again, it worked. I tried to do a second one, again but this time with another piece from the garage. It worked. There were two giant pawns in my backyard. It seemed, for some reason, I could only use the chess pieces from the garage. I changed the chess pieces back to normal and put all of them back where they belonged. I was instantly overcome with exhaustion, dropping to the ground with my body quivering. I laid back on my grass and didn't have any other choice but to rest. The adrenaline had worn off and my body was feeling the effects of constant use of my new ability. After an hour or more I finally stopped trembling and back went inside. I put the chess board from the garage under my bed and put all of my dad's other ones back in his closet.

There was a box on the top shelf. I pulled it down. Inside the box were some pictures of us, pictures of his parents and my mom. At the bottom was a tape. On the side it read "Home Videos of Zane". I took out the tape, moved into the living room, and put it into the VCR. I hit play and it was my dad trying to figure out how to work the camera. My mom said that it was already on. He stumbled around and finally got it working. He zoomed in on me. I was no older than ten or twelve months. My parents were talking about how cute I was. The doorbell rang and my dad ran to the door. It was his ride from the military. He left and the tape skipped a couple years.

It was me again. This time I was about three years old. I was playing with a deck of cards. I was surrounded by toys, building blocks, dinosaurs and other things like that. My dad kept calling my name and I kept looking up at him. There was a knock at the door. My dad sat the camera down and it was just me playing with the toys. A few minutes later he came back and put a bag on the floor; he was leaving again. He picked me up and said something to me. I started to cry. He put me back down and I began throwing a temper tantrum. I was smacking everything around me. I was crying hard. Tears were running down my face. My little hands started to glow and I hit one of the cards on the floor. A circle appeared the same circle that appears when I use the pawns. The card disappeared and a small pocketknife came out of it. My dad picked me up quickly and moved me away from the circle. He picked up the pocketknife and showed it to me. He gazed at me looking very upset. He kept asking me how I did it. I started to cry again. I grabbed the knife and my hand started to glow. The knife was sucked into the floor. The tape stopped."

"Is that all?" Cyrus asked.

"No. The screen went fuzzy. It cut to my dad talking to the camera," I explained.

"Son, if you are watching this tape . . . well I'm not too sure what to tell you. Either I gave it to you or something bad has happened to me and you've found it. Anyway, I'm not positive what you did. I tried to get you to do it again but you couldn't; at least not with anything other than that one deck of cards. All you could do was make that purple pocketknife appear every time. I took the deck of cards away from you and I tried to do it. I couldn't, I'm not like you. You're special son. I've always known it. I just felt like you were going to do something important some day. But I bet all fathers get that feeling," my dad said.

"I couldn't help myself, I began to cry uncontrollably. I missed him so much, I loved him and wanted him back," I said tearing up a bit. "The video continued."

"Anyways, I hid them after I gave up trying to make the circle appear. I didn't want you to know what you could do. I didn't want it to control you. But I guess it is no longer my choice if you are watching this. I'm not going to tell you where they are but I will give you a hint. If you truly believe that you are ready to accept what you can do then you need to look deep inside yourself and there is only one way to do it. Can you truly see yourself?

I guess that about raps it up. I just want you to know that I do love you, with all of my heart. It is hard for me to show my love because I leave you so often. I'm very sorry but it is my job. I have to protect the ones I love. I hope someday you can understand it a little better but . . . I don't know. I love you son."

"The tape stopped and the screen was consumed by static. I wiped my eyes and took the tape out. I went into his room, put it back into the box that I had found, then sat down on the bed. I couldn't believe everything that was happening. I felt sick to my stomach. I just wanted to watch the video over and over again. I missed him so much. I knew that it wasn't going to bring him back. I had to focus on what was happening now. I thought about his clue. I didn't quite understand what he meant. I thought about it for a little while. I walked around the house. I stopped for a second and sat down on the stairs.

I looked at the mirror in front of me, realizing what he was talking about. He hid them around or behind a mirror. I ran all over the house checking all the mirrors; but there was nothing there. I fell to the floor, remembering about the one we had in the attic. It was my grandma's. My dad said to me once that it the only mirror that he could see himself in. It never made sense to me. I thought he was just crazy. In the attic, it was dark and everything was covered in cobwebs. I hadn't been up there in ages; I don't think anyone had. I found the mirror, and walked over to it and looked at myself. I searched around the mirror and found the cards taped to the bottom and pulled them off. I opened the case that they were in and looked at them. They looked just like normal cards. I pulled one out and tried to do the same thing that I did with the chess pieces. Nothing happened. I was a little disappointed at first but I realized it wasn't gong to be easy controlling this thing that I could do.

I went back outside and into my backyard. I brought my dads chessboard with me. I took out a pawn and did my thing. Then I tried to do the same with the cards that my dad left for me, but nothing happened. I had to try and do something different to get them to work. I tried really hard to focus my energy into my hand. It had worked; my hand was covered with the colored energy. I slammed the card on the ground but no circle appeared. I tried over and over again; failing every time. I sat down to regain my breath. Trying to use my power wore me out. I thought about the tape, the first time I brought out that pocketknife I was very upset. I stood back up and just thought about my dad and how I never got to see him. I thought about how he always left us and I never got to really know him as a man. All of that emotion built up inside me and my hand was raging with energy. I ripped a card out of the case and it started to glow. I could feel it feed off of my energy. I slammed it into the ground and the circle appeared with small pocketknife coming out of it.

I picked it up. I couldn't believe that I actually did it. I could now use the chess pieces and the cards. I kept thinking if all I could make was a little purple pocketknife. So I decided to try something else. I took out another card and did it again. Another pocketknife came out. I put the pocket knifes back into the ground and the cards shot out and up into the air. I caught them both and held them in my hand. I took out a couple more cards and held them in stack between two of my fingers and my thumb. I charged my energy into my hand and put the cards into the ground and the circle appeared. It was there for a few seconds and nothing was happening. Then something slowly started to come out of it. Suddenly it shot up and out of the circle. It was a blue bladed sword with a purple handle. I caught it before it landed. I could make more than just the pocket knife. I had taken my power to a whole new level."

"That's amazing. Your power developed rather quickly. No wonder you are so good," Cyrus complemented.

Perin walked into the room.

"Zane, I would like to speak to you in private," he said. "Sorry if I'm interrupting Cyrus."

"No worries Perin. We just finished," Cyrus said.

I got up off the couch and walked out side of his office and into the hall with Perin.

"Zane I believe that you are one of the top people on this island. You've shown as much potential as the heads do with your power. These sessions with Cyrus have only improved your skill," Perin said. Two of the project's heads came out from behind a corner holding a tall bag.

"What is going on?" I asked.

"I've talked to the heads and the Boss about this and they all agree. I've showed them tapes of your training," he said.

"Wait, what?" I was confused.

The two heads unzipped the tall black bag and took out a long white coat. It had a purple trim and the projects symbol on the back, except it was blue purple and white.

"Zane I would like you to became the eighth head of Project Dominium," Perin handed me the coat.

I took the coat. I didn't know what to say. I was astonished by his proposal.

"I'm sorry, Perin, but I don't think that I'm ready yet. You may think so, but I don't believe I have what it takes as of right now," I kindly refused.

"That is quite alright. I'm not upset. You can keep the coat to remind you of my offer. My offer will always be standing; whenever you are ready."

"Thank you all. It means a lot to know that you can trust me with such an important position."

Chapter XXXIV

ADEN: BAD BLOOD

July 5, 2007

I got off the plane and walked into the airport. I was on my way to see Reece. I hadn't heard from him in about a week. I decided that I was going to pay him a surprise visit. I walked outside and hailed over a taxi. One pulled over and I got into the back seat.

"Where to?" he asked.

"Winter Park. 159 Ocean Avenue."

"You got it kid."

The ride was about twenty minutes long. I began to grow more and more excited each mile closer. I could have flown, but I didn't want to draw any attention to myself. The taxi parked outside of Reece's house. I paid him and he drove off. I walked over to the door and knocked. I could hear people inside. His mom came to the door.

"Oh, hello. It's Chris right?"

"Hi, I wanted to stop by for a surprise visit."

"Um, why didn't you just call?" she asked smiling politely.

"I tried, but none of my calls were answered. I just really wanted to see Reece. I've kinda started to think of him as my younger brother."

"Well, isn't that sweet."

"So do you mind if I go in and see him?"

"Actually, Chris. I don't think that would be a good idea," she stepped outside and closed the door behind her.

"Excuse me?"

"My husband and I think that it's weird how much you want to be around our son. You're a young man and he's just a boy. I don't want to have to call the police. Plus Reece isn't here. He is at a . . . um, a summer camp and he won't be back for some time."

"I don't believe you," I said very rudely. I pushed open the door. "Reece, it's Aden. Come on down."

"He's not here. Please leave," she moved me out of the doorway.

"Where is he? Tell me the truth!"

She backed up and stopped at the door.

"He's in a better place."

"What!! Tell me where he is," she opened the door and was about to close it behind her but I held the door open with my foot. She was scared. Her hands were shaking. "Tell me where he is, NOW!"

"Honey, this isn't a joke. We need more soap."

"What does that mean?"

"She moved out of the way and her husband came around the corner with a shotgun.

"Leave my house now. You've got one chance to leave before I kill you and burry you in my backyard."

"Tell me where you sent Reece. Tell me, before this gets messy," I said without wavering.

"Your time is up kid."

He pulled the trigger. The blood that I kept around my ankles reacted, shot up, created a barrier, and protected me from the shotgun bullets. I filtered the bullets out of my blood and made a whip and disarmed Reece's father. I ran at him and covered him in blood and slammed him to the kitchen floor. I had the ability to cut him open and drain all his blood in the blink of an eye; but I didn't want his blood anywhere near my body. His entire existence disgusted me.

Reece's mom picked up the phone. I shot a single needle straight through it knocking it out of her hand.

"Where is he? For the last time, tell me. This is as nice as I'm going to be! Don't test me!"

"We sent him to a place where he could be helped. He's sick. They said they would help him. Some sort of island facility," I could see the way she looked at me. She was terrified of me. Her hands were shaking and her eyes large.

"I can't believe you sent him back there! I'm going to save your son again but this time I'm not bringing him back. You don't deserve him," I walked out of the house and I hardened the blood that was covering his deadbeat dad.

I couldn't believe that Reece was back on the islands. I hoped that I would never have to go back. Finding Faxon had become my biggest priority.

I ran over to a car and ripped the man out of it. I drove back to the airport but I didn't have enough money to buy a ticket. There was nothing that I could do. I had no other choice. I had to get home. I used the blood I had left to leech blood away from innocent bystanders, doing it very carefully. I didn't need to draw attention to myself. It didn't hurt them; they only felt a little lightheaded afterward. It took about an hour but I got all that blood that I needed. I created wings and flew from the top of the parking garage. In hours, I was back home. I grabbed my car keys and just began driving around. I made sure that my cell phone was on just in case Faxon called me.

I left my mom a note. It read "I'm not sure when I will be back. I have to help a friend. I'm sorry I have to leave, but I'll be okay, and I'll be back as soon as I can. I love you. Please don't worry."

I needed a plan. I couldn't just fly to the islands and steal him back again; they'd be expecting me and Perin would have everyone ready to tear me apart. I'm surprised he hasn't sent an army to retrieve me by now. My phone rang. It was a number that I've never seen before. It had to be Faxon. I picked up my phone.

Chapter XXXV

Faxon: Knowledge is Power

July 5, 2007

I was on my way to see Travis. He was the next person on my list to ask for help. I had been putting it off since the day he escaped. With Stel successfully maturing his power, he was a much needed asset to me. I was headed to his house to put forth my offer which I already knew he was willing to except. I still had to work on Bastian though, who would be an equally important member to the team. I rummaged through my brain, the warehouse of information, to quickly look for Aden and see what he was up to, except I was halted by an excruciating headache. I got a fragment of what I was searching for. He needed my help for something. I put on my coat, departed from my building, walked outside and preceded down the street to the center of town. I bumped into a man, borrowed his cell phone to call Aden.

"I'm glad you called I need your help. It's Reece," he said frantically.

"Okay, don't panic. I'm in Pennsylvania. I'll go to the tallest building. Fly over here as fast as you can. We don't have much time."

The call ended and I ran back to the man that I lifted the phone from.

"Sir, I believe you dropped this," I said handing him his phone.

"Oh," he checked his pockets. "Thanks, my life is on this phone."

"Yeah, you wouldn't be able to go an hour without it, Paul. Your boss would kill you if you lost all that work," I laughed and patted him on the shoulder.

"Excuse me? Who are you?" Paul asked with a perplexed look.

"You're going to be late for your meeting if you don't get moving." He looked at his watch.

"Oh shit, you're right." He started running down the sidewalk.

A trolley coasted slowly down the street. I grabbed on and let it take me. It was only a matter of minutes before I got to the tallest building. After I caught a glimpse of it, I leaped off the trolley, walked into the building, and traveled straight to the stairwell to begin my trek to the top. When I got there Aden was already waiting.

"I'm here, now tell me how to save Reece, He's back on the islands."

"What? How?"

"You don't know?"

"I haven't been using my power for a little while. My headaches were getting slightly unpleasant."

"It's a long story, but it doesn't matter now. I just need to get back."

"If you go alone they'll kill you."

"I know. I'm surprised they haven't sent anyone after me already. But if I don't have another option then I'll go alone."

"Take my advice; they will to be on high alert. They will shoot you down so fast you won't even hear the bullet leave the barrel."

"You have to come with me."

"That's not possible. I wouldn't last any longer than you would. We'd probably die faster if I was there."

"What the hell am I supposed to do? Can't you think of a plan?"

"I know someone who can help you."

"Who? Is he close?"

"It's Bastian, He's in Kansas. There is a plane leaving now. You should be able to catch it." I pulled out a pen and paper writing down Bastian's information, his address, where he was last at, everything recent.

"I'm not going to have time to get a flight."

"Just fly high up into the sky, wait for the plane to fly by, and grapple on to it. Then sit back and relax. You should be there late tonight."

"Thank you, Faxon. Which way is the plane?"

"It's just leaving now; from the west. Good luck convincing him."

Aden flew off into the sky.

I had to hope that Aden would be able to convince Bastian. He was a stubborn kid, his mind and emotions constantly changing. I didn't want Aden to go with Travis, even though it seemed like the obvious choice, but Aden was the only one who could convince Bastian. I had a good feeling it was going to be by force.

Being sidetracked by Aden had pushed my plans for Travis back one more day.

THE NEXT DAY

I let a small amount of information pour into my mind. I found Travis' location. He already knew about me to some degree from Stel and Alexander. It was only a matter of time until I needed his help too. All I had to do is pitch him my idea about the islands and he'd be all over it. This was going to be the easiest conversation I've had in a while, I thought

I got back to the streets and hailed down a taxi. Again, I let a minuscule amount of information drip in.

"Hey, Arnold, how's the streets treating you?" I asked getting in the taxi.

"Do I know you?" he asked.

"I own half of the taxi's in this town. You better know me."

"Excuse me? Are you stoned, sir?"

"No, if you want I can give you the names of the drivers and the license plate numbers."

"Sir, what are you expecting? A pass on the fair?"

"I sure hope so, 'cause if not I'm going to call Frank and tell him how unpleasant one of his drivers is."

"Why don't we just call him right now." Arnold took out his cell phone and dialed Frank's number. "Excuse me boss, I don't mean to bother you, but there is some bum telling me that he owns half the taxi's in the city."

"Give me the phone," I said gesturing it away from Arnold.

"Yeah, Frank. It's James. How's Caroline doing?"

"Richards?" Frank asked.

"The one and only. I'm sorry for taking up your driver's time, but I got mugged and need to get to a friend's house quick. Could you mind telling your driver to give me a lift. I promise I'll repay the dept."

"Yeah sure no problem. Put him back on. Oh, and say hi to your girl for me. How old are they again?"

"Sara is twelve and Amy is seventeen."

"That's great. I'll talk to Carol about setting up a dinner date, and we can finally catch up. Well I'll see you around."

"Thanks Frank." I handed the phone back to Arnold. He got a quick earful. Then the conversation ended.

"Sir, I'm so sorry."

"No big deal. Stop thinking about it, just drive, I don't have much time to waste."

"Yes, sir."

Chapter XXXVI

TRAVIS: EVERYTHING?

July 6, 2007

"I'll kill you, Travis!" I heard behind me.

I turned around and saw Nadim running at me. He must have been watching me since the day at the gym. I held out my hands and was about to turn into air, but I wanted to wait for him to be right in front of me. He was getting very close when all of the sudden, a ragged looking man jumped over my neighbor's fence. He would die if Nadim hit him. The bum turned his head and smiled at me.

Nadim was right in front of him. The bum moved out of the way and grabbed Nadim's arm and put his foot in front of Nadim's and dropped him to the ground. After Nadim was down the man put his thumb on Nadim's back.

"I . . . I can't move," Nadim said.

"That's right Nadim, you can't. As long as I have my thumb on this very point on your back the most you can do is talk."

"Who are you?" Nadim asked.

I watched him take down Nadim like he was nothing. I was more than impressed, I just hoped he was on my side.

"I want to help you. I don't want to be your enemy."

"What do you mean?"

"You can't trust the people on the islands."

"Why not?"

"They lied to you, that's why."

"What do you even know about them?"

"Well, for one thing, your sister isn't in the hospital being taken care of by top doctors."

"Yes she is!"

"Sorry, Nadim, but she died last year. Your parents couldn't afford to keep her healthy and with you gone they couldn't get as much work done with the crops."

"That's not true! I've been getting letters from her every month!"

"Sorry, those are fake. Why do you think they were typed?"

"The project gave her a computer."

"No they didn't."

"She is alive!"

"Nadim you can believe what you want but they lied to you and told you that they would take care of your sister if you went with them. They never held up to their side of the bargain."

"How would you know!?"

"Because, Nadim, I know everything. I'm the one that the islands fear. I am Faxon,"

"Never heard of you."

"They keep everything secret on that island, of course you've never heard of me. I will release you. I want you to just go back to the islands and have them send you to go see your sister. They won't allow you to go see her because she is dead. They won't even let you talk to your parents. You are on the wrong side, Nadim." Faxon removed his thumb off of Nadim's back.

Nadim stood up slowly. He stared at me and then looked at Faxon. Nadim turned away and started running.

"I hope he finds the light. He isn't very bright. I bet that they will find another way to deceive him. It's very saddening actually."

"So you're Faxon. I've heard so much about you, but at the same time so little," I said. "And now I've finally come face to face with you."

"Well, this is me," he said shrugging his shoulders. "I know I'm not what you expected, but I enjoy the way I look. It makes me feel comfortable. Let's go for a walk."

"I first heard about you from Bastian. He wasn't very happy with you."

"He still isn't. He's going through a very rough time right now. His power has got him questioning himself."

"Then I heard about you from Alexander."

"I know."

"And then from Stel. You and her were close."

"Yes we were, but I don't bother her anymore. I know she doesn't want to destroy the islands like you and I do."

"Yeah."

"She did a great job on you though. Even though you should definitely not have survived, it's more than a miracle that you did. You are now probably one of the strongest people around, Travis."

"Really?"

"Definitely. We both know that you could have easily disposed of Nadim right there. He wouldn't have stood a chance and you did great in the fight with Nadim and Aden."

"You saw that?"

"I see everything. Well basically everything."

"I don't understand."

"My power is extraordinary, to say the least."

"Well, what is it? Show me."

"It's not something I can show you, but I can tell you. I know everything that has happened and is happening. I am omniscient, for the most part. I can't see into the future or anything like that, but I can know what every person in the world is thinking. It all started about four years ago; actually way before that. You see, my power didn't awaken until about five years ago. It came fast and hit me hard. I received massive headaches that actually made me lose consciousness on more than one occasion. It was about a full grueling month until I could go an entire day without passing out. It took a long time before I learned how to filter the information. With the help of one of the instructors, I then developed a program to locate people with powers. It only took the two of us about a whole day to do it. The program was remarkable. I later found out what the islands were really doing. I didn't react right away. I waited until the right moment, then I escaped with Stel."

"Wow."

"You're telling me."

"How long were you on the islands for before you got your power?"

"Almost eight years, and before that I made frequent trips to and from there. It wasn't an easy idea to grasp once I discovered the truth."

"Why don't you just take out the islands by yourself?"

"They have created something that stops me from receiving any information from there. It's like a massive field blocking my senses."

"Oh."

"That is why I'm trying to create a team that will do it for me. I'm old and can't really fight all their soldiers at once. Sure, I know everything that is happening, but I can't dodge a bullet or have it bounce off me like you can."

"You make a good point, but I'm still unclear about what they are doing. I read some files on a computer, but it only got me more confused."

"This is where my power comes in handy. I'll tell you everything. How the islands came to be, what they are really about, the theories, and about . . . the First."

Chapter XXXVII

FAXON: FROM THE BEGINNING

July 6, 2007

"It all started in 1946, after World War Two, when the government started looking for any countries with advanced weaponry. They noticed something on their radar, some sort of energy source that was being emitted from a group of islands located far off the Florida coast. They went to the islands equipped and prepared, but they couldn't find anything dangerous so they left. They completely ignored the blips of energy for about ten years. Then a new person came in charge who had a companion with him. His companion had a "superpower". He could create a purple dot on a person's body that would eventually spread into a deadly virus and slowly eat away at you every time you strained your muscles.

Everyone was afraid of him and called him a freak. The commander wanted to further explore his companion's strange "superpower". He knew that if there was a person who had a strange ability then there would have to be more. He came across the islands and decided that he wanted to know what it was about. Nearly every person told him it was a waste of time and that there was nothing on the islands except for trees.

He disregarded their advice and sent a group onto the islands; three helicopters, one for each island, filed with a dozen soldiers a piece. The first two landed on what are now the Industrial and the Homestead. They found nothing and started getting back onto the choppers. The third chopper landed and the men examined the island.

Meanwhile, inside of his home, a man sat terrified of what he was hearing. Well, first let me give you a quick summery of the man's life. He is a Native American from the Dine tribe. He is the one who gave us our powers. He has been alive for centuries. His tribe abandoned him and shunned him away to the middle of the island. At that time the islands were one but it started to break apart due to quakes and water tremors. Anyway, he sat inside of his home and was terrified of the sounds that he heard outside. Then the men came across the man's home, his hogan. They stopped. The man heard footsteps outside. He hadn't seen a person in over a couple hundred years. He wasn't sure what to do because he wasn't supposed to leave his home. The men contacted their commander and asked him what to do. He told them to engage the small dome shaped building and let him know the findings afterwards. The men approached the dome guns pointed and ready to fire. Inside man heard them approaching. He opened the door to his home. The troops stopped and looked at each other.

"Stop!" the soldiers yelled. "Don't move!"

The man couldn't understand them. He didn't speak our language yet. He took another step outside and they started to unload their clips on the First. He turned his body and held up his arm to protect himself from whatever was coming. The bullets hit him, and flattened, leaving him uninjured. He knew that they were trying to hurt him. He turned to look at the soldiers and one of them was running at him. He held his hand out to block the man and wind shot out from it. The soldier went flying and crashed into the others. They turned back and looked at the man. He stood up straight and held his hands out; shooting streams of air out and hitting the soldiers. Some of the soldiers went flying, one hid behind a tree and called for back up. The other two choppers landed on the island and the reinforcements came running out. The man saw them coming at him and he knew he had to protect himself. He had just found out that he had this newfound power, he knew he could use that to protect him.

He shaped the wind around his body like a dome and pushed it out knocking down all of the soldiers. The First started to get tired and the wind wasn't doing too much other than holding them off, but he continued to fight. He was about to release the energy out of his body that gives people powers. Centuries of it happening and still it hurt him. He couldn't hide the pain. He dropped to his knees and started to illuminate white and emit a strange glow. He released the energy and it covered him like a blanket and then shot into the sky in the form of a beam. He tried to stay awake, but he was too exhausted.

The soldiers were awe struck. They had never seen anything like it before. They quickly grabbed him, tied him up with rope, and threw him onto one of the choppers with all three flying back to the base. When they returned, they told there commander what had happened. He was very pleased. He waited for the man to wake up, which didn't take too long. When the First came to he broke free from the rope binding him as if it were mere thread. The commander was pleased when he saw and the man started freaking out. The commander had some troops try and calm him down, but he wouldn't let anyone near him. He shot streams of wind at anyone who approached. The commander laughed due to his excitement. He had his soldiers back off and he entered the room and approached the First slowly and carefully.

The commander held out his hand and the First immediately shot him back with wind. The commander got up and tried it again. All he wanted was a hand shake. He figured that the man wouldn't be able to understand him. After a few attempts the commander and the man were sitting down eating together. The First no longer felt threatened. He felt his body start to burn. He started to glow and emit the white light again. The commander immediately ran out of the room and into the control room and turned on the radar that detected the strange energy source. It was now coming from their building. The commander realized that the young man was discharging the energy.

The commander had his men trace it. The energy became smaller the further it traveled. They found that it went to a hospital somewhere in Utah. He sent a squad to go check it out. No one could say for sure what they saw. One of the doctors swore he say a flash of light after the baby was born, but no one else saw it. It seemed that after the energy leaves his body it isn't very easy to see.

The flash of light that the doctor saw was the energy that the First gives off. That energy that leaves his body is what gives people their powers. The government monitored that girl for the next six years. One day they saw her on the playground talking to a group of squirrels and they understood her. Not the most destructive power in the world, but still a power nonetheless. The government kidnapped the girl and brought her to their home base. They questioned her and made her use her power. The commander showed his boss and persuaded him to let him develop a place where everyone of the freaks could go. The plan was approved and construction began immediately. The commander drew up plans for three different main buildings. They had no purpose until a few years later.

The men investigated the area where they found the man. On the back of the home there was a word written in some form of Native American. They had a translator come and decipher it. The word meant the Abandoned One. It was the First's god given name. He despised it because it was an accurate description on him.

The commander and the First began to grow on each other. It only took the First a few days to pick up on the American language. He was speaking perfect English in less than a week. The commander was impressed. Everyone respected the First. He did undergo many experiments, some of which with blood testing. I've tried to figure out what happened to his blood, but it was as if it dropped off the face of the earth around the time that I was brought in to Project Dominium. He didn't mind the tests. He knew that it was for the good of everyone.

Each time the man gave off this energy they would follow it and track that person until their power became clear. They didn't find every single person. It was actually very rare when they did find the exact location that the energy went. The ratio was somewhere around one person every thirty-six energy releases. He released the energy on average about twenty-four times every three and a half weeks. The First had no idea what they were doing.

The commander had to leave for a few months because his wife was going to give birth. On the day that the commander's child was born the First expelled energy and it was tracked to the hospital that the commander's son was born in. The commander didn't believe it. He had mixed feelings about his son at that point. He didn't hate people with abilities, but he did consider them freaks.

Theories started to develop about the First. These theories gave him the name "The First". It was believed that he is the first person with a power. They believed that he could control them because he granted them power. That is untrue. There was an incident in the late seventy's. Four people with abilities went on a killing spree on the west coast. The commander stopped it with the help of two of the people with abilities. He captured and killed them.

He began to think that maybe they would all turn out like that. The completion of the construction on the islands was nearly finished. The commander's mind was changing; he wasn't sure how to feel about the people with abilities. There was another incident in Australia where a man was robbing banks using his power. That was the last straw. He knew that the islands had to be a prison for the people, not a sanctuary. He planned to disguise the place as if it was one though. He had a giant dome constructed underwater and in between the three islands as an addition. The dome was very special and used the latest in technology.

He came to realize that if he really wanted to rid the world of people with abilities then he would have to kill the First as well. The commander was worried that since the man was giving off the energy and making people have special abilities, after the First died so would everyone with an ability, even the commander's son. He knew what had to be done. He went for a walk on the islands with the man and showed him what had been created on his old home. The First seemed displeased, but understood that times change. He told him about his life as they came across his old home, where they found him. He was in shock. He hadn't seen it in many years. The commander didn't want to destroy it. In fact he didn't want to do very much to that island at all. He wanted to save it for the First.

The commander took out his gun and held it to the First's head. He apologized and pulled the trigger, but the bullet hit his head and flattened. He turned around and looked at the commander. He was startled, but not surprised. The First was saddened and disgusted. The commander explained himself and the First was more than upset. Soldiers came out and surrounded him and he looked down at the ground. He had thought he was finally accepted for who he really was. A tear dropped from his eye and he looked up at the commander. He didn't fight his captivity, willingly going into the newly constructed dome; a replica of the man's old home, on a larger scale and underwater. It was dark and terrifying. The First was not surprised that what he had became foul. Just when he was accepted he was put right back where he was before. The gods had cursed him for his life and wouldn't give him a chance to renew it, was all he thought.

The commander theorized that if the First was the one giving off the abilities then he could only be killed by someone with an ability, but he only had a handful of people with abilities at his disposal. Most of them were much too weak to do any real damage and the rest of them weren't trained for combat. The commander sent his companion and two others into the dome to attempt to kill him, but he fought them off and kept them away using his wind power. The First was caught off guard by one of the men and the commander's companion touched him on the chest. He looked down at his chest and saw the mark start to spread. Then a circle formed around the dot and they canceled each other out, leaving no mark. He grabbed his head and suddenly received a colossal headache. A tiny sphere of orange light appeared in front of his forehead then surrounded him. It was comparable to the energy that he distributes. The energy expanded around his body and continued to grow. The commander's companion was the first to be inside of the energy. The other two men tried to run at the energy, but were pushed back and outside.

The energy covered the inside of the dome. It was just the First and the companion. The companion tried to fight him, but it was futile, he was far too strong. One punch made the companion fly across the dome.

"Just leave me alone. Let me rest in peace. You accept me and then shun me away. Just let me be. Leave here and don't come back," the First said.

The companion left and told the commander what happened. The commander found another person with a power and tried to send all four of them in at the same time. It couldn't be done. The energy that the First released only allowed one person to enter. There could only be two people inside of the energy at once, one of which being the First.

The commander decided that if he really wanted the First to be killed he would have to find stronger people to fight him. After putting him inside the dome it became harder for them to track his energy. When he did release the energy, some of it was converted into electricity to power the islands, which was why the dome was originally designed. The commander had only one choice and that was to train the people that he had. He made them stronger, assigned them trainers, and the project continued to grow. The islands were given labels: The Homestead, The Industrial, and The Hokee. The Hokee, named after the First, the name given to him by a man named Sani. That is the island that leads to The First and his prison. The commander had two other people with him to run the islands, his companion and another woman who didn't have an ability. Years passed and more and more people with abilities came onto the islands without knowing what they were really doing. The commander created a trial called the End of Chaos. It was where five of the top "students" would go and try and kill the Hokee. No one ever came back alive. The commander told the other "students" that they were sent home because they did well on the trial.

Hokee had no other option but to kill the ones who came into his dome. They tried to kill him and he had to defend himself. During the fights he had gained more and more skills. Hokee only grew stronger as time passed and the commander noticed. The commander finally grew too old and had to give up the project to someone else. He turned it over to his son, Jacob Perin. His son appointed new heads to assist him. He chose six others, some with powers and some without. You already know that he runs the project well. His father remained on the islands for many years after he retired, but his father has disappeared. Not even I know where he is now. All I do know is, before he left, he created some sort of device. The information is too blurry for me to understand it.

The trial is about to happen again. It is about that time. We have to stop it from happening. We can't keep having people die for a useless cause. Anyone who fights the First most definitely would be killed."

"Then why don't we save him?" Travis asked with concern.

"It's not that easy. He is kept under very close watch. The ones protecting him are very strong."

"It's nothing I can't handle. I know what I can do and I know that I can easily take out the islands."

"You are over estimating yourself. I'll get you help. At this very moment one of my people is trying to convince Bastian to go to the islands with him. You know him, it's Aden."

"What? Aden works for you?"

"Yes, he infiltrated the islands for me, but not to destroy them. He went there to save a friend and that is why he is going back. If he succeeds with Bastian then by the time you arrive, they should already be there. As a team you can wipe them out in one strike."

"Sounds good to me."

Chapter: XXXVIII

PERIN: THE TRIAL BEGINS

July 6, 2007

The trial was about to start. Each year everyone gathered to hear who would be taking part in the trial. I knew that the students talk to each other about things. There was nothing that could be done to control their level of association with each other while still maintaining order. As long as they thought they were breaking the rules then there was no need to worry about an uprising.

"Now we all know why we are here. We are here to praise the ones chosen for the End of Chaos trial this year."

The students started to clap.

"You too could be sitting up in one of these five chairs this time next year, that is if you work had enough. Some of you are strong and some of you have a long way to go. Remember, training always pays off."

I had most of the instructors and all of the heads up on stage, excluding McGrand of course. I wanted everyone to know who was going on the trial. There were a total of about two hundred students in the auditorium. The I.E.S was all over the room, just in case. I told Zander to be ready at any minute to cover the room in his darkness domes and put everyone to sleep if anything started to happen. With everything that had been going on lately I wanted to be ready.

"Ladies and gentlemen, I want to recognize the ones who have worked as hard as they could to make it here today. I want to thank all of the instructors that help you all learn how to control your powers and better understand them. I want every single one of you to know that you are important. With out you none of this would be possible. Every one of you is special and has helped toward achieving our main goal, protecting the world!"

The kids clapped.

"Okay now I want to introduce the five students who have been selected for the trial this year. Zane Kinsley, will be the first to take the trial," The crowd roared with excitement. I knew he had made a name for himself in Fight Night. Everyone knew his name. Technically he was an instructor but it wouldn't be the first time I sent an instructor to the trial.

I really didn't want to have to sacrifice Zane. He was one of my strongest fighters. If all went according to plan he won't stay dead long after the trial. Reece would arrive by then. As long as we had him then our attempts to kill the Hokee would be unlimited.

"Next up is Tyson Gawl." The crowd clapped.

Tyson was decent help. With his ability to regenerate his limbs he would be able to tire out the Hokee.

"Then Makale,"

If Zane failed, Makale would be able to finish the Hokee off. He was by far our strongest student. He had zero limits and unlimited potential.

"Faye Deria."

I had chosen her just as filler. She has shown a lot of progress but it would be over by the time Makale is up.

"And finally Kaden Sputem."

Again, just another filler. His progress had been great but no real importance. This was the best team that I had in a long time. There was no way I could fail. The Hokee would be killed and Project Dominium would be complete. I knew the price that I had to pay, but if my father was willing to pay it then so would I.

The crowd continued to clap and cheer.

"Everyone please, silence." They quieted down. "Thank you. We are about to proceed to begin the trial. Hopefully, this is the year that the trial ends and the world becomes free and safe. Wish us luck."

We walked off the stage and outside to the helicopter. The chopper hit the air and we all headed over to the third island; The Hokee. We landed on the landing pad, exited the chopper, and proceeded to where the transit was. Then got onto the transit and began our decent underground. The Hokee is being held in a dome deep below the water. The entire complex was incased in a sphere. You could see it from inside the transit. The kids admired in curiosity of what they were looking at, but none of the students new it even existed. The sphere was massive; about the size of three football fields in diameter.

"This is it everyone. You are the five chosen ones for this year's trial." I said exiting the transit.

The transit took us inside the sphere but outside of the Hokee's dome, which had lights all along the ceiling. The interior was metal just as the exterior. There were also small rods coming down from the ceiling. Every time the Hokee released his energy the rods would electrify. Thanks to a technopath the energy that the Hokee releases can power one of the islands for an entire month. Generators on the Homestead store all the left over energy. There was housing for the instructors that were stationed there at all times monitoring the dome. They lived comfortably but exclude from the rest of the project.

Unfortunately, I'd been too busy to worry about anything other than the trial. Its preparation was of utmost importance. The past weeks had been more than a thorn in my side. With Aden's betrayal always on my mind I'd admit it was hard to stay focused, but he was too predictable. He returned Reece to his parents, just where I wanted him to be. If Aden had kept him it may have actually been a challenge to get him back. As for Reece's parents, just one quick check and Reece was back in my custody. Before we left I sent a team to go retrieve Reece. I carried a walkie talkie in order for them to notify me once he was brought back to the islands. I wanted to wait to start the trial until we got him back, but I feared that Faxon was building an army, I knew he had Travis, Aden, Bastian, Stel and who knows how many others. He'd soon be planning an attack. Sadly, I owed Faxon. Most of the students were here because of him. But that fact would not excuse his betrayal. I fear he was already in route to stop the trail from happening. I had to start immediately. When Reece arrived, I'd just revive any one who was dead and send them in again.

"Are you ready Zane? You are the first one to enter."

"What exactly is the trial?"

"Win the fight."

"What fight?"

"Enter the dome and it will all be explained. There is a great evil inside of that dome, Zane. Eradicate it."

Chapter: XXXIX

ZANE: THE LAST TRIAL

July 6, 2007

"I'm ready, Perin."

"Then go."

I began walking toward the dome. I arrived at the door, opened it, and went inside. As I walked in, I felt my body pass through a strange energy. It wasn't painful but it did give me chills. It was dark and I couldn't see anything. I took only a few steps forward.

"Hello?"

The lights started to flicker and then turned on completely. I looked around the dome. I was looking up at the ceiling expecting to see something big, like a demon of some sort, but there was nothing. I brought my head back down and was startled by a man sitting in lotus position, legs crossed, in the middle of the dome.

"Who are you?" I asked.

"I have many names."

"Well give me one."

"The First."

"The First?"

"Or Hokee."

"What? That is the name of this island."

"I know. They named it after me."

"What? Who are you?"

"I'm the "evil" that you must destroy," he stood up.

"You are?"

"Yes," he looked up at me.

He had long black hair, skin that was a dark tan, and he wasn't wearing a shirt, just old Native American pants. He had a spearhead around his neck, and his muscles were very apparent. Height wise, he was about six feet.

"Are you ready to do this or what?" he asked very unhappily.

"Fight you?"

"Yes, every year a group of you come down here and I have to kill every one of you. None of you will just leave. All of you say that I must be killed to protect the world."

"I never signed up to kill anyone."

"You signed up to stop the evil one, did you not?"

"I was told that was what the trial was about."

"I am supposedly that evil; you have no choice but to fight me."

"I . . ."

"As far as I am concerned you can leave."

"I can just walk out?" I looked back at the door.

"Be my guest."

I turned around walked out of the door. Everyone looked at me.

"What!?" Perin said. "Did you kill him?"

"No."

"Then why and how the hell are you back out here!" Perin asked. Everyone was confused and amazed.

"He said I could leave, so I did," Perin paused for a moment.

"He tricked you. Are you really that naive? He doesn't want to be killed so he tricked you. He let you leave because you are a threat to him and his plans."

"What plans?"

"He plans to destroy the entire world if he isn't stopped. Don't be fooled by him Zane. You are smarter than that. If you want to protect the people you love then you will go in there and fight him with all you've got."

"I'm sorry. I had no idea Perin. He just didn't give off an evil vibe."

"It's fine, just don't be fooled again."

"It won't happen a second time," I went back inside of the dome ready to destroy the evil being.

The lights were off again. They turned on and he was sitting in the middle still. He stood up.

"I'm not falling for your act this time," I took out sixteen cards from my deck, and put them into the ground summoning a hammer with a blue head and a purple handle.

"Impressive. That's definitely something new."

"Let's do this!" I screamed and ran at him with my hammer.

"I want to let you know that I am sorry in advance for anything that happens in this fight. I do not wish to harm you, but I must in order to protect myself. I only wish you knew the truth. You are so misguided and gullible. Wait . . . is that the right word? Gullible? Adjective meaning easily deceived or duped. That is correct."

"Shut up!" I smashed the hammer down to hit him but he jumped back and I missed. "I'm not going to let you trick me. Perin said you are evil. I believe and trust him."

"I remember him when he was a mere child. He was actually adorable, but a lot has changed since then. If you are this clouded by his thoughts and have no will to think for yourself, just like all the others before you, then my only choice is to kill you."

"Give it your best shot."

He held his hand out and I saw something forming on his palm.

"FINE!"

A large blast of wind erupted from his hand and was rushing toward me. I quickly took out a pawn from my pouch and summoned it to protect me from the current just in time.

"You're very special. You are the first person that I fought with a power like this."

"That is why I'm going to stop you."

"I am sorry, that will not happen."

Hokee ran at me extremely fast and punched my pawn as I stayed hidden behind it. The punch was outrageously powerful; it completely destroyed my pawn, shattering into thousands of pieces. I was surrounded by them as I flew back due to the force of the explosion. I got up and saw him standing still, so I summoned three more pawns around me. I left my hammer on the ground, focused, and it turned back into cards. I put eight more cards into the ground and summoned a sword. The pawns started to move. I was going to use them as a defense and wait for a time to stab him. Hokee remained stationary, waiting for me to come to him. I accelerated my pawns' movement and ran behind it. A pawn moved toward him, and he punched causing it to burst just like the last one. It was killing me inside to see my father's chess pieces being destroyed but I knew that it had to be done. He would understand. He always told me that I was going to do something great someday, something that would do the most good. I lunged at the man with my sword pulled back, ready to stab him, moving through the debris of the chess piece. I could see him standing; I extended out my sword. He saw me and tried to jump back, but it didn't help, I caught him on his left arm. It wasn't a fatal strike but it was a start.

My other two pawns came on both sides of him. Hokee was startled and surprised.

"You are one of few people to draw blood from me, congratulations. I'm sorry, but I have to end it here."

He put out both of his hands, doing the same move from earlier. I could feel the power behind it. He shot the blasts and I had zero time to react. Once the wind hit me, I dropped my sword. The current carried me all the way to the other side of the dome and I smashed into the wall. I stood up and brushed myself off. My back really hurt, but it wasn't serious. I went to grab my chess pieces but my pouch was gone. I looked up and saw him walking toward it.

"Are you missing something?"

I had no response. I didn't know what to say. There was nothing that I could do. I still had my cards and my last piece. I never kept the white queen in the pouch with everything else. She was my dad's favorite piece. I couldn't use her yet. I needed to get my other pieces back and create a defense so that she could strike him.

He opened the bag and took out one of the pieces.

"This is for the game of chess."

"Yeah."

"How do you make the pieces come to life?"

"It's my power."

"I have found that I can do what others can do."

"What?"

"People that I fight, I can do what they do. I'm not sure how but I can. For instance, I once fought a man who could make high pitched sounds that could paralyze an opponent."

Hokee opened his mouth and made an ear scratching sound. It felt as if my brain was going to pop. My entire body went numb and I dropped to the floor, then he stopped the sound.

"See, I am not sure how I can do these things, I just can. If I watch someone do something I can do it." He held the chess piece in his hand. "I've been fond of defeating people with their own power. That is what I'm going to do with you. This is how you did it right?"

He slammed the chess piece into the floor. I waited in fear. There was no way he could do what I could do. Nothing happened. There was no summoning circle or anything. Hokee lifted his hand and the chess piece was smashed into dust. There was nearly nothing left. I took out some cards.

"You have no idea how to use my power. You wanna know why?" I asked walking towards him.

"Why?"

"Because I'm special, because I have the greatest responsibility of all: Killing you!"

"You are so misguided. Only if you knew the truth, you wouldn't be in this dome. You'd be on the outside living your life instead of being in here losing it. It is a shame. All of you are so young, with full lives ahead of you. I have had to kill you because your minds have been molded by the people outside of this dome. They have brainwashed all of you and you haven't even done anything about it. You believe every word they say while they use you for what they want. They want me dead so badly because they think that if I die than the world will be ridded of powers and abilities.

They do not want any of us "freaks" to be walking around the streets. That is why you are here. You are here to kill me and rid the world of powers."

I didn't know whether to believe him or not. He sounded sincere and I still didn't feel any evil from him, even as we were fighting. It's his word over Perin's. Perin has been with me since the beginning. I couldn't turn on him now, I thought. I had to do this, whether or not he is telling the truth.

I put groups of cards into the floor. Three swords came out of the floor; one blue, one white and one purple. I grabbed them and ran at the man.

"Please stop this now. I don't want to kill you. I'm tired of killing you kids. I just want to be left alone," he held out his hands and shot wind at me.

I moved out of the way of the first few blasts but then he hit me. I dropped and got back up then ran around picking up my cards.

I turned my swords back into cards. Then put all fifty-two cards into the floor at once.

"I'm ending this now. The Queen and I are going to finish you."

"Do you know what happens every year? Kids come in here and never leave because they are killed by me. They tell you that they get sent home but they do not. They never see anything again. I am the last thing they see before they die. I gave them their power and I take their life."

"What do you mean?"

"You have your power because of me. I am the first person to ever have a power. I gave every single person their power."

"How? I don't understand."

"I can not even begin to explain how."

Is he really why I have my power? Did he really give it to me?

"I just thought I would let you know the truth."

"It doesn't change anything. It's my life or yours. Honestly I don't want to kill you or anyone but I no longer have a choice," I explained.

"You are a good dog. You obey orders quite nicely. It's too bad you are on the wrong side."

"I'm done listening to you. I know what I have to do whether I believe in it or not," I put all fifty-two cards into the floor and the summoning circle appeared. A large lance came out. It had a blue spearhead and a white staff with a purple bladed butt.

"Very nice," he complimented.

"I'm not finished," I took out my father's queen: the white queen. She was attached to a string around my neck incased in a plastic tube. I put her into the floor and the circle appeared. "I hope you're ready, because she's a real bitch."

The Queen started to come out of the summon circle. She was radiating blue, white and purple. She was stunning, holding a sword in her hand and wearing a crown on her head. Her body was motionless; a statue. She broke out of the motionless state and swung her sword, not speaking any words, and not having to. I knew that I could control her with ease.

"Let's remove him from the game," I said to her.

She gave me a nod and sprinted at the man. She was my father's favorite piece. I remembered the first time my father was teaching me the game. He told me how important and powerful she was and how to use her properly. I had taken what he taught me then and applied it to my training with her.

"This is going to be very entertaining," he said as he put the pouch on the ground.

I sprinted at him with my lance as well. The Queen got to him first. She tried to cut Hokee and he barely dodged the strike. I came to my pouch and picked it up. He tried to blast her with air but it was futile, she wasn't going to be knocked over by some heavy wind. The Queen continued to slash with her sword but he continued to move in the nick of time. I appeared on the side of him and I could tell he had forgotten about me. I swung the lance around and thrust it at him. Hokee slapped it to the side and was blindsided by the Queen, landing a slash on his left arm. He pushed himself away from the two of us with his wind, moving a considerable distance away.

I opened my pouch and took out two black pawns and the black knight. The black and white chess pieces had different attributes but looked the same other than their opposite colors. The black pawns moved slower but were much more durable than the white ones. The black knight was faster than the white but took more of a toll on me to use. I summoned the pieces and sat upon the black steed.

"Queen, don't let up," I instructed.

She darted toward Hokee twirling her sword.

"You attack and unarmed man Queen, that is not noble," he said.

She threw her sword at him and followed with haste. He dodged the sword and watched as it stabbed into the dome's interior wall. He turned around and she was in front of him with her fist pulled back. Hokee braced himself as she threw her punch colliding with his face and knocking him back. She threw punch after punch, landing a majority. He did the best he could to block it, but all my energy was focused on her. I remained stationary to channel energy to her more effectively. Hokee began to punch back and was dodging more of the Queen's attacks. With each blow he landed a crackling noise followed leaving the affected area slightly cracked and damaged. The speed of their fight increase and she was back on the offensive, pushing Hokee back towards the wall and her recently thrown sword. The Queen did a leg sweep knocking Hokee airborne. She quickly spun around and kick him mid air launching him at the sword stuck in the wall. Hokee's back cracked as it made contact with the swords hilt. He fell to the ground and quickly uppercutted the Queen, grabbed one of her arms and tossed her far away. He pulled the sword from the wall and held it reverse style.

It was my time to strike. I directed my pawns on what to do and I galloped toward Hokee with powerful speed. He launched spheres of air at me and I moved out of the way effortlessly. I reached him and began stabbing at him with my lance. He protected most of the attacks and then slid under my knight and got behind me. I quickly move in an L-shape away from his powerful attack. The Queen was back on her feet and she wanted her sword back. Her and I rushed toward Hokee and fought him ending with the Queen gaining back her sword. He backed away breathing heavily.

"You have skills that I have never seen before with talent that is unparalleled," he spoke.

"This is no time for compliments." Again the Queen and I preformed a combined assault. Hokee began to spit out brown liquid into his hand with it shaping into a star about the size of a cd. He ran passed me and over to the Queen sticking her with the brown star, pinning he sword to her chest. In seconds red veins began exiting the star from each point and began covering her body.

"She is forever motionless. Now that I have removed your strongest piece, I can end the match," Hokee spoke as I noticed my Queen still being able to move except it was as slow as molasses. All I had to do was buy some time until she could free herself. I moved a pawn to my backside for protection and beckoned Hokee to me. He whizzed to me and jumped into the air, firing blasts of wind at me, and landing on my left side. I deflected the attacks and started striking him, but only scratching him as he dodged. I moved my other pawn behind him and he slid in front of me. I pulled my knight's reins back causing it to lift up on its hind legs then kicking Hokee backwards with great force.

He slid on his back and rolled. He got up and wiped his bloody lip and stood up holding out his fist. A green strap came around his wrist and continued to shape into a thin glove with three small boxes on top of it. Out of boxes came black arrows, which as soon as their form solidified, he shot them at me. I hit them with my lance and he began to make them again. As fast as I could I galloped at him hit the arrows away from me as I moved. I was directly in front of him and brought my lance down breaking his arrow shooting contraption and piecing his hand. He jumped back and grabbed his hand in pain.

Unexpectedly, my Queen was free from Hokee's trap. She swung her sword with immense force, cutting his left side and sending him rolling on the ground away from us. He was stopped by a pawn and spit the brown liquid into his hand again covering up his large wound. It was time to end it. The Queen rushed at Hokee with her sword raised high, bringing it down on Hokee. He formed air in both hands in combined them into a ball stopping the blade and holding it in place. They each were pushing hard to hit the other. I moved my other pawn on his left side, leaving only his right side open, and having no way to escape. I charged at him with haste and pulled back my lance, I was seconds away from him and he was trapped. The fight was about to be over and I would complete the trial.

"CHECKMATE!" I yelled as I went to stab him.

A yellow energy appeared above his head and began to spread downward encasing him in a yellow transparent stone and protecting him from my attack. The lance collided with the rock and pieced it. I pushed as hard as I could and came inches from Hokee's face. He filled the inside of the rock with air and I slowly began to crack the exploded, knocking me off of my knight and causing the Queen to fall backwards.

"It has been long since I had felt fear. I did not know I could perform such a technique," he said as the Queen and I got up.

He ran at he Queen and his entire fighting style changed. He went ferociously on the offensive attacking the Queen. He only punched areas that were already cracked. Each one he landed took chunks out of her body. I jumped in and started attacking him but he was brushing me off as if I were a measly fly. I continued to attempt to strike him with my lance but I couldn't land a hit; he was too fast.

His entire focus was on the Queen. She started dancing around dodging his attacks. She began to use my two pawns as defenses and he was starting to get very upset. He hit a pawn multiple times smashing it and leaving himself open. The Queen came to his right with great speed and sliced him with her sword. His chest was cut badly and he jumped back in pain.

"You are good Queen, but I can not allow this to happen any longer. We are both fighting for the same thing, but only one of us is right; and that is me. You fight because of lies you have been fed, and I fight to protect the portion of mankind with powers. I gave them life and if I die it could be taken away. I can not allow this fight to continue any longer."

As he was talking I ran behind him using my last pawn as a shield. I jumped out and tried to stab him but he caught my lance and he threw it with me attached across the room. After I got up I noticed that the cut was already starting to heal itself. He moved quickly at my queen, who was caught off guard by his speed.

"Maybe I underestimated you and your skills. I apologize for that, but I will not die, I cannot die. I fight to save your life." He grabbed his chest. "NO! Not now, please."

I wasn't sure what was going on. He punched my queen and she hit the ground and rolled; pieces of her chipped off and scattered. He put one of his hands on the floor and held the other up in the air. It was as if he was draining something with his hand in the air. The floor started to crack in a line moving toward her. Then the line turned red and a stream of fire shot out from the ground and was about to destroy my queen but I quickly sent her back into her summoning circle and turned her back to normal.

I sat up and was out of breath, holding the lance still ready to fight. The man dropped his hand and hugged himself.

"Please no," he cried.

It was my final chance to kill him, but something was wrong. I couldn't even bare to watch. I wanted to get up and kill him but my body wouldn't let me. It was refusing to fight him. His body started to glow white and continued to glow brighter and brighter. He screamed in pain. I sat and watched. I could have ended the fight at any time while he was in the state he was in. I could have just walked over and stabbed him in the heart but I no longer had the urge to. My body was tired and I no longer felt it necessary. I no longer knew what was right and what was wrong, and unsure whom to believe.

The light exploded out of him, covered the entire dome, and then it was gone. I looked over to see if he was okay. He was standing up.

"I now know why. I can do anything. I now have no limits." He vanished.

Instantly, he appeared in front of me. I was startled.

"Teleportation," he said. "I understand everything now. I understand these gifts that I have given to all of you. I know what they are and how to use them."

I was speechless.

"You were telling the truth when you spoke of yourself being special. You gift is one of a kind, Zane. You, like me, can give power to other things. But the catch is they are specific to only you. You gave the power to your father's chess pieces, to the deck of cards, not me. That is why I was unable to use them. I have this same power, granting abilities to three objects."

"Are . . . are you . . ." I stuttered.

"I have no reason to kill you, Zane. You are a great fighter. I just hope that you can see the truth now. I am not your enemy but your friend. I must leave here now. I now have the opportunity to. I just need to find someone that I can trust."

He closed his eyes, I could tell what ever he was doing was hurting him very badly. He grabbed his head.

"I found you, Tobias." He vanished again.

I looked around but he was nowhere. I pulled myself up and gathered up all of my cards and chess pieces. I walked out of the dome. I was hurting bad; I had at least one broken rib.

Perin looked at me, noticing that I was in bad shape. That wasn't his priority though.

"I saw the rods electrify. He released the light. Did . . . did you kill him?" Perin asked with his eyes wide.

"No, he teleported out of the dome." Perin grabbed me and pulled me close.

"What the HELL do you mean? He isn't supposed to be able to leave that place. When the hell did he learn to teleport?" Perin was very angry.

"He released some sort of light, and all of the sudden he could do it. He said he had to find someone he could trust. Someone named, Tobias." Perin threw me away. He called for back up immediately. Everyone got back on the transit. Nothing was said the whole ride up. When we arrived back on the Hokee, Perin told everyone to go ahead, except me.

"Zane, I am very disappointed. The First hasn't left this island for as long as I have been alive," Perin said very seriously.

"Perin, I'm sorry. I fought to my best ability, but . . ."

"But, you failed!" He screamed then grabbed his face to calm himself down.

"He said a lot of things in there, the First did. Were the things he said, true? Perin?" Perin began to roll up his sleeves and loosed up his tie.

"Zane, I'd like to show you something."

BIDZIIL: MID TOWN IN PHILADELPHIA

I teleported from the dome into Tobias' apartment. He was the only one I could find quickly that was strong enough and I could trust. My head was killing me; there was an immense amount of information being flooded into my head and there was nothing that I could do to stop it.

"Tobias!" I yelled. He came running into the room.

"Who the hell are you? How did you get in here?"

"I teleported." I squeezed my head. It hurt so badly. "You can not let anyone take me away. I am a friend, please protect me."

I could no long stay conscious.

Chapter LX

FAXON: BIDZIIL IS FREE

July 6, 2007

My head exploded with pain and I screamed in agony.

"Shit, Faxon. Are you okay?" Travis asked.

I couldn't even speak. Seemingly an endless amount of information was pouring into my mind. It was Bidziil. The trial had already started. He fought with Zane and he was injured. A boy, Rupert, was just born, with a power. There was loud scratching all over my head. I dropped down and struggled to stay conscious. I hadn't had an attack to such and extent in months. I was just getting used to the large amounts of information and learning how to organize it better.

The boy; his power. He knows all powers and how they work. Bidziil has everyone's power, and he can do anything that anyone else can do. He gave birth to the power therefore he can wield it. He was in New Jersey with a man named Tobias. 1340 Front Street. My brain nearly shut down, but I quickly held consciousness and sustained all the information. I held off on feeding any more information into my head. It was causing me too much pain.

"Faxon, are you okay?" he asked again.

I stood up and took a deep breath, and then another.

"I'm going to be fine, Travis."

"What just happened?"

"Information."

"What?"

"I was hit by a lot of information at once. Sometimes my mind can't handle it all and starts to shut down."

"Oh."

"It tends to hurt a bit."

"I noticed."

"Bidziil has escaped the islands."

"Who is Bidziil?"

"Bidziil is the man in the dome. He is the First and the Hokee."

"Wait, so is he okay?"

"I don't know. The trial has just begun. He escaped after the first fight. A child was born and he exploded with the energy and gave the child power. Bidziil's power is not only to give others power but also to have every power that he gives off. The particular child's power was to know and understand every power. Bidziil has this power and now, he knows what he can do. He teleported off the island and went to Tobias' house."

"Who is Tobias?"

"He is someone with a power," my brain shot with pain. There was too much information trying to get in. "You have to go get Bidziil and make sure that he is okay."

"How?"

"Go to Tobias' and get him. Make sure, at all costs, he is protected. If anything happens to Bidziil then we could all die; in theory."

"Where is he?"

"1340 Front Street. You need to go now."

"What about you?"

"I'll be fine. I've dealt with this pain for a few years now. It will eventually subside."

"Are you sure?"

"Yes, I'll go into the alley and relax. Trust me I'll be fine. I'm not what's important right now. We need to protect Bidziil."

"Okay, but don't hold it against me once I leave."

"Just go."

My thoughts were echoing in my head and the pain was growing worse. Travis turned his entire body translucent and absorbed the air. I could hear what he was thinking. He was very worried about me. He was one of the best that I could have found.

"Bye."

He disappeared away in a gust of wind. He broke his body apart and began traveling towards Tobias's apartment. Stel did such and amazing job upgrading Travis. The odds were somewhere near one in a billion that it would work.

I got up and crawled into the closest alley. I already looked like I was a bum so it's not like I wouldn't fit in. I planned to lie down and just let all the information come in, but if I did I would surly lose consciousness. Then that would create another problem. Once I awoke I would again be attacked by information. At this point there was really nothing that I could do. I had no other choice; the pain was getting too unbearable. I allowed all the information to come into my head. Pain shot all over my body starting from my brain. It was like a million volts of electricity were surging through me. There was no way for me to stay conscious.

Chapter XLI

TRAVIS VS. Tobias: A TRUE TEST OF POWER

July 6, 2007

I moved the man into my guest room. My parents had paid for my apartment while I was going to school; they lived in Rhode Island. They knew what I can do and they are very supportive of me and my decisions. I promised them that I wouldn't use my power to get what I wanted, only for what was right. Helping the stranger had to be considered something good.

I had no idea who he was but he gave me a good vibe; I just knew that he wasn't a threat to me. Plus he obviously had a power, considering he teleported into my home. He looked very strange though. He had no shirt, only tan leggings and long and black hair. He was well toned and had dark tan skin. If I had to guess, I would say he was part Native American.

I put a pillow under his head and made sure he was comfortable. He was completely out. There was no walking him up.

I flew around until I found Front Street. I found the duplex and flew in. I returned back to normal and landed on his floor, making a loud crash.

I jumped, startled by another loud crash coming from my living room. I ran out of the guest room to see what the noise was, closing the door behind me. There was a guy getting up from my floor. He was wearing a long white coat.

"What the hell is with people landing in my living room? Who are you?" I asked.

"Where is Bidziil? Is he okay?" I asked Tobias.

"Excuse me?"

"My name is Travis, I'm here to protect Bidziil. I have to make sure he is okay."

"Sorry Travis, but you aren't going near him. He told me before he passed out not to let anyone get to him. I don't know how you got in my apartment but you are going to have to leave," I said politely.

"I can't leave. I need to help him." I said sternly.

"Then unfortunately I'll have to make you leave."

"Don't take me lightly Tobias."

"How do you know my name?"

"A man named Faxon told me. Does it ring a bell?"

"No, never heard of him."

"He is a very smart man. He told me to come here and protect Bidziil and that is what I'm going to do, protect him. I'm not here to start any trouble."

"If you don't leave now I'm going to make you leave. I'm sorry but you're not seeing him. Once he awakens he'll make the decision whether to see you or not."

"If anyone comes after him I need to protect him."

"You're the only one around right now and I'm going to protect him from you."

"He has to be taken somewhere safe."

"You're not taking him anywhere; he's safe here."

"Yes I am," I started to move toward the hallway that Tobias was blocking.

"Get back! Please!" I didn't want to hurt the guy.

"No!"

"Fine!" I pictured a golem. The golem was a gray color, about six feet tall and had a pointed head. Its arms were bulky with no hands only two rounded fingers that were separated by about three inches. It was fully created in my mind. I concentrated and my dresser started to deteriorate into particles. The particles moved in front of me and formed into the golem. It was now a living thing. Travis stopped dead in his tracks.

As I was walking toward him his dresser started to break apart into nothingness. Then suddenly this huge rock creature appeared in front of him. It came out of nowhere.

"Golem, do away with him," I instructed.

The golem ran at me. I had no time to react. He hit me and I started to absorb its rock. He grabbed me and pushed me back to a window, breaking it and we both fell outside. As I was falling from the third floor I absorbed the air and flew down safely. The golem made a large crater once he hit ground.

That was pretty effective. I ran over to where the window used to be and looked down into the alleyway behind my apartment. All I saw was my golem. The kid was nowhere to be seen. All of a sudden, I could see skin and a coat start to form out of air; then he was there. It was clear that he had a power, but was it like mine, I questioned. I had clearly gotten into something way bigger than I knew.

I moved away from the window and pictured a giant bird. It had long white wings and white feathers covering its entire body. My couch started to fade away into particles. I jumped out the window and the bird grabbed my shoulders, carrying me down to where they were. The bird flew into the sky and deteriorated.

I looked up as a giant white bird was carrying Tobias down. His power was very odd; I became curious as to what exactly it was.

"Golem, he is a threat. You must stop him."

My golem ran at Travis. Travis' body turned a clear white and then he disappeared. Again, he seemed to become the air.

"Golem!"

The golem came at me again and I moved out of the way, without turning into air. It was slow enough for me to dodge on my own. I could go right after Tobias but I wasn't trying to hurt him, only convince him that he can trust me.

"Okay Tobias, if this is the way you want it. I'll destroy your rock friend."

"I highly doubt that."

"Watch me," I put my hand on Stel's wedding ring and turned my hand clear white.

It became diamond; quickly spreading all over my body until my entire body was completely diamond. Nothing could hurt me. The rock creation was going to be a walk in the park.

I watched as he absorbed the diamond into his body. It was nothing like my power. He could become anything he touches. I'm had to do something big to take him down. I couldn't let him have Bidziil.

"Go Golem!" I yelled.

The golem charged at me swinging his arm. He reached me and punched me. My feet dug into the ground and I moved back a little, but taking no damage. In my diamond state I was basically indestructible. I punched the golem multiple times; each punch taking chunks of rock off and denting his body.

"Is that all you got," I laughed.

My golem stood no chance against him. He is way too strong. I watched as he destroyed my golem punch by punch. With one swift kick he crushed it to pieces. My head went crazy. It was as if someone had hit me in the skull with a baseball bat. It had happened a few times before. It was because a creature I had created was destroyed. I had to do something to at least hold him back until Bidziil woke up. I pictured another golem, but this time, with much more power and detail. He had fire in his hands and I imagined metal spikes all over his back. The dumpster to my left and the fire escape ladder deteriorated and the new golem appeared in front of me.

"What is it with you and golems? Can't you think of something else?" I asked mockingly.

"Just shut up and fight."

My golem charged at him just like the last one did, but this time would be different, I would win.

I stood waiting for the golem to get close to me. I held my arm out and stopped it in its tracks, and chuckled. With my other hand I punched hit and tore a portion off its shoulder. The golem backed up and shot a wave of fire at me. I didn't try and move because I didn't need too. I was diamond; I wouldn't be hurt by fire.

Travis started walking out of the fire. I was baffled.

"Do you really think a little bit of heat is going to bother me?" I asked.

I didn't respond. I just told my golem to keep fighting.

The golem tried to hit me again, I kicked out one of his legs and he dropped. Then punched off his head and it disintegrated.

"Anything else?" I asked.

My head began to hurt more. I thought of another golem. The trash cans broke apart and another golem appeared.

"Please. This is just getting boring and pathetic."

This time I ran at the golem. I was tired of holding back. It was fun and everything, but I had to save Bidziil. I beat the golem down to barely nothing. In its last attempt to fight, it shot a wave of fire at me. I turned my body clear white, absorbed the flames, grabbed all the fire around me then shot it back at the golem and he exploded.

My headache was only getting worse. I could barely stand. He was diamond and so quickly became fire. He was too powerful. Only if I could think straight it would be easier. The headache was stopping me from using my full potential. I created the first thing that popped into my head. Pieces of the ground broke down and two green winged men appeared. They were thin with bird like faces.

"Is that really the best you got?" I laughed.

I focused as hard as I could but the pain was hindering my abilities. A sword popped into my head. A ladder deteriorated and swords appeared in both of the men's hands.

"Not a bad addition but I'm made of fire. You can't cut me. You know, just for fun." I returned to normal and the two men flew at me. I jumped back, stepped in a small puddle of water, and absorbed it. They sliced me but it was ineffective. The blades passed right through me. "Maybe next time guys."

I moved at the men and punched one. My fist just splashed on his chest. I couldn't keep a solid fist. Either I was too tired, or I just wasn't familiar enough with a liquid form. They then tried attacking me with their fists, but those too went straight through me. My liquid form offered no real advantage over them. I rolled into a ball and tried to get away from them for a second in order to change into something more efficient. They spread out their wings and flew at me, leaving no chance to change. They were on the full offensive. I unraveled and shot streams of water at them. I then held my hand out, expanding it into a sheet and one flew into it. I rolled it up and captured him, then separated that part from my body. The man dropped to the ground making a splash. I shot more streams at the other one to buy some more time, but the first one dried off and flew at me. I moved over and returned the water that I used to capture him. I stretched myself out and covered them both in a bubble. They tried to break out but I kept pulling them back in. They both started to fade away. My bubble exploded and the water splashed everywhere. I pulled myself back together and returned to normal.

"What is this guy?"

Everything that I threw at him he has handled perfectly. I could barely keep my eyes open, but I couldn't let Bidziil down. I had to protect him. He had chosen me to keep him safe. I just didn't know what else I could do. I'd tried everything.

"Just take me to Bidziil, please?" I asked.

"No." I said stumbling while trying to get up. I fell down. I could feel my eyes getting heavy. My brain was throbbing in agony.

Tobias fell to the ground and passed out. I guess he just couldn't handle it anymore. His power took too big a toll on him.

Chapter XLII

Travis: A New Mission

July 6, 2007

I walked over to Tobias. He was definitely knocked out. I picked him up, absorbed wind, then surrounded him and carried him back up into his apartment through the hole in the wall. I laid him down on his floor and ran into the rooms in his apartment until I found Bidziil. Seconds after I found him I heard a door open. I took out my lighter and struck it, and ran my hand over the flame absorbing it. I moved slowly out of the room.

"Put your fire away Travis. It's only me." I heard Faxon say. "Let's hurry up and get out of here. We need to get Bidziil to a safe place."

"I know." I turned my hand normal.

Faxon walked into the room.

"Let's get him out of here."

I bent down to pick him up. His eyes began to move; they opened. He stared at me and I was petrified. Looking into his eyes was like nothing else I'd ever seen. I could see his power, his importance, and his fear. There was no other way to explain it. He grabbed his head and screamed. Faxon pushed me aside and kneeled next to Bidziil.

"Listen to me; I know what you are going through. The headaches are devastating at first. You have to focus on one thought. Or just listen to the sound of my voice. Just focus on something. Now push everything else out. Find a place in your mind and direct everything there. You can dispose of it later."

I stood watching Faxon help him.

"Is he going to be okay?" I asked.

"I'm fine," Bidziil said as he was standing up. "Thank you Faxon. You are one intelligent man."

"Thank you," he laughed. "I never thought I would be talking to you."

"I know what you are trying to do, what you've been trying to do. I really appreciate it, but I can't allow you to take part in your quest any longer. I will be the one to destroy the islands. After I figure out how to keep my mind in tact I will go and eradicate them. Just against me they don't stand a chance. I have every power they have and then some."

"I understand but it would be safer if you had some back up. I have very good candidates in mind." Faxon stated.

"I know. Travis, Bastian and Aden, and now you are thinking about Tobias as well. With Tobias' power alone I could have the islands destroyed. I just have to learn to control my mind and all of these new gifts I have."

"I'm not allowing you to do this alone." I said. "Whether you like it or not, I'm going to be there."

"You were an idiot to ever allow yourself to have Stel use her power on you. You should have died. Even with your ability to absorb anything, which protected you from Amity's mind control, it still should not have succeeded. Yet for some reason you are alive. I believe you are destined to live. The Gods have a greater task for you. This is not it. This is my task and my task alone."

"I have to go make sure Tobias is okay." Bidziil teleported. Faxon and I were both startled and ran into the living room. Bidziil was moving Tobias onto the love seat. He laid his hand on Tobias' chest. It began to glow. Tobias woke up.

"You!" Tobias said.

"Thank you for trying to protect me. You did a fantastic job." Bidziil complimented.

Tobias turned around and looked at us. We walked over to him.

"You were telling the truth." Tobias said with sorrow in his voice. "Sorry I didn't believe you."

"It's no big deal. I would have done the same thing." I said.

"So, what's this all about?" Tobias asked.

"You see, Bidziil is a very old man. He has been around for centuries. He is the one who gave you your power," I explained.

"What? He doesn't look a day over twenty four years old."

"I don't age past my prime," Bidziil said.

"Amazing. How did you give me my power?"

"During birth, a light is released from my body, and it goes and finds a child and grants them a power. I have no control over whom it goes to or when it happens. I just know that it hurts when it does." Bidziil explained.

"Wow. Unbelievable."

"Yep." Faxon said.

"So why did you come here? What were you running from?"

"I was trapped on an island after people discovered what I could do. There was a project created to study me and my gift. Then other people with powers started showing up. They were captured and studied as well. At first it was harmless then some people outside of the islands figured that since they had powers they could do whatever they wanted. They began to kill, thankfully they were stopped. The project changed from studying to imprisoning. They discovered that I was the one giving out powers. The project was turned into trying to find a way to kill me. They got people to come to the islands telling them they will learn how to use their power. Partially it is true, they actually do learn how, but the place is a prison. Every so often a group was sent to try and kill me. They don't know what they are getting into. They enter my confinement believing they are going to stop a tremendous evil. They attack me and I have to defend myself. Unfortunately, I had to kill many people, innocent people. I escaped and came here because I knew I could trust you." Bidziil explained.

"How did you know you could trust me?"

"I gain every power that I give out. Faxon's power is to know everything that has happened and is happening. I searched quickly in my head for a person for a good heart and I found you, so I teleported here."

"Now what? You're free, what are you going to do?" Tobias asked.

"I'm going to go back to the islands and destroy them." He said. "And no, you're not coming."

"What!? Why not? I can be a great help. I mean sure I actually have no idea what I'm getting myself into, but I know I want to help."

"You've helped enough already." Bidziil said.

"Tobias you . . . can . . ." Faxon began talking but he was losing his breath.

"Faxon . . . are . . ." I began gasping for air.

It was happening to everyone. I looked around and I saw Perin in the doorway. He walked in followed by Cal, Zander and someone else. Cal was dehydrating us. I could barely move, my body was too weak.

"Bidziil you thought that you could escape the islands?" Perin asked.

Bidziil was pissed.

"Without any oxygen going to your heads it is going to be very hard to use any powers." Perin laughed.

"Zander now!" Faxon yelled.

Perin looked at Zander. Zander looked confused.

"What is he talking about?" Perin asked.

"You got me. This guys a bum." Zander said.

"Hahaha, I see what you're trying to do. You're trying to make me think that he's working for you. You're hoping that I'm going to freak out and cause a scene that will buy you time to think of something. Not going to happen you DUMB BASTARD!"

It was getting even harder and harder to breathe. I was trying to use my power but the most I could do was change my fingertips.

"Enough talking. We have to get him before he starts fighting back. Kaden, Zander now." Perin yelled.

I heard Zander snap his fingers; black.

I opened my eyes and shot up off the floor. I looked around but Perin and his group were nowhere to be found. Faxon stood up and ran out the door. I absorbed the air and followed him. He was outside looking around frantically. I turned back to normal.

"SHIT!" Faxon yelled. "They have him again."

"What do we do?" I asked.

Faxon ran into the alley that Tobias and I fought in.

"For some reason I can't find them. I think they're in their chopper put I can't hear their thoughts."

"What do you mean?"

"I'm not sure; they must have found a way to hide their thoughts. I've got to think of something." Faxon started walking back to Tobias' apartment.

"We have to save him." I said.

He just kept walking scratching his head. I followed him back up to Tobias' apartment.

"Where did he go? Did they take him?" Tobias asked.

"Of course they did." I answered.

"What are we going to do about it? We have to rescue him." Tobias said.

"I know, but I'm waiting for Faxon to think of something." I replied.

"We need to get back up. I'll contact Aden and Bastian. The four of you should have no problem getting him back . . . maybe. If you all work together it about . . . a sixty six point eight percent chance you will succeed." Faxon said. "I just don't know how long it is going to take to get you all together. Bastian doesn't even want to talk to me. Aden is trying to get him as we speak. I need to make a phone call. Please excuse me."

Faxon picked up Tobias' phone and walked into the other room.

"I don't mean to insult you, but Travis you can do what you want. You don't have to wait for Faxon's approval. If someone tells me how to get to the islands I'll go," Tobias said.

"No that's just stupid. You are strong but not strong enough."

"Then come with me," Tobias said. "Together we can rip these islands apart and save Bidziil."

"You know nothing about this place Tobias."

I didn't know what to do. Faxon was thinking hard. Tobias was strong and so was I but I didn't know if we could do it with just us.

"Bidziil gave us these powers; we should thank him by saving his life. If we don't leave soon it could be too late," Tobias said trying to convince me.

I looked around trying to make a decision. I was worried about Faxon. He walked back in the room.

"Don't worry about me, Travis. It's clear you believe you can handle yourselves. Tobias barely tapped his power when he fought you earlier. He is stronger than that. Bidziil healed him to perfect health. Together you two should be fine. It turns out that Aden and Bastian are already on their way there. If you leave now you should be able to get there in time to save Bidziil. They are going for a different reason. None the less they will be there. As a team you will succeed. I believe in every one of you."

"How are we supposed to get there?" I asked.

"I've got that covered," Tobias said.

He ran over to his window and started to climb up onto his roof.

"Follow me!" He yelled.

Faxon and I followed him up onto the roof. Tobias stood there with his eyes closed. I could see veins bulging out of his forehead and his face was turning red. He was concentrating incredibly hard on something. Maybe he was making some kind of flying golem.

Tobias let out a grunt. His face was blood red. Gravel from the roof started floating into the sky, pieces of the metal fans on the roof started to decompose and float up into the sky as well. I looked up and the pieces were forming something. More things on the roof started to decompose and move into the sky. This continued for about ten minutes. There was now a black jet in the air. Tobias let out a sigh of relief. He dropped to his knees panting.

Faxon and I ran over to him. He looked up at us and smiled. "What do you think of that?"

"Very nice. We're going to be riding in style."

"You are something else, Tobias. I'm surprised that I didn't see you earlier," Faxon said.

"It's cool. No worries. I'm just glad that I can help out now. It's good to know where my powers came from."

"We should probably get going, we don't want to waste any more time," I said.

"You're right. You two need to leave now." Faxon stated.

"Then let's go," Tobias stood up. "Ship! Board us!"

Two holes opened up from the bottom of the ship and a light pulled us up.

"Good luck! I won't have any contact with you once you reach the islands. Please be safe and covert. Avoid any fights if you can. Don't do anything stupid, you must find the others!" Faxon yelled to us.

"Okay," we yelled back.

The light pulled us into the ship. I looked around. It was very high tech. It looked like something out of a Star Wars movie.

"Just sit back and relax. The ship has a built in healer. Just sit down and the ship will fix you right up. It'll bring us both back to full fighting condition." Tobias went to the head of the jet and started touching buttons and throttles. We started to move. "We should have no problem with anyone coming after us. I set us to stealth mode and autopilot. Where exactly am I going, cause as of right now we're just going to go straight until I pick a destination."

I got up out of the chair.

"Um . . . it's somewhere off the south coast of Florida." I looked on the display map that the ship brought up. I pointed to the area that the islands should be in. "Somewhere around there."

"Alright. Ship, that's where we are headed, Let's move." We turned around and headed higher into the sky.

"Now just sit down and let the ship do its thing." Tobias said.

Chapter XLIII

ZANDER: PERIN'S NEW PLAN

July 6, 2007

Perin. Cal, Kaden, and myself pulled up to Tobias' apartment.

"Okay boys, this is your most important mission yet. There can be no screw-ups. We have to do this quick before they spot us. We know that Bidziil, Faxon, Tobias and Travis are in the building. Cal, I want you to begin dehydrating the second you walk in. Kaden, I want you to continually pause Bidziil. Zander, I'll give you the signal when I want you to act," Perin pulled out his gun and cocked it. "Let's do this."

We ran into the building, Cal ahead of the group, clinching his fist tight. That's how he focused his ability. He concentrated on not harming us with it. Perin was behind him and I was behind Perin, and Kaden was last in line. We quietly ran up the stairs. We got to Tobias' floor and went into his apartment. They were already affected by Cal's ability.

"Bidziil, you thought that you could escape the islands?" Perin asked.

I could see how angry Bidziil was.

"Without any oxygen going to your heads it is going to be very hard to use any powers," Perin laughed.

"Zander now!" Faxon said.

Perin looked at me. It was the moment I was supposed to act, but I didn't. I pretended as if I had no idea what he was talking about. I've been lying all those years so it was just another day.

"What is he talking about?" Perin asked.

"You got me. This guys a bum." I said.

"Hahaha, I see what you're trying to do. You're trying to make me think that he's working for you. You're hoping that I'm going to freak out and cause a scene that will buy you time to think of something. Not going to happen you dumb bastard!" Perin yelled.

They were all gasping for air.

"We have to get him before he starts fighting back. Kaden, Zander now," Perin yelled.

I snapped my fingers and covered them with my dome. Kaden paused time inside of it. I ran inside and grabbed Bidziil, then we all ran out of the building quickly and jumped into the van. Yukanzo was waiting for us.

"Go, teleport us out of here quickly. We have to get him locked up right away," Perin instructed.

If you can hear my thoughts Faxon, the game isn't over yet. This was not the time for me to act. I have not betrayed you. You know what you have to do now. It is your only option. Send the best you can get, you must not allow Perin to do anything to Bidziil. I can't stop the islands alone, please be quick.

Yukanzo teleported us back to the Industrial. Cal continued to keep Bidziil dehydrated and Bane and Wanda were brought into the mix. Bane was able to slow down anyone's brain functions so that they are not able to access their power, let alone think straight. They brought him to one of the warehouses and kept him under constant surveillance. His brain patterns were low and he was barely breathing. Plus, he wouldn't be able to escape Wanda's force field if he gained consciousness anyway.

Perin called in all the remaining heads and myself into a meeting room.

"Why is he here?" Emily, the third head, asked.

"Because he is going to be McGrand's replacement. He is now the seventh head," Perin said.

"The Boss said that it was okay?" Kalcos, the first head, asked.

"He insisted on a seventh head. So I appointed Zander," Perin informed.

"You didn't even discuss the decision with the group. I am the first head and I demand an explanation!" Kalcos screamed.

"What about Zane?" Oran, the sixth head, asked.

"He is not part of this establishment any longer. Zander is our number one student and has been with us for years. He is the new seventh head. We don't have time for this problem right now. We need to focus on Bidziil," Perin said.

"Every attempt to kill him has failed. Not to mention he has escaped the dome and I'm sure he can do it again," Emily assumed.

"He is a threat that needs to be stopped immediately," I declared.

"It's not that simple," Oran replied.

"We can't keep him the way we have him for long. If he regains consciousness then we are all dead. He'll kill us all," Victoria, the fifth head, spoke.

"What if we all attack him at once, that is the one's who have powers," Franz, the fourth head, suggested.

"That could work. It is worth a shot," Emily said.

"Why is the Boss not here?" Kalcos asked.

"I don't know," Perin answered.

"He should be here. In a time like this we need his guidance and his ability. He would be able to completely eradicate Bidziil with one strike. There would be nothing left," Kalcos added.

"What if we use Bidziil?" Perin asked.

"What do you mean?" Oran asked.

"We all know the theory about Bidziil. If he dies then everyone with an ability dies along with him. That is why I am so reluctant to put him down."

"Stop talking as if you are in charge! I am the first head. I am higher ranked than you. The Boss should be talking to me, not you," Kalcos was furious.

"This is not the time," Perin said ignoring Kalcos's ferocity "In our database there is a female with an ability to swap souls and powers with someone. The idea has just dawned on me. She could take Bidziil's body and power and we could use it to our advantage. In the process of swapping her old body dies; meaning once the other got into the body it wouldn't survive. This way the ones with abilities get to keep their lives, in theory. Plus we'd get the strongest being in the world to fight for us."

"Why would we want him on our side, World domination?" Emily asked.

"No, well maybe. We could keep the world in check. Why not? If we have the power to do it then we should," Perin explained.

"I don't know about this idea," Victoria said.

The door opened and soldiers came in.

"Heads, there is an aircraft headed toward the islands as we speak," the men said.

"Let it be. Victoria I want you to keep an eye on the aircraft but make no confrontation. Oran, did you have any luck retrieving Bastian or Aden?" Kalcos asked.

"I believe they took the bait," he answered.

"Good, Go to the Homestead and prepare a team for their arrival. You have my full permission to use anyone you like. Bastian is our priority, not some damned soul girl. We are doing things my way," Kalcos said. "We are going to keep an eye on Bidziil until then."

"Fine," Perin said.

Everyone cleared out of the room. Perin pulled Emily, Franz and I aside.

"Emily, Franz, I want you to go find this girl that I was talking about," Perin directed.

"The soul swapper? Franz asked.

"Yes. Find Yukanzo, he'll have all the information you need. You should be able to retrieve her effortlessly. Please do it quickly," he said.

"Yes sir," they both said and then took off.

"Sorry about putting you in the spotlight there for a second. In time they'll get used to you," Perin said.

"Am I really the seventh head?"

"Yes you are."

"Thank you, Perin. This means a lot to me. I won't let you down."

"Good. We should get to the holding room."

Chapter XLIV

ADEN VS. *Bastian*: FIGHT FOR CONTROL

July 5, 2007

I hung onto the plane until it landed. I quickly took out the directions that Faxon gave me and started heading toward them. I had no time at all to spare. I needed to find Bastian. I pulled out my wings and tried to fly without drawing attention to myself, which in the night sky wasn't too difficult. I landed behind a grocery store and continued to follow Faxon's directions. It was only a matter of minutes until I started to see the buildings that Faxon described; the plaza and the restaurant. I looked to my left and saw the park that he said Bastian was last at. I ran past the gate, but he was nowhere to be found. I left the park, walked behind an apartment building and covered my hands in blood, spiking the blood and started climbing the building. I got to the top then looked around. My phone started to ring, another unknown number.

"Faxon?" I answered.

"About half a mile west. He's walking on a street called Coulage. Go quick." He hung up.

I moved the blood from my hands to my back and made wings again and started flying west. I landed at the start of the street. I saw a man walking; he was wearing a black trench coat. Bastian was wearing the same thing the last time I saw him.

"BASTIAN!!!" I yelled hiding all my blood underneath my clothes.

The voice sounded familiar. The islands would regret comin' after me another time. I was stronger and I understood that I can't get rid of my power, I'd fully embraced it. I wasn't the same as I was when they kidnapped me. I turned around. It was that kid that was with Faxon at the airport, Aden I believe his name was.

"What do ya want?" I asked.

"I need your help."

"What do ya need my help for?"

"I need to get back to the islands. I need to rescue Reece."

"So why did ya come to me? I'm not stoppin' ya from goin'."

"I won't be able to it alone. I'm good but they'll kill me if I go alone."

"And ya think that I'm goin' to help ya, I'm not goin' back to those islands. Ya don't know what I've been though."

"Then get revenge on them, help me save my friend, it's my fault that he's there. Please, I need your help."

"I'm sorry man, you're on your own."

"I'm only gunna ask nicely one more time, Will you please help me?"

"Go home kid, you're goin' to get yourself hurt talkin' like that. I'm not goin' to help ya. Ya got yourself into this mess and ya can get yourself out of it." I turned around and started walkin' back to my house.

"That's it!!!" I screamed. "I don't care how strong you think you are, but I'm going to convince you to help, even if it's by force."

"Hahaha, oh man." I turned back around. "When I beat your ass ya leave me alone, got it?"

"Bring it tough guy." I let blood pour out of my sleeves.

I didn't know what happened to him but he was already bleedin'. His blood started to shape into somethin', he was moldin' it. He must have been able to control blood. I needed to do somethin' quick. I opened my coat and took Ien out, put him on, and flew to the end of the street and over to the junk yard.

I chased after Bastian. He must not have wanted to fight in a public area. I molded my blood into whips, wanting to use my distance attacks to my advantage. I launched the whips at him, which he dodged quickly.

He was definitely fast. It was goin' to be like when I fought Pruen. I flew up into the air and continued to dodge his lashes.

I retracted my whips and changed my tactic, beginning to shoot needles at him and hitting him many times. I could see the needles sticking out of his body. I wasn't going to hurt him that badly, just enough to change his mind. I needed to make him help me save Reece.

I tried to keep dodgin' his attacks, but they were too fast. I dropped to the ground and took shelter behind a junked car; takin' a deep breath and removin' Ien. The aerial advantage meant nothin'. I put Ien back in my coat.

"You don't understand Bastian, I can't lose. Reece saved my mom's life. I owe him everything. Please, let's just stop this and go to the islands now. It will save me some time. Plus this way you won't have to get your ass kicked."

Reece saved his mom . . . I could understand why he owed him, but that didn't mean I was goin' to jeopardize my own life just for someone I didn't even know. I opened up my coat; I needed to end the fight quick. He was the only one that could do it. I took out the werewolf mask. I had to try and stay in control. I came out from behind the car holdin' Wer in my left hand, terrified of puttin' it on another time.

"Gunna try another mask?"

"I'm goin' to end it with this mask."

"Sure, you will." I said sarcastically.

"It's over." I put the mask on. I heard a horrifyingly loud howl.

Immediately, he started to change. Hair from the mask spread all over his body, traveling down his spine and then down his legs. His bones snapped, creating an awful sound. He was hunched over a little and his legs changed. I watched his nails grow longer and jagged. The mask he put on started to come to life. The snout broke out and cracked forward. The mouth opened and started biting. Its eyes blinked and stared with ferocity.

He let out a fearsome howl, then his hands grabbed his head and he dropped to his knees.

"Maybe not."

I immediately wrapped up the werewolf and started to constrict him.

I opened my eyes and was inside my head. The werewolf was ravagin' my mind. I stood up and yelled at him.

"Hey!!! Cut it out!"

He turned around, howled, and charged at me. Feathers began to form out my face revealing Ien. I flew up where he couldn't reach me. As I flew away from him, he began to chase me, so I dropped down and he stared at me with his mouth agape.

"I'm not goin' to get anywhere just flyin' around. I've got to show ya that I'm the boss, not you."

He howled again. I removed Ien and called for Dac. A black cloud appeared in front of me. I put my hand into it and pulled out Dac, then attached him to my face. I had learned that in my mind I could call on my masks to help me fight. The werewolf ran at me and I turned my entire body intangible. He tried to rip me apart, but he couldn't hit me. I stood there and let his attacks go through me, he couldn't comprehend that it was futile. I put my fist through his chest, moved it around, and he jumped back and howled in agony. I ran at him and he tried to attack me again, but I ran through him. He dropped to the ground, letting out a cry.

"Ya listen to me," I said. "I run the show. Ya just sit back and enjoy the ride."

He stumbled to his feet and looked at me. I knew he understood me. He realized that he had lost so he nodded his head and there was a black flash. I opened my eyes. I was back to reality.

Aden's blood whips were holdin' me tight, but I was the werewolf now. I had full control over his power. I tamed the beast inside me. I flexed and ripped out of the whips and I looked straight at him grinnin'.

It was probably the most frightening thing that I'd ever seen. I watched him rip out of my restraint as if it was a paper bag. I thought he just wanted to make it look like I had control to throw me off guard. He lunged at me with speed that scared me. I was nearly paralyzed by my fear, but that didn't stop my blood from protecting me. It moved in front of me and blocked his claw. He was just as strong as he was fast. I kept jumping back as he attacked my barrier. I was slowly getting over the fear.

I was tearin' through his defense. My strength was unbelievable and I had the speed to match. The werewolf was now my strongest weapon. He alone could help me win any battle.

I pulled in my barrier and changed it to a spike ball, shooting it at Bastian's chest, making contact and pushing him back. I had to find someway to detain him. I made the blood cover him. Then I created spikes and stabbed them into the ground. Unfortunately that didn't last. He let out another howl, broke out, and started to come at me again.

I broke out of his hold, it was stronger than the first but I still couldn't keep me. The ball he shot scratched my chest but there was barely a wound. I let out another roar, it didn't feel normal. When the sound hit Aden he seemed to be paralyzed. I had to take my opportunity to strike now. I ran at him with full speed.

It wasn't easy to not be terrified, but I just didn't focus on fear, I kept my mind on my goal, rescuing Reece. I let my blood cover the ground in front of me. He was only seconds away, I forced spikes out of the ground and almost caught him in my trap, but he stopped just in time. I moved my blood through the cracks in the ground, got it behind him, forcing my blood out and shaped it into scythes. I swung them from behind him, but he turned around and stopped the blade with his forearm, leaving a cut. I could have drained the blood from him but I didn't want to kill him. I returned the spikes to their liquid form, shaped one hundred needles, and then shot them all at Bastian, holding back the strength of the needles so I didn't do a tremendous amount of damage.

I was peppered by needles. I felt each one dig into my skin. It was painful, but I could handle it. The scythe, which I stopped with my left arm, turned liquid and wrapped around my arm. It ripped me to the ground; my shoulder slammin' into concrete leavin' a good sized dent. I broke free from the scythe and got up, breakin' off most of the needles on my body. I charged at him slicin' through his blood barriers as they came up. Finally, I landed a hit on him, just barely scratchin' his face. I jumped into the air and lunged at him, but he pushed me back with a stream of blood.

I wiped the blood off the side of my face. I had to find a way to end the fight quick without killing him. I didn't want to have to wait another day to leave for the islands. I gathered all the blood around me and drew it to me. He stood up with his eyes fixated on me.

Maybe helping him wouldn't be so bad. If I let the islands stand, then they could just keep taking people and torturin' them just like they did to me. We could kill two birds with one stone; save Reece and finally finish the islands for good. Suddenly, I was hit hard from my left side. I didn't even see him make a move. I smashed into a beaten up car. I got up and realized that the blood wasn't what hit me; it was . . . a massive mushroom.

The thing came out of nowhere. I moved away from it. It knocked Bastian down in werewolf form; It obviously packed quite a punch. I looked over to see if Bastian was okay. He was starting to get up. We made eye contact and didn't speak a word, yet we knew what each other were thinking. He shook his head. I had a feeling things between him and I had become very good.

Chapter XLV

GABE: FINDING OUT THE TRUTH

July 6, 2007

I woke up at the time that I usually did, around seven-thirty. I was scheduled for another training session, but this time I was training with another student. My instructor talked to one of the heads into letting a double training session take place. I took a shower, put my clothes on and headed down to the main office. I looked outside and saw a ton of soldiers walking around.

"What's going on?" I asked the lady at the front desk.

"No one knows anything."

"That's weird. I wonder what's happening. Anyways, could you page my instructor?"

"Yeah sure," She picked up the phone, dialed his number, and then looked at me. "The line is busy."

"His line is never busy. Thank you," I walked away and then went back to the desk, "Actually I'm just going to go to the gym, I'm gunna sign out."

She handed me the clipboard and an ankle bracelet. I signed the sheet, put on the bracelet, and walked outside toward my instructors building. One of the soldiers approached me.

"Excuse me. You are going to have to step back inside. There is a disturbance." he said.

"The alarms would be going off. I'm scheduled for something."

"Everything is canceled. Go back to your room."

"No."

"Then I'm going to have to escort you back." He tried to grab my arm but I moved back. "Do not resist."

"I'm not going back to my room. Not yet."

"Don't make me use force." He put his hand on his gun.

I kicked his gun and took off in between my building and the next. I took the back route to my instructor building. They chased me the entire way, but I never let them get a good shot at me. I came to the back of the building and broke in through a window in the back; heading up to my instructors room. I heard him talking to someone, so I stood around the corner.

"We are going on full lock down in less than one hour. Do you think your student is able to fight yet?" the man said.

It sounded like Perin. I was positive it was him.

"No, I don't want him fighting. This is not his battle. If this is all going to be finished now I don't want him to be a part of it."

"In theory if it all ends tonight then he'll be dead either way. So why not just let him fight?"

"Because he's my student and I said no."

"You've become friends with the boy, haven't you?"

"Yes. I admire his determination and his skills."

"These freaks are all the same, I told you not to get attached."

"And what's the difference between them and the Boss, or the other heads?"

"Power."

"You're saying that they won't die because they are strong?"

"In theory."

"That's idiotic."

"I'm done talking with you Ken. You are being released for insubordination. I'll have some soldiers bring you to your grave."

I ran down the stairs and out the window, back into my building, and up to my room. I grabbed everything that I needed and put it in my backpack. All of the sudden, the lights in the entire building went out. Then a siren began to go off, followed by flashing red lights. Perin's voice came out over the intercom.

"Students, please remain calm. Everyone report to their designated rooms and do not leave until further notice. The islands are on full lock down. This is not a drill. Disobedience will not be tolerated."

The announcement continued to play repeatedly. There was no way that I was hanging around and waiting to see what happened. I tried to get out of my room but the door was locked. I looked around to see if I could find something to pry the door open with. I ran into my bathroom and smashed the mirror, grabbing the metal boarder that held the glass together and snapping it in half. I got the tip in-between the door and the wall, enlarged the metal, and cracked the door open. I looked around the corner and saw soldiers going down the stairs. I had to be quick so I wouldn't get caught.

The red lights were still flashing everywhere. I ran down a different flight of stairs, and at the bottom I saw Hannah hiding.

"Hannah!" she turned around startled and then ran over to me.

"Gabe, what's going on?"

"I don't have time to explain. We just have to get out of here now."

Two soldiers came out of a room.

"You two. Freeze!" one yelled.

I threw Hannah behind me and took a toothpick from my belt, throwing it at the two soldiers and enlarging it. It hit one sending him flying, impaling him to a wall. The other turned around to look at his companion. I ran up to him, while he was staring at his friend and kicked him to the ground, knocking him out. Hannah and I proceeded to try and find a way out. She drained the electricity from every door that we came across so it would open easily. Behind one of the doors was a man named Saeed and a girl named Callia, both of which were also escaping.

"Do you know what is going on?" Saeed asked me.

"Now isn't the greatest time to talk. Let's just keep moving," Callia said.

"You heard the woman," I said.

Soldiers spotted us. We turned around and ran down a separate hallway. I opened my backpack and took out a stick of clay. I quickly laid it down on the floor and stuck toothpicks in it, enlarged the toothpicks, and created a wall to separate us from the soldiers. We continued down the hall when suddenly we walked into nothingness, causing us to stumble backward. Saeed put out his hand and touched the nothing. It was like an invisible wall. Hannah and I stood up and touched it as well. Unexpectedly a man came around the corner. He was tall and bald with pale skin, and his clothes were black and tight.

"Makale," Saeed said with fear and disgust.

Chapter XLVI

ADEN AND *Bastian*:
MUSHROOM FIGHT

July 5, 2007

I molded the blood into a whip but with a spiked ball at the end of it. Bastian got up and ran at the huge mushroom that was at least six feet tall and the cap being at least three feet in diameter. It had arms and legs coming out of its stem and it was a puke green color.

I ran at the giant mushroom and it ran at me. I saw Aden's whip out of the corner of my eye smash into the mushroom and push it into a car. I ran over and jumped on it, beginnin' to tear it apart with my claws. I bit into its arm, ripped off it, and then spit it out onto the street. The mushroom began to melt into a watery substance. I stepped off the car and looked at Aden, who was starin' at somethin'. I looked over and there was a man leanin' up against a tree with his arms crossed.

"And you are?" I asked.

"My name is Oran," he responded.

"The Seventh head."

"Very good, Aden. I'm glad you remember. You should just save me the trouble and help me return Bastian to the islands."

"I think I'll pass. Draining your blood and turning it into a weapon to kill more soldiers on the island sounds much more appropriate."

"You need a lot of help little boy." he said condescendingly.

"I don't need help killing you."

"You first years are always so naïve." He walked over to a car and put his hand on it.

It began to melt and shape itself into another mushroom. Bastian let out a howl.

"These guys are cake, let's rip him apart just like the last one."

Bastian roared. I assumed he agreed. I shot a sheet of blood at the mushroom and covered it, wrapping it up and throwing it toward Bastian.

The blood covered mushroom rolled toward me. I stepped on it with my foot and dug my toenails into it. Swiftly, I stabbed my hand into the mushroom. It began to melt just as the last one did. Aden launched a blood net at Oran, hittin' him perfectly. He was trapped. I began to run at him, but he put his hand on the net and it started to melt. I stopped. Puddles of blood surrounded him, and they started to form into small mushrooms and they marched at me and began shootin' scales from their caps.

I blocked the scales from hitting Bastian by pulling them the ground. I waved my hand and all the little mushrooms turned back into puddles. After all they were made of blood; I could mold them to my liking. I looked where Oran was standing but he was gone. He must have ran away. I drew all the blood back to me and hid it under my clothes, as usual. Bastian removed his mask and put it in his coat.

"So ya really want my help?" I asked.

"I *need* your help. I can't do it alone. There will be too many enemies to fight. Once I save Reece I'll have to protect him and fight as well. It won't be easy."

"We'll leave tomorrow. It's already very late and I'm not goin' to fly there at night."

"But it'd be smarter to go at night. We'll get the jump on them."

"I'm too tired I've been trainin' all day, and the fight with ya didn't leave me with too much energy left."

"I'm tired too, but I need to save Reece. That's all I care about."

"We'll go back to my place and sleep for the night, and leave in the morning."

"Okay. If that's the way you want to do it, then I won't argue."

"Good, just follow me. My house isn't too far from here." We walked for no more than twenty minutes before we got back to my house. *"My dad isn't home; he's on a fishin' trip. He won't be back for a couple days. Make yourself at home. I'm goin' to take a shower. There's food and drinks in the fridge."*

"Okay man, thanks." Bastian went upstairs. Within a minute I heard the water running. I went over to his fridge, took out some pasta that was in a container, and put it in his microwave. My stomach was growling as I watched the time count down. I took it out and ate every last bite. The water upstairs stopped running, shortly after Bastian came downstairs.

"Feel free to take a shower, I'm goin' to bed. The couch in the den folds out and there are blankets in the cabinet. If ya need anythin' feel free to wake me up, or try too at least," he laughed.

"So, we're cool now? No hard feelings about the fight?" I asked.

"Yeah, everythin' is good. It's about time that these people pay for what they did to me."

"Now that's the attitude I like."

"See ya in the mornin', Aden."

"Night man." He walked back upstairs. I cleaned up my mess and went into his den. I took all my blood and made it into a few large spheres and put them on one of the stands. I went up to the bathroom and took a shower. It felt good to get clean. I got out and dried myself off then back downstairs. I didn't even bother pulling out the bed, being much more tired then I thought. I laid down and passed out.

THE NEXT MORNING

I woke up to the smell of pancakes. I walked out of the den and into his kitchen, it was about ten thirty.

"I made enough for two. Eat up; we're goin' to need it today." Aden and I ate breakfast and cleaned up. I wanted to try and make another mask before we left. I was told by the werewolf to not force it, but I

tamed him, I should be able to do the same if somethin' goes wrong. If not, Aden was with me. I'll admit that I was a little jealous of him. He was really strong and seemed to have complete control over his power. I could feel that I was so close. I needed to try one more time before we left.

"Come outside. I would like your help."

"With what?"

"Ya have full control over your power, I don't. I'm goin' to try and make some more masks. After I do that, then we can go."

"Okay, no problem." We walked outside and he pointed to a small tree outside of his back yard.

"Can ya cut up that tree for me? Like into logs?" Aden shot four disks of blood out and cut down the tree. "Can ya make me as many logs as ya can that are at least a foot long?"

"Coming right up," I made a chainsaw whip and cut seven logs out of the fallen tree. I gathered up all the logs and carried them in a blood bag to Bastian. We sat in his back yard surrounded by all his masks. I thought it was kinda weird but whatever allowed me to get Reece back. He had a log in front of him and his eyes were closed. "So do I just sit here and wait for you to do something?"

"I'm tryin' to learn how to focus my episodes. When I make a mask I go into this strange state and I don't know how to control it. The last time I forced an episode the werewolf was created and reeked havoc on my town."

"I would greatly appreciate if that didn't happen. If you made something more powerful than the werewolf, I don't think I'd be able to stop it, and I'd hate to be delayed any longer."

"I'm not goin' to force an episode, just try and allow one to come to me."

"That works for me."

I sat, siftin' through my head, waitin' to hear a voice and capture it. Ten minutes had passed and nothin' was happenin'. My eyes began to tingle. I opened them and I could see scratch marks start to interfere with my vision.

"Dude, your eyes."

"What about them?"

"It looks like someone scratched them or something, leaving behind yellowish cut marks."

"This is what I want, but I don't hear any voices." My hands started to shake. I put my hands on the log and started to shave off pieces, havin' complete control over what I was doin'. It was never like this before, I thought. I stopped, took some deep breaths, and closed my eyes. I opened them, after about thirty seconds, and I could see just fine.

"Why did you stop?"

"It wasn't the same. I wasn't bein' guided by anythin'. It wouldn't have gone anywhere. I would have just ended up with a carved log. I have too . . ." I heard a small voice speak to me.

"I'm here." it said.

Immediately, I closed my eyes and began searchin' for the voice. After about a minute I heard it callin' out to me again. I opened my eyes, saw the scratches and my hands began to shake.

"Aden, grab me another log please!"

Aden made a blood whip and pulled over another log. I grabbed it and began to shave and carve it. The voice was speakin' to me the entire time, instructin' me on what to make the mask look like. My hands were goin' so fast that I finished in about seven minutes. My eyes went back to normal and my hands stopped shakin'.

"That was the craziest thing that I've ever seen! Absolutely amazing!"

I picked up the mask. The mask was very strange lookin'. It had four oval spikes on its head and two long skinny oval pieces hangin' from the sides of its cheeks. It had some weird markings on it; mainly swirled shaped. I put it on. I saw flash of light and a strange color that I couldn't even describe with words.

I was standin' on a brain; which I assumed was mine. A small lookin' creature crawled out of a space in my brain. I walked over and helped pull it out. It only had three fingers and wore a robe that covered its entire body, and was a dark color with very bright stitching.

"Thank you," it said.

"Is this my brain?" I asked the bein'.

"In a sense, Yes. This is my home. You can walk on it and no damage will be done. I promise."

"Oh, that's good to know. My name is Bastian," I said holdin' out my hand.

"Gei is mine. It's nice to meet you. I'm glad you heard my voice."

"So am I. I've never met one of ya that has already had a name before. Is it too forward of me to ask what ya can do?"

"No not at all. I am an extremely intelligent creature. I use all of my brain when I think. I can look over a situation and understand everything at once and produce one simple non biased opinion."

"That's interestin'."

"You should go to the islands. I know you have already decided to. I'm just giving you my opinion."

"Oh, well thanks."

"I know you are trying to figure out your power, but now it's not the time. You have an amazing gift and it should be used to protect and save. I will point you in the direction of another mask, but after you create this one you must go to the islands. Agreed?"

"Okay. That sounds good enough to me. Thank ya, Gei."

"You're welcome brave one."

Gei's body turned into vapor and was swallowed into the mask. The mask floated away from me, and I followed it. It stopped, turned, and looked at me. It whispered "look here." The flash appeared again. The light cleared and I was starin' at Aden.

"So what happened?"

"I was told what to do. Can you grab me another log?"

I put the log in front of him. It was almost twenty minutes before he started to open his eyes. He opened them slowly and the scratch marks were way more distinct, darker and thicker, with a combination of black, yellow and brown. He was moving much slower this time. There was much more feeling put into making this mask, it seemed. I watched as his nails, which had to be as hard as steel and sharp like a knife, scrape the wood off the log. Minutes passed and the mask was nearly finished. There wasn't much detail to the mask, it looked very smooth. It had two small spikes coming out of the top right corner of its forehead; almost like sharp pimples. It didn't have a mouth or eyes, only indents where the eyes should have been. I actually liked the mask a lot. It reminded me of me when I covered my face with blood. Bastian's eyes cleared and he put the mask on the grass.

"Okay, let's get these things painted and get movin'."

"Awesome." We went up into Bastian's room and I watched him paint the masks. One he painted teal with the eyes pink. The swirls he painted purple and black and the other mask, just plain white.

"Okay, I'm ready to go." I put the two masks in my coat.

My phone started to ring. It was an unknown number. I answered it.

"Aden, this is very important. You have to listen to me. The islands are going to be on high alert. It isn't a good idea to go. The two of you need to wait. Come to Pennsylvania. There are two other kids with powers that can help you. You already know Travis, he is going back to destroy the islands. The other one is Tobias. He is a very powerful young man. They can help you find Reece, and then together you can finish the islands for good."

"Maybe we'll meet up with them, but I can't wait any longer. I need to save Reece. Bastian and I can handle it."

"You don't understand. Things have changed. Don't go."

"Sorry." I hung up the phone.

"Who was that?"

"Faxon. He was warning us. But I know we can handle it."

"Absolutely. When this thing is over, there won't be anythin' left of those islands." We walked outside, I put on Ien, and Aden grew out blood wings from his back.

"Let's fly."

Chapter XLVII

Travis and Tobias: Attacking the Industrial

July 6, 2007

"We're almost at the island," I said.

"Good. I can't wait to tear them apart," I said getting up out of my seat.

I created the jet as a perfectly intelligent life form; one that would be able to account for all variables in any situation. The jet knew what it was doing. I saw Travis get a little scared when the ship began to tremble, but it was nothing to worry about. The ship had found a clearing just big enough for us to fit.

We landed and a door slid open on the right side of the ship. Tobias and I stood up.

"You ready for this?" I asked Tobias.

"As ready as you are."

"Good luck," The ship said to the both of us.

"What? The ship can talk?" I said confused.

"Yeah. Everything that I create is a living organism," I answered.

"Okay . . . well thanks ship,"

"You're welcome Travis," the jet said as I was leaving.

I released the ship from my mind and it began to deteriorate into nothingness.

"Well here we go. Let's try and get this done quick."

"Yeah, I mean all we have to do is fight of a ton of super powered people, save an outrageously old Native American, destroy three islands and save the innocent. Yeah let's just make this quick," I said mockingly.

"You're an ass," he joked.

"At least we get to start this thing with a laugh," I replied as we walked toward the buildings in the distance.

"And where exactly do you think you're going?" a woman's voice asked.

Travis and I stopped. We both began to franticly look around to spot whoever was there. A woman came out from behind one of the trees in the distance. I was ready to create some creatures and Travis' hands were ready to absorb.

"Do you really think that you could just come onto the island unnoticed and just waltz right in and save the day?" she asked.

"Actually, yeah. I did."

"Don't be smart with me boy. You don't know who I am. You're just a weakling outsider who doesn't know the meaning of power," she said.

"Who are you?"

"Travis, my name is Victoria and I am the Sixth Head of Project Dominium."

"And I assume you're here to say join us or die?"

"Perin wanted to ignore you boys and your ship. He said you were not a threat that he couldn't handle himself. Instead, I've decided to take the matter into my own hands and do what is necessary for us to succeed."

"And that would be killing us now."

"Correct."

"Not gunna happen."

"Wrong!"

She swiftly moved her hand up and shot a wave of some kind at us, making an made an ear piercing sound. We were struck and thrown back by it. Tobias and I got up. I absorbed the ground through my feet and Tobias created a man made of ice.

"That was just a thirty percent sound wave. A small taste of what I can do."

"Thanks lady." I quickly pictured a satellite looking machine in my head; a machine that generated a soundproof barrier. It was now a solid picture in my head. The ground around me started to form into it. The second it was fully created, it covered itself and I in a soundproof shield.

"What did he just do?" she asked.

"You should have never underestimated him, or me," I said staring her down with the man of ice.

"No matter. I'll rip your skin off with this next one," she shot out a second sound wave.

The wave knocked down my man of ice and Travis. The barrier wouldn't be able to reach them unless they were close to me. Hiding behind the barrier the entire fight wouldn't end in us winning.

"Hahaha! Good thing I don't have skin," I said standing up with small pieces of me falling off. I had to change into something unbreakable.

"I'll give you some more backup." I created a man of fire and a man of stone to help Travis.

"Thanks." I saw a puddle of water not too far away. "Let's get her guys."

The man of ice shot out a beam at Victoria's legs, freezing her to the ground. The man of stone ran at her along with the man of fire, and I began running toward the puddle.

"Damn you!" she screamed.

She sent out a third wave out from her mouth, bigger than the first two combined. The sound rippled the air and knocked me down, completely destroyed the man of fire and the man of stone. My body went back to normal. She broke out of the bind and shot sounds at the man of ice. All of the sudden, it began to rain. I absorbed the water as it fell on my body.

She wrecked my men. Each time a creation got hit, it was like taking a hit straight to my head. I could still keep the machine in front of me running though.

"What's the matter? Little baby doesn't want to come out and play?" she asked shooting sound with the push of her hand and the flick of her fingers.

I ran at her and surrounded her with my water. It seamed like it was working until she screamed and my water rippled violently, exploding and splashing me all over the place. I pulled myself back together and returned to normal. My body was shaking with pain.

"I'll admit you two are more than I bargained for. I haven't had any fun like this in a very long time," she said.

"You're welcome, but I'm done playing games and wasting time. Let's see if your sound has an effect on this," I absorbed the wedding ring and became diamond. Feeling the power of diamond course through my body was unlike any other absorption.

"Unbelievable!" she gasped.

I slowly walked toward her. She blasted me about three times and then gave up as I stood right in front of her. I thrusted my palm at her chest and she flew backward and hit a tree, her head and face bleeding.

I released the soundproof shield generator and ran over to Travis. He changed back to normal.

"Now what?" I asked.

"Let's just leave her. She shouldn't be able to cause anymore damage. Plus I'm only looking to kill one person on this island."

"Who is that?"

"Don't worry about it."

"Rough subject. Backing off," I said as we walked toward the buildings again. "So do we just storm in there guns blazing?"

"I'm thinking we take the more stealthy approach."

"Works for me."

We heard a loud crackling and looked ahead and saw a huge dome of electrically energy. The crackling was freighting loud and was almost ear piecing. There was another loud crack and then it was gone.

"What the hell was that?"

Chapter XLVIII

Gabe: There Is No Escape

July 6, 2007

"Who is this guy?" I asked Saeed.

"He is Makale, the strongest person on this the island."

"What!" Hannah and Callia said in fear.

Makale stood there staring at us with no expression on his face. He looked at us, picked up his hand and started swinging it around.

"What the hell is he doing?" I asked.

He acted as if he tossed something at us. The next thing I knew we were all pulled together. I tried to move, but I couldn't. It was as if a rope tied us up.

"What the hell do we do?" Hannah asked as he pulled us closer.

"I don't know," Saeed said. "I can not move."

He started dragging us through the halls. I looked around and watched other kids trying to escape, but failing because the soldiers tranqed them. He pulled us passed a large hallway and I saw a girl with two mechanical birds flying around her and she was with three other people. They were fighting a man and a woman who looked like instructors.

I could see Saeed trying to get his hand free and get the sword that was at his waist. He unsheathed his sword and cut the invisible rope, causing us to roll and Makale to stop moving. Saeed and I stood up. He held out his sword and Makale turned around and beckoned Saeed to come at him. Makale acted as if he was holding a sword. Saeed slashed and Makale blocked it with his invisible sword. It was weird to watch Makale protect himself with nothingness.

"Girls, stay close," I instructed.

I took a toothpick out of my belt and waited for the right opportunity to hit Makale. Saeed and Makale's swords clashed continually. He was perfectly positioned in front of a window so I ran at him. Saeed moved out of the way and I enlarged the toothpick and launched it at Makale's stomach. It hit him and he shot out the window. Saeed and I ran over to see him fall. He was surrounded by glass. Right before he hit the ground, he bounced on nothing, and stayed suspended in the air on something invisible.

"Damn it!" I yelled. "What the hell is this guy?"

He got onto the ground and started playing with something invisible. It looked as if he was loading something. He held it up with his shoulder and it suddenly started to rain. I could see the outline of whatever he was aiming, which was a long cylindrical object.

"Move!" Saeed said pulling me back.

All of the sudden there was an explosion where the window was, leaving behind a large whole.

"What was that?" I asked.

"He shot something at us. We have to be careful. He is dangerously powerful."

"I don't care. I'm not afraid of this dude," I said taking out the Angel. "I'm going to take him out. Just get them to a safe place, I'll deal with him."

I ran and jumped out the hole in the wall, stabbed the Angel into the wall and slid down.

"Look you crazy-looking freak. You leave them alone. Just worry about me."

He shot another rocket or what ever it was at me, I saw it coming and dodged. It blew a hole in the wall behind me.

"You're a shitty shot." I ran at him and attacked him with the Angel.

He made something new and was fighting me with it. I made some distance between us and started throwing enlarged toothpicks at him but he was dodging of blocking them with nothingness. He pulled something out and shot me. I felt the bullet hit me in the shoulder making me drop the Angel. I picked it up with my left hand and ran after him as he stood there waiting for me. I was no match for him with my left hand. He knocked me off my balance and then punched my shoulder wound causing me to scream. He kicked out one of my legs and beat me to the ground. I tried to crawl away but he put his boot on my back. I could see Saeed running out of the building.

"That's enough. You fight me now." Saeed stared him down and Makale lifted his foot off of me.

I slowly started to crawl toward the girls. They sat me up and pulled me away. Saeed wasn't holding back. It actually looked like he had the upper hand. He cut Makale's arm. The rain began to fall harder. It seemed to make Saeed stronger. He was incredibly focused. Their swords were clashing non-stop. Saeed dodged a slice, turned behind Makale, and kicked him in the back of the knee and cut Makale's back. Makale moved out of the way before Saeed could stab him and created a gun and shot Saeed in the leg. Saeed fell to his knees.

"No!" I yelled. I picked up the Angel and stood up.

"No! Stay here Gabe," Hannah said.

"I can't just watch him die." I walked toward Makale. "Hey, jackass. You're not done with me yet."

He turned and looked at me, holding up his hand, looking like he was holding a gun. Multiple recoils affected his hand but there, was no sound. All I felt were the three bullets passing through me. Everything began to spin and I heard Hannah scream. Callia and her came and helped me. I had to fight to stay conscious. I heard Hannah crying and I felt her head against mine. A spark went through my entire body. I opened my eyes. She was glowing with a blue aura.

"I'll kill him," she whispered in my ear.

"You need to take him and go Callia. I don't know what's about to happen but it won't be good," Hannah said with the sound of crackling electricity all around her.

She stood up and started walking toward Makale. The blue electrical aura began to grow bigger. Callia grabbed me and dragged me inside of the building. I couldn't see anything. Then all of the sudden there was this flash of a bright blue light and a loud crash, like thunder.

Chapter XLIX

ADEN AND *Bastian*: THE SEARCH FOR REECE

July 6, 2007

I was ahead of Aden because his wings could only do so much. I stopped, let him catch up, and he stopped when he got to me. "I have an idea."

"And what's that?"

"Create some of those blood whips and attach them to my legs. I'm faster than you and this way you won't be far behind."

"Okay, that's a pretty good idea," I made the whips and held on to Bastian.

"I'm goin' to go as fast as I can. Hold on tight." I rocketed away. I had never flown that fast before. Ien was workin' at a limit that I could never imagine. The buildings below me were less than blurs.

"Stop!"

I was startled and halted as fast as I could, with Aden almost crashin' into my back.

"What?"

"Look over there," I pointed to the sky.

There was some black thing growin' in the distance and objects were being ripped up into it. It was starting to gain a shape.

"What do you think it is?"

"I have no idea. Most likely somebody is using a power. Do ya want to go check it out? It could be dangerous."

"Reece is more important. It doesn't look *that* dangerous anyway. Let's just keep moving. Sorry," It began to look like a jet. "It probably wasn't going to be used to destroy the city. At least, I hope not."

In a matter of fifteen minutes, all that was under us was water. We would arrive at the islands shortly. The view was beautiful and this time I actually got to enjoy it. No helicopters shooting at me, and no black magical sleepy balls in front of me. Once we got to the islands, nothing was going to stop me from saving Reece. I checked behind my back to see if my knife had fallen out or not; still there. Soon the islands became visible.

I flew to the island closest to us. Aden detached his blood whips and glided down to the island and I just dropped. There were trees everywhere. I took off Ien and put him in my coat and Aden hid all his blood. We started walking deeper into the woods.

"I wonder how far until we find something."

"I'm not sure. We're just goin' to have to keep movin'."

We walked for almost an hour. We came across what looked like a hut of some kind. We walked inside and there were thousands of scratch marks all over the wall. Bastian ran his fingers over it.

"They are tallies. Someone was countin'' somethin'. Days maybe."

"Do you think this was a prison? It's extremely old." Dust and dirt covered everything. Plants had found their way inside and began growing all along the walls.

"Possibly. This entire place is sendin' chills down my spine. Let's get out of here."

"Yeah, let's move."

We kept walkin' and we saw somethin' on the ground that looked like a tattered white coat. We ran over to see what it was. It was a man. We both were worried. The man's coat had a purple trim with the island's symbol on it. He also had a pouch attached to his belt. He had, what looked like, rug burns all over his body.

"He might be an instructor. We should probably keep moving, before someone comes looking for him."

"Right." We ran through the woods and stumbled across a hatch. "Should we go in?"

"Absolutely. It could bring us to where Reece is."

"Then what are we waitin' for?" We entered the hatch and there was barely any light. We heard footsteps and took cover behind pillars.

I poked my head around the corner. There were about ten soldiers talking. They were in a separate room about a hundred feet away. One of them had to know where Reece was being held. I let blood drip out of my sleeve and molded it to a whip. I shot it out and grabbed one of the guys, pulling him to me.

"What the hell are ya doin'?"

"Where is Reece?" I asked furiously.

"What!" The man said.

I could hear the others freakin' out, shootin' into the darkness.

"Come out, whatever you are!!" one of the soldiers yelled.

"The little boy. He is somewhere on these islands."

"I have no idea you freak!"

The other soldiers started comin' closer.

"Do you know where he is?"

"I don't know anything about a boy."

The soldier turned on their lights and the room became slightly illuminated. It was clear we were in some kind of prison, with cells and bared rooms everywhere. I took out my knife and stabbed his stomach. I pulled my knife from his gut and all the blood out of his body with it. It took all my strength to do. My arms were dead tired and my head was throbbing, as if I just tried to lift a car. With the little energy I had left I molded the man's blood into a golem and sent it after the other soldiers. I watched as they tried to kill it, but bullets wouldn't do anything other than pass through it. It gave me enough time to catch my breath. Bastian was still hiding in the shadows. He must not have wanted to get his hands dirty so early on. He must've understood that it had to be done. They weren't going to stop unless we stopped them. It was us or them, and I chose them. The golem grabbed one of the men and smashed his head into a cell.

I couldn't stand by any longer. It was a blood bath. I ran into the room and over to Aden.

"Aden, what the hell are ya doin'?"

"I'm going to find Reece at all costs. These men's lives mean nothing to me.

"We are supposed to be doin' this stealthfully. I could have just run in here all werewolfed out and done the same thing, you need to keep your cool. This can't happen again." I turned my head and watched as Aden walked away. There was blood everywhere. His golem was holdin' the last livin' soldier up against a wall and he was kickin' and screamin' like a child.

"Where is the boy, Reece?" The soldier was trying to talk, but couldn't. "Golem, let him breathe."

"I don't know," he gasped.

"Golem, I have no use for him." The golem broke the soldier's neck.

I stood in the middle of the blood filled room, holding out my hands, I could feel every ounce of the blood. I pulled it all towards me. My golem was pulled toward me as well and enveloped me. I opened my eyes and there wasn't a drop of blood anywhere. I was tightly covered in it, all of it. I solidified all the blood, turning it into rock solid armor.

It was amazin' to watch him change, but he was becomin' blood hungry. His head had three spikes stickin' out of the front and His chest was covered in, what seemed liked, scales. Long thorns were at the ends of his elbows and shorter ones from his feet. His arms and legs were layered with hardened blood started from his shoulders and thighs going downward. He walked down the hall way and up some stairs. I had to knock some sense into him. If he wasn't goin' to stick to the plan, then the entire mission would've been a waste of time. I opened up my coat and took out my latest mask, the one that Gei guided me to; Vaz.

I walked up the stairs and shot the door at the top open. My blood was more powerful than ever, and it was intoxicating. I walked slowly through the doorway. I looked to my left and to right. There was a man to my right, who began to shoot at me. I stretched out a solid spike and stabbed it through the man's leg, dragging him to me. I covered his body with blood but left his head uncovered.

"Where is Reece?" I asked calmly.

"The healing boy?"

"Yes." I pulled the man up from the ground and held him in the air. "Where is he?!" I screamed.

"Even if I knew, I wouldn't tell you."

"Wrong answer," I threw him down the hall and smashed him into the wall. I slowly walked toward him. My armor began acting on its own, shooting three-inch spikes at the man with none of them hitting vital areas.

"Are you going to tell me where he is?" I could see his blood dripping down the wall.

"I don't know!"

"Liar!" I retracted all the blood and made my blade and stabbed him in the shoulder with small strings of blood stretching out on their own and stabbing him in other areas.

"OKAY!!! I'LL TELL YOU!" he screamed in agony.

I removed my blade from his shoulder and the strings came with it.

"He's being held on the Homestead. It's the island next to this one. Don't get confused with the Industrial, which is directly across. Leave this building and go right."

"Thank you," I covered his entire body this time. I could hear him gasping for breath. I turned around and Bastian was just coming up the stairs. He was wearing one of his masks, the new one that he had painted white.

"Aden, you're losin' sight. You need to get a grip. I understand you're pissed off, but ya need to calm down. They did terrible things to me, Things that still haunt me in my sleep. If I can keep myself under control then so should you," I spoke in a deep stern voice.

"I'm fine," I said pulling the blood off of the man. "Now back off."

"Can you keep your cool?"

"I am cool." Again my armor acted on its own and shot needles at the soldiers face killing him.

"No, you're not." I walked down the hallway towards Aden, shatterin' the glass windows in the hallway as I passed them. The glass floated in place after it was broken. "I need to knock you out of this blood thirsty

state you are in." I drew all the glass in and made it float around me. I pieced some shards together, creatin' a long blade. The shards didn't become one; they stacked on top of each other. I ran at Aden. He shot needles at me. I moved shards in the way and they collided stoppin' each other. When I reached Aden I held the glass blade to his throat.

He was controlling the glass, like I controlled blood. I made my blade with my left arm and held it to his throat. The blood started to move on its own. I could feel it about to shoot through Bastian. I pulled it back and withdrew the blood from my face.

"You're right. I'm losing control. I'll stay focused, I promise."

"Good." All the glass around me dropped to the ground. "Then let's keep going."

"We have to go to the Homestead, That's where Reece is."

"Then that's where we're goin'."

Chapter L

PERIN AND Bidziil: AWAKE

July 6, 2007

"Sir, there was just a huge explosion outside of Dorm Building Three," an advisor ran in and told me.

We were monitoring Bidziil. He was being contained in Wanda's most powerful force field and his mind is being suppressed by Bane. Just for an extra safety precaution, Cal was also dehydrating him. He had no chance to get free. It wasn't solving the problem but it was buying me time until Emily and Franz got back with the girl.

"I had sent Makale to deal with the escapees."

"He hasn't responded since the explosion," the advisor stated.

"He can't talk. How could he have responded in the first place you idiot?"

"What I meant to say was, that no one has responded," he explained.

"This is becoming a nuisance for me. Have all the kids been appended and sent to Amity's facility."

"The men are rounding up the rest of them."

"Make sure they all get there. She needs to erase everyone's memory of the past twenty-four hours, just in case this doesn't work out."

"I'll go make sure everyone knows the orders, sir." He ran out of the observation room.

"Gina, go gather up heads. Bring them here. I want to have another quick meeting." Gina was a loyal assistant of mine with a great gift.

"Yes sir."

Zander and I stood and watched as Bidziil was kept down. They should have been returning with the girl soon. All he needed was just one moment to gain control and kill us all. I had a four-year student, Sarah, monitor Bidziil's vitals, that's what her power was after all. Her eyes turned purple and red veins grew around her eyes. In about twenty minutes my assistant came back in with Kalcos, and Oran.

"Did you get Bastian?" I asked Oran.

"Perin, I have already gone over this matter with him. Stop acting like you're the Boss. I'm tired of hearing you bark out orders."

I turned around and grabbed a paper off the desk behind me, showing it to Kalcos.

"This is directly from the Boss. He has put me in charge of the project at this time. Now Oran, please answer my question." Kalcos snatched the paper out of my hand and began reading it. He punched the wall behind him and sat down in a chair.

"He's on his way here with Aden. They were spotted on our radar not long ago."

"WHAT! They are working together! This cannot be. Faxon must be behind this. Damn it! Where is Victoria?"

"She has not responded to any calls. The jet she was monitoring had vanished," Kalcos said.

"I DON'T like this. I feel something is about to go wrong."

Emily, Franz and Yukanzo came into the room.

"We have the girl," Emily said.

"Perfect. Now we can get this under way."

"But she is not cooperative. We had to knock her out to get her here," Franz explained.

"Then bring her to Amity. She will be cooperative in no time."

"Also, there has been an intrusion on the Hokee. Guards bodies were found drained of their blood."

"Aden! That means they've arrived. He's going to be after Reece, I know it. They're going to be headed for the Homestead. This is just perfect. We can have Bastian as well."

Yukanzo's radio went off.

"Sir, two blips just landed on the Homestead."

"I'll go and deal with them," Oran said. "I will not mess up this time I swear it."

"Go quickly."

"Emily and Franz, go bring the girl to Amity. Zander, get our friend out from captivity. He said that he is willing to help us."

"Who is that?"

"Room number 109."

"He has been down there for some time. What has he been doing?"

"Controlling his power; learning how to use it better. He will be a great asset. Go tell him to look for any threats and bring them to me. Give him a means of communication to us."

"Yes sir." Zander left along with Emily and Franz.

"Yukanzo, bring me Nadim, he has been loyal. And find Makale." He teleported out.

Kalcos watched as Sarah began to shake. I looked over at her.

"What is going on?"

"His vitals," she said quietly.

She shot back with the chair and her hitting the wall, knocking her unconscious. Kalcos and I looked out the one-way mirror looking down at my group and Bidziil.

Thoughts . . . return . . . mind . . . think . . . must . . . get . . . out. Slowly . . . began to . . . regain my . . . ability to think. I opened my eyes and looked around. I could barely breathe. I tried to move, but I could not. I was steadily breaking out of whatever state I was put into. I saw Wanda, meaning I had to be in a force field. I let my hands take in energy readings from the ground. Everyone around me was at one hundred percent, they weren't holding back anything. My body must had manually began to counter their abilities. I rose to my knees and tried to air blast the dome, but it was futile. Slowly, I was gaining my energy back. I held my hand on my chest. I was at forty two percent. Within exactly seven minutes and forty-two seconds, I would be at one-hundred. It would have been smarter to wait, but after calculating all the variables, I could easily dispose of everyone in the room with just fifty-one percent. There was Perin and Kalcos in the office, the unconscious girl, Wanda, Bane, and Cal. I was ready. I started punching the barrier and I could feel the hits going straight to Wanda's head. She was weak enough to over power, after that. I generated my own barrier, forcing it quickly out of my body. My barrier grew inside of hers and pushed on it, giving one more push and her barrier shattered like glass. I allowed mine to fall.

She dropped to the floor; out for the count. I looked at both Cal and Bane. Cal had his fist tightly clenched and Bane had his fingers locked behind his head. That was the way that they both concentrated their power. I made a thirty percent air ball and shot it at Bane, then walked over to Cal. He was trying so hard, it was humorous. I held my hand up just like him and began to dehydrate him.

"How does it feel Cal? This is how it feels every time you do this to the people you capture. It is like you're dying, but so much more painful. It is torture. You gasp for air but yet you are helpless." I generated a gravity field around him and increased it to ten times the normal gravity. I listened, but he could not even groan in pain.

I took a deep breath; having used multiple different powers took its toll on me for a moment. I had to constantly keep the worlds information at bay in my head. I had not had as much practice as Faxon, but I was doing alright.

I looked up at the mirror. They were next. I ran toward them, when all of the sudden, I began to hear the wind breaking above me. I looked up and there was someone falling, I stopped, stunned by shock. The person landed on me, with the weight of tons, leaving behind a large crater and a cloud of dust. He got up off of me and stood staring. It was Ryder. I quickly stood up and prepared to engage in combat. I tried to gain the information coming out of his head, but I couldn't. It was being blocked by some static interference.

"Trying to read off me?" he asked. "That isn't going to work."

"What? I do not understand. But it doesn't matter. I will dispose of you quickly."

I watched as he changed his shape and structure into that of a Rhinoceros, running at me with full strength. I held out my arms and stopped him when he got to me, my feet driving into the floor and leaving behind skid marks. I looked him in the eyes, smiled, and threw him into the wall creating an explosion of dust and concrete. I heard Bane walking toward me. I teleported behind him and air pushed him up to the ceiling. Again, Ryder caught me of guard, blind-siding me in boar form. I was knocked to the ground, but quickly regained my balance and absorbed a piece of metal on the wall with only both my arms. I was unable to turn my body into metal because I didn't have as much training as Travis. When I gifted a person with a power I only received the base power. I would have to train just like them to make it grow and evolve.

At times, it was as if two blurs were fighting, not people. Ryder was actually holding his own.

Ryder and I ran at each other, colliding, and matching each other blow for blow, until I changed back to normal and air blasted him. I then surround him in a tornado. I directed it up and then straight into the ground, leaving behind a huge indentation.

The dust settled and I saw nothing. He slowly picked himself up, and I he was changing again. By the time he stood up he was taller than six feet with arms long and full of muscle. His legs were thin and toned, and his hair long covering his shoulders and chest. His mouth was full of sharp grinning teeth; unlike no single animal that I had ever heard of. It seemed that he was multiple animals, creating some new beast, a chimera of sorts. He ran at me with speed to exceed my own, colliding together again, all the dust around us was pushed up and away. We grabbed each other's hands, pushing each other, with the ground cracking at our feet. He was pushing me down into the floor. He was stronger than me.

Ryder lifted me off the ground and threw me across the room. Before I hit the ground, I flew and landed on my feet. He started walking toward me grinning and laughing.

"You may have every power in the world, but it's clear you have not figured out how to use them yet. It's obvious that you can utilize your super strength and speed, but I can keep up with you. You have an unimaginable amount of powers at your disposal, but I have the whole animal kingdom behind me. In my newly discovered chimera state, I have just as much power as you do, and more." Ryder spoke as he walked towards me.

I began shooting air blasts at him, but they did not phase him. I quickly cycled through my head, filtering though the never ending amount of data I was receiving, for an ability to use. I chose hastily and began to increase the acidity of the water molecules around me. Then I drew them close to my body creating an acidic veil all over me, a combination of two separate powers. I then stretched my arms toward Ryder with great speed. He dodged the first strike, but was unable to dodge my second arm, leaving a burn from the acid.

He ripped a chunk of the floor out and launched it at me, running at me after he threw it. I dodged the rock, but not his kick. I was forced to the wall to my left, while the acid burned the rock wall around me. I allowed the veil to fade and began to look for another ability. There was a flash of light and I was knocked out of my head. I dropped to my knees. It was happening again. The light.

Bidziil fell to the ground and released his energy, blinding Kalcos and myself. When the light cleared Bidziil was unconscious and so was Ryder, unable to handle the pressure of his new form any longer. He did well, and the mini generator that my father had developed had worked wonders. Yukanzo teleported into the room with Nadim.

"Yukanzo, go and grab chains, ropes, ties, any form of restraint. Also get one of the portable prisons and bring it to Dock Five."

"Yes sir."

Chapter LI

TRAVIS AND Tobias: GATHERING OF ALLIES

July 6, 2007

"I have no idea, but I think we should go check it out."

"Definitely."

We ran toward where the electrical explosion came from, which was a good distance away, running was taking us too long. By the time we got there, we'd be tired out and wouldn't be able to help anyone. I closed my eyes and pictured an inner tube. I extended the hole so it could fit two people, covered the hole in the middle with a piece of metal flooring, and added a computer. I uploaded all the artificial intelligence data it needed, placing an engine in the back and turning it into a hover craft, finally I gave it exact directions on where to bring us. It was complete.

The trees around us started to break down and deteriorate. I looked over at Tobias and his eyes were shut. He was creating something. I watched as the material from the trees was being drawn behind us.

"What are you making?" His eyes opened and the trees stopped breaking down.

"Jump!"

I did as he said and jumped with him as some sort of circular craft flew under us. We landed inside of it and bounced a little. "What is this thing?"

"It's our ride. I figured I'd save us some time and energy."

"Good call," I sat back and enjoyed the ride. It was a matter of minutes before we got to the site. We jumped out of the craft and landed near a massive crater. I could see the electrical energy still flowing through it. We looked around and saw a charred body a blonde girl in the dead center. I ran over to her and rolled her over. It was Hannah. "Oh my God."

"What?"

"I know her."

"She seems fine, just unconscious. I'll whip something up. Hold on." I closed my eyes and began to create.

I looked around and more things began to deteriorate; parts of the building, chunks of the ground around us, and trees from behind us were all being drawn above Hannah's body. It was a pink blob of, what looked like, metal and then began to form into a diamond shape. A head popped out of the top and two bight yellow eyes lit up. It was a robot with no legs; just a torso and a head. It was no bigger than two feet.

I opened my eyes and saw my creation, just as I pictured it, as usual.

"You destroyed all of that, just to make this dinky thing?"

"It takes more material to make something powerful. It doesn't take much to make my favored golem because it's is a simple creation. There is nothing to him; it's just a large rock creature, but when I want to make something that does something special it takes a lot more."

"Oh, that's pretty interesting. So what does this little bot do?"

"She'll scan her body and then heal her completely; every wound, scratch, cut, bruise, and even fatigue. She's going to be just fine in about twenty minutes."

"That's great. Can you stay here with her while I go look for anyone else?"

"Yeah, no problem."

"Awesome, thanks." I ran toward the dorm building. There was a gapping hole in the side and a few floors up too. I rested my hand on the wall before walking in absorbing it into my arm. I heard voices and clenched my fist as I turned the corner. It was Callia and Gabe, who was badly injured. I changed my fist back and ran over to them.

"Callia, what happened?"

"Travis, oh my God. You were the last person that I would ever expect to see here. How did you get back? I thought you escaped," she asked.

"I did, I came back to save everyone and destroy this place."

"Big hero."

"That's me. We have to get Gabe to my friend and his robot."

"What?"

"Let's just go," I absorbed the concrete from my arm to my entire and then picked up Gabe, who was unconscious and losing a lot of blood. I carried him back into the crater and Callia followed behind, then put Gabe down and looked at Tobias' robot. On its back there was a timer with thirteen minutes left. Tobias made another robot and started repairing Gabe.

"Tobias this is Callia. Callia this is Tobias."

"Nice to meet you. What happened to your friend?"

"He was trying to protect us. Have you guys seen Saeed?"

"No, but . . ." I looked back at the charred body.

"Oh no," she ran over to it. "There is no way this is Saeed. His sword is nowhere around. He must have gotten away somehow. I just know he's alive."

"I hope so. I honestly do."

"So what exactly happened?"

"There was a lock down and Saeed and I tried to escape. He had a really bad feeling and I've never doubted him before. Then we found Gabe and Hannah, who were also escaping. We were attacked by this extremely powerful guy, but he's dead now."

"Well what was the explosion?"

"Oh, that was Hannah. She saw Gabe almost die and she started to spark up. The next thing I know there was that explosion."

My robot was finished healing Hannah, and she began to open her eyes. Her head was resting on Travis' lap.

"Am I dreaming?" she asked.

"No Hannah this is real. Are you okay?" I asked.

"But I thought you escaped."

"I did, but I'm back now to end this whole thing."

"Wait, where is Gabe? Is he okay?"

She looked around and saw my robot hovering around Gabe scanning and healing him.

"What is that thing?"

"I made that. This one healed you," I pointed to the one hovering next to me.

"That's an interesting ability."

"So are electrical explosions."

"Is he gone? Did I kill him?" she asked.

"Yeah Hannah. You did. There is barely anything left," Callia answered.

"One less problem, but now what do we do?"

"Wait for my robot to finish healing Gabe and then we go on our way. Continuing what we came here to do."

"I want to help," Hannah said.

"You're welcome to tag along but when things start to get rough, I want you and Callia to lay low."

"That's fine, but we should look for Saeed. He would be a great help to you guys. His power has advanced a lot. I saw him with my own eyes. He's fantastic."

I looked at Travis. "It wouldn't kill to have some help. To be honest I have no real idea what we're getting into." My second robot beeped. Gabe was fully healed. Hannah got up and made sure he was okay. My second robot came over to me. "Travis I don't know about you but I'm a little beat."

"Yeah, I'm feeling a little tired too," Tobias closed his eyes and the two robots began glowing bright pink, forming into energy. The two energies then combined and formed a new single robot with pink eyes. The shape was essentially the same but I assume that it was greater than the two separate. A door opened on the front of the robots abdomen and two small bottles came out. Tobias grabbed the bottles and the robot deteriorated.

"Drink this. It's going to restore our energy," I said tossing him the bottle. We both drank it and in seconds I felt better and so did Travis. Hannah and Gabe stood up and walked over to us.

"Hannah, just filled me in. I'll be glad to help you guys out. This place is going down," Gabe said.

"I saw your fight with Zane. You did awesome. Glad you're willing to help," I said shaking his hand. "I'm Travis and this is Tobias."

"It's nice to meet the two of you. Thanks for the reboot, Tobias. I really needed it. I feel brand new," Gabe said.

"Anytime man."

"So, now we're off to find Saeed?" Callia asked.

"Let's go." We walked out of the crater and there was a man standing outside of it. He had purple pants and was wearing a protective vest with a black shirt underneath. I was ready to create one of my golems right behind him.

"Adair?"

"Travis. It's good to see you," Adair said.

I had completely forgotten about him.

"I heard you escaped. Nice job. Why are you back?"

"To destroy this place."

"Well, I heard you guys talking and if you need Saeed, I watched soldiers carry him away."

"Really! You have to take us to him. He's really badly hurt. He needs our help," Callia said frantically.

"You were the guy that fought against Cal on fight night, right?" Gabe asked.

"Yes," Adair answered.

"Man you did awesome."

"Thanks, so did you. We don't have time for any more small talk. We should get moving before it's too late," Adair said.

"You're right we have no time to waste. Soon someone is going to come and check out what happened."

We all followed this Adair fellow. I just had a bad feeling about him, but I didn't want to cause a big scene and call him out. Travis knew him, so it was good enough for me. We were close to the building that Adair saw the soldiers carry Saeed into. He said it was only fifteen more minutes of walking.

"FREEZE! Don't move!" We heard from behind us. We all turned around and there were about two dozen soldiers with their guns aimed at us. There was no way for us to escape.

"Tobias, I want you to create a bulletproof wall. I'll handle these guys. You keep going," I whispered.

"No, we can help you."

"Just do it, please. Everyone just go on without me. I'll finish this up in no time. I promise. I want to do this."

"Fine." I broke down some unnoticeable things, not wanting the soldier to see. Travis began to walk forward. The wall appeared in front of us and after that, all I heard was gun fire. We began running toward the building.

As soon as the barrier went up, I absorbed the air around me. I separated myself and flew through the group of soldiers, pulling myself together and turning back to normal.

"Stop, men!" a voice ordered.

A man walked out of the group and looked at me.

"I saw you move. That was very quick, but quickness is my specialty. So you're a teleporter huh?" the man asked.

"No." He must've been an instructor. Someone had to have sent him to check out the explosion.

"Sure looked like you teleported. Can we just skip this, you fighting back thing? I'm going to beat you so fast . . ." He disappeared. " . . . that you won't know what happened." He was behind me. He moved quickly. I took out my lighter, struck it, and absorbed the fire; my body engulfed in flames. Their bullets would pass right through me, and what ever he tried would be useless.

"That's something I've never seen."

I turned around and looked at him. "Try and use that speed on something you can't touch." I tried to punch him, but he ran away. "Is that all you can do is run?"

"Kill him," he ordered.

The soldiers began to open fire on me, but it had no effect. I walked toward them and they backed away in fear and continued to shot at me. I threw a fireball at them, hitting a soldier and causing a distraction. I ran into the middle of the crowd and allowed myself to lose structure; my fire spreading everywhere, consuming the soldiers. Some got out, but must were burnt to death. I regained my shape and went after the six others. I flew at one, lit him a blaze, and threw him at another. Then, I shot fireballs into the air and they rained on three others. The last soldier took off into a building and there was no sense chasing after him.

The speed man watched in horror. He had no idea what to do. "Scared?"

"Extremely."

"Just gunna run away?"

"Of course not. I was given a mission and I'm going to fulfill it."

He started to run circles around me. Suddenly, he had created a vacuum by running so fast. I began to lose my breath. The oxygen was getting ripped out of the center of the vacuum, my fire was dying quickly. I absorbed the ground with my foot and felt it flow all throughout me. My entire body was solid and the tornado had no effect on me. He stopped running and stared at me from a far.

"What are you?"

"Everything."

"I'm not leaving 'til you're dead." He ran at me and began punching my stomach. I grabbed his arm. His knuckles were covered in blood.

"Then I guess you're never leaving." I sent my absorbed rock into his wrist and began returning to normal, starting with my feet and working its way up and out of my body and into his. The rock passed through his wrist and spread throughout his entire body. I let go after I was back to normal and he had become solid rock. He didn't have my ability, so he wasn't going anywhere. He was dead; his brain now just a large pebble.

I returned to the group. They were waiting in front of the building.

"Hope they were no trouble," Adair said.

"None at all."

"Then let's go rescue your friend."

Chapter LII

PERIN: BUYING TIME

June 4, 2007

Yukanzo teleported back with his arms full of chains and ropes.

"Thank you. Teleport Nadim and I down to Bidziil." He grabbed the two of us and the next moment, we were standing in front of Bidziil's motionless body.

"Yukanzo, go check on Emily and Franz. I want to know the progress of the girl. Nadim, start tying up Bidziil. We are going to bring him to the docks and put him in the ocean. Is the prison there?"

"Yes sir it is. I will go check the progress of her and return."

"No, bring the girl and everyone else to the basement of Instructor Building H."

"As you wish." He teleported away.

Nadim was done restraining Bidziil. It wasn't going to hold him for long, but all I needed was a little time.

"Grab him and let's go." Nadim picked up Bidziil and threw him over his shoulder. We left the room and proceeded to go outside. There was no quick way to get to the docks because we had to go through three buildings to get there. My phone rang.

"Yes?"

"Sir . . . huge . . . with . . . Bastian . . ." There was too much interference with what was going on behind him. It had to be one of my instructors. I hung up the phone.

"Who was that?" Nadim asked.

"Someone. They have informed me that Bastian is on the island. There must be a fight on the Homestead where they landed. Hopefully, Oran can handle them."

"Oran is strong. He can do it."

"Let's hope so. We have to keep moving. If he wakes up, then he'll kill us both."

"Yeah, we should." There was a door ahead of us. I opened and closed it behind me, leaving Nadim on the other side. I didn't want him to see what I was going to do. After, I opened the door and let Nadim through. He looked at the repeating holes in the walls ahead of us, which were just big enough to fit through. The path led straight to the docks.

"What the hell! How did this happen?"

"I had someone create a short cut for us. I planned ahead."

"Wow, Perin. Great idea." He was so gullible.

He dropped Bidziil and started dragging him so he could fit through the path, arriving at the docks much faster than planned. Nadim threw Bidziil inside of the five by five-foot square prison. It was similar to a dog cage, but it was made of metal four inches thick. He picked up the cage, after he locked it tight, held it over his head, without even straining, and threw it into the ocean; not very far out. There was a chain attached to the prison, he grabbed and tied to the dock, so I could come back and pull Bidziil up when the girl was fully mine.

"Sir, your arm. It's bleeding. Badly!" Nadim said in shock.

"Oh, yes," I spoke casually.

"What happened?"

"It's nothing." I walked over to him and he ripped off his sleeve so I could wrap it around my arm. I called Yukanzo. "You need to grab Ryder and Reece."

"Yes, sir."

"How is her progress?"

"She is very strong willed. Amity is working as hard as she can."

"She needs to work harder."

"Good news, sir. Ninety percent of the students have been wiped clean of the lock down."

"The students don't MATTER! All I care about is this one girl!"

"And I thought you should know the intruders are in the H building."

"Damn it! They're too early. Just do as I told you. Get Ryder and Reece, and when she is done, bring everyone to the H building basement, Room Two."

"I will do as you say. It shouldn't take too much longer. Amity is making great progress."

"Do not bring Amity. Save her for later."

"Okay, sir."

I hung up. My arm was in pain. I didn't have time to worry about it. Reece would heal me and I'd be fine.

"We must go to the H building."

"Then let's go."

Chapter LIII

TRAVIS AND Tobias:
ROUGH GRAVITY

July 6, 2007

We opened the doors quietly and looked around. The entire building was empty.

"They keep all the prisoners downstairs," Adair said. "Don't be fooled. It looks empty but we will be ambushed soon. I wouldn't doubt it. Everyone be on your guard."

He opened a set of double doors and we started walking downstairs, where it started to get dark. We came to, what looked like, a dungeon full of random things; like desks and furniture.

"Are you sure you're bringing us to the right place? Maybe we're in the wrong building."

All of the sudden, we were all slammed down to the ground by sheer pressure. I turned my head and watched Adair continue to walk ahead.

"You tricked us," I mumbled. It was hard to breath and impossible for me to move. Everyone was in pain. I had to do something. Adair began to float.

"I was locked up because of you, Travis," Adair said. "You told Perin that it was me that left on fight night. He sent me straight to the dungeon. I was beaten, burned, shocked, stabbed and then . . . healed. Then they did the whole thing over again. I went through agonizing pain because of you. I wanted to die, but they did the opposite. They continued to heal my body. Over and over the process continued, until became part of their team. I gladly accepted their proposal. It was much better than the alternative. Then I was told that you sold me out, even though we both left that night. Over the weeks, I honed my power even more; increasing its duration and strength. Now because of what you did, you're going to watch your friends die."

During the psychopaths rant I tried to use my ability but my head felt too heavy and it was hard for me to concentrate. I couldn't keep a good picture in my head. Adair had to be affecting the gravity level; it's the only thing that explains all the things going on at the same time.

The weight grew stronger. I could feel my bones about to crack. I tried to focus as hard as I could to use my power. My hand turned clear white and I began to slowly absorb the brick floor.

"None of that, Travis." The weight was lifted off of me and I began to float. I looked down at Adair.

"I'm sorry, Adair. I was going to tell you but I guess it was too late. I'm so sorry."

"It's *way* too late, Travis." Random things around him started to float. He grabbed a nearby desk and threw it at me. I had nowhere to go and nowhere to move. The desk hit me and I was crushed against a wall. He held me there, continuing to put pressure on me.

"This is just what I wanted," he laughed. "But before I kill you, you must watch your friends die."

They all began to hover just like I did. This time he grabbed a bookshelf and threw it but it turned into particles with other objects around the room, including the desk pinning me to the wall. It was Tobias; he was trying to make something.

"Perin, go away. I can handle this!" he yelled looking around.

All the matter was drawn onto Tobias, covering himself in it. He dropped to the ground and was no longer affected by Adair's power.

"What the . . ." Adair was confused.

"Anti gravity suit. None of your pressure is going to work on me."

"I don't need my ability to kill a weak kid like you. This will just make it more interesting." Adair dropped to the ground. "Bring it on kid."

He grabbed a chair and threw it at me, but I caught it and threw it back, crashing to the ground before it got to him. I wasn't going to waste any time. I ran at him and punched, but he dodged it and followed up with a hit to my stomach but my padding cushioned the blow. I continued to try and punch him, but he was too fast. I finally landed one on his the face. After that, I didn't miss again until he flew upward. He started soaring around the room, kicking hovering objects at me, delaying his defeat. I dodged everything he kicked at me, deteriorating one object and turned it into an attachment for my suit; a chain launcher. It was oval shaped and attached to my wrist. I had to tie him down, so I launched the chain at him, he dodged effortlessly; I retracted it and ran at him. If I got closer I could get a better shot with my chain, but he started flying around the room. I shot to chain at him, but as soon as it exited the launcher in plummeted straight into the ground. He began throwing more random objects at me. The chain was hindering me from dodging them all. A desk and a chair clipped me. A couch was about to crush me, but I pictured an attachment to the chain launcher, that caused it to be in affected by gravity changes, and broke down the couch before it could harm me.

I shot the chain at him and it tied him up, ripping him toward me. I deteriorated almost all the random things in the room and turned them into a set of boosters for my back and a metal glove on my right hand with another booster attached to it. I activated all the boosters and rocketed toward Adair; my metal glove colliding with his face. The force of my punch sent him flying through a pillar and then through a wall into the next room. I released all my attachments and fell to the ground. His gravity effects wore off.

I ran over to everyone to make sure they were okay. Everyone was pretty beaten up, so I had to make another one of my super drink robots. I closed my eyes, pictured my robot, and the entire room started to shake. I open my eyes and my robot was in front of me. I looked around the room and it was like someone took a cookie cutter to it. I had to use something to make my robot, and I didn't want to use the entire room, so I broke down pieces of the wall and stretched my reach outside of the room and used things outside.

I opened the chest of my robot and took out five drinks, passing them around and drinking one myself. We were all ready for whatever was passed the door ahead of us. I was hoping it was Bidziil so we could get him and I'd make another ship and get us all out of there.

Chapter LIV

ADEN AND *Bastian*: MUSHROOM FIGHT II

July 6, 2007

We landed on the hanger of the Homestead. My body was still covered by blood armor. My wings were liquid form but the tops were solid. There were three black jets on the hanger. We looked around and there was a single large building and a small forest behind it. There was about thirty or more soldiers that ran out of the building.

I looked at Bastian and smirked.

I opened up my coat and I took out Alden. I ran at the soldiers and they began shootin'. I could see the bullets comin' toward me. Alden was at his peak just like Ien was. I was movin' fast enough to dodge the bullets; weavin' all around them and not gettin' hit once. I reached the line of soldiers and began fightin' them while Aden stayed back and was shootin' needles at the squad. He was pickin' them off one by one. I watched the needles shoot through them. It was as if they were gettin' shot by bullets. They tried to attack me, but they moved too slow. I caught one man's fist, spun him around, and then kicked him into a crowd of others. A blood whip came crashin' into the troops eliminatin' the remaining ones.

I ran to Bastian. He took off the mask. "Let's get inside. We have to find Reece."

"You two aren't going anywhere. We still have a fight to finish," Oran said walking out from behind a jet.

He put his hand on the jet and it melted, beginning to shape into a giant mushroom, doing the same with two others. The mushrooms were at least eighteen feet tall. They were black and had arms and legs just as the ones before did. Some parts of there body were metallic. One had metal pieces where eyes should have been. Their caps cast a shadow all around them only making them look even more sinister. Bastian and I looked in horror. I began shooting spikes at one of the mushrooms. "Let's try and focus on one at a time."

"Sounds good."

I took out my werewolf mask and put it on. I changed form and ran at the mushroom that Aden was focusin' on. I jumped and slashed at its body. When I landed the mushroom smacked me with its arm and I went rollin' on the ground. My werewolf wasn't goin' to work on them much. They were too massive, close combat wasn't goin' to work. Aden was still attackin' the same one.

I shot spiked balls at the one mushroom. I had to dodge the other two while attacking the same one. They moved faster than I would have guessed. The other two came at me ignoring Bastian, seeing as how I was doing most of the attacking. My attacks weren't doing much though. I drew all the blood back to me and made both of my arms into blades. I ran toward Bastian, slicing the legs of the mushrooms in passing.

I got back up and continued to attack the one mushroom. It was poundin' the ground tryin' to hit me. Luckily, I was fast enough to dodge its giant fists. I scratched its hands as they were on the ground, woundin' it in the process. It was clear that the creatures didn't feel pain. I could attack its hand all day with no avail. I had to get a killin' blow. The mushroom tried to punch me again; I jumped backwards avoiding the swift strike.

Suddenly, my waist was wrapped in blood. I looked back as Aden was about to be attacked by the other two. He threw me up into the air, as close to the cap of the mushroom as possible. I looked back and Aden created a barrier with is left hand to block the fist of one of the mushrooms. Then unexpectedly blood spikes shot out of the *mushroom's arm. They only went about half way but it was still and impressive attack.*

I dug my claws into the edge of the mushroom's cap. I hastily pulled myself up onto the cap and began to reek havoc. I sliced it again and again. I dug my claw deep into the left edge of the cap and dragged it all the way to the other end cuttin' off a large piece. It fell to the ground as a pile of slush. The mushroom was angry. Bubbles started to appear all over the cap, poppin' at the same time and forcin' me off.

I saw Bastian fall followed by a rain of goop. I ripped the blood spikes out from the arm of the mushroom, got some distance from the other two, and continued to focus on the first. I shot larger needles at it and it seemed to be taking a lot of damage. The mushroom then began to push something out of its chest. I saw a head of a missile. The missile shot out with destructive force. I created two giant blood hands and caught it.

The missile exploded and I was blasted back. My blood splattered all over the place. The explosion made the mushrooms stumble; one was knocked down. I regained my balance and created wings. I flew at the one who launched the missile. I didn't want to give it the chance to do it again.

I drew back all my blood, that splattered everywhere after the explosion, and made the long blade with my left hand. I began slicing the mushroom that I was focused on before. I was able to fly fast enough to dodge its swipes. It tried to take out my wings but I quickly retracted them to dodge its attack. Then reform them to continue flying.

Aden was doing great. The explosion seemed like it didn't even phase him. I had to find a way to help him more. I hid behind a piece of concrete, opened my coat, took out Gei. and put on the mask. I was inside my head and Gei was sittin' on my brain meditatin'.

"Gei, I need your advice. Look outside. There is a battle going on. I can't think of any mask that can help me. They are too big."

"What about Ien?"

"Flyin' won't help me right now. I want to help, not escape."

"What about Wer?"

"I already tried. The mushrooms are too big for him." She stood up and looked at me.

"You can't think of a single mask that can help you?"

"No," I said sadly. "I don't know what to do."

"Then try two masks. That way you can use two abilities at once."

"How do I do that?"

"Sorry, but you have to figure it out on your own. You can do a lot more than you think." She flicked me in the head and there was a flash of light.

I was knocked out of my own head and Gei's mask fell off my face, landing in my hands. How am I supposed to use two masks at once, I asked myself. I don't have two faces. I put her back in my coat and looked at all my masks. I pulled out Ien and stared at him. My vision became scratchy, like it did before I made a mask. A jagged dark yellow line appeared in the middle of Ien. It was beggin' me to pull it apart. I could sense it. I didn't want to pull it apart though. I had no idea what would happen to Ien if I did. Unfortunately, I had no other choice.

I gently pulled Ien apart. I didn't even have to apply any strength. It split into two halves; each half had jagged edges. Quickly, I put the two halves back together and the mask became whole again. I turned it around lookin' it over. The mask was fine. For a second, I was frightened. I focused my eyes on the mask, again the dark yellow line appeared and I split the mask apart. I put down the two halves and opened my coat. I needed a mask that could provide the most help. I needed long distance and close range capabilities. Ien gave me speed and height advantage, now I needed some force behind it. I looked at my newest mask, Vaz. He was the glass controller. He would provide exactly what I needed. I pulled him out and a similar line appeared down him then pullin' him apart just as easily.

Like Ien, Vaz and I had an instant connection. I picked up the right half of Vaz and the left half of Ien. I put both of the pieces together. It was a perfect fit. I tried to put the leftovers together but they didn't combine, I then put them in my coat pockets. I stood up and watched as Aden continued to try and fight them off. He was still attackin' the *same one, and managed to remove its arm while I was gone. He needed help, and we were the ones that were goin' to deliver it, I thought. I put on the mask and I heard a bird's cry and glass shatter at the same time.*

In my head, I looked on the ground and it was covered in glass. It was Vaz's home. I looked up and feathers were suspended up in the air. Ien and Vaz were standin' in front of me starin' at each other. I ran to them as the glass broke and cracked beneath my shoes.

"Please don't be upset. I need ya both. One of ya can't do it alone."

"You want us to work as a three?" Vaz asked.

"Yes. I should've talked to you both separate before doin' this, but I had no time. I'm sorry. Our friend Aden needs help. He can't win this fight on his own."

"I do not know you, but if Bastian has chosen you than he did it for a reason; Aden needs us, Bastian needs us. We must work together," *Ien said to Vaz as he held out his hand.*

"I agree. As a whole we can do this." *Vaz grabbed his hand. The glass from the ground was drawn to Vaz and it swirled around him. The feathers from up in the air did the same to Ien. I could no longer see either of them; all I saw was glass and feathers in tornados. The two small tornadoes combined together then exploded.*

I was back, watchin' Aden attack the mushrooms. Now I could be of use to him. I flew into the air and looked at the buildin'. I shattered all the glass and pulled it to me. Then I began flyin' surrounded by glass with it trailin' behind me as well.

Bastian came out of hiding. Finally, he was going to help. I saw the werewolf fall and I feared he was out for the count. He was wearing a mask I had never seen before. It looked like he had combined two of his masks together. I didn't know he could do that.

I combined shards of glass and fired them at the mushroom Aden was attackin'. One of the other mushrooms' arm started to freak out. Suddenly, guns shot out of it. It began firin' everywhere. I dodged its bullets and flew behind another mushroom. The bullets hit it causin' it to stumble backward. I combined shards and made a three-foot long blade which I used to stab the mushroom with multiple times to direct his attention on me. It began shootin' at me gain. I flew underneath the arm and behind the mushroom. I used my blade to chop off the machine gun arm. It fell to the ground as slush with the machine guns clearly visible.

He was kicking ass. Two controllers with the ability to fly; it spelled game over. I hacked off the other arm of the mushroom, and then shot my chain whip through its head. I flew with the whip still in him, pulled him, and knocked him over. I stayed at a distance and used my whip and spiked balls to attack the other ones; constantly drawing my blood back to me for continuous use.

There was only one left to worry about. The others weren't dead, but there was no way that they could get up. I combined the shards into a crescent shape and held it out in front of me. I flew around the last one standing and cut him all over.

I flew up next to Aden.

"Watch this next move. This will finish it for them. Then we can go in and find Reece."

"Let's see what you got."

I flew at the legs of the mushroom holdin' my crescent out. I gained maximum speed and flew right at its left leg, completely removin' it like a knife through butter. The mushroom fell and smashed into the ground. I watched as it began to bubble up and started to turn into goop. I turned and another mushroom was walkin' toward me. I launched the crescent at its chest; I didn't notice that its chest was bubblin'. I saw a missile head just barely poke out. My crescent collided with the head, and there was a giant explosion. It hit me and I was shot back. All I saw was smoke and debris.

I surrounded myself in a solid blood ball. It protected me from the debris but not from the force. I let down my barrier after about a minute of waiting and there was still a lot of smoke that hadn't cleared. There were remains of the mushrooms everywhere, black slime all over everything. I ran toward the building. Nearly half of it was in rubble. Reece was still inside somewhere. I retracted all my armor created two giant hands and started clearing the debris.

I was hoverin' over the water. It took me a second to get my head to stop spinnin'. I flew up back to the landin' pad. My coat was tattered and dusty. I checked to see if all my masks were okay, and luckily they were. Most of the smoke cleared. I saw Aden clearin' a path into the building. I hoped Reece wasn't affected by the explosion. I flew over to Aden and then took off my mask, pieced them back together and put them back in their pockets.

"Aden, I'm sorry."

"It's fine. Reece is going to be okay. Just step back and let me clear the debris."

"Okay." I watched as he finished clearing a hole through the debris.

"Let's move."

Chapter LV

Aden and *Bastian*:
Faxon Breaker

July 6, 2007

I walked in first and Bastian followed behind me. I was out to make sure that Reece was okay. We came to a long hallway with doors on each side and walked down it. Each door had a name on it.

"Dude," I put my hand on Aden's chest and stopped him.

I looked over at the door. It had Reece's name on it. I kicked it open and ran inside. There was a bed and a television but no Reece. Under the television there was a VCR with a tape in it. I walked over and pushed the tape in. Perin came on the screen.

"Aden, sorry to disappoint you. Reece isn't here. I knew you would come back looking for him. His parents and I have an agreement. I gave them a sum of money and they said I could have him. You see people are afraid of what they don't understand. They saw him as a freak. I gladly took him off their hands. Reece is very important too me just like he is to you. He is going to be a great asset to the islands. I wish you the best of luck, because if you don't leave now, I'll kill you myself. You should have just stayed with us." The tape ended.

I shot needles at the television, shattering the glass and making it spark.

Aden didn't look happy. I could hear his blood rushin' and pumpin'. It sounded like a train movin' through his veins. I didn't want him to get blood hungry again. I had to calm him down.

"He's still alive. We can rescue him. I promise. If we've got anythin' in common, it's our hatred for Perin. Just do me a favor. Leave a little life in him so I can have my revenge too."

"No promises. Let's keep moving. Maybe he's still in the building somewhere." I had to keep my cool. If I lost it again I wasn't sure what would happen. I had to stay positive, Reece was okay. He was fine. Nothing bad was going to happen to him.

We left the room and we heard people's voices. We followed the voices and we came to another long hallway. There were people frantically running in and out of one room all wearing white lab coats; possibly scientists. There was a window that allowed you to see in the room. It looked like they were fixing some machine.

"What do ya think it is?"

"No clue, but I do think we should go break it."

I looked at Aden and smiled. "That is a great idea."

"What can I say? I have great ideas."

"We should totally hang out more after we save your friend and destroy this place."

"That goes without saying."

"Awesome. How about I deal with the scientist and ya go break that machine?"

"Lead the way."

"Good, cause I wanna try out one of my other masks." I pulled Pruen out of my coat and put him on. "He stretches."

Bastian's voice changed. It became squeaky and high pitched. I still didn't quite understand his power but it was powerful and he used it perfectly. I let him go ahead of me. His arm stretched out and grabbed one of the scientists leaving the room, pulling the scientist toward him quickly and then letting go. The man went flying down the hall, his clipboard bouncing off the wall and smashing into the floor. It was a relief to not have to fight another huge battle. I was beginning to get weak. Bastian broke the window and jumped into the room.

Everyone was freakin' out. I reached out, grabbin' another guy, and pullin' him back. "I bet ya ran tests on me and my friends." I opened my coat and showed him all my masks. "Look familiar?" I grabbed his neck and threw him out the window that I came through.

A woman was running down the hall trying to get away. She was about to go into another door, but I made a blood whip, grabbed her foot, and she tripped and hit her face on the ground. I pulled her back to me and held her up. "Don't run away. You're just as bad as everyone else on these islands. I'll let you live if you can tell me where a little boy named Reece is."

"I have no idea," he gulped in fear.

"Oh, wrong answer."

"Wait! They do keep some people on the second wing. It's directly behind this building. If you go through that door and keep walking you'll get there in a jiffy."

"We've already been there." I whipped her back down the way she came and her body slammed on the ground.

I took out a mask that I only used once, the one that tried to kill me, the death mask. I held it in my hand. I figured I could try it on someone else. Gei told me that I could do a lot more than I thought. It wasn't like these guys were fightin' back. I stretched out my arm and shoved the mask on a scientists face, feelin' it suction to her face. I held onto the mask and pulled the two of them into the air. Suddenly, she was released from the mask, dropped to the floor bleedin' from the ears, eyes, and mouth. It worked; the mask was no longer completely useless. I continued puttin' the mask on other people's faces, there was only three left in the room as I was doin' it to one of them, the last one made a break for the door. He was about to open it when the door was shot open by Aden.

"Good timin'," I said puttin' the death mask and Pruen away.

We walked around the machine and there was one more person curled up hidin' behind it. Aden covered her in blood and stuck her to the wall, removin' the blood around her head to let her breathe.

"What does this machine do?" I asked nicely.

"We call it the Faxon Breaker," she cried.

"What? Why?"

"There is a man named Faxon that has a really powerful ability. As long as the machine is running he can't get any information that comes from here. It creates an electronic pulse that covers the islands. Please don't destroy it."

"Sorry, babe. This thing is toast." I sent blood inside the machine and turned it into spikes. They broke out of the machine and sparks flew everywhere. "So does this mean we can contact Faxon somehow?"

"I think so, but how? He has always contacted us."

"We don't have time to worry about contacting him. We need to stay on point. Let's search this building and then move on to the next," I said as we left the room. We found nothing in the build and were about to leave when three phones rang simultaneously. Bastian and I looked at each other and smirked. It was Faxon. We both knew it. I walked over to it and picked it up.

"Aden, I'm glad to talk to you. You guys are doing great, but you're not on the right island. Bidziil is on the Industrial and so is Reece. You need to get to Dock Five right away. There is no time to waste. Quick go," he hung up the phone and I put it down.

"What did he say?"

"We have to get to Dock Five on the Industrial. That is were Bidziil and Reece are."

"Awesome, let's finish this thing." We ran out of the room and the phone rang again. I ran back and picked it up.

"Hey Bastian, how are you?"

"Better,"

"No hard feelings" You know I'm truly sorry for what happened."

"We're cool, don't worry."

"Great, good luck. You're kicking some major ass. Keep it up. I just wanted to say thank you, and to tell you that there is another team on the islands. They'll be able to help you but you have to go help them first. They need you." He hung up. I ran back to Aden.

"So?"

"He just wanted to say thanks and to let use know that there are others on the islands."

"We are running out of time. We have to get to the Industrial."

Chapter LVI

TRAVIS AND Tobias: THE BOSS

July 6, 2007

We all drank what Tobias gave us and were all completely revitalized. I stood up and began walking for the door ahead of us.

"Travis, wait!" Gabe yelled. "We should make a plan first. We have no idea what is beyond that door."

"What's beyond that door is another challenge. We can't make a plan if we don't know what to plan for," I said.

"He's right. We have to just go and hope for the best. I'm sure we can handle it."

"Alright," Gabe said helping up the girls.

I opened the door and walked in with everyone following behind me. The room was empty, except for some other doors. We all looked around waiting for something until the door that was directly in the middle of the others opened. Five people walked through it. One was the guy who broke into my apartment, Perin. The others I had never seen before: a man in a white coat with a black symbol on it, a man dressed in a suit, a black guy and a girl.

"What a surprise, I never would have thought you would have made it this far. I'm very surprised Adair didn't kill you all. It seems that I have underestimated all of you," Perin said condescendingly.

"You have no idea," I said. "I'm going to kill you myself, Perin."

"I don't see that happening, Travis. You are far too weak to kill me."

"We'll just have to see about that."

"Or we can just stop all this fighting and you can join me and my efforts. We aren't as bad as you think."

"Never! I know what you are up to. I know your plans. I read the files. Faxon has told me the whole story. I know it all from the beginning."

"My plans have changed since then. Killing Bidziil seems to be impossible. I have decided to take control of his body and power."

"You make it sound like it's so simple."

"That's 'cause it is." Another door opened and Nadim and some girl walked out. "Ah, perfect timing. This is the girl who will become the new Bidziil."

"What!? How is that possible?"

"She is just as special as most of us in the room. She has the ability to swap souls with another person. She will remove Bidziil from his body and take it over. In the process her old body will die, and Bidziil's soul will go into a dead body. Bidziil will be removed from this plane of existence and I will have control over the most powerful being on the planet."

"That is crazy. I can't let you do that."

"*We* can't let you do that," Gabe said.

"You all are so ignorant. I'm not giving you a choice in the matter."

"We are going to stop you and save Bidziil."

"I will use him for myself. He will become my personal slave. In theory he will stop releasing his energy and we will gain all of his power."

"But what about the Boss. You have to obey his commands," the girl said.

"Emily, you don't understand." Perin grabbed her wrist. "You know what the Boss can do, don't you?"

"Yes, I read the report that the last boss left behind."

"Well then this should clear up some missing information for you." The skin around her wrist started to disintegrate, leaving behind a very blood wrist. She ripped her arm out of his grip and grabbed it with her other hand.

"I don't understand; it's not possible!" The muscle fibers were visible. He had almost burned her to the bone.

"It's true. Now all of you know. I'm the Boss. And these islands belong to me," the other men helped her up. "You all obey me. I've always been in control."

"I can't believe it was you this whole time. I should have known. It was all too coincidental," one of the men said.

"This changes nothing. The project still continues and so does the mission. I chose all of you for your skills. If anything this just makes it easier."

They all kneeled down to him. "Yes, Boss," they all said.

He was in charge of the entire project. I couldn't give him the chance to use his power on me. Another door opened and four more people walked out, a young boy, a pale man, two other guys, and a woman.

"These are some loyal students; Makale, Bethany, and Ryder. As for the young boy, he is Reece. He is the most important of them all," Perin said.

"No," Callia said quietly.

"It can't be. How is he still alive?" Gabe said.

"What?" I asked.

"That is Makale. Saeed and I fought him earlier. He was caught in the electrical explosion with Saeed. He should be dead."

"That means that . . . Saeed," Callia began to cry uncontrollably.

"Now we can get this party started. Ryder, Makale, Bethany, these people are a threat; I'm going to leave them for you two. Yukanzo, Emily Nadim, Franz, and Kalcos: take the girl to Dock Five. That is where Bidziil is. Have the girl take his body. I will stay here and make sure they are disposed of."

"Yes, sir. Right away," the black man said. They all grabbed onto him and he teleported them away.

"This ends here Perin!" I yelled.

Chapter LVII

TRAVIS AND *Gabe*: PERIN'S POWER

July 6, 2007

The boy moved close to Perin. The fight was between the six of us; a fair three on three fight.

"Are we going to start this or what?" Bethany asked.

"I'll make the first move." Tobias deteriorated things in the room and created a brown bark skinned man, wearing blue jeans and no shirt. He flexed his muscles and spikes broke out of his skin. "Go get'em."

I absorbed the diamond on the ring as Gabe took out a customized toothpick. One of the guy's body structure began to change, transforming into something. His nose bent upward and his skin looked hard. He ran at us.

"Makale is mine. You guys get the other two."

"I'll deal with the rhino." I stopped him in his tracks. He was pushing back hard, but it was useless. I wasn't going anywhere, but he was. I picked him up and I threw him into a pillar. It exploded and he crashed in to the ground; dust covered the room.

I ran at Makale with the Angel. He was ready for me, having already created some sort of weapon to defend with. Every time I slashed at him, he protected against it. He was an impossible opponent to fight hand to hand with. I backed up and began running all around the room and Makale followed. I placed toothpicks in strategic locations and enlarged them but he dodged the majority. I turned around to look at him, and he stopped running at me.

"You're good, but I'm better," I put my hand on the wall and enlarged a toothpick that I put into it, expanding and crashing into Makale's left side. He was knocked down. I had to finish him quick. The dust was blown away. He got up and we started clashing weapons, matching each other blow for blow. He was fighting fair this time; he could've pulled out a gun and shot me whenever he wanted, but for some reason he didn't.

Dust covered the room. Gabe was being chased by Makale and it didn't seem like Ryder was getting up. Tobias' spiked man and I ran toward Perin. The spiked man shot spikes out of his hand at a figure in the dust cloud. We heard them make contact, but the dust cleared, sadly, it wasn't Perin. It was Bethany with blood pooling underneath her. I looked back and Tobias had giant mechanical wings on his back. We turned back around and Perin hadn't moved. The spiked man shot spikes at Perin, but he stayed stationary. The projectiles were just about to hit him when they were suddenly turned to dust.

"What!?"

"You can't hurt me with a power like mine." Perin said with confidence.

"You're just like everyone you are imprisoning and torturing. Your as bad as they come, Perin. Your power is garbage and you still don't stand a chance against me."

"Let me explain to you what my power is. I can deteriorate any solid material. That means if I wanted to, I could turn you to dust. Regardless of whether or not you're made of diamond."

"Then do it tough guy. What's stopping you? Don't have the guts?"

"My power comes with a cost. For every amount that I deteriorate I must lose the same amount myself." Perin held up his hand and parts of his skin looked to be burnt away.

Reece grabbed onto him and healed his wounds. "But with training I've been able to have to give up less amount of myself to deteriorate more. It is very hard to train because of the side effects. That is why Reece is so important to me. If for some reason the girl does not succeed in taking over Bidziil, then some day I will be able to kill him just by looking at him."

"Well that's not the case now is it? You won't get to live long enough to master your power."

"We'll just have to see about that." My coat began to shred. I had a burning sensation all over my body. I could feel my arms begin to itch and burn.

"Travis! Absorb!" Tobias yelled. He was holding a big gun that he shot at me. It released a long strand of electricity that I absorbed when it hit me. My body was glowing blue. I looked up at Perin. He could no longer deteriorate me. I wasn't a solid. My body was complete energy. I tightened my muscles and drew energy into my right fist and let out an electric beam, hitting Perin and leaving a burn mark on his chest. He began convulsing on the ground.

Makale looked away and over to Perin. It was my chance. I stabbed him directly in the heart, enlarged the Angel more, and it ripped through his back. His blood shot out everywhere.

"Look out!" Tobias yelled. I turned around and Ryder was running toward us. The gun in Tobias' hand faded away and another one appeared, firing net and capturing Ryder. He pulled him back and flew out of the room. I changed back to normal and walked over to the girls.

"You all did great," Hannah said.

"He's dead Callia," I dragged his body over to her. *"This time you know he's dead."* She spit on his body and ran out of the room.

"Travis look."

I looked behind me. The little boy was helping Perin up. There wasn't even a mark on his chest from where I electrocuted him. Only a mangled hole in his fancy suit. He dusted himself off like nothing happened and spoke.

"My little friend here has the ability to heal. His instructions are to heal me whenever I get hurt and to listen to my ever order."

I hadn't realized it until then. The boy's eyes were glowing blue. It was her; Amity. She was on this island somewhere and I was going to find her after I killed Perin.

"Where is she Perin?"

"Who?"

"Amity. Where is she?"

"Oh yeah, that's right. You have a bone to pick with her don't you? Is your little girlfriend? Amber, Right? I bet you miss her. This all could have been avoided if you never left. It's all your fault, Travis. How does it feel to know that you killed her? Do you have restless nights because of it? Does she haunt your dreams when you sleep? Does it burn your insides every time she crosses your mind?"

I grabbed my lighter and absorbed its flame. "I'll show you how much it burns." The fire rose to my shoulder. "No one is going to be able to recognize you when I'm done with you." I slowly walked toward Perin, slowly being fully consumed in fire.

"Everyone get out now. Go to the dock and save Bidziil. I'll handle Perin myself." They took off running up the stairs. The boy hid behind Perin. I raised my body temperature higher and higher, slowly treading towards him with my feet melting the stone floor below me. Perin held out his hand and the floor was rapidly turned to dust. I began floating and then launched at him full speed. I grabbed him by his tie and it turned to ash; his clothes began to catch fire. He tried to protect himself against me but it was a waste of time. I grabbed his throat, picked him up and slammed him against the wall. There wasn't even blood. I was so hot it was evaporating.

"Do you think you can stop me, Perin? You brought this on yourself! You're the one who found me! I would have never known about my power if it wasn't for you! I'd thank you, but you don't deserve it!" I threw him at the pillar behind us. "Tell me what hell's like." I let my fire shoot out of my hand in a stream, covering his body. All I could smell was burning flesh. After the smoke cleared, all that was left of him was a charred corpse. There was no way he would be able to come back after that. I did the same to Makale and Bethany's body as well. The little boy was nowhere in sight. The spell must have broken off and he ran away. I changed back to normal. I had nothing left to do but save Bidziil. The big bad boss was dead.

Chapter LVIII

ADEN AND *Bastian*: A FRIEND NO MORE

July 6, 2007

Bastian and I flew to the Industrial and looked around. We were only on Dock Two. We began running down the pier and reached Dock Five. No one was around. We noticed a chain attached to a hold where the end of the chain was in the water. All of the sudden, six people appeared out of nowhere. They backed up, took out guns and started shooting at us. I quickly made a blood barrier and protected us.

"Who are these guys?"

"Well some of them are heads of the project. One used to be my partner and another one is Yukanzo."

"Details, what can they do?"

"Nadim has super strength. Yukanzo can teleport. I don't believe those heads have powers. We can rule Oran, McGrand and Perin out. The only other one with a power is Victoria, so our odds are good."

"You stay here. I'll deal with them." I took out Dac and was about to put him on when a man appeared behind us.

I shot a blood ball at him, but he teleported away appearing further way.

"What are you all doing back here, Aden? You should leave before this gets messy for you."

"I think you should be the one to leave, seeing as how you're good at running away."

"This is my last warning." He had no idea I was stretching out a blood trail at sneaking it behind him.

"What's the worst ya can do, send me to China?" He pulled out a gun and aimed it at us.

"You've made the wrong choice." I turned the trial into a bladed disk and shot it at his gut with about a quarter of it coming out of the front of him. He dropped to his knees and fell on his face.

"I'm really tired of all these 'last warnings', aren't you?"

I put Dac on. "I won't even give them a chance to speak," I walked through Aden's barrier. They tried to shot me but their bullets passed right through.

I drained all the blood from the teleporter and added it to my barrier, making an opening so that I could see what Bastian was doing.

One of the guys came runnin' at me. I kicked my left foot through his right and he dropped to the ground shakin'. There where two girls and two guys left. One girl and guy were tryin' very hard to protect the other girl. A man in a white coat was walkin' toward me with two handguns.

"I may not have a power, but I'll kill you."

"Ya can't touch me."

"We'll see." *He began unloadin' his clip, but the bullets did nothin'.*

I slowly walked toward him. He was jumpin' all over the place and doin' all these crazy tricks and flips as if they would make his bullets hit me. I got up to him and knocked his guns out of his hands, then put my hands into his shoulders and he dropped. I removed my hands and punched through his head. He fell to the concrete with his eyes bleedin'. I moved toward the last three. The two protectin' the girl ran at me. I put both my hand through the man's chest and then put my hand through the girl's throat. I removed Dac and began walkin' towards the girl. She wasn't movin' had a blank look on her face. Suddenly, I was grabbed from behind, ripped back, and slid across the concrete. It was the first guy I attacked; my kick must not have done enough. He picked me and threw me into the air toward the forest.

While movin' through the air I opened up my coat. I was seconds away from hittin' the ground and I took out Bon and put him on. My entire body froze up, becomin' stiff. I crashed into the dirt, leavin' behind a crater the size of my body. I made the mask fall off, put him away, and was about to put on Ien until I heard fightin'.

I ran through my barrier, covering myself with it, and molding it into my armor. Nadim sprinted towards me, and tried to punch me but I moved out of the way and tied up his hand and ran behind him. The blood armor felt like it was giving me extra speed and strength. It made me feel good, but I had to stay in control and couldn't let the blood take over again. I pulled him toward me and punched him. He broke out of my restraint and started punching back, but I moved out of the way every time he swung. I was way too fast for him. He was getting pissed. I put both my hands together, made a whip, and hit him from the side to send him crashing into the nearest building. I shot a net at the last girl standing. She seemed to be out of it. Her eyes were glowing blue and she had no expression on her face. She couldn't have been a threat. I grew out my wings and went toward the area where Bastian landed.

I went to where I heard the fightin'. There were trees knocked down everywhere, and it seemed like some of them had just vanished. I came to a person standin' next to a movin' tree and a giant caterpillar. The tree had two wholes for eyes and was usin' its roots as feet, and the caterpillar had two huge spikes at the end of its body. It appeared the they were bein' controlled by him. I heard a loud grunt and then I saw Ryder come runnin' at the tree. The tree tossed him aside like a bug.

"Ryder!" I put on Alden and ran at the kid, but the caterpillar got in my way. I bounced off the middle of him and rolled back.

"Bastian, oh my god! I'm so happy to see that you're okay," Ryder said.

"What are ya doin' here? How did ya get here?"

"I came to find you. I heard that you were in trouble. I flew here and this guy attacked me. Help me kill him," *Ryder answered.*

"Don't listen to him, Bastian! I was sent by Faxon. Travis and I came here to save Bidziil. Faxon told us to find you and work together. You have to believe me," the man asked.

"It's all lies Bastian. He works for Perin. He's trying to get you to turn on me. You know me better than that, Bastian. I'm your friend. Friends look out for each other."

I didn't know what to do. Ryder was my friend. It didn't make sense how or why he was here, but I also I had no idea who the other guy was. Clearly he was powerful and could have been trained by the islands. He could have been workin' for Perin, but he did mention Faxon. I took out Gei and hoped she would offer some help.

I was in my head again, standin' on my brain. I looked around and Gei was nowhere in sight.

"Are you honestly back again?" *Gei asked from behind me.*

I turned around and looked down at her. "I'm sorry, but I need your help again."

"With what?" *She asked angrily.*

"There is a fight goin' on outside and I need to know what side to help."

"Young man, there is always a fight going on with you. How am I supposed to help you now?"

"I need your unbiased opinion. There are two people; one is my friend and one is someone I have never met, except he knows Faxon. He sounds believable. I need to know which one to help."

"Just give me one second." *She disappeared and came back in seconds.* "I had to review the data you had just processed. The facts are these; you and Ryder are friends. You know nothing about the other man. You have doubts about Ryder and his honesty with you, due to the day at the lake. The other man is not giving off any indication that he is lying. He is clearly a powerful person. He could be powerful from island training. He does know of Faxon and Bidziil. That is all the information that I have on the situation. With it, I can make the conclusion that Ryder is the one you should help. You do not know this other man. This is my decision."

"Thank ya, Gei."

"You need to stop this."

"Stop what?"

"Coming to me whenever something has gone awry."

"I don't understand. That is what you're here for."

"Since you have found me, you have been with me three times. I am not the same as the others you use. You need to become more independent. You already know everything I know. I just help access information. You do not need me to make decisions. You can do it all on your own."

"I guess you're right, but still you are useful and I wouldn't want to ignore you."

"Just like you have ignored the color mask?"

"What?"

"He was one of the first masks you have created and yet you have only met him once. You haven't bothered to make a connection other than that."

"I never really gave it a second thought."

"You need to use us all. We can all offer some help at some time; as you have seen from the death mask. He is an asset. The color mask is part of you too. You know how time works in the masks. I'd be like he just kicked you out of his home. You should give him a chance after this is all over."

"Or maybe before."

"That's the attitude I like about you. Now get out of here. And I don't want to see you for a long time. I can calculate all the information that has been put into your head and then figure out how many days it has been. I'll know if you come back in just a few hours. I don't want to see you for a while and I mean it. You can function without me, I promise."

"Yes ma'am."

"Now leave." *She kicked me and there was a flash.*

The mask fell off my face. I looked over at Ryder. "This guy is finished. I took out Wer and was about to put him on, when I heard a noise and looked up. It was Aden with massive blood wings floatin' down to us. He landed next to me, looked around, and withdrew his armor.

"What the hell is going on?"

"You must be Aden, please you have to help me. I was sent by Faxon. He said you and Bastian could help Travis and I. Bastian is having trouble believing me." Tobias spoke.

"Wait, did you say, Travis?" I asked.

"Yeah, do you know him?" he asked.

"Yes, well I'm sure we're not on good terms right now, but yes I do know him." I chuckled.

"Then please help me. We are supposed to work together. These islands can no longer stand. We have to stop them and save Bidziil," he pleaded.

"You must be Tobias then."

"Yes, thank god. Will you help me?"

Ryder jumped up in werewolf form and knocked over the tree. He was about to attack Tobias.

I couldn't let anything happen to him. I quickly shot out a blood blast and hit the guy. He was struck and knocked out of the air. Tobias ran behind the giant caterpillar.

"What are ya dong?"

"Faxon said he was getting Travis and Tobias to help us. I'm not turning down free help. I've picked my side. You can do what you want, but I suggest you fight along side me. I trust Faxon more than anyone. You should too. He would never lie to us. Tobias is our friend."

"But Ryder is my friend."

"Then how did he get here?"

"I . . . don't know."

"Why is he here?"

"I don't know."

"How well do you know him?"

"I don't know!"

"Then it's clear what side you should be on." Ryder got up and roared then changed back to normal.

"Bastian, please. Trust me," Ryder begged.

"I'm sorry, Ryder. If you are truly my friend then you will stop this fight."

"I've had enough of all of this. I'm tired of this game," Ryder said. "I'm just going to kill all of you."

"What?"

"I was never your friend, Bastian. I was only trying to gain your trust so that I could kidnap you again, but now that the plans have changed, we don't need you anymore. You are just as useless as everyone else that is trying to destroy us. I'm finally going to do what I've wanted to do since the day we met; kill you."

"I should have known. You can try but you won't succeed. I'm much stronger since the last time we fought."

"And so am I."

"I want both of ya to leave. I can handle him on my own. Aden go with Tobias and help Travis."

"You can run, Aden, but I'll kill you for betraying the islands as soon as I'm done with Bastian."

"In your dreams."

"Aden just go." I put on Wer and lunged at Ryder.

Tobias ran over to me and said, "You really should go. There is a bigger fight in the basement. Travis and the others could use your help."

"Are you sure you two will be okay?" I looked over and saw Bastian throw Ryder into some brush.

"I think we can handle it."

"Okay," I ran toward the building.

I let out a howl and ran at the bush. I could hear bones crackin' and muscles rippin'. It was the sound of Ryder changin'. I jumped at the brush and somethin' jumped out at me, collidin' with me in the air. Ryder grabbed me, spun me around, and then he threw me to the ground. I picked myself up and looked at him. I had never seen him like that before. His hair was long and dark and everythin' about him was huge, from his muscles to his height. He was visually terrifyin'. His eyes were a golden color and his teeth looked sharper than razors with his claws being jagged and long. He was like no animal that I had ever seen before. Even in my werewolf state he was horrifyin'. I was goin' to kill him regardless of what he was.

I ran at him and slashed with my claws, but he caught my hand, grabbed my throat, and slammed me into the ground. I tried to break free but it was too difficult. He was much stronger than I was. Worse, I could see he was barely tryin'. I bit his arm and kicked one of his legs. His grip loosened and I broke free and got up and ran into the woods to hide and think of a plan.

"You can't hide from me, Bastian. Your death is inevitable," he laughed sadistically.

I wasn't sure what to do; so I removed Wer and put him back in my coat. I looked at all my masks to figure out a plan: the death mask. It was perfect. I could plant it on him and kill him quickly, but how was I supposed to get close enough, I questioned. If I used Pruen he'd be able to see me comin'. I looked at the color-changin' mask. I had to try it. I took it out and put it on. Maybe it could offer more help than I thought. There was a splash of colors and I was inside her home. I walked around for a while and finally saw her standin' in the corner. Her entire body was continuously changin' colors.

"Hey, what's going on?"

"Leave me alone please. You don't want to be near me. I'm just a nothing who can't do anything right," she said depressingly.

"What are ya talking about?"

"I already told you, I'm useless. You don't need me. I can't even control what I can do."

"What do ya mean?"

"My power. I can't control it. I'm a waste."

"No you're not. I'll help ya. We can work together and learn how to use your power."

" . . . Really?"

"Of course. That's what I'm here for right?"

"Maybe."

I held out my hand and she grabbed it. Suddenly, she was gone and I was wearin' the mask. I could still hear her talk though.

"I'm goin' to learn how to use your power." My body was rapidly changin' colors with multiple colors one me at one time, never stayin' the same for more than three seconds. I focused on one color and my body changed to it, holdin' shade for a while.

"How did you do that?" she asked.

"If there's anythin' that I've learned to do, it's focus. I just thought about the color then my body would change to it."

"Wow, I'm gunna try." The mask floated off my face and his body grew out of it. I watched as she tried and after a few minutes, she got the hang of it. "I'm doing it! I'm actually doing it!"

"Yes, ya are. You're doin' great." After a few more minutes, she was changin' perfectly. I had to find a way for her power to be useful. *"Can you turn your home into a forest please?"*

"Why?"

"I would like to try somethin'."

"Anything for you." In the blink of an eye we were surrounded by trees.

"Can ya combine with me again?"

"Sure." The mask was on my face and I started walkin' around. I focused on all the colors around me and my body began to blend in with everythin'. It was just as I thought; she was a chameleon.

"You can put your home back to the way ya like it." I said and everythin' went back to normal. *"I'm glad ya let me help you. You're about to be very useful."*

"I owe you one."

"We'll call it even, Chameleon." I focused and left her home; the mask was still on my face. I concentrated on everythin' around me and was beginnin' to blend in with the surroundin's. Ryder wasn't even goin' to see me comin'. I took out the death mask and began to move stealthily toward him as he was walkin' around lookin' for me. I jumped onto a tree and grabbed a branch, waitin' for him to get close. Once he was near I jumped off the tree and landed the mask on his face. He let out a muffled cry and after a few seconds he smacked me out of his body and I went flyin', still holdin' the death mask. I hit the ground

and watched him come closer. His right eye was bleedin', but that was it. He didn't die like everyone else did. Again, he proved himself to be too strong.

Tobias ran in front of me and a tree deteriorated to the left of us. Suddenly, a wooden golem appeared behind Ryder and attacked him. Ryder turned around and began to tear it apart.

"This guy is way too strong. We have to go and get help. We can take him out as a team." The golem was turned to splinters. Ryder laughed as he walked toward us.

"I've got my own team." I opened my coat and showed him my masks. "Together we will beat him. Just sit back and watch." I jumped in front of him and took out Bon, puttin' him on and spreadin' out my arms. I could feel my body begin to tighten up. He wasn't gettin' past me. When I first talked with Bon, he was able to speak with me telepathically so I figured I could do the same. I focused on Tobias and began to talk to him with my mind.

"Run."

"What? No, I'm not leaving you with him."

"I won't move an inch. He's strong, but not this strong. Now run." Tobias got up and ran. Ryder was standin' in front of me droolin' and laughin'.

"I don't care about your friend. He'll get his soon enough." *He grabbed my head and tried to pick me up, but couldn't so he let go and laughed.* "I'm done with your stupid masks." *He punched the mask, but it didn't fall off. He took two steps back and then punched me with his left hand and then with his right, continuin' relentlessly. The punches felt like a heavy breeze. He was tryin' hard; hittin' me all over. I felt not one bit of pain. Except I was becomin' exhausted from continuous use of Bon. I had to fight to stay indestructible. Ryder needed to tire out before I did.*

"What, is that all you got?" I said telepathically.

"I'm just warming up." *He jumped back and got a runnin' start, puttin' a lot of force into his next punch. I won't lie, I felt a tingle. I could see sweat drippin' from his face. He was breathin' heavily. His body began to shift and I heard bones crackin'.*

"No!" He yelled. "Not yet! I've got plenty of energy!" *He continued to hit me movin' all around me tossin' punches and scratches. He backed off and kneeled down tryin' to conserve energy.*

I let Bon fall off, grabbed him as he was fallin', and took out Alden and put him on. Instantly my body was full of energy.

"You're notasstrong asyouthought, huh?" *I said hastily.*

"I'll kill you!" *He screamed.*

He grabbed a tree and pulled it out of the ground and threw it at me like a spear. I quickly dodged it, the roots from the tree ticklin' the mask. I looked up and he was runnin' at me, so I started runnin' away weavin' in and out of the trees. He couldn't keep up. He was too tired. He stopped, and was breathin' even more heavily. I turned around and watched him change back to normal.

"What's thematter? Can't keepup?"

"I'm out of here."

I ran at him and punched him in the face, takin' out Pruen while he was on the ground. He got up and I saw him begin to change. I wrapped him up with my arms and legs and squeezed tightly. I could feel his bones crack and break, but it wasn't from me; he was changin' again. I lifted him up and threw him into the ground, then pulled back my arms and legs. All of the sudden, he flew into the sky. I took off Pruen and put on Ien, flyin' into the sky chasin' after him. He was no match for Ien. I grabbed him, punched him numerous times, then kicked him down toward where we were. I flew at him as fast as I could and pushed him into the ground leavin' a large crater followed by a cloud of dirt. I stayed on top of him punchin' him.

He changed his body structure into a bear, grabbed me and started to squeeze. I tried to fly away, but I couldn't escape. I used the beak on the mask and pecked him in the left eye. He quickly let go and I flew back, spottin' Tobias near us.

"Can you only make those golem guys or can you make other things too?" *I asked gasping for air.*

"I can make anything."

"How about somethin' out of glass. It doesn't have to be anythin' special. Just like a statue or somethin'."

"Whatever you want."

A tree deteriorated and then reappeared as glass. I took off Ien and put on Vaz. I shattered the tree and drew all the glass around me. Ryder stood up holdin' his eye.

"What lengths would you have gone to, Ryder? What would you have done to get me back?" I shot a long glass shard into his shoulder. It hit him and pinned him against the tree behind him. He screamed in pain. "Would you have bribed me? Used the ones I loved against me?" I shot another shard at his leg. His entire left half was pinned to the tree. Again he cried. I shattered more of the glass around me into smaller pieces, no bigger than a dime. "Would you have taken innocent lives to get me here?" I pushed them at his right half. He screamed again, he was in a lot of pain.

"STOP!" *Vaz yelled.* "This is torture. I will not allow this. No one deserves this type of punishment. Just kill him."

"I'm sorry, you're right. But I will not let you kill someone. You are too pure. I will not make you do that." I pulled out all the glass that was in Ryder, causing him to fall to the ground, blood oozin' out from his body. I took him off and took out Dac, walked over to Ryder and shoved my hand into his chest and grabbed his heart. "Goodbye, Ryder." I squeezed it and ripped my hand out. I removed Dac and walked over to Tobias.

"I'm sorry ya had to see that,"

Chapter LIX

TRAVIS AND ADEN: THE END

July 6, 2007

I walked upstairs. It was all finally over. There would be no one else after us. We could save Bidziil and find some way to make sure the project was destroyed for good. I came to the top of the stairs and Hannah, Callia and Gabe were waiting for me.

"How'd it go down there?" Gabe asked.

"Let's just say that they won't be coming back for us. We need to head to the dock and save Bidziil."

"Hopefully Tobias is okay and he'll meet us there."

"He can handle that guy." We started walking out of the building when someone came through the doors. I put my hand on the wall and absorbed it, just to be cautious. He was wearing a red hoodie and black pants. It was Aden.

"Travis, wait. Before you attack let me explain."

"No need. I already know. Faxon explained our last encounter. So where's Bastian?"

"He's with Tobias fighting off Ryder. Tobias told me to come help you guys."

"We don't have time to talk. We have to get to the docks and stop the other heads and instructors before they kill Bidziil." Gabe reminded.

"Bastian and I came from the docks. We killed all of them. None of them are left standing."

"Did you save Bidziil?"

"Who is that?"

"Faxon hasn't told you about him?" I asked in confusion.

"No."

"Then why are you here?"

"To save my friend Reece. He's a young boy who saved my mom's life."

"He was just with Perin."

"What!? Where!?"

"He was down stairs but I think he ran away."

"I have to go find him."

"It would take too long. This place is huge. If we save Bidziil, he will find Reece. I promise."

"What can he do?"

"Everything. He's the one who gave us our powers. He can do everything we can."

"What? You're kidding?"

"Not at all. I'm surprised Faxon never told you. All of that doesn't matter now though. We have to go save him. Are you coming?"

"If he can help me find Reece then I'm coming."

"Awesome. How were Tobias and Bastian doing?"

"They'll be fine."

"Hopefully, they'll get there soon." We left the building and ran to Dock Five, seeing a chain going into the water. "He must be down there in the ocean." I absorbed the ground and started pulling up the chain.

I didn't want Travis to be the only one pulling. I made blood whips and helped him out. We heard something coming in the distance, so Travis and I continued to pull the chain while Gabe watched our backs.

"It's Tobias," Gabe said.

We turned around and looked. Tobias and Bastian were riding in some type of vehicle. They jumped out and the thing disappeared. They ran toward us I wrapped my blood around the chain and held it to the ground while Travis walked over to Bastian.

"It's so great to see you again."

"You're Travis? I almost killed you the day I escaped from this place," Bastian said with surprise.

"You're the reason I escaped. If it wasn't for you none of this would have happened the way it did. I wouldn't be as strong as I am now. I owe you a lot."

"I guess so, but no need to thank me. Let's just destroy this place," Bastian said.

"First we have to save Bidziil."

"Who is that?" he asked.

"You don't know either? How has Faxon not told you about him? If you're not here to save Bidziil then why are you here?"

"To destroy this place. I don't want anyone to have to go through what I went through."

"Understandable, but we can do that after we save Bidziil."

"Why is he so important?"

"He gave us all our powers. He is the most powerful being on this planet. He can do everything we can do."

"Impressive."

"That's why we have to save him, plus if he dies, we may all die too. That's only a theory though."

"Excuse me?"

"What!" everyone said.

"Failed to mention that, sorry. It's only a theory. Let's just get him out."

A crate disappeared and out of nowhere a brown spiked man appeared to start helping us pull up the chain. In about a minute we had it pulled up. There was a crate attached to it.

Finally, we had it out of the water. I absorbed diamond, stabbed the crate, and cut a hole in it. I ripped off the entire side and took Bidziil out. He was unconscious.

"That's where I have to stop you. You all have done enough, thank you," a voice said from a distance.

It was Perin's voice, but I burnt him to a crisp. He couldn't have still been alive. We all turned around and saw him standing on the roof. It looked like he was alone.

"I'm going to have to take Bidziil from you. He is property of this project," he said.

"You aren't getting him. He isn't anyone's property!" Tobias yelled.

"He is ours and we are taking him by force." Doors opened at the base of the building and soldiers came out followed by some more of Perin's puppets. Nadim was the only one I knew but there were a few other guys with them.

"The only one I know is Tyson. I don't know what his power is but he was selected for the End of Chaos trial. I'm assuming he is powerful. I've never seen the girl though," Gabe informed.

"I'll deal with the soldiers. Tobias, Hannah, Callia and Gabe, get Bidziil out of here," Bastian instructed.

"I'll handle Nadim."

"You will all die here. I've died twice today and I'll keep dying. It won't make a difference because I've got Reece." *I watched as he walked out from behind Perin.*

"You bastard!" my blood wings ripped out and I flew up at Perin.

Everyone started to move and attack. I ran at Nadim. Bastian opened his coat and was about to put on a mask. Hannah, Tobias, Callia, and Gabe took off with Bidziil.

-*Bastian* vs. Soldiers and Vlad

I threw on Alden and ran at the soldiers, disarmin' most of them. I knocked them down, threw them into each other, and kick and punched them. By the time I stopped movin' all the soldiers were down.

One of the men ran at me; he was fast. I looked down at his feet and they were beginnin' to be wrapped by, what looked like, orange electricity. He was gettin' faster, but with Alden I had the upper hand. He was close enough to me where he jumped, kicked horizontally, and a semi-circular of orange electricity shot toward me. I ducked and he was in front of me. He did a back flip and kicked me in the face. I felt the electric shock though my entire body, then I took Alden off of my face and took out Ien.

"My name is Vlad and I will kill you, Bastian. I won't let you harm these islands any longer."

There wasn't even a point in talkin' to him. He was too set in his ways. I just had to get rid of him and help the others. We locked eyes and he ran at me. I flew into the air, spottin' Aden fightin' someone on the roof top. I had to stop Vlad and help Aden. I flew down behind him so the docks were facin' his back. We locked eyes again and I lauched at him with great speed, spearin' into him and flyin' towards the water. He was tryin' to break free from my hold, his legs makin' contact with my body and hittin' me with an electrical surge. Luckily, I was already over the water, droppin' Vlad into the ocean and quickly flyin' back to land. I had to catch my breath for a second; I was beginnin' to get very tired. All the fightin' was finally takin' its toll on me.

-TRAVIS VS. NADIM-

I absorbed the gold band from the ring into my right arm and then I absorbed the diamond with my left. I jumped and came down on Nadim with my fist of gold. He fell to the ground. I picked him up with my diamond arm and ran him into a crate and began punching him violently. He pushed me off and I skidded back.

"I've wanted this since the day I met you in that battle box," Nadim said.

"I bet you never thought you'd lose," Nadim ran at me screaming. We exchanged blows. I never let him hit me in the body, blocking all of his punches with my arms. One hit from his fists on my non absorbed body and I'd be out. I stopped playing it risky and changed my entire body into diamond. His punches felt like heavy breezes of wind. He took a swing at me and I grabbed his fist.

"That was your last punch." I twisted him around and kicked him in the back as hard as I could. He flew across the ground and crashed into a cargo container. I ran toward the container but when I got there Nadim was unconscious. I had to go make sure Bidziil and the others were okay.

-*Gabe* vs. Tyson-

We were running away from all the fighting, carrying Bidziil over my shoulder. The girls were watching our backs and Tobias was in front. Tyson came out of nowhere. I quickly set Bidziil down and took out a toothpick and stabbed Tyson in the arm and pushed him back into a wall. He began to laugh, ripped off his arm at the shoulder, and seconds later, a new one grew back.

"Wanna try again?" he asked.

I enlarged the Angel and stabbed him in the stomach, pulling it out and he dropped to the ground and I ran back and picked Bidziil up to keep moving. I heard loud footsteps behind us. It was Tyson, who had grown four more arms. I put Bidziil down again and ran at him. I tried to cut him, but he had too many arms, making it impossible to dodge all of his punches; always punching me before I could land an attack. He grabbed both my arm so I was unable to swing and kept hitting me. I kicked out his knee, head butted him, broke free to cut his hands off at the wrist, and kick him far back. In seconds his hands began to grow back. I placed toothpicks on the ground and waited as he ran towards me. I enlarged them, piercing his arms and legs, trapping him. I ran back to the girls and Tobias and continued running.

ADEN VS. PERIN

I flew at Perin. Makale stepped out from behind him and mimed a gun and tried to shoot me, but I quickly made a barrier and stopped the shot. I molded the blood into a ball and fired it back at Makale, hitting him in the face. He struggled to take it off; I formed a bunch of sharp tipped strings stabbing them into anything solid around him, tying him down and blinding him. I landed in front of Perin and was about to stab him, but he picked up Reece.

"I wouldn't do that if I were you, Aden." He slowly began to back up. "I'll break his little neck if you try anything. Now why don't you join us? It will be for the best. You and Reece can work together. You will never have to leave his side."

"I'd rather just kill you and take him with me."

"Haha! Aden you poor sap. Maybe someone else should deliver my proposal to you." *Some girl walked out from behind a wall. She was looked about Reece's age.*

"Come on, Aden. Join us," she said as her eyes began to glow a faint blue.

I looked towards the roof to see if Aden was okay. It was her. I could final get my revenge. She caused me so much pain. I absorbed the air and separated myself, coming back together on the rooftop. I blasted air at her and Perin, knocking them prone. Perin let go of Reece, Aden grabbed him, and made sure Makale was still having trouble. He covered Perin in blood and slammed him on the ground. I returned to normal and walked slowly to Amity, kicking her to the ground as she tried to get up. She tried to use her ability on me.

"Remember me?" I absorbed diamond and held her down. Her eyes began to glow a bright blue. "You know that won't work on me. I was strong enough to fight it off weeks ago, but now it's just a sad joke for you to try it now." The pain she put me through was not going to go unpunished. I held her down as she struggled; there was only one way I was going to let her die. I held her arm down and was about to cut her wrist with one of my diamond fingers.

"MAKALE!!" She screamed at the top of her lungs.

I was suddenly struck by a projectile and knock off of her. She got out of my hold and began running on the roof.

All of the sudden, black domes began appearing everywhere. It was Zander coming to help Perin, and doubtfully alone. He missed me and hit Amity. I couldn't kill her while she was incased in his darkness. I jumped off the roof, landing right in front of Zander. I grabbed his wrist and was about to break it when he yelled at me.

"Wait Travis! Look around. I'm not covering your guys. I'm covering everyone else. Is Bidziil okay?"

"Why do you care?"

"'cause I'm on your side. I've been working for Faxon since he left this place. He wanted me to act at the apartment, but the final battle had to happen here. Everyone, please come closer. We don't have much time. Perin made a call to someone and whoever it was; they're on their way here now. We need to be prepared."

We were all gathered together; Gabe, Aden, Bastian, Callia, Hannah, Reece, Tobias, Zander and myself. Gabe put Bidziil on the ground.

"He's still unconscious. What do we do?" Gabe asked.

"Wait for him to . . ." Bidziil's eyes opened and he stood up and looked around.

"Hello everyone. Nice to meet you all. I am Bidziil," I said slowly standing up.

"There are helicopters coming to the islands. We have to think of a plan to end this all now," Zander said.

"I am tired of putting people in danger. I will go somewhere far away where no one can find me."

"That won't work. They will find you. As long as you keep exploding someone will find you. If you destroy this project how long will it be before someone starts another one. This needs to end here. Now. Today," Zander said.

"There is no way to."

"You have to have some power in you that could help us now," I said.

"There is one power. The power that Perin planned to use on me."

"The soul swapping one? But someone has to die for that power to work," Zander stated.

"That is why I will not use it."

"Well, you have to do something. This can't keep going on. We need to put a stop to it." Zander retorted.

"What exactly is the power?" Bastian asked.

"It is not what Perin explained. He does not fully understand. My body would turn into complete soul energy and combine with another person's. The stronger of the two souls gets to keep the body."

"So no one actually dies?"

"Not entirely. The two souls would combine into one. I would still be me, but the other person would be gone, except for their power. I would look like them and have their ability, but I would be myself. There would be no more releases from me."

"And what would happen to your powers?" I asked.

"Gone. I would only have the ability of the other soul. I would have his body and his power. Nothing left of me except, my mind."

"I'll do it, take me. It's the only way that we can end this entire project. They will think you're dead and another project won't need to be created. Please, Bidziil. Just take me," I begged.

"No, Travis. Not you."

"He's gunna take mine," a voice said from behind us.

A mangled man came walking out from around the side of a building. His clothes appeared to be burnt way and so did parts of his skin. Zander asked, "Zane?"

"Zane, what happened to you?" Gabe asked.

"Perin did, but that doesn't matter now. I heard everything. Bidziil, take me. Go through my head and read my thoughts; I've got nothing left to live for. The islands were my life. Now that I have come to see that my entire life was a lie, I just want to do some good."

"I'm not going to end your life, Zane."

"You have no other option. This has to stop today."

"I'll dispose of everyone on the islands and then I will go away forever."

"Only if was that simple, but Bidziil, you know it's not. It won't end today. Your only option is to take my body; take my life," Zane explained.

"You can not be serious."

"Never been more serious in my life," Zane said.

"This will not be easy for me. I can not allow myself to do this to you; to anyone."

"Bidziil, enough of the bullshit! Quit dancing around the idea of it already! There is no other option! Just do it! I'm giving you my permission! I'm demanding it!" he yelled.

"Fine. Everyone it was great knowing all of you." I teleported all of them back to their homes except for Zander, Zane and myself. We could see the helicopters coming in the distance. I froze them in time and finally had a moment to think, to take a breath. If it truly would end, then I had to dispose of those with dark desires. I did not want to play the role of a god, but it seemed that it was up to me to decide the fates of hundreds of people. I spent about five minutes of frozen time to get to know everyone on the island, thanks to the birth of Faxon. With his gift it was simple to do. There were many on the islands that were just misguided and did not deserve to pay the price of death for the things that they have done. Sadly, there were some that I could not risk returning to the outside world. They could not be helped. I ran through possible scenarios, but even if I wiped there minds clean some would use their gifts for evil. It was not my place to judge the whole world at that point. I kept all my thoughts and powers focused on the people of the islands. I sent everyone that deserved a second chance to their home, but some had no place to go so I sent those people to a relative's house or anyone that could care for them. Their minds where wiped clean of the islands, and of there knowledge of their power if they even one. The minds of all of Faxon's spies I left untouched. They had been doing the best they could to stop Project Dominium from continuing and they deserved to remember that fact. The scientists and doctors were all mainly good people for the most part, just happy to be involved in such a big project "saving" man kind. I could assure them, they would be happier at home, out of harms way. As for everyone else I teleported them to the Hokee. They did not have the option of a second chance. I then teleported into Perin's office and grabbed a few blank disks. I put one hand on his computer and other on the stack of blank disks and transferred all the information onto each cd.

I grabbed a sheet of paper and began to write a note to everyone who had helped me.

"I will deal with the islands. You all did a great job. I appreciate everything you have done for me, but I have to finish the job. On the back of this paper is everyone's number so that you can all keep in touch, if you wish. There is also a disk with all of the projects files on it. After today you will be the only ones to have this information. Outside of the islands the government has no known involvement in the happenings here it seems. They just supply money and officers and do not ask questions. Strange as it seems, it is an agreement the Perin's father made before starting Project Dominium. I hope you all have long happy lives. Good luck and I wish you all the best."

I sent a copy of that note to Tobias, Bastian, Aden, Travis, Hannah, Callia, and Gabe. I deteriorated all the furniture in the room, made three bombs and set the timer for ten minutes, and teleported a bomb onto each island. I sent the tape that Perin left for Aden to him, because Reece and Aden were the only ones I did not send home. They were sent to the child services department in Florida. All the pieces were in place. The blast from the explosion would kill anyone that was left on the islands, which honestly wasn't very many in compassion to the total number of people on the islands.

I returned to Zane and Zander and surrounded us in an extra thick barrier and covered it in wind, setting the bombs off early using my tecnopath abilities. There were three simultaneous explosions. It took nearly ten whole minutes before the dust began to settle. I used my wind power to clear it faster, revealing no sign that any buildings even existed there; only dirt, some trees, and a craters. Zander watched in amazement. Everything he had done in the past years was not for nothing. He had helped in saving everything and everyone. He was proud, just by the look on his face you could tell, but there was also sadness. The islands were his home. That's all he knew. It was time for him to start a new chapter in his life, just like me. I looked at Zane.

"Are you ready?"

"Yes, Bidziil."

"Then so be it," I released my soul and my body was flooded with energy. I walked toward Zane and then my energy surrounded him. His soul came out and tried to defend his body, but it was much too weak compared to mine. I took Zane's soul and combined it with my own, entering Zane's body. I looked around through Zane's eyes, everything appearing different. There was no information constantly flowing into my brain. I did not have to constantly reroute thoughts just so I could think straight. Finally, I could hear my thoughts. The helicopters began flying again, landing on the Industrial to pick us up. They were from the government. Zander and I gladly went with them.

Chapter LX

FAXON: EPILOGUE

From the moment that the islands were destroyed, nothing was the same. Bidziil had returned everyone back to where they belonged. Travis was in his room; Bastian was standing outside by his pool, Tobias was back in his apartment, Aden and Reece were standing in the waiting room of the child services building in Florida, Callia, Hannah and Gabe were back at there own homes as well. They all had a paper in their hands. They read it and weren't very happy about Bidziil decision.

In less than twelve hours, everyone had contacted each other. They all had to know what happened to the islands. Tobias created a jet and they flew to them. All that was left were a few trees, debris, and huge craters. They didn't want to admit that it was all over and it was time to move on with their lives. I had made one phone call to each of them to tell them they did great and they should move on. After that, I exiled myself from their lives. It was hard not to think about them.

Travis wanted it to be him. He still beat himself up over what happened with Amber. The fact that he did have a chance to kill Amity tore him up. He felt that Amber was never truly avenged, until he went to her grave about two weeks later, sleeping there for two days. Didn't eat, didn't speak, barely even breathed; he felt like he was with her again and he knew that not killing Amity was for the best. Amber wouldn't have wanted him to kill in her name. He enrolled in the University of Pennsylvania and started on his path to becoming a lawyer like his father: a path of justice.

Bastian went away for school. He moved to Boston, Massachusetts to study history. His father was proud of him for pursuing his dreams and not settling for anything less. He looked for me for about a week straight. It was very hard to stay hidden from him. He had so many questions he wanted answers to. Some I could give him and some I was instructed not to answer.

Tobias continued college and told his parents what happened. They were so proud of their young hero. He had been talking with his father and there was going to be a big business opportunity in Japan that would be offered to him if he graduated on time and if he wanted it. It sounded appealing, but he was given plenty of time to think it over.

Aden showed the tape to child services. He explained the situation to them and Reece confirmed it all. Reece's parents were arrested and Aden was offered a part time job, but he couldn't leave his mom in West Virginia. The department made some calls and got him an internship at child services in his area. Reece was sent to his aunt's house in California. He was happy there and called Aden every Thursday to keep him up to date on his life.

Gabe, Hannah and Callia all went to the same college in Maryland and got an apartment together. They had no idea what to do with the gifts that they had, but they figured it would be easy to discover their paths together.

As for Bidziil and Zander, or should I say Zane and Zander, they were questioned thoroughly about Project Dominium. The government had little to no data on it. The one file they did have on the project was empty except for some pictures and blueprints of buildings. They only knew that there was a facility on the islands, but nothing about its usage. As well as having no information on Bidziil or people with powers. They ended up closing the project and sending Zane and Zander to New York for school. They paid for their apartment and gave them enough money for a few years to live on.

As for me, I just go around helping people that I know need it. I keep an eye on the ones that Bidziil let go, referring to them as "The Spared". I offer them any help that I can give them, usually finding them jobs or places to live. It's hard for them not knowing what has happened to them or where all the years have gone. There isn't much I can do, but I do my best to offer answers. I do not inform them of their past years or their abilities. That is something they must figure out on their own.

I've begun holding back my power more and only letting small amounts of information seep through. It is better this way. Project Dominium is over and now everyone can live their lives in peace.